"[An] emotionally rich, incandescent debut novel. *The Ocean in Winter* is a page-turner of a book with a family mystery at its core, and profoundly explores the ways in which women struggle to rebuild their lives after grief and trauma. You won't want to put it down once you start."

"A compelling portrait of a wounded family seeking a path forward . . . Rich in dialogue, action, and a keen sense of place, *The Ocean in Winter* pulls the reader into the swirling vortex of three lives shaped by a family legacy that will not let them go."

"This tale of love, loss, grief, and connections is one that could shatter your heartstrings. It is a saga of family turmoil that hints of the supernatural—a world of spirits that try to alert of danger, the past, and the way forward."

The Ocean in Winter

The Ocean in Winter

Elizabeth de Veer

BLACK
STONE
PUBLISHING

Printed in the United States of America

First edition: 2021
ISBN 978-1-9826-7464-9
Fiction / Literary

1 3 5 7 9 10 8 6 4 2

CIP data for this book is available
from the Library of Congress

Blackstone Publishing
31 Mistletoe Rd.
Ashland, OR 97520

www.BlackstonePublishing.com

For Amelia.

Prologue

I am hurtling through Massachusetts at a rate of speed I cannot understand; the wind blows my cheeks, but it does not feel cold. I know only generally where I am going: deep into the state's northeast corner where small towns cluster at the coast like grapes, nestled by a fragile barrier island at the mouth of the Merrimack River. The towns, blanketed now in briny mist, go by these names: Rowley; Newbury; Newburyport; Salisbury; and, inland, the city of Amesbury, the rough-edged river-fed mill town where my sisters and I grew up, a place I left when I was eighteen and never returned to. The town was too small for me, I suppose, and too much had happened for me and Amesbury to pretend that we had ever been all that close.

A storm has been raging here all day, but now the rain has stopped. In this strange moment, I come to stand on the doorstep of a house in the town of Newbury that I have never seen before, an old farmhouse whose white paint and green trim are cracked and peeling, wooden beams rotted. Behind me, I leave no footprints in the cold mud.

What year is this? I think for a moment. Wait, how do I not know the answer immediately?

It's 2014. The answer comes to mind like a vague memory, as though the question itself does not matter. The house belongs to my oldest sister, Alex. Time is confusing to me right now—how long has it been since I saw her? Years, I think. But how many? Four, five, six? More? Maybe seven. I pushed her away. I pushed everyone away, far away, all to protect my ugly little secrets. Regret lingers in my throat like bile; I've made so many mistakes.

I glance through the front window; the room beyond is pitch black. The electricity in this area is out and has been out for a couple of hours. How do I know this? I'm not sure. In the woods beyond this clearing, trees creak high and long like old rocking chairs, swaying slowly in one direction and then the other. The effect is eerie, ghostly.

Many secrets stand between me and my sisters, Alex and Colleen, but not all will be revealed tonight. Tomorrow, after dawn breaks, one of these secrets shall become known. Others will unfold in the days to follow. Far from here a little boy sleeps soundly in his bed in the city. My awareness of him is so intense, I can almost hear his soft steady breath. *Goodbye, sweet Caleb. Mama loves you, though she never did a good job of showing it.*

I stand for a moment at the threshold of this house and take a deep breath of damp, mossy air, while a chill wind presses against my neck and blows my hair in my face. Alex is inside alone. She is not waiting for me, in fact, she is not expecting my visit. I raise my fist to the door and rap my knuckles against it. One moment passes, and then another. Nothing happens, so I knock again. Finally, Alex opens the door a crack.

"Hello?" she whispers. "Is someone there? Colleen?"

"Alex, it's me," I say, pushing my hair away from my face. "Riley."

"Riley?" she says, incredulous. Then she opens the door the rest of the way. She points her flashlight toward me; I squint in the light and raise my hand to shield my eyes. From the shadows Alex stares, her pale face wide-eyed with fear and surprise. Slowly her expression registers recognition and then she gasps.

"Riley!" She pulls me inside and slams the door to leave the wind and wildness behind us. She throws her arms around me and hugs me hard and long; I do the same. There is a damp towel over her shoulder. Her wool sweater smells dusty, and the air reeks of plaster and paint.

"Hi, Alex," I say.

"Where have you been?" she says, touching my arm as though she does not believe that I am real. "We've been searching for you. Are you okay? Wait, how did you find me?"

"That's a lot of questions," I say.

"Let me look at you," she says, and she holds my face in her hands. She's shorter than I am, which is surprising because she is eight years older, and I remember her as tall, although I suppose the last time I saw her I was already over a head taller. In my childhood memories, she's a grown-up, which I guess she has been since she was eleven, since the day she saw what she saw. In the pale shimmer from two utility candles in paper cups, her skin looks tired, her eyes sunken as though she has not been sleeping. Her eyes bear the beginnings of fine lines at the corners; she, too, has aged in these past years. The dark, curly waves of her hair are streaked with a few gray strands, tied back in a sloppy ponytail. She looks strong, like she's someone who knows what she's doing. The kind of person I always wished I were or would someday become.

She takes the towel off her shoulder. "This house, of course one of the windows is leaking," she says, drying her hands on the towel. "Oh, Riley!" Her smile fades; now she looks worried. "You look different."

"It's been a long time, Alex," I say. "I think you visited me in New York, and we haven't seen each other since then."

Alex frowns. "I think almost seven years. I'm sorry, Riley. It's been too long."

"I know," I say, smiling a little.

"I should have visited you more," she says. "I was bad about taking time off from work, until I quit. But you know, I was always thinking that you might come home too."

I nod. "I should have," I say. "It's hard to get away, sometimes."

"Well, can't really blame you," she says, grinning. "You glamour girl, you. You know, for a long time I tried to keep track of all the ads you were in. I even clipped them and kept them in a binder. But then, there were so many, I couldn't keep track. You're a big deal, sweetie!" She smiles at me awkwardly, like she's waiting for me to agree, which I don't.

I smile flatly, shrug.

Finally, she beckons me to follow her into the house. "Well, come in. I have snacks in the kitchen."

Alex walks ahead of me, the yellow flashlight beam slicing through the darkness like a dull butter knife. She turns to look at me as though she does not quite believe I am real. "Wait, did you come all the way from New York alone through the storm? How did you get here? I didn't see a car."

"Oh, right," I say. I make my voice sound sleepy, like I don't entirely understand what she's saying. "The car . . ." Flighty gestures complete the effect. "I don't know, there was some mud on the tires, so I just left it out there . . ."

"Wait, your car got stuck in the mud?" she says, looking out the window. "Where is it? I'll call Triple A."

"Oh," I start. "No need. I'll get it later."

Alex looks at me closely, scrutinizing my face and my story. "Well, I guess it doesn't matter right now," she says. Outside the windows, a brief and sudden flash illuminates the world like daytime. No thunder; the blaze is silent. We stop in our tracks to register the shocking light.

"I think the worst is over," she says, her hands on her hips. "Just lightning now. But it's still so cold for March. It's been a cold winter. Was it this cold in New York? Riley, you must be freezing. Do you want a blanket or something?"

"I'm okay," I say. I pull my sweater tighter around me, only I realize it isn't a sweater but an oversized men's suit jacket, which I wear over a long-sleeved T-shirt. I think the man who owns this gave it to me. I almost remember. Then, yes, I see his face, handsome and warm, his smile kind as he wrapped this around me. His eyes were dark and gentle. Where did he go? He brought me home. He delivered me safely to my door, and then he left me alone to rest.

He said he'd take me out to breakfast. But now, I don't think he will.

I follow Alex across unstained wood floors, empty of rugs or carpeting, through rooms so empty the walls seem to float in time. As we walk, we are like the children we never were, stealing into an abandoned building, sneaking, insubstantial as sprites. The eight years between us is a lifetime in the lives of children. And all our lives are divided into *before* and *after*—before our lives changed, Alex was a sporty kid who played baseball with the neighborhood boys and didn't have much time for younger sisters. After our lives changed, she became our everything, the glue that kept our lives together. She did what she had to out of necessity; she never settled into roles or became comfortable playing house. She missed Mom. We all did.

We come to the small kitchen; a round table sits in the corner with two chairs, an old refrigerator and an electric stove with curlicue burners that would glow red, if switched on. If there were electricity.

"Colleen told me not to open the fridge when the power's out, as if my one jar of mustard might go bad." She rolls her eyes and takes two juice glasses down from a shelf. "Let me get you some wine, at least. I have crackers too."

"That's all right," I say, smiling. "Hey, what happened with India? I thought you were going to be there for a long time."

She sets the flashlight on the counter and opens a box of Saltines, spreads them out on a plate. Then Alex opens cabinets and closes them, one after another, in search of something. Finally, she finds what she's looking for, a can of spray cheese. "Here it is," she says.

"Alex? Why did you come back from India?"

"You're standing in the reason," she says, sighing. "This house. Colleen told you I went to India, but she didn't tell you about the house?"

I pause, unsure how to answer. I have not spoken to Colleen since before Christmas. "You tell me. How did you end up here?"

She purses her lips in thought. "About two years ago, I met this woman on a bus in the middle of a snow storm in Boston. It was snowing and the traffic was stuck for hours. We just started talking and became friends, I guess. But she had ovarian cancer. She didn't have any heirs, though, and she'd been trying to figure out what to do with this place. When she found out I was from Amesbury, she offered to leave me the house in her will. I didn't want it, I told her that over and over, but she"—she sighs—"convinced me to say yes. And then she died while I was in India."

"Oh, no," I say. "I'm sorry for your loss."

She gives me a half shrug. "I was sorry to come back from India early. But you know, it was kind of a spur of the moment decision to go at all. My friend is volunteering at a small village clinic, and I wanted to see it and help out. I didn't make it to the village."

"That's too bad," I say.

"I got in a few weeks of traveling anyway," she says. "I saw the Taj Mahal, the Ganges River, I saw the place where the Buddha became enlightened."

"And then you came back?" I ask.

"Yup," she says, looking around. "Well, not only for this place. Colleen was dealing with some things. And we didn't know what was going on with you."

"I know," I say. "Sorry about that."

"It's okay," she says. She squirts three or four crackers with canned cheese, neon orange swirls, and carefully arranges them on a plate.

"Alex, can I ask you something weird?" I say. She nods. "I always imagined you with kids."

I make the comment without much thought, but I feel her react with a deep wince. She looks at me as though in disbelief, and then shakes it off.

"Me too," she finally says. She looks down. "It just doesn't work out for everybody, I guess."

"Don't say that," I say. "There's still time."

"Wait, did Colleen tell you to talk to me?" she asks. "Look, I don't want to go over this anymore. I tried. I really did. At some point, you just accept things the way they are and move on."

I blink, confused. "Alex, I—"

She talks over me. "It doesn't matter now, Riley. I can't have a baby, and I can't afford to adopt, so I'll have to settle on being the best aunt in the world to Maddie and Ethan. You need to see those kids, Riley. They're teenagers."

"Wow," I mutter. "Funny how fast it all goes by."

"Come on," she says to me. "Let's go to the other room." We walk into the living room. I sit on a high-backed wooden chair; Alex sits on the floor, her back against the wall.

"Please eat something." She gestures to the plate of crackers, white squares adorned with plastic-looking cheese food swirls. "You must be hungry after that drive. I know it's not fancy . . ."

"No, they look great," I say. I look at the plate, but I can't really imagine putting those in my mouth.

Alex stares at me; I wonder if she can see through me. "Riley, where have you been? We've been trying so hard to find you."

I don't know how to answer her questions, any of them, including am I hungry. Am I? I can't tell. I don't know. And where have I been? Everywhere and nowhere. I don't have an answer for that either.

"Sorry, Alex. Past few months, I've just been completely crazy." I try to laugh; I try so hard to act casual. "I've been working a lot. There was a special project. And it really did take all my time." I pull my jacket around me, tight against the cold and draft. My gut churns with the aftershocks of my special project. Earlier there was intense nausea and cold sweats, but now, a sense of calm washes over me. My project must have settled into the depths of my biochemistry. I almost don't understand how I am still conscious, but here I am.

"Riley, didn't you get any of Colleen's phone calls?" Alex asks. "She's been frantic searching for you."

"I'm sorry if I worried anybody," I say. "But now I am where I need to be."

"Yes," she says. "You're home."

I smile slightly, but I do not explain that that's not what I meant. The room becomes so quiet, the stillness itself takes a shape like there's another person in the room. And the truth is, there is another person between us, a person made of silence: our mother. Finally, I speak. "Tell me about that day." It is the question I ask every time, and she knows I will ask it this time too. "I don't remember it. What happened?"

Alex turns toward me, looks away for a moment, and bites her lip. Eventually, she speaks. "Riley," she says, her face still turned away from mine. "I don't like talking about it."

"I know," I say. "But I can't remember her. Why don't I remember, Alex?"

"You were little," she says. "It was 1989, twenty-five years ago this spring. Can you believe that? April second. What's that? A month from yesterday."

"Twenty-five years," I say. "Tell me again. I was too young for school, right? So, why wasn't I with her?"

"You were at a friend's house," she says. "We picked you up on the way home from school."

"What did you see when you opened that door?" I ask. "She was in the bathtub, right?"

"Don't do this, Riley," she says, rubbing her eyes. "Try to remember who she was. She was a gifted artist. She loved you, loved all of us." Her face looks strained as she says this.

"Thanks," I say. "That's a lovely little speech." I stand up to stretch my legs, then look out the window behind Alex. The darkness beyond is so thick and uninterrupted, it's like being blind. Alex has never forgiven our mother for taking her own life, so I don't buy the she-loved-you business. I lean into the window, a small seat there, and crumple myself up inside it. I don't want to meet her eyes when we talk about this next part. "You were eleven, right?"

She won't say no to me for very long. Nobody does.

Then finally, "Yes, eleven. We were walking home, and I had to pee," she says, standing. Her tone is matter-of-fact. "That's why I ran ahead of you and Colleen. I remember crashing through the front door and dreading that Mom would be mad at me for making too much noise." She pauses and wanders over to the wall beside the empty fireplace, arms crossed, her face twisted in a kind of half grimace. The pain of remembering is written on her face, the anguish of crawling through a tunnel between then and now to see that they are the same time, the same place. You have walked many miles for many years, but you have not progressed from where you started. This is always the truth.

"I ran upstairs and opened the door to the bathroom. And then . . ." She pauses. I look over at her; she has no expression and she's staring at the wall, spellbound. Like she's watching it all happen again.

"What?" I ask.

"The metal doorknob, cold in my hand," she says slowly, stretching the fingers of her right hand. "I was still holding it when I saw what was in the bathtub." She laughs a little. "I didn't need to pee anymore."

I look over at her, and the anguish on her face makes me cringe. "I'm sorry, Alex, I just want to understand. Was she . . . completely underwater?"

I hate asking her to revisit that place, but I feel and have often felt like I need to be walked through these moments. I don't understand what happened, and I can't make myself believe it; I need to feel it through the eyes of the sister who went through it. *I am so sorry, Alex.*

Alex nods. She does not cry as she talks about this, but she used to. "Her eyes were open. Her mouth was open. She didn't look real, but I knew she was gone. And then in one instant, I knew . . . I couldn't let you and Colleen see her like that. And I knew that everything in our lives that was good and easy was over."

"Did you think it had been an accident?" I ask.

She shakes her head. "I knew it wasn't," she says. "She was wearing a bathing suit. Why would someone wear a bathing suit in the bathtub? She knew somebody would find her. She must have known, actually, that one of us would find her. And you know she didn't like the idea of her children seeing her naked in the bathtub, but it didn't bother her so much that we might see her dead in the bathtub."

"Maybe she wasn't thinking clearly," I say. "Maybe all she knew in that moment . . . was pain."

Alex shakes her head and looks steely eyed straight ahead. "You're probably right. And I guess the part we'll never understand is why there was so much pain."

"No, I think we never will," I say, but my words falter in my throat as I speak. "Alex, do you ever hate her for what she did?"

She hesitates, then speaks. "I used to. I always thought she wouldn't have done it if she loved us." Alex stops for a few moments, and I look over at her. She has not moved; her eyes are still firmly on that spot on the wall. "You know, she was thirty-five when she died. I'm a year older than she was then. My whole life, I thought the world would end when I turned thirty-five."

"But the world didn't end," I say.

"No," she says. "But that's how old I was when I found out that I would never become a mother. So, in a way, it did."

The wind is still howling through the seams in the windows; it sounds like an animal in agony. It gusts, and the flames of the candles flicker and fold in response. Alex walks over to one of the windows and jimmies it open, then slams it, and the howling quiets a little.

"I wish I was angry at her," I say. "I wish I'd known her enough to be angry or miss her."

"What do you remember?"

"Not much." I smile a little. "I remember a hotel room with a rickety table and a TV that got extra channels."

Alex nods. "That night we slept in a hotel room."

"Why?" I ask.

"Our house was considered a crime scene," she says, pulling her hand through her hair. "Complete with yellow police tape. We weren't allowed home until the next day."

"I remember you and Colleen and Dad being sort of dazed. I was jumping on the bed and nobody told me to stop," I say. "I don't think I understood—or believed—whatever people were telling me about Mom. But I knew something was wrong because everybody was just sitting there, letting me jump on the bed."

Alex smiles a little. "We were in shock," she says. "We probably didn't even notice."

"I can't remember anything about Mom," I say. "Sometimes I think I remember, but then I realize I'm just thinking of photographs. Or imagining things people told me. Everything secondhand."

"I know," she says. "We all feel like we didn't know her."

"Tell me something about her. What did she love?"

"She loved you," she says. "She used to wrap you up in a little blanket and coo to you and rock you to sleep in the rocking chair. And if any of us made too much noise or woke you up, she threatened to sell us to the gypsies."

I smile slightly.

Alex shrugs. "She loved music. Jazz," she says. "She was tiny, skinny. She had blondish brownish hair, same color as yours, but straight and long."

I look at Alex: her lips are thin, her features broad. Everybody says Alex looks like Dad's side of the family, and I can see that. She has a strong peasant build. If someone gave her a makeover and a good haircut, she would be pretty. But she wouldn't want that. If she didn't recognize herself, she'd feel like the ground had fallen out from beneath her.

Sometimes I don't recognize myself. But then, I've always been a shape-shifter.

"Did her face look like mine?" I say.

She nods.

"I wish we knew why she did it," I say. "I wish she'd given us some piece of her to hold onto. Do you know what I mean?"

Alex pulls an old wooden chair to where I am sitting, sits, mounts her feet on the wall, and pushes herself back so that the chair is teetering on two legs. Like she used to do when we were kids. She sighs. "I don't think there's any way to know."

"She must have been so sad," I start.

In the darkness, I hear Alex grunt. "She had kids, Riley," she says. "I mean, aren't kids supposed to give you a reason to stick around when things get hard? Don't they give your life some great feeling of worth? Some kind of meaning? Isn't that what people say?"

I shrug. "Maybe she felt like she'd screwed up. Like she couldn't get anything right and it was too late to try. Maybe she felt like we'd be better off without her."

Alex's voice ascends with frustration. "Why would she have felt that?"

"I don't know," I say. "But she wouldn't have done it if she wasn't in pain."

"Maybe," she says. "Well, she didn't leave a note. So we'll never know for sure how she felt."

I stare out the window; I can barely see the shadowy profiles of trees leaning in the wind. I speak out loud, but quietly. "Actually, Alex, I do. I know for sure how she felt."

"What did you say?" she says.

"Nothing," I say.

Alex keeps talking then, although I don't exactly hear her words. I am concentrating too hard on the thing I need to say. The thing I have specifically come here to say.

"Alex, I have to ask you something."

Chapter 1

My breath puffs in little white steam clouds, one after another. My feet pound frozen asphalt that creaks and crackles. This winter has been bitterly cold, almost too cold to run outside, and sometimes I think I need a treadmill to make it to spring. But I don't know where I'd put it. On *Today*, they said people's exercise equipment almost always ends up unused and abandoned, just a place to stack boxes or holiday decorations; the idea of which makes me physically ill, the wasted time, money, and square feet, plus the eyesore. Instead, I do layers, thin ones, a progression of thicker ones, and a lightweight jacket on top. And to protect against the wind, I rub my cheeks with Vaseline; I feel it now, slimy and frigid. A few strands of hair, dyed whitish-blond, have slipped loose from my short ponytail and are sticking to the oily residue. It makes my face itch, and I want to stop and tuck the strands out of the way, but if I stop for a moment, I will freeze in my footsteps, so I keep going. And that's what I need to do now, just keep going.

I come around a corner on the road back home. In a moment, I will see my house, a lovely new two-story Colonial with an attached garage and a big yard. Once it is within view, I know I will make it, so I push on. A breeze pushes icily scalding air into my lungs. But I am the champion, my friends.

And . . . there it is. Home.

I follow the mailman by about thirty seconds, so I jog to the mailbox on the curb. I try to open the metal door, but the hinge is stuck, so I struggle with it. I kick the post with frustration and give the door a hard tug. Finally, it opens. I would ask Eric, my so-called husband, to fix it, but he moved out, and now I need to figure out these things on my own.

On my own. I frown at the thought.

On my own is something I have never wanted to be. But right after Christmas, when he seemed irritable and distracted, Eric informed me that he would be moving into the downtown Newburyport condo that we have owned since our daughter was born. We have been renting it out for two or three years at a time, but our renter moved out before Christmas, and I guess Eric saw his chance. I gulped back tears of shock and hurt. Was this a midlife crisis? Would he come back home eventually? Was he open to counseling? His answers were lukewarm and unenthusiastic. *Sure*, he said, *we could try counseling. Maybe*, he said. Maybe he'd consider moving back in.

I don't know what happened. I thought we were happy. At least, I thought we were happy enough.

I sniff back another wave of tears; no more weeping today. A quick flip through of the envelopes: electric bill, summer camp brochures—do I already have to start planning for summer? It's two degrees out here!— grocery store sale flyers, department store ads. And one other, an envelope that I addressed and mailed three weeks ago, returned to me unopened, marked "undeliverable" and "no such resident."

It's the letter I sent to Riley. I hold it, look at it. Oh, little envelope, you got all the way to New York and came back; why couldn't you just find her?

I am sweating, and my fancy science layers are starting to freeze around me, so I go inside. In the warmth, my blood begins to thaw and flow through my limbs and into my hands and head. The sensation is dizzying. As my heart pounds, I microwave my morning coffee and sit down at the kitchen table. A month ago I told myself that if this letter came back and I still didn't know where she was, I would go to New York and track her down.

The last time I talked to Riley was on her birthday in early November.

We only talked for a few minutes; she told me friends were taking her out to dinner. I invited her to join us for Thanksgiving; she said she'd have to check her schedule. After that, I texted, called, and emailed her about Thanksgiving. No response. I figured she was busy, probably off to some exotic place for a photoshoot for *Vogue*, and couldn't make it. Then I started asking about Christmas—as I do every year—and the radio silence continued.

Then I started trying to reach her through every channel I could think of: text, email, Instagram messages, and telephone. I told her, *Don't worry about the holidays, but let me know if you're all right.*

Nothing. So I resorted to paper. First a Christmas card with pictures of the kids, where I begged her to get in touch. That card was returned. Now this letter. And now I am worried. Where is my sister?

I force myself to get up, go upstairs, and shower, then dress and head out for errands: grocery shopping, then to Staples for something Ethan needs for his computer. Half my life is spent behind my car's steering wheel; this is where my mind wanders. Driving down Route 1A past pizza places, farm equipment outlets, and doggy day cares, I am antsy; I chew on my thumbnail. A kind of nameless urgency is bubbling within me.

Riley, where are you?

When I reach home, there's still time before I need to pick the kids up from school. I fire up my laptop and do the social media walkabout that I've been doing at least once a day, sometimes more. First, Tumblr. It's mostly photos of Riley posted by various fans. A few new ones, but nothing useful. Then, Twitter. It's a million little inside conversations that are almost unreadable. I try to make sense, but trying to follow those threads literally hurts my eyes. Next, Facebook. She hasn't added anything there since last November: there are some photos and short videos of Riley and her friends, a couple of humorous memes about coffee, a smattering of photos of kids in a New York playground where someone tagged Riley, but she's not in the photos. God, social media. Why do random people think they can just go around tagging people whose lives are more interesting than theirs? It's so bizarre.

Then I check Instagram, and that's just a useless stack of poses, one after another. Riley at magazine shoots, Riley with her friends, Riley without makeup, Riley looking serious in a black top and jeans, Riley using a filter that makes her eyes big and cartoony. Photos still crop up there from time to time, but they don't feel real. People comment, and sometimes Riley responds with a quick quip. I guess there's no point in checking Snapchat, but there's probably some other new social media sensation where Riley's making her presence known. I can't stand looking at all these posts, the way they tell me something and nothing at the same time. It's exhausting.

Where do I go from here? I don't want to call her agency again. I can't listen to the tinny voice of the girl who answers the phones tell me again that all she can do is take my number and message, then give it to Riley. My sister is not responding to me; what am I supposed to do?

Finally, I look up the property manager for Riley's apartment. My heart beats as I dial the number. A man answers the phone.

"Hi there," I say, working the friendly tone. "My name is Colleen Newcomb, and my sister, Riley Emery, was, until recently I think, renting an apartment from you." I look at the address on the envelope. "She lived on West Twenty-Second Street. In Chelsea." I pause to let him respond, to acknowledge that he knows this property. But he does not.

"Do you know the place I mean?"

"Sure," he says.

"A letter I sent her was returned, and I just wanted to check with you because she didn't mention she was moving. Is she still living there, by any chance?"

He sighs heavily into the phone. "I can't disclose that, lady."

"Oh," I say, trying to sound a little flighty. "Of course, it's just, like I said, I'm her sister, and she's so busy that she probably moved and hasn't gotten around to telling me the new address." I grip the edge of the counter and stare at a spot where some sugary liquid has dried to a shiny slick. This man doesn't know what's at stake. "I don't want her to think I forgot her birthday. Can you just let me know if she's still living there?"

"Like I said, I can't disclose that information," he says again. "Have a nice—"

"Wait," I say, desperate to keep him on the line. "Can't you just—"

"Sorry, lady, I can't just."

"Okay, fine," I say, my voice thickening. "Just tell me this. True or false. Riley Emery no longer lives in your building."

He sighs again, heavy and irritated. Finally, he says, "True."

Confirmed. But still, it hits me like a blast of cold air from my morning run. "Okay," I say. "I suppose you can't tell me if she left a forwarding address?"

He chuckles. "If she left an address with the post office, her mail would be forwarded to her, huh, now?"

"Yes," I admit. "I guess it would be."

"All right," he says, and I hear him shouting out to someone in the room before he hangs up the phone.

What's next? I type into Google, "New York Missing Persons." First result: "Missing Persons Clearinghouse – NY DCJS – Division of . . ." I click the link, scan the page. I don't quite understand—it looks like a public resource to help find missing people. Well, that's what I need. I call the number.

"My sister is missing," I explain after quick introductions. "I don't know what to do."

The voice on the other end is female, patient and understanding. She asks me a few questions about Riley: age, abilities, and whether she might be impaired in any way. Finally, she explains to me that Riley's an adult, and since there's no reason to think that she's cognitively impaired or lost in the city, they can't help me. I thank her and hang up.

I snap my laptop closed and stare at it. The problem is that my sister *isn't* missing. I am the only person who doesn't know where she is. And now that I realize that, I'm officially panicking.

My hands shake slightly as I call Eric at work. He answers. "Hi," I say curtly. "Sorry for the last-minute notice, but I need to go to New York, and you have to come home and stay with the kids. I'll set up the guest bed for you. What time can you be here?"

"Colleen, what are you talking about?" he says. "I can't just change my plans on a moment's notice—"

As he talks, my body fills with that familiar hot impatience. No, you don't, Eric. For years, you've been given a pass to go anywhere, anytime—two-week international business trips, late-night dinner meetings, early-morning jaunts to CrossFit, last-minute trips to Chicago to meet with corporate. This time, you stay home.

"It's not a girls' weekend, Eric," I bark. "I don't know where Riley is."

"What do you mean? You still don't know where she is? Did you try calling her agency?"

I want to slap him. "Yes, Eric, I have used every mode of communication I can think of. On top of that, I've called her agency, many times; I've called her property manager. I have no idea if she's ignoring me—" I pause. I sigh. But then, she must be. Ghosting, I think the kids call it. But why would she do that? Did I do something? "Anyway, I haven't heard from her and nobody will tell me anything, and I have no idea where she is or what is going on."

He sighs as though this is all a big inconvenience. "You can't go there, Colleen," he says. "You hate big cities. You'll get lost. New York is huge."

I hate him for talking down to me; he has no right to do that. The worst part is that he's right, I do hate big cities. When he went to law school outside of New York, I never ventured in by myself and wouldn't go near Manhattan unless I was meeting Riley.

"Eric, I'm not asking for your opinion or even your help. I just need you to spend the weekend with the kids. Maddie has soccer on Saturday morning. Ethan has a birthday party in the afternoon. I'll make a schedule with addresses and everything you'll need. Tonight I'll pick up a pizza for dinner, and I'll leave you a chicken and salad for tomorrow. What time will you be here?"

"I'm not a babysitter, Colleen," he snaps.

"No, you're not, Eric. You're their father. It's one weekend," I say, clenching my jaw. I hate the anxiety of this conversation. *You are my husband*, I want to yell. *You're supposed to support and encourage me.* "Can you be here by six? I'll leave as soon as you get in the door. You won't even have to talk to me. Okay?"

He sighs. "I'm sorry," he says. "I don't mean to be a jerk. I'll be there."

I close my eyes, relieved. "Thanks. If this comes up again in the future, let's please try to act like adults."

"I'm trying, Colleen," he says. And that's how his voice sounds. Trying.

I glance at the big calendar on the wall, which is covered with notes about the kids' activities. And one thing on Tuesday mornings, marked only "C."

"Listen, we have another counseling session this Tuesday. Same time. Can you make it?"

"Oh, right," he says. "I might have a meeting then, but I'll see if I can move things around."

"That would be great," I say. And the next words tumble from my mouth as though someone else says them. "You know, it would be a big help if you'd actually try to participate in the process and not just sit there with nothing to say. You're the one who's unhappy here, in case you don't remember." He says nothing for long enough that I wonder if we've lost the connection. "Hello?" I say.

"I can't really talk right now. I said I'd try, and I will. What more do you want?"

I laugh to myself. What more do I want? I want to turn the clock back to when we were a family. "See you tonight," I say.

In the evening, Ethan and I pick Maddie up from practice, and we head into downtown Newburyport to pick up a large pepperoni pizza. On the way home, I explain to them that I'm going to New York so they get a whole weekend with Daddy. Ethan, my ten-year-old, doesn't look up from the game on his phone but puts his fist in the air and announces, "Excellent! Weekend with Dad!"

Maddie, beside me in the front, glares at me. "Can I go with you? Caroline's mom brought her to New York to see *Wicked*. She posted like a hundred pictures."

I stop the car at a red light on High Street. "I'm not going for fun, Maddie. I need to track down Aunt Riley." And part of me believes it might just be that simple, a matter of finding my sister in person, confronting her about why we haven't heard from her since last fall, why she won't return my calls. Maybe all she needs is a reminder. She's just distracted, that's all. Could it all possibly be so easy, so innocent?

But my daughter is relentless. "I can help, Mom," she says. "Oh, maybe we can get tickets for *SNL* or *Today*. We could hold signs and get on TV. That would be cool."

"She gets to go to *SNL* while I have to stay home with Dad?" Ethan shouts. "That sucks."

"Stop, kids. Everybody, just stop," I say. "I am going by myself. This is between me and Aunt Riley. I'm sorry. We'll do a family weekend in New York another time."

Ethan huffs and goes back to his game. Maddie crosses her arms and pouts. "I never get to go anywhere," she says. "It makes me want to jump off a bridge."

Makes me want to jump off a bridge. I pull the car to the side of the road and jam the brakes so hard, the tires squeal. I turn and look Maddie hard in the face. "What did you just say?"

In the streetlight's glow, my daughter stares at me in abject shock. "I don't know."

"*What* did you just say?"

Ethan regards her with curiosity, while she glances around the car for a clue. Neither of them remembers the words that just tumbled from her mouth. Maddie looks panicked. "We . . . never go anywhere?"

"The other thing, Madison Dodge Newcomb. What was the other thing you said?"

"Umm," she starts. She stutters. And finally, eyes lowered, whispering, she repeats it. "Makes me want to jump off a bridge."

"That's the one," I say. "We do not joke about that in this family, you understand?"

"Geez, Mom," Ethan says. "It's just something people say. She didn't mean it. She's not going to go throw herself into the Merrimack River."

"I don't care if it's something people say," I snap. "We don't joke about jumping off bridges. Not in this family. Do you understand?"

They both nod, and nod quickly, eyes cast down. On the way home, the car is quiet. My children believe that my mother died of breast cancer. This is what I tell everyone, even Eric, even my friends. But in this family, we don't make light about ending our own lives.

At home, I make a salad and stack a plate with fresh vegetables and a bowl of homemade hummus to go with the pizza. Then I sit with the kids and go over their weekend plans.

"Maddie, I washed your soccer uniform and packed it up in your duffel bag," I say. "For the game, make sure you bring a sweatshirt, that place gets so cold. And bring a couple of bottles of water and one or two granola bars. There's a new box of the kind you like in the pantry. Here, I'll get those out."

I would like to just load up her duffel with snacks and water, but I am trying to teach her to think about these things herself.

"You don't have to, Mom," Maddie says. "I can find them."

"If you see the box on the counter, you'll remember," I say. "Also, the game is in Exeter, and that's a half an hour drive. Make sure your dad packs something substantial to eat in the car, a couple of apples and a yogurt, maybe."

She rolls her eyes as she crunches on a celery stick. "Okay," she says.

"Eat some carrots," I say, turning the vegetable platter. "You need the Vitamin A. You too, Ethan. By the way, Charlie's mom told me that he really likes the new climbing gym in Newburyport so I got him a gift card, and I wrapped it up in a box with a couple of Ring Pops."

Ethan puts a few carrot sticks on his plate and mutters, "Thanks," through a mouth full of pizza.

"Don't talk with your mouth full, please," I say. I nibble on a slice of cucumber, but I'm too nervous to really eat.

At six fifteen, Eric walks in the door. I glance at the clock on the microwave, amazed. Fifteen minutes late counts as on time for him.

"Hi, everybody," he says.

"Hi, Dad," they respond. The kids don't get up to greet him, but he walks behind them and kisses their heads.

"Thanks for coming," I say. "I still need to pack. Pizza's on the counter. Help yourself."

"Colleen," he says as I cross the room without meeting his eyes. "I'm sorry, I shouldn't have been so gruff on the phone. It was just the sudden notice. I'm always happy to help with the kids. Okay?"

"Thanks," I say. He looks me in the eye, and I smile a little. The Eric of another era, kind and helpful. With a gentleness that used to feel like a respite from the world. He used to know what I needed before I did. I don't know when things changed.

"The sheet on the counter lists everybody's weekend plans," I say. "Ethan's birthday present for Charlie is on the credenza. I'll be ready in a few minutes."

Upstairs I pull out a weekend bag and toss in a couple of sweaters and slacks, a cosmetics bag and a few toiletries. Maddie appears and stands in the doorway of the bedroom.

"Mom, do you really think Aunt Riley is missing?"

My daughter, her hair pulled back into a ponytail, curly strays tamed with a stretchy headband. She wears yoga pants and her Red Sox hoodie, her lounge clothes. Standing there in the doorway, I'm struck by how long she has become, how skinny and gangly, limbs that stretch in all directions. Someday she will be a lovely woman. And that possibility terrifies me.

"Maddie, aren't you freezing?" I say. "I wish you'd wear slippers around the house, at least in the winter. You're just getting over that cold. I'd hate for you to miss a whole season of skiing, especially now that the Corwins have that condo in North Conway. Emma's mom told me that once they get things set up, they'd love to have you join them up there—"

"Mom," she says. "Stop. I'm not sick, and I'm not cold. I'm okay."

I know she gets tired of me butting in. She doesn't understand that I want their lives—hers and Ethan's—to be perfect. When I was her age, the only person who cared if my feet were cold was me. Nobody worried about whether I was sick, hungry, cold, scared, lonely, whether I had what I needed or what I liked. That's a mother's job, and I didn't have one. Maddie doesn't know what growing up was like for me, and I don't want her to.

"Well, good," I say. "Still, I put the flannel sheets back on your bed. I know you said you were too warm at night, but it's been in the single digits lately—"

"Okay, Mom, that's fine," she says, raising her voice over mine. "Thanks. What about Aunt Riley? Do you think she's hurt?"

"Well, I hope not," I say, folding a sweater and placing it in the bag. "But I don't know where she is, and I can't get in touch with her. I don't know what's going on. And I'm worried."

"Do you think she's alive?" Maddie says. "Or do you think they'll find her, like, floating facedown in the East River?"

"Madison Dodge!" I shout. "Don't even say that. I don't know what you're watching on YouTube, but when I get back, we seriously have to talk about screen time."

"Oh, God," she says, whining.

"Aunt Riley is not dead," I say, zipping my bag closed. "She's somewhere, I just need to figure out where. I mean, she's probably just working, right? And moved and changed her phone number and forgot to tell me."

"And she shut down her email, and she's not posting on Instagram," Maddie says. "When you put it all together, the whole thing is kind of freaky. Did you ask Aunt Alex what she thinks? She might have some ideas."

I scoff and put my suitcase on the floor. "Alex is in India." Maddie is right, my older sister frequently has good ideas. But she's in another hemisphere. So, for now, I need to handle this. On my own.

"I will find Riley, Maddie. I have to."

"I hope you do," she says. "I want to meet her. I want to see what she looks like up close, like, when she's not all glammed up for the magazines."

I smile slightly. "I always forget, you haven't met her since you were a baby. Riley's just a regular person who models clothes in glossy magazines, Maddie. She's not Cinderella."

"Oh, I know, but . . . the whole thing is weird," she says. For a moment, she seems satisfied enough, and her eyes glaze as she looks absently around the room. "Hey, Mom, can I ask you about something else?"

"Sure," I say.

She walks into the room and plunks onto the bed. "Do you think Dad . . . Are you and Dad getting back together?"

I start to open my mouth to give a quick answer, and then I change my mind; I sit on the bed beside her. "Maddie . . ." I start.

"And don't give me some political answer that doesn't mean anything," she says, staring hard and pointed. "Just tell me the truth."

This child before me, this girl struggling to come into her own, who is this? Some say she resembles me, but as I look into those dark eyes, I see a young woman who looks like someone I have never met, a person in the process of becoming. She's feisty; she always has been. I admire that part of her, but she also has a jadedness, a world-knowing, and darkness to her that makes me worry. I have a bad feeling she learned that from me.

"Honey," I say. "I don't know what's going to happen. Your dad and I need to figure out how to . . . not just fix things, but start over." My face twists, and I feel a faint sob shake through my body, but I resist it.

The expression on her face softens and saddens, and her body curls forward as though her confidence has sprayed out of her like a balloon leaking helium.

"He's been gone less than a month," she says. "Can't you . . . I don't know . . ."

"All I can tell you right now is that we're working on it." I grab her hand. "But Maddie, please know, we will always be a family. Your dad and I love you and your brother so much."

"But if Dad goes away," she says, her voice low. "For good, I mean. Will you be all right? I mean, I think about your mom. I've read that people can get so stressed out, they actually give themselves cancer."

I look at her eyes, this little girl who used to do cartwheels on the beach and make cupcakes out of Play-Doh. I don't want death to be a presence in her life the way it was in ours; I don't want her to worry about things like bodies in the East River or people giving themselves cancer.

I pull her toward me and stroke her hair. "Nobody is going to give themselves cancer."

After a four-and-a-half-hour drive, I arrive in Manhattan, thrilled but terrified to be someplace new. The GPS takes me directly to the hotel, and shortly after eleven p.m., I check in. The room is tiny and cramped with a double bed and a reading chair that I need to squeeze past to get to the bathroom. The view isn't much, just a row of brick buildings with layers of buildings beyond it, and more buildings beyond those.

I sit down in the soft chair and stare out the window at the city for a while. I wonder if she's out there in the darkness; maybe I am looking straight at her now but can't see her. Then I notice, beside the chair, a stack of glossy magazines in a basket. A while ago, *Today* investigated hotel rooms and used ultraviolet light to show all the body fluids that never get cleaned from the bedspreads and walls, but I defy Savannah Guthrie and pick up a magazine—I don't really want to touch the TV remote, but I probably will eventually. It's a couple of years old. I flip through pages and stop on a shiny perfume ad featuring a young woman dressed in brightly colored feathers, with darkness behind her. She holds a mask on a stick away from her face and gives a coy, mischievous smile. The line of cleavage from her breasts peeks out from behind the feathers. I look at the picture for several moments before I realize: this is my sister.

And that is how Riley works: she appears where I do not expect her, in a place where I was not looking for her. And when I do find her, I barely recognize her.

I wake up early in my hotel bed, then brave the remote to switch on the news; temperatures today will be relatively mild, midforties with low wind. After the winter we've been having up north, that sounds like spring.

I lose myself again staring out the window as light rises to shine on the adjacent brick buildings. If she were dead, I would know it in my body; I am sure I would. I pour water from the sink into the coffee brewer and push the on button. Riley. She's changed her address, phone number, and email address, all without telling me or Alex or Dad. But why? Did she have a bad breakup? A stalker? A problem with work? Taxes? People don't just fall off the face of the earth.

Do they?

I sit on the edge of the bed and drink my coffee. She could be hurt, alone, scared. Or, then again, maybe her boyfriend is a member of the Saudi royal family and she's with him on his yacht right now, lying on a beach chair off the coast of Dubai. Maybe she needs to keep quiet about it because he's married.

Maybe she's in the witness protection program. Maybe she's a spy.

I think about these things, and there is a pull on my insides, a sour kind of ache of something I half know but don't want to admit. Maybe Riley started using opioids again. And if that's happening, we really need to be worried. Riley, where are you?

For the next few hours, I wander the cold city. I visit Riley's old apartment building, a low-rise walk-up in Chelsea on a side street lined with little trees, leafless for winter, and shops and cafés around the corner. She said it was a one bedroom with an extra little room that she used for storage. It was simply flooded with sunlight, she told me, with quiet neighbors and an amazing place for coffee just steps away. The one time I visited her here, she was having the place painted and didn't let me come inside. As of last summer, though, she was considering looking for a condo or a co-op, maybe a place with a doorman, maybe closer to Fifth Avenue.

Any chance she found her next place and just went there, not even bothering to let the post office know? I fidget with my gloves. No. That wouldn't keep her from responding to every other possible communication she received from me.

I don't know what I expected to do once I got to this building. I can't get inside, and even if I could, I'm sure her apartment is either empty and locked, or is already home to a new tenant. Instead, I stand outside and ask the people who come and go if they've ever met or seen my sister, and if they have any idea where she might have gone. One man thinks he saw her a few times. He said she sometimes had a little boy with her, but she doesn't have a child, so I think he must have her confused with someone. One woman saw Riley in the halls occasionally but never talked to her. Several other people recognize her from her picture but don't know where she went.

Just to see what happens, I buzz her apartment from the panel inside the main door. Nobody answers.

The weather report lied; it's plenty cold today. What next? Deep breath. All right, I think. Her agency has refused many times to tell me where she was over the phone, but if they knew I came all this way, maybe someone would tell me in person. I look up the address for JCW Modeling Agency on my phone; there it is. I walk downtown. My heeled leather riding boots make a loud clacking sound as I walk the sidewalks. I like that sound; it makes me feel like I know where I'm going, like I have confidence. Like I'm getting somewhere.

A half an hour later, I am in downtown Manhattan, standing among a maze of buildings so high my neck hurts to look at them. I walk into one; I show my ID to a guard and sign in to ride the elevator to the eleventh floor. When I step out of the elevator and push through glass double doors, I am in another world. Models are everywhere, fluttering about like winter moths: tall and young, some with painted faces, some with hair pinned back, awaiting cosmetics. One or two notice me, eyes landing upon me, then darting quickly away. I am not twenty-one and emaciated; I am not one of them, and I am summarily dismissed.

After a few moments, a woman with glasses and a phone emerges from the crowd and looks me in the eye. "Hi, are you from Chanel?"

"Hi," I say over the din. "No, not Chanel. I'm looking for Riley Emery. Is she here, by any chance?"

"Riley?" she says, as though the possibility is absurd. "Is she supposed to be here?"

"I'm not sure," I say as three girls squeeze behind me. "You're busy for a Saturday."

She sighs. "Last-minute model call from Jeroen Lenemans for a magazine piece. First it was happening, then there was a problem with the concept, then the weather, then the location changed. Now they're supposed to go to some studio, but the place is locked up. So now we're . . . ugh, never mind. Who did you want? Riley? Is she doing a job for you?"

"No," I say, suddenly realizing that I should have said yes. "I'm just trying to contact her."

Suddenly she looks at me like she's seeing me for the first time. "Who did you say you were?"

I hoist my purse over my shoulder and grip the strap. "Just a friend," I say, giving her as warm and carefree a smile as I can.

She eyes me suspiciously, but then a young woman carrying several hangers of clothes rushes up to her and starts asking questions, frantically demanding answers in that way that young people do. "Marina," she finally says, pressing her temples. "These aren't the right—can someone just get Jeroen's assistant on the phone?"

Marina groans under her breath. "I told you, they're on a plane, flying back from Paris. And the flight is delayed because of bad weather in Chicago."

"I know, but . . ." Then she looks back at me. "Okay, I need to get on the phone. Wait here. I'll find somebody who can help you."

She goes off poking at her phone, and I stand where I am, quietly kicking myself for not saying that she was supposed to be doing a job for me. If she thought there was money involved, she would have gotten Riley on the phone right there and then.

The woman does not return, and finally, I decide that she has been swallowed by the crowd. Quietly, I slip out, and on the sidewalk beyond the leviathan building, I watch taxi cabs zip past. I feel small, hopeless, and genuinely scared. I don't know what else to do, so I look at my phone. No messages, no calls. I glance through the news headlines. My phone knows I am in New York, so the stories on the top of the feed are all based around here. Taxi driver road rage, the crime rate, someone (a man, not Riley) found murdered in the East River. A headline about some kind of massive financial scam that's been uncovered. The blurb reads, "A private investigation found evidence that the investment company was conducting a pyramid scheme, similar to the one instigated by Bernie Madoff in 2008 . . ."

Private investigation. Could that work? I could pay someone—a professional people-finder, no less—to find her.

I walk a block to the next Starbucks where I order a coffee and grab a table. I look up private investigators in Manhattan. A surging thrill of panic jolts through me as I look at reviews on Yelp, and I almost can't believe I'm doing this. I find a few names and addresses that appear to be nearby and read the reviews. Two or three seem like good choices, so I start making phone calls. The first one just rings; no answer. The second, a woman answers, and my mouth goes dry, and I stammer and hang up.

I put my phone down and get a drink of water. This is madness, I say to myself. What am I doing? You are looking for Riley, I say back. You need to find Riley.

I go back to my phone and look at the next name. Nate Hensler. The reviews say he's great, very smart, thorough, and reliable, and that's enough for me. My heart pounds as I dial the number. After a couple of rings, a man's voice answers, impatiently declaring, "Nate Hensler."

"Hello," I say. The panic starts again, but I push through it. "Is your office . . . are you open today? I mean, on a Saturday?"

"I'm open whenever people need me," he says. He speaks fast and aggressively, as though he's in a rush; I guess that's a New York City thing. "What can I help you with?"

I pause, gulp, swallow. "I have a missing person. My sister. I don't think she's hurt or kidnapped or anything, she's just . . . not communicating with me."

"Um hum," he says. "And did you two fight or have some kind of a falling out?"

"No," I say. "That's the strange part. We're close. I mean, we were close. I've tried finding her everywhere. She's a model. I've called the agency and checked her social media. As far as I can tell, she's still working. Last time I talked to her was last November, and I've been calling and texting. I called the property manager for her apartment building, and all they'll tell me is that she doesn't live there anymore." I choke back a wave of tears. "The police won't help because she's an adult. And I have no idea, she might be avoiding me on purpose, but I don't know what to do."

"All right," he says, although his voice sounds distant as though he's looking at something else. "Sounds like you have a case. Do you want to come in to discuss it?"

I nod, aware that he cannot see me. "Yes, please. I'm in Midtown now. I could be there in an hour. Would that be all right?"

"Sure," he says. "What name should I put down in the appointment book?"

I clear my throat slightly. I consider making up a name, but I tell the truth. "My name is Colleen, *C, O*, double *L*, double *E, N*. Last name is Newcomb with a *B*."

"All right, Miss Newcomb-with-a-*B*," he says. "See you in an hour."

"It's 'Mrs.,'" I say, for whatever it's worth. "Mrs. Newcomb. See you then."

Then I walk. I need to walk. I need to go. I need to pound the pavement along with the other busy people in the busy city. I need to rush around and feel the cold air on my cheeks and in my throat and lungs.

I wish I could run, but there's no time for that now.

I walk through the city with my hands in my coat pockets for warmth. I stop at red-light intersections, then continue, not really noticing anything but the rhythm of my own steps. When I notice that I am starving, I step into a café and grab a salad. My hand shakes as I bring the fork to my mouth. Hiring a private investigator isn't what I came here planning to do, but at least it's something. Riley might have started using again, and this is the idea that scares me down to my bones. Before Alex left for college, we three sisters promised to keep each other safe. We made a pact. I can't let that go now.

One hour later I stand in front of Mr. Hensler's office building, heart pounding. I close my eyes and lean my forehead against a brick wall. I sip from the bottle of water left over from lunch. Finally, I comb my hand through my hair and pull the heavy glass door that opens into the lobby of the simple brick building; I walk up the stairs to the second floor. I push open the door, and a little bell jingles as I go. The office is small with one window and a metal desk that looks old but sturdy. An open laptop sits atop with a simple brass lamp on one side, and on the other, a stack of papers, a pile of books, and a few scribbled-on yellow legal pads.

The man sitting behind the desk is clean-shaven and younger than I would expect, probably in his early thirties. As soon as I walk in, he stands up. He's slender, of medium height, and has sharp features, intense dark eyes, and dark hair that's a touch on the shaggy side. His clothes are casual but tidy, dark jeans and a sweater.

"Mrs. Newcomb-with-a-*B*, I presume," he says, extending his hand.

I shake his hand; his grip is firm, decisive. "Hello," I say.

He gestures to the chair in front of the desk. "Please, have a seat."

I take off my coat, then sit and clutch my purse in my lap. Beside the desk is a table with a Keurig coffee maker and a box of pods, beside that a water bubbler, and three chairs. The one window does not provide much sunlight on the room, but on the wall are three abstract paintings, two featuring bright colors, another one is a study in interlocking gray boxes. I gaze at them for a moment.

"So," he says, "how can I help you, Mrs. Newcomb?"

I feel like I've walked into a film noir, but I'm here, so I may as well do this. "Mr. Hensler—"

"Nate," he says.

I nod. "Nate, I need to find my sister," I say. Tears well up in my eyes, and for a few moments, I cannot get any words out or the tears will come too. He offers me the box of tissue on his desk.

"Sorry," I say, dabbing my eyes.

"That's okay; take your time," he says.

When the tears are done, I talk about my sister's life, where we grew up, how she got to New York. As he listens, he scribbles notes on a yellow legal pad with a sharp yellow pencil. He asks a few questions about the situation: the last time I heard from her, whether anybody else in the family has been in touch with her—no—and whether she had any friends in the city we could contact—I never met her friends and I don't know their names.

When he's done, he sits back for a moment and fidgets with three or four cube-shaped silver magnets, his gaze on the wall behind me.

"Generally, when a person is missing, there's a reason for it," he says, the magnets in his hand clicking as they tap into one another. "In this case, your sister might be fine. She might be out of town working. But you're worried. Why? What are you not telling me?"

"For starters, it's been a number of months," I say.

He nods slowly. "Yes, a number of months. Anything else?"

I gaze down as I whisper, "Umm," I start. "She had a point in her life—"

"Sorry, Mrs. Newcomb, I can't hear you."

I clear my throat and take a breath. I hate having to say this aloud, and I cannot make myself meet his eyes as I speak. "She used to have . . . to do, to take drugs. But she beat it. She did. She went to rehab, and when she came out, she was recovered."

He crosses his arms and thinks about that. "Of course, the stereotype with models, or maybe it's just the way it is, is that a lot of them do use drugs. It's an intense lifestyle, right? Flying all over the place, working at all hours, eating almost nothing, exercising like mad," he says. "But your sister went to rehab and was all recovered. You're sure about that?"

I shrug a little. "She said she was."

And now that I think of it, how do you know if someone has really recovered from addiction? Until you know for sure they haven't.

He scrawls down some more notes. "All right," he says. "Is there anything else about her background or your relationship that might explain what's going on?"

I am filled with the hot energy of an anxiety attack, but it levels out, and I don't hyperventilate, which is a relief. I shake my head.

"Your case sounds pretty straightforward," he says, looking over his notes. "Actually, there's a lot I can do on the computer as long as I have an official name and a social."

"I've been trying that myself, but I haven't been able to find anything."

He smiles a little to himself. "As a licensed investigator, I have access to databases that most people don't. I can search utility bills, credit card numbers, and a few other things. If my online resources don't turn anything up, the next step is surveillance."

I nod. Okay, surveillance, that's when things get serious. "How would that work?"

"Well," he starts. "I'd have to find some kind of lead, try to figure out her general location. Then I'd follow her around for a couple days and see what happens."

"And how much does all this cost?"

"My fee is two fifty an hour," he says. "I could probably find your sister with about three or four hours online. Then I'd make a physical approach to confirm that she is where she seems to be. To get started, I require a retainer of 50 percent of what I think the job will cost. I could probably find her for fifteen hundred, with seven fifty up front; that would cover a few hours online plus a couple of hours of surveillance."

I give him a half nod. "Okay," I say.

"If you'd like to go ahead with this, I need to ask you a few more questions. Some of them may feel intrusive, but I ask you to try and answer them as best you can." He clicks, clicks, clicks on the computer.

"Okay," I say.

"First of all, can you describe her to me?" he says. "Including tattoos, birthmarks, anything else interesting."

"Well, she's beautiful," I say. "Not quite statuesque like some models, but tall, around five-ten. Slim but strong. Have you ever heard of Lily Donaldson or Gemma Ward? Oh, or Lily Aldridge?"

"Names are familiar," he says, typing.

"She's in that generation of models," I say. "She's not really a super-model, but she had some real notoriety for a while. A couple of years ago, she was in a series of ads for Maybelline that I saw all over the place. She's also worked pretty regularly with *Vogue* and *Harper's*. Oh, she was once on the cover of *British Vogue*. At one point, she was doing a lot of work with Grace Coddington. You know who she is, right?"

"No," he says. "What was the name? Grace . . .?"

"Coddington, she's the Creative Director at *Vogue*," I say. I sigh. He doesn't look like he's getting it. I stop myself from asking if he's heard of *Vogue*. "Riley, anyway, she's always busy, going from Paris Fashion Week to New York Fashion Week and flying to Costa Rica for a shoot, then to LA for a commercial. She has medium length wavy blond hair, though some-times it's closer to light brown. Her eyes are light blue. Ears pierced. No tattoos that I know of. No birthmarks that I recall."

"Um hum," he says, typing.

"You've probably seen her in ads. She's done L'Oréal, Dior, Chanel," I say. I pull up my phone and bring up the portfolio photo on her agency's website. "Here she is. Give me your email address, and I'll send you some of her work."

He leans across the desk to look at my phone. "May I?" he asks, and

I hand him the phone. He scrolls through some of the pictures on the browser and shows me one of her looking a little more normal. "Is this how she looks in general, when she's not working?" he asks, turning the phone toward me.

"Yes," I say.

"I'll print this picture out later," he says, handing back the phone. "If that's what she looks like walking around town, I probably don't need to see more than this. If she is, in fact, in town. It sounds like she could be anywhere."

"She could be," I say. "I assume her agency would know if she's traveling, but they won't tell me anything."

He nods, typing. "Okay. First language is English?" he asks. I nod. "Does she have a car? Or any vehicle?"

"No," I say. "I mean, as far as I know."

"We already talked about drug use and abuse," he says, glancing at his computer. "How about medical issues. Disabilities, recurring illnesses, allergies, any medication she needs to have?"

"None of the above," I say.

"Personal habits," he says. "Does she cook dinner at home or get takeout? Does she run through Central Park or exercise at a gym or a yoga studio? Do you know anything about her friends?"

"I don't think she cooks," I say. "I don't think she runs on the street; she prefers cardio classes or like, interval training. She usually works with a trainer, but I don't know who."

"What about her headspace," he says, pointing at his head. "Phobias, psychosis, anything else you might know about her mental state? She doesn't sound violent, but can she become violent, if provoked?"

I shake my head.

He looks at me. "Any chance she's in a relationship with someone violent?"

That one surprises me. "Oh, I hope not."

"Okay," he says, writing that down. "Parents, living or dead?"

I clear my throat and look down. "Our father is alive. Our mom died when Riley was four."

"Died how?"

I pause. I wish I didn't have to say this, but maybe it's important. "She took her own life."

"Oh, I'm sorry," he says, and with raised eyebrows, he types something. "What was your mom's name?"

"Why?" I ask.

He looks at me directly. "I like to have as much information as possible."

I nod. "My mother's name was Suzanne. She was married to my father, George Emery, but her maiden name was Montgomery."

"Okay," he says, typing.

I'm nervous and I'm talking too much. "She was from California," I blurt. "Aside from that, we don't know anything about that side of the family."

"California," he says. "Do you mind if I look into her background?"

"Sure," I say. "I don't imagine you'll find anything there that can help my sister. Are we good for questions? What's next, do I sign something? Oh, do you take credit cards?"

He pauses for a moment and looks at his computer screen. "I think that's all I need for now. I can print out a contract."

"Good," I say.

Nate keeps typing, and a minute later, he prints out two pages. Fifteen hundred—with a first installation of seven hundred fifty. That's a lot of cash, especially while we're paying two mortgages. But then, I only have one Riley.

He puts both sheets in front of me and shows me where to sign. I fill out another form with information about Riley, and then it's time to pull out the credit card.

"One thing worries me," I say while he runs my card through the device on his phone. "Riley is in the public eye. You might turn up something that she wouldn't want made public. Please respect my sister's privacy."

He glances at me with those dark eyes. "Actually, Mrs. Newcomb, that's a part of my job I take very seriously," he says. "I never forget for a moment that I'm working with someone's real life and the things I find out may have serious consequences for them."

"I'm glad to hear that," I say. "So, when can I expect to hear from you?"

"Do you want me to email you a receipt?" he asks.

"Sure," I say, and I tell him my email address.

"Right now, I'm in the middle of another case," he says. He's punching buttons on his phone, presumably checking his schedule. "I may be able to find some time this week, but probably not until later in the week."

"All right," I say. I stand and put on my coat and scarf. "Mr. Hensler, please find Riley. I need to know where my sister is."

Chapter 2

Monday, January 27, 2014
Alex

The skies over New Delhi are overcast, but I have only seen them through the thick glass of the windows in the Indira Gandhi Airport. Since early this morning, I have been crowded in among the hordes of Indian travelers; the process of changing my airplane ticket so I can go home, back to northeastern Massachusetts, has been way more complicated than I expected. I grasp my original ticket; I will show it to anyone to prove that I have paid my way. But the sleek brown faces in crisp uniforms of red, white, and blue behind the British Airways ticket counter keep assuring me that every seat on every plane is booked until further notice. I wasn't supposed to go home for three more months, but I'm flying back early to deal with a legal problem: I inherited a house. And, as I am learning, airplane reservation systems are not so flexible in India. One seat to London, I keep telling myself. All I need is one seat to London. How hard could this possibly be? Plenty hard, apparently.

Now it is ten o'clock at night, and all I've eaten since morning is a bowl of rice and curry. Every person I have talked to today has started the conversation by looking around my shoulders for a husband. *I'm sorry*, I want to tell them, *I am* thirty-six *and unmarried, so you can speak to me directly.*

The airport is cool from air-conditioning but reeks of body odor and hair oil. Still, I like the way it smells; this is India, where a walk on a city street endows the nose with every human smell possible in a single moment: spiced food cooking in rich coconut oil, thick body smells, perfumed flowers used in worship, car smog, and a million others. I am sad to leave this place so soon—two months in India only scratches the surface—but then, this whole adventure always felt a little fairy tale-ish. Today the clock strikes midnight, and this Massachusetts Cinderella is turning back into a pumpkin, maybe a prize-winning one at the Topsfield agricultural fair, but a pumpkin nonetheless.

I want to come back. I will come back. I just have to go home, sign some papers, sell a house, and I'll be back before the monsoons. And next time, my airplane ticket will be one-way.

I watch people file onto the day's last plane to London, and a gate agent calls me over to tell me that the seats are filled. My eyes burn with exhaustion; I smile and thank her, then I sit down to breathe before deciding what to do next. The doors of the gate close behind the travelers, and suddenly this room that has been crowded and hectic since early morning is cool and silent. My ears are ringing from the constant, incomprehensible blare of loudspeaker announcements; I am grateful for the quiet and the chance to collect myself.

One lone gate agent remains behind a desk, typing furiously. I go and stand before him, waiting for him to notice me.

"Yes," he says, glancing at my face.

"Hello," I say. "I'm trying to get a flight to London. Do you know if there's a seat available on any of tomorrow's flights?" I smile. "I only need one. I'll take a middle seat next to the bathroom."

"Let me check," he mumbles, then keeps typing and glancing up at the screen before him. Finally, he speaks. "Nothing right now. Check tomorrow." He jerks his neck to the side and looks at me and smiles. "Good luck."

I grip the strap of my backpack. "Thanks," I say. I never imagined that it would be so hard to go home. Well, I imagined it would be hard, but not for logistical reasons.

I set my two backpacks down on a seat whose torn black vinyl exposes the bulging yellow foam underneath, and, relieved of the weight, I stretch my shoulders and my neck. Then I open up my daypack to stash my airplane ticket and passport—keep those safe, remember where they are; they feel useless now, but if I lose them, I have big problems. Backpack open, I spy my travel mate—a dog-eared copy of Lonely Planet's three-inch-wide travel guide to the subcontinent of India. I pored through it and stuck colorful Post-it tabs on the pages of the places I wanted to visit. This volume informed every choice I made, from hotels to doctors to how to haggle the price of a rickshaw ride. Other travelers had iPads and smartphones, accessing information online. I know I'm old fashioned. I like my book.

I hoist on my big backpack and strap my smaller one to my front, then head outside. The moment the automatic doors open, my face is enveloped in air that is cool for January but still humid and thickly scented with diesel fuel and fermenting urine. A cab takes me to the closest hotel; a room costs forty American dollars, a lot by Indian standards, but I pay. It's close to the airport, plus, the space is clean, the bathroom private, the water hot. All the best amenities. I brush my teeth—thank heaven—and shower, then watch TV, the Starz network. It's an *Everybody Loves Raymond* marathon. I doze off listening to canned American laughter.

At three thirty, my phone rings with the requested wake-up call.

I settle my bill, then the same cab driver takes me back to the airport. He does not try to talk to me; I am grateful. When I tip him, I give him half of the Indian currency I have in my wallet, leaving me with just enough for something to eat. It is a gesture of extreme optimism and a tip so generous it must create a little karma in my favor.

Four a.m. and the airport is already filled with smells of people and curry. Generations of families bustle about, men in suits, women in saris, toting steam trunks stacked on airport dollies.

I wish I wasn't leaving. I was one week from reaching the small village in the southern state of Kerala, where my friend Maura has been living for months. She is twenty-five. When we met at Mass General three years ago, she said her plan was to work for a couple of years, then go to India to volunteer as a nurse in a small clinic she'd read about. And last April, she did it: she'd saved up her money and honed her skills, and she was ready to go. Saying goodbye to her at a three a.m. "bon voyage" party in the break room, featuring coffee from a Dunkin' Donuts Box o' Joe and cake, I listened to her talk about the clinic. The big hospitals in India were a mess, she said, and people were so poor that they often let little problems go without medical attention. And little problems could fester and become big ones, possibly life-threatening ones. So this clinic was an effort to encourage people to seek help early.

She hoped to put together a health program for women and girls, she told us. Sex education and hygiene, that kind of thing. I didn't know a single thing about India, but suddenly I envied her. On Facebook, she posted pictures of coconut and banana groves, rivers, lush, green landscape, and thin-faced children with tattered clothes. In her Indian clothes, dancing with the children, or eating a meal from a simple, tin dish, she quickly lost her Boston pallor and looked . . . happy.

My whole life, I'd never left the country. I decided I was ready for an adventure.

Maura, I emailed. *I want to come to see the clinic and help out. Can I stay for a while? I can sleep on your floor. I'll fly into Delhi on December third. Can I take a train to where you are? What do you need me to bring?*

Wonderful, we can use your help! she wrote back. *We need sterile gauze and alcohol wipes. India is amazing; you should travel around before you come to Thirunelly. It's incredible all the things they're doing at this clinic to help the community. Cell service is spotty, just email me. You can take the train to Kottayam, and we'll pick you up.*

Somehow the next part was easy: I bought a ticket, quit my job, and moved out of my apartment. I shipped boxes of gauze and alcohol wipes to the clinic so I didn't have to carry them. Then, I packed, said my goodbyes, and left.

I decided to take two months to see the country before I would go to the clinic. India was a shock to the system as soon as I got off the plane: the smells, the noise, the crowds. Traveling in India is unlike anything else, but with my trusty LP (Lonely Planet guidebook), and by talking to others, I started to get the hang of it. I stood in the women-only line to buy train tickets and always asked whether there was a women-only train car. I ate with my hands and learned how to get through the intestinal distress that I seemed unable to avoid, no matter how careful I was. I bought a *churidar* and learned how to wrap a *sari*. I did a week-long yoga retreat in Rishikesh and spent a week in Kolkata volunteering with the Missionaries of Charity.

But then the worst happened: Marjorie died. I was in the small town of Mahabalipuram, on the eastern coast, when I exchanged a dozen emails with my dad and talked to him three times over two days. Lawyers were calling Dad about this house, and it was freaking him out. I realized there was nothing else I could do. I took an airplane to Delhi and emailed Maura from an internet café in the airport.

Change in plans, I wrote. *I'm in Delhi. I have to go back home for a while.*

That's too bad, she emailed back. *I was looking forward to seeing someone from home. Life happens. Hope it all works out.*

Life happens. Death does too. Marjorie. Before I left Boston, I hadn't seen her in a while. I almost hoped she'd forgotten that she'd wanted to bequeath me her birding cottage. We were strangers until the snowy night in Boston when we were the only two people on a bus, stuck in unmoving traffic. I was wearing a knit hat that I'd bought from Colleen's daughter as a school fundraiser; it had a patch on it that said, "Newburyport."

"Your hat looks warm," she said, sitting beside me. "Are you from the North Shore?"

Nope, Marjorie didn't forget. She may have had ovarian cancer, but her mind was working just fine.

I lean my backpack in a corner. Anxiety surges through me; I feel it inflating me like helium. I show my ticket to another gate agent, and she responds with a flurry of typing. I imagine she's typing in a chat window, "There's a crazy sleep-deprived American here. Send security." Finally, she tells me she has made a note of my request and will call me if any empty seats become available. This is all I can hope for at this point. I smile, nod, move quietly on.

Next, I find a food stand selling *idli*, soft, warm rice cakes and a spiced lentil soup to dip them in. It is delicious and comforting. I relax a little now and long to close my eyes, just for a moment, but I dare not sleep. There is always the chance that they might call me, and if I miss my name, I will have to simply live in this airport until the sun explodes.

Instead I go to the international calling booth. I lost my cell phone about a month ago when I was riding in an open jeep up in the hills of Sikkim in northern India. When I was checking the time, the jeep hit a rock, and my phone flew out the window and into a deep valley. Even if I could have asked the driver to stop, the phone was simply gone. Luckily, I'd backed up my photos, so only a few were lost. I was going to buy a new one when I got to Kerala, and bought a cheap digital camera to hold me over. But actually, I loved being unreachable. I felt free.

At the calling booth, I pay by credit card to dial the number I wasn't really planning to call until I was stateside. But I have some time, may as well get something off my to-do list.

My sister answers. "Hello?"

"Colleen?" I say. "It's Alex."

"Alex!" she shouts. "Are you home?"

"Nope. Still in India." I rub my eyes; the dust and smell of the streets of this country will never wash out of my clothes or my skin. "Changing my ticket has turned out to be . . . kind of an ordeal."

"I'm sorry," she says. Her voice also sounds tired. "But, Alex, I'm glad you're coming home."

For a moment, I do not respond. I feel like my family's need is pulling me right back to where I started, like a giant rubber band. Finally, I sigh. "What time is it there?"

"Nine p.m.," she says. "I wish there was some way they could transfer the house to you without your having to come back."

Yes, the house. A house I have never seen, left to me by a woman I barely knew.

"Me too," I say to Colleen.

"The place has been empty for a long time, right?" she says. "So, why couldn't the lawyers wait until you got back?"

I scoff. Good question. "They started harassing Dad, and he got overwhelmed. It seemed easier to come home and deal with it. But that was before I tried to change my flight."

"Right," she says. For a moment neither of us speak, and there's a lot we need to talk about, but this isn't the time. "How was it?" she finally says, trying to make small talk. "India, I mean. What's it like there?"

"It's amazing," I say. And that part is true, but what I say next is not. "I'll tell you all about it when I see you." I can't imagine trying to explain what these months have been like. To anybody, but least of all Colleen, who values perfection above all things. I don't think she'd understand the strange, mystifying beauty of this place.

"Any news about Riley?" I say.

"Nothing," she says. "Alex, I'm worried."

"Have you tried calling the police?"

"They won't do anything. She's out there, she's working still, so we know she's not *dead*," she says. "Technically, I mean, legally speaking, she's not missing. I just can't find her."

"That's strange," I say. "That's not like Riley."

"That's why I'm worried. I'm . . . Alex, I'm considering some options. Well, we'll talk about it when you get home."

"Okay," I say. "Hey, Colleen, Dad told me about you and Eric. About the divorce. I'm really sorry."

Silence on the other end. "Eric and I are separated, Alex, we're not getting a divorce. We are in the process of putting our marriage back together. Our children deserve a family, and they are the priority. We both feel that way."

"Okay, good," I say. I never liked Eric much, so I think it's just as well.

Colleen says something else about getting their marriage to a "better, more honest place," but I don't hear what she says. A man in a British Airways uniform is standing before me, gesturing for me to come.

"Colleen, I have to go," I say. "I'll call you tomorrow, okay? When we're in the same country."

"Okay," she says. "Alex, I'm glad you're coming home. Really glad."

"Me too," I say. My sisters are in trouble, and after all, we had a pact. And when you have a pact, you don't get to linger at the edge of the world with dancing gods and transcendent temples. You need to go home and take care of your sisters, just like you always did. Because, if you don't, and the worst thing happens, then you will feel for the rest of your life like you failed them. And since you already feel that way about your mother, you know you don't like how that feels.

But still, it's hard not to feel disappointed. Why do other peoples' needs always come before mine?

I grab my things and make my way across the tarmac to a plane, executing an anxious international escape, like a political refugee. My heart pounds with posttraumatic stress for the first two hours of the nine-hour flight to London. Finally, after a beer, I relax and fall asleep. When I land in London, I call my father to tell him I am on my way. He offers—insists, even—on picking me up at the airport in Boston. I am surprised because he doesn't like to leave home, but his voice sounds determined, so I agree. He probably feels bad about not being able to manage the lawyers. Well, and maybe he should. At least a little.

Around six p.m. my flight lands at Boston Logan Airport. I get myself through customs, and then I am in a place that is familiar and strange at the same time—the air is cold and crackling dry, and everything smells clean and sanitized. I am surrounded by people milling about in their sloppy western clothes, who swig coffee drinks from giant Styrofoam coffee cups and constantly stare at their phones. A part of me is confused; yesterday I was in New Delhi with so much color, noise, people, heat, and dust, and now I'm in Boston, where Dunkin' Donuts and the Red Sox reign supreme.

Oh, the Red Sox. Walking through the airport, there are banners on the walls, tchotchkes in gift shops, plus people everywhere bedecked in logo-emblazoned hats, scarves, sweaters, jackets. This city, still basking in the glory of three World Series wins in nine years by its scruffy little underdog team, won the World Series again last fall against the St. Louis Cardinals. I was in the hospital working a twelve-hour shift, but I watched pieces of the game in the hospital waiting room whenever I could steal a moment.

But the lazy summer baseball afternoons are far from where I am now, a cold winter's evening, battling jet lag, looking for my father. My backpack rolls down the conveyer belt, then I wait, watch, look around; still, no Dad. Finally, I call him at his house from a payphone. When he answers, I am not surprised.

"I wanted to pick you up, honey," he says, "I just couldn't get out of the house."

And that's how it is with Dad. There are days—many, many days—when he cannot make himself leave the house. He gets groceries delivered and occasionally treats himself to bacon and eggs at the diner down the block. He finds everything else he needs within walking distance or from a friend or neighbor.

"So, what now? Commuter rail?" I eye the clock on the wall. It's just after six p.m., but the sky outside is pitch dark. And I cannot calculate what time my body thinks it is.

"Sure," he says. "Let me check the schedule." I hear him balance the clunky old phone receiver on his chin while he unfolds the brochure. "There's a train at seven. Can you get there in time? I'll pick you up at eight fifteen in Newburyport."

I can get there, but I wince when I consider managing Boston in February, wearing the lightweight jacket I brought to India. "Sure," I say. "See you then."

A shuttle whisks me to the subway, and a subway brings me to North Station. I find a seat among the commuters leaving their Boston workdays. The car fills with a smell like burned rubber; it reminds me of India, but this locomotive where everyone is sitting quietly is so different. The train lurches forward, the engine churns, and then we are moving through towns and neighborhoods on the outskirts of Boston, some humble, some wealthy, some old and historic, some working-class.

The North Shore. Why does coming home make me feel so homeless?

Before I went to India, I closed my eyes tight and shut down every part of my life.

I quit my job as an ER nurse at Boston's Mass General, where I worked for ten years; gave up my apartment in a charming neighborhood in Brookline; sold most of my things; gave loads of others away to friends; and parked my car in my father's driveway. I wasn't planning to come back.

Just before we reach Newburyport, the train hits a dark stretch of nothing. I touch the cold window. The train on the tracks, rolling in rhythm, the car, nearly empty, and out there, revealed in stray slivers of light, the marsh, great and wide, grassless and dense, frozen for winter.

Somewhere on the outskirts of that, a house that will soon be mine.

The train stops in Newburyport, and when the doors open, I breathe in a burst of cold, crisp air touched with sweet wood smoke. So different from the air I was breathing yesterday—yesterday or two years ago?

My father stands before me, waiting on the platform. He's tall, his body softly imposing and slumping a little; his hatless head shows hair that is gray and thinning. He doesn't have gloves either but keeps his hands in his pockets.

"Hi, Dad," I say, and we embrace. "Thanks for coming."

He leads me to his car. "You must be tired."

I smile. "It's been a long couple of days."

We walk across the empty parking lot to the Buick he's had since we were kids, rusted and dented, but still running. I throw my backpacks into the trunk and get inside.

My hands are freezing. "Hey, can we turn up the heat?" I reach toward the controls.

"Don't," he says, pushing my hand away. "The engine could overheat. You want a blanket? I think I have one in the trunk."

"No, thanks," I say. I pull my scarf around me. "Do you really drive around with no heat? It must be in the twenties."

He sighs. "I could spend a few thousand to get it fixed, but what's the point? I don't drive much."

I smile to myself. He was always stubborn, and old age isn't helping.

"Speaking of cars, I'll need mine tomorrow. Did you get a chance to—"

"Yes, yes," he says with an exasperated tone, as though he does me favors every day. "Frank at the garage put in a new battery, then did an inspection. I had to talk him into giving you a sticker. I have a list for you, for when you get settled and all that."

Oh, great, a list. "Thanks, Dad."

"Glad to help," he says. He drives onto the little chain bridge through a stretch of pine trees across the Merrimack River. The river beneath rushes fast over rocks and bridge supports, and the water is studded with chunks of ice that glisten in the streetlights' glow.

When I look at him in the dim light, I see his face as it looked to me for years: stiff, expressionless, never complaining or celebrating, just taking it all in. I always believed in my heart that he was being strong so we could fall apart. But there were times when I wished he would express a little of what was beneath the surface. Just so we knew that we were all going through the same thing. Well, he just wasn't that kind of dad.

"I know you are, Dad," I say. "And I appreciate that."

Chapter 3

Riley

In the morning my eyes open slowly, and I am on a mattress on the floor, wrapped like a corpse in a sheet that is not mine, my artificially lightened hair tangled on a pillow that does not belong to me. In that moment I can't quite remember where I am or if there's something I need to wake up for. Maybe I don't need to at all. I lie there for a while, the white city light streaming through the blinds, and the first thoughts that come to me are about the thing I might do, the thing I mustn't do, the place I shouldn't go.

All I can think about is getting high.

To distract from that thought, or maybe because I like it, I touch my body, touch small breasts, hard nipples. Fingers trickle down my belly, then reach inside; it's wet, a little at first, but as I touch, it gets wetter. My breath is hard. Finally, it starts and the pulsing seizes me through my center. I sigh, whimper in pain and pleasure, and then it is over. Now my blood is flowing, and my mind is a little clearer.

Still, I am thinking about the thing I should not think about.

Two months ago they kicked me out of my place, and I don't know why. I lived there for a couple of years, always paid my rent on time, and never made any noise. I mean, I was never there; it was really just a locker for my stuff. And I didn't even have that much stuff, so you'd think they'd give me a discount. What they gave me was an hour to pack up and leave, and that was only because I sweet-talked the thug who'd locked me out. He kept saying that I hadn't paid my rent, but I know I paid last month, just before the parade. Wait, if there was a parade, maybe it was Thanksgiving and not Christmas. And I know I owed them something from last fall, after Caleb left. Just a couple of months, though; it couldn't have been more than two or three. Four, tops. I mean, I was gone a lot. And it's not like I have an assistant to help me figure these things out. Why are people so mean?

Lucia took me in before Christmas, when I was a poor little strung out match girl. I am forever indebted to her. Lucia Agosto, a socialite who models sometimes, sometimes acts, and also runs a small art gallery in SoHo where she shows her friends' works. Beautiful, graceful, funny Lucia lets me stay in this Manhattan studio, her crash shack—with east-facing windows, an elevator, and a small terrace—while she is abroad. In this case, abroad happens to be at her dad's ex-wife's island off the coast of Italy while Lucia dallies with the affections of a very famous and married movie star who's filming on location. Ludicrous Lucia. Loose Lucia. Licentious Lucia.

Rent, I will certainly pay rent. *At some point*, she said, *no rush*. She herself doesn't know how much this place costs since her father pays for it. And I am obviously not the only one with a key to the place, because since I've been here, more than once, people have let themselves in in the middle of the night. Once, two people made each other's dreams come true on the living room couch. Ugh, get a room! Oh, wait, you did.

There's no bed here. Why doesn't Lucia have a real bed? I feel like she told me, but I can't remember. Did it have something to do with bedbugs? Yes, she told me; someone in the building had an outbreak, and she decided it was easier to just throw the whole bed away. Plus, she's planning to redecorate as soon as one of those reality-show decorators can come and knock down a couple of walls.

I untangle from the sheet; the morning air is so cold, and me, dressed for the wrong season in my T-shirt and boy shorts. Stumbling off the bed, I wander into the bathroom and look at myself in the mirror. There she is, everybody, Riley Emery. I wave and smile gratefully, hold my hair on top of my head and blow kisses to the invisible people around me. I snap a pretend selfie and post it to a pretend Instagram. Immediately, I get pretend likes. "Gorgeous!" they type. "Love you!" and "You still got it, baby!"

Cameras all around, snapping, snapping. I practice my poses, sideways with head to side, then face the camera, other side, head back, laughing, pouting, eye roll with shoulder forward. I want it. I work it. I own it.

I am used to being watched. "You," I say, pointing at the mirror. "You behind the camera. I know you're there; I feel you see me. I feel you need me." It comes like a little shiver in my bones, thrilling and horrifying at the same time. I give you that expression, smoldering— "smoldering," that's someone else's word, not mine. What does it even mean? Embers, not blazing or crackling, just hot enough to emit smoke. It's the eyes. My face points down, but the eyes point up to show this reluctant desire. Or longing so profound it defies language. Or maybe I'm constipated. Either way, the feeling is so intense.

My head hurts. I can't remember how many pills I have left, not including the secret stash. Either way, I need a few more. I go to the kitchen for a breakfast of five raw almonds and some leftover green juice. It tastes like a city garbage truck on a hot day, but what can you do.

I walk around, pick a shirt, some jeans, and a sweater off the furniture and throw them in a laundry pile, though I'll probably end up wearing them later. I check my phone. A text from my agent, reminding me about a photo shoot this afternoon. Thank goodness she keeps getting me afternoon gigs. It's just too hard to get out of bed some days.

Then I see the photo, the one family photo I have. It's me, my sisters, and our mother. I am little in this one, maybe three. Mom sits behind us girls, and Alex gives one of those huge forced smiles, so big her eyes shut. Colleen, my middle sister, smiles nicely, but her attention is off to the side. Only Mom and I are looking directly at the camera.

My mother. She would be gone less than a year after that was taken.

Every time I look at that picture, I wonder what Mom would think of me now. She was an artist and a free spirit, so I like to think she would understand my life, might even be proud of me. After all, she created pictures, and I create pictures too, just in a different way. But there are things in my life that I'm not so proud of, things I wish I could change.

Caleb, for one. And with that recorded, the list is complete. Would Mom hate me for not taking better care of him? *Who are you to judge, Mother dear*, I would say. *You ended your own life and abandoned three daughters.*

I need coffee, so I'll have to go out. And if I'm out anyway, I may as well visit my buddy, Sammy Baskin. He sells me the pills that make my head swim, make my skin crawl, dull my senses, and open my mind. I'm clean; I don't shoot up. Just pills now. Plus, the occasional hit of cocaine, because the pills make me spacey. But that's just sometimes.

Today's shoot. I check my phone for the time and address; yes, it's at one o'clock. I shower, wash and style my hair, then grab the clothes on top of my laundry pile and dress. Now it's eleven, so there should be plenty of time. Time has been an issue lately, Marcella getting cranky about what she calls my "propensity for procrastination." I check my phone; it's forty degrees outside, so I throw on a tight sweater and a scarf and my favorite pair of aviators. I stop for coffee and an apple at that new place down the street, and then I take the subway uptown. I text Sammy while I wait for the train.

> You around?

Twenty seconds later, he texts back:

> Always.

Sammy isn't what you'd expect. I think he graduated from NYU last year with a degree in something mathish like business or economics. A friendly, sandy-haired college boy with an amazing condo uptown, complete with exposed brick walls and a lovely wine refrigerator that keeps whites and rosés at the optimal temperature. A lot of the girls I know use him because he's so nice. And his place is clean and on the way to things, so it just makes the whole experience that much more pleasant.

I get off the train and start to walk toward his place, and suddenly a cold breeze from the river comes up behind me. My phone buzzes; there's a text. It's from Marcella, my agent. Probably sent by Bernie, her assistant.

> Don't forget: shoot
> today at one.

I text back:

> On my way!

I wish Sammy's place was closer to the subway; it feels like a long walk. I'd take a cab, but something is going on with my bank account, and until I figure out what, I have to be careful with cash. I guess I'm not working as much as I used to, but the account balance I'm seeing at the ATM is still insanely low. Which is really weird, because I am not making those crazy rent payments anymore. So what's going on? I must be waiting for checks from the agency. Or maybe somebody put my money into some other kind of account? I kind of remember something like that, but I can't remember exactly what, and the records are back at the apartment that they locked me out of, along with my clothes and my shoes and all my stuff. That's the worst part about being evicted—no time to pack up all those amazing shoes I got for free. Whoever ended up with those Manolo Blahnik shoes owes me a thank-you note.

My phone rings. Probably Marcella. I look at the caller. It's not Marcella; it's Colleen. Again. I roar into the wind, exasperated. I don't need this! Who gave her this number? I canceled my last phone because I didn't want to talk to her. I am not answering; I don't want to hear it ring. I click ignore. Colleen makes me feel bad, the very fact of her, how easily she does everything, has everything, is everything. And it's like my friend Valencia said that one time when we were smoking pot on someone's balcony: we don't need to talk to people who make us feel bad. *We must stop letting them make us feel bad*, she said. *We must turn them off.*

Val, I said, *you are totally right.*

The phone rings again, and I check it. Colleen. Again. Ignore. This is getting ridiculous. Why can't she leave me alone?

I get to Sammy's building and push the button to his place; he buzzes me in. I reach his unit and push the door open. It's a party, clearly; half a dozen young men are hanging out in their boxers and T-shirts. Sammy, a cigarette dangling from his mouth, and another guy are planted in front of the TV playing some Xbox game like they are at war, furiously banging their thumbs on a plastic controller and shouting. I walk over and gently put my hand on his shoulder.

"Riley!" he says joyfully. "How's it going, girl?"

"I'm good." I slide my hand down the back of his T-shirt, touching his skin. "Look at you. Are you winning?"

"Yeah, yeah," he says, shouting at the TV, not really responding to me. "Hey, one of these guys is my brother, and the rest are his friends. They're from North Carolina, in town for a few days for my brother's bachelor party. This is Riley," he calls out to them. "Say hi, guys."

They all say hi. "Hey," I say, swinging my hair just right, smiling a little. They're all nice young men, all sort of pasty and dorky looking. A particularly shortish, chunkyish one leans in and offers to shake my hand. "I'm Wade," he says. I guess that's supposed to be Sammy's brother? I don't really care, but I smile and say, "Hi there."

I squat down and whisper in Sammy's ear, "Can I just get a little something, baby?" I breathe in, blow a little. He likes that.

"Yeah, yeah," he says. "Hold on." Someone else takes over for him at the console, and I follow Sammy to a room in the back. He takes out a box filled with tiny Ziploc bags, each containing pills. "Same as usual?" he says.

"Yeah," I say. Fentanyl. It's like an eraser for pain. I like it because it gets straight to the point.

"Whatever the lady needs," he says. He smiles as he pulls out a Ziploc bag. "Also, I got some good grass the other day. Coke too. It's good. I tried it."

I think about it. "Maybe a little coke. I'm kind of supposed to be quitting," I say, and I smirk.

"Now, now," he says as he prepares my little stash. "We don't talk that way around here."

We both laugh nervously. And then my phone rings. I pull it out. Colleen again. Can't she leave me alone for one moment? "Jesus Christ," I say under my breath.

"Everything okay?" he says.

"It's my sister." I click the ignore button. "She's fine. Last year, she was just really getting on my nerves. Then I realized it's just a matter of time before she figures out that I . . ." I stop, swallow, chew my lip. *That I'm taking these stupid pills*, I want to say. And the moment she figures it out, she'll make my life a living nightmare until I stop. And frankly, I just don't have the energy for another stint at rehab. So I have to pick, the addiction or the sister.

"I can't deal with her right now," I say. "So I stopped answering. And now she's getting mad."

"Dude, you're ghosting your own sister?"

I shrug. "I just need a . . . family vacation."

He smiles. "Good one," he says, and he hands me the stuff. I pull some money out of my pocket and hand it to him. "Thanks," I say.

"Oh," he says. "Plus, an extra forty for the coke."

I make a pouty face. "Can you put that on my tab for next time? Money's a little tight right now."

He throws his head back, showing a muscular, sinewy neck. "Riley! I totally would, but you already got a balance. And the thing is, I work on small margins, you know that. We're friends, right? And I'm here for you, I really am." The cigarette between his fingers, he strokes my shoulder. "I can't let my customers run a balance, dude. That's a policy."

"Sammy," I whine. "Come on. Please? I sent you three customers last month." I touch his arm and lean in a little. Then, I pull slightly at my top so it falls open, showing a shadow of cleavage. I pull it down a little more to show the nipple. I watch him watch. I watch him like what he sees. I watch the hardening in his shorts. "You've got company right now," I whisper. "But baby, I can come back tomorrow. I can come back whenever you want."

"Yeah, yeah, yeah," he says. "Models."

"Thank you," I say, and I kiss him on the cheek.

I follow him back out to the room where all his friends are sitting around in their underpants, eating out of Styrofoam containers. "Can I have a drink of water?" I ask.

"Anything you want," he says, returning to his console. "Hang out. What's on the schedule for today, Wade?"

"Museum of Natural History," Wade says. "Tucker wants to see dinosaurs." Everybody laughs.

I slip into his kitchenette and fix myself a glass of ice water from his refrigerator. I take a drink, and then I take out a pill; I am happy just to see it. I put it in my mouth, right up against my cheek, and it begins to dissolve. I hate myself, but I feel better. And then I feel even better. And then even better.

I think I am in love with Sammy. I think I will stay in this kitchen for the rest of my life.

After a few minutes, the initial shock wave of bliss and lethargy passes, and I look around the room at the guys all in their T-shirts and shorts. They keep talking among themselves about their plans for the day, for the next days ahead. I stand there smiling; they are so sweet, these young men with their lives before them. College graduates who will get desk jobs and marry nice girls and raise well-adjusted kids. I'm not sure what's ahead for Sammy; he once told me that his plan is to deal drugs for a year to finance an MBA, and once he has that, he's going to quit forever. And maybe he will or maybe he won't; he might get shot or sent to prison. Although he's kind of pretty; it does seem to me that things usually work out for pretty people.

One guy sits in the corner reading the paper with great concentration. He drinks coffee from a paper cup and eats Cheetos out of a bag. He's thin with a tight, angular face, has a goatee and light-brown hair clipped short, kind of a military cut. He looks so familiar. Who does he remind me of? I can't place him.

The sick feeling in my gut precedes the memory itself, and my mouth fills with acid. Memory takes over. I am four years old. My sisters are at school. My mother is dead, which I tell myself—or maybe someone told me—is like she's on a vacation she won't come back from. Our neighbor, Mrs. Rhinehold, always so nervous and strict, watches me until the girls come home from school. Sometimes her son, Arthur, is there; he's a teenager, a little older than Alex. He goes to the middle school, but sometimes he has to stay home for a couple of days when he can't figure out, as Mrs. Rhinehold explains it, how to play nice with the other kids. Alex and Colleen don't like him, but to me, he is kind.

At least, at first, he is.

Sometimes, Mrs. Rhinehold goes to the market and leaves me alone with him. He gives me the cookies that I'm not allowed to have, the ones in the package. He lets me use the nice, new markers instead of the thick, broken crayons that Mrs. Rhinehold puts out in a yellow-and-black Chock Full o'Nuts coffee can.

Then, things change. Arthur brings me to the basement to fold laundry. Why? I don't like it down here. It's dark and scary and it smells bad. Scurrying footsteps in the walls; rats, he tells me. Or giant spiders. He'll protect me, he says, but I have to do what he says. Do what he says. And then, my underpants are down around my ankles and he's doing something, and I know Mrs. Rhinehold would be so mad at me. But he says that if I tell anybody, he'll twist my arm hard, so it burns, and if he does that hard enough, he could tear it clean off, like a baby doll.

I promised I would never tell a soul. But why is he doing that? Why does it make me feel so bad?

Sammy's brother's friend sits quietly, reading, I think, the stock market indices. Some memories you carry around with you always, and some you only bring out for special occasions. Arthur memories; I thought I'd lost those long ago. Packed them airtight in a Chock Full o'Nuts cannister and buried them in a corner of the yard.

I go to the bathroom; it's cluttered with hair products and shaving cream cans. I kneel on the floor and throw up quietly. When I'm done, I make myself stand up, look myself in the face. Damn it, I hope I didn't throw up a pill. What a waste.

I wipe my face with a dirty, damp towel and shake my hair into place.

I go back into the apartment and put two more pills into my cheek.

Sammy at the Xbox, shouting, roaring, as he controls a jet flying between buildings.

I kiss his head. "Ciao," I say.

"Later, Riley," he says.

"You boys have fun," I say. "But not too much fun."

"Bye," they all respond.

On the sidewalk, on the long walk back to the subway station, reverberations from the memory. My eyes fill with tears, then I am crying. There are shops and cafés up ahead, and I want to go there; I want to be someplace happy. I check my phone for the time: one thirty. I don't know how it got so late. Was I supposed to be somewhere? I can't remember.

My phone beeps to tell me I have a voicemail. I decide to listen. Maybe it's a friend who wants to hang out tonight. I would like that.

"Riley," Colleen says. "Are you there? Please call me. Your agency finally gave me your new number. I have to talk to you. I need to know that you're okay. We miss you. If I've done something, honey, I never meant to. We don't have to have some big long talk. I just want to hear your voice. Please call me."

I want desperately to throw my phone down hard through the wrought iron slats of a drain to the sewer. But I simply can't. I cannot be unreachable. I cannot fail to take and post selfies or the World of Fashion will forget I was ever born. I cannot be out of reach of Child Protective Services.

Colleen, however, I do not need to talk to. I stop walking and look at my phone. I'm so mad, I'm trembling. How does she keep finding me? Colleen, you have to leave me alone. You all have to leave me alone.

Then I lose it. "You are not my mother!" I yell at the blank phone. And I grasp the phone in one hand and bash it against a telephone pole. If it were a bug, it would be crushed. If it were a person, it would bleed. If it were a pill, it would be in my veins. Dissolved.

When I feel better, I slip it back in my pocket and keep going. I am dizzy with rage, but here I go. I keep going.

Chapter 4

Wednesday, January 29, 2014
Alex

Dad pulls into the driveway and turns off the car. There it is, the house on Greenwood Street. Not much has changed over the years. The picket fence used to be white, but now it's gray and leaning; one gutter hangs off the side of the house, but it has been like that since I started high school. Paint flakes off the sides in gray curls, the window sashes are split, concrete steps are crumbling. The house sits flat on the busy street with a small yard that used to have an old rusty swing set that Dad finally hired someone to cart off last year. We spent a lot of time in that yard, rushing through sprinklers in the summer, building snowmen in the winter. It was an almost perfect childhood. Almost.

I step into the cold night, my breath puffing like cigarette smoke. Dad pops open the trunk, and I reach for my pack. "Let me get that," he says. I hand him the smaller one but swing the big one onto my shoulders. "I can take that one too," he says.

"I know you can, Dad," I say. "I'm okay." I like the weight of it. It makes me feel like I am still traveling, like this place is just the next stop on my journey.

Together, in dim electric porch light, my father and I walk up a couple of stairs to the front door. As we pass the stoop, I remember the cold June night just before Colleen's wedding when she was barely twenty-one. The three of us sat on the steps and poured our father's rum into warm cans of coke until we were so drunk we couldn't see straight. Above, there are the windows to the bedrooms, including the one I snuck out of once to roam around with Hudson Phipps, my high school crush. I wonder where he is now; I'm sure he's not too far. People from Amesbury rarely wander far from home.

Riley made it out. And me, I almost did . . . I came so close.

These are things I have not thought about in months and years; people I forgot ever lived. Then I come back to this town, this house, and suddenly, it's all real again. I hate that. I have always hated that.

Before I walk inside, I need to see the small second-floor middle window; I need to look at it on purpose so I don't feel it looming there, staring at me. And there it is, the window to the bathroom, the bathroom with the bathtub, the bathtub that swallowed my mother.

All right. I see you.

Dad unlocks the front door; I walk in and swing my backpack on the floor. Only then, for the first time during that forty-eight-hour day, do I feel the ache in my arms and my back, my whole body swooning.

"Hungry?" he says, switching on the light in the living room. "I can make you a sandwich."

"No, thanks," I say. I look around, but I cannot see the floor, can barely see furniture. Everywhere are piles and piles of piles: warped cardboard boxes filled with stuff; old wheels extracted from small rolling things; heaps of newspapers; stacks of magazines, catalogs, papers, junk mail, children's drawings; old records; and broken toys.

I have never seen the house like this before, and now that I am, all I can imagine is that there are rodents making happy little homes down below, where we can't see them; they could easily be carrying airborne bacteria, even the Hantavirus, which can be fatal. Big piles like these restrict airflow and encourage mold, insects, bacteria, and all of this can contribute to illness, especially respiratory problems. Not to mention that it can cause a tripping hazard, and, especially in older populations, a fall of any kind can break or fracture bones. Which, in my father's case, could easily mean the end to his independence. Which could mean the beginning of the end.

I've seen a lot come through the ER. You get to know the world in a different way when that's where you work.

"Dad," I say, trying to keep my voice calm. "What is all this?"

"It's nothing," he says. "Just a little clutter."

"But where did it come from?" I ask. "Why is it here?"

"Well," he says, scratching the back of his neck. "I decided to take everything out of the closets and just dump it in the middle so I could look at it and decide what to get rid of. But I haven't . . . had a chance to look at it yet."

"But, Dad," I say, "you can't live like this. This isn't safe." I look at him, my father. His mind is not right if this is how he's living. Is this some kind of early dementia?

"I'll get around to it. Your sister wants to get a dumpster and pitch everything in." His face looks tired and terribly sad. "But she doesn't understand. I need to look at it."

"Dad, let me help," I say, taking his hand. "We can do this. We'll sit down and go through everything. Together. I don't want to get a call that my father tripped on a pile of, what, old toys, and broke his hip and has been lying on the floor in pain for a week before anybody found him . . ."

"Knock it off with the emergency room sagas," he says, gesturing as though he is pushing the whole thing away. "Fine, fine, I'll clean up." He walks away from me and into the kitchen.

"And, Dad," I say, following him. "When's the last time you had a physical?"

"Had to have a medical person in the family," he grumbles. "I'm healthy as a horse."

"It's just a good idea . . ." I pinch myself to keep from saying anything about his age. "We need you healthy. That's the only way you can keep living here by yourself. Okay? Just go see your doc and have them check your blood pressure and your cholesterol. Maybe get a stress test. I promise it won't hurt." I pause. "Although a flu shot might not be a bad idea."

"Thank you, Nurse Emery," he barks. "Now, what do you want to eat?"

"I'm not hungry, thanks," I say. I load up my backpacks and head up the stairs that are covered in the same green carpet from my childhood. "I just want to stretch out and sleep."

"The bed is made and ready," he says, sounding proud. "Clean sheets, even. Mrs. Moschella got me a couple of ladies' magazines for your bed stand."

"Mrs. Moschella?" I say. Dad's longtime girlfriend who, as far as we know, Dad has never kissed or taken out to dinner. "How is she these days?"

"Fine," he says. "Might need knee surgery, but that's how it goes. Can I pour you a bourbon?"

"No, but thanks." I reach the top of the stairs. The hallway and the rooms up here look mostly free of the debris that pervades the living room. That's a relief. I push open the molded door to the room we three girls used to share. Two twin beds now sit where a pair of bunks were once stacked, plus a third bed against the opposite wall. The beds are made and covered with faded pink bedspreads, twists of pink fringe hanging off the sides. Same ones from when we were little.

When were we little? It didn't last long. After Mom died, Colleen and I had to grow up overnight so we could take care of Riley. For many nights after, the three of us huddled into Riley's bed and listened to her unending questions: What happened to Mama? Where did she go? When will she come back? With no good answers, we simply told her over and over that Mommy was in heaven now, an angel watching over us. Riley was prone to insomnia even when she was a baby; after Mom died, she had so many sleepless, tearful nights. The only thing Colleen and I could do was to hold her close.

I sit down on the bed and glance at the magazines that Mrs. Moschella picked out. *Good Housekeeping* with a section on healthy muffin recipes. A few moments later, Dad knocks gently on the door. He is carrying a glass of milk and a peanut butter and jelly sandwich on fluffy white bread.

"Don't tell me you're not even a little hungry," he says. "And if you're not now, you will be the moment you're almost asleep."

I smile. "I can't refuse a home-cooked meal." I take the plate from him while he sets the glass of milk down on the table between the beds.

"How was India? I want to hear about your trip."

I appreciate his interest, but I am out of words. "Tomorrow, okay? I'll pull my pictures together and give you a slideshow."

"Good," he says. Then he looks down, slightly sheepish. "Sorry I couldn't make it to Boston."

"It's okay, Dad," I say. "I know it's hard."

"Yup," he says.

Daddy, I cannot be here without going back there, back to that day. And I hated that day.

"Well," I say. "Thanks for the sandwich. Good night."

His head hangs, and he gives me a small flat smile before he leaves my room. I watch his hands swing at his side, big and bulky, white as fish flesh. Strong mailman hands. Yes, he was a mailman; he doesn't care if his car is unheated in the middle of winter. He probably doesn't even notice the cold anymore. Then I remember my mother's hands, so fragile and slender, wielding a paintbrush on canvas, the smallest gesture creating a line on the surface, and that line denoting shape, movement, an entire story. What was it like, the first time their hands touched? They were mismatched for sure, but I always felt a real affection between them. Sometimes I feel bad for my father; I don't think he knew what he was taking on when he asked her to marry him.

I take a bite of sandwich, but my gut is truly not up for food. The milk is cold and fresh, so I drink it, but even that tastes strange. I go to my backpack and pull out what I need: pajamas, which still smell like India, and my toothbrush. I pull down the shades in the room and shed jeans, shirt, and sweater—peel is more like it, especially the bra, which my body gives up like scaffolding. My cotton pajamas are too thin for winter, so I pull out a pair of long athletic socks (thankfully clean) and an old sweatshirt that says UNH.

Then it is time. I need a sink, a toilet. I will not be ready for bed until I go to the bathroom. And there's only one in this house.

Deep breath. Toothbrush in hand, I walk down the hall, past my father's room where he is watching the news on a tiny cathode-ray tube TV that's so old, I'm amazed it works. Then, the small, narrow bathroom is before me. I stand in the doorway. I do not go farther. Soon after we buried Mom, Dad replaced the old claw-foot tub and put in a standing shower with cheap plastic sides. I push open the door, and the room looks just as I remembered it: floor covered in subway tiles, blinds drawn, plastic sink in an old vanity. And the textured plastic doors of the "new" shower, stained beige in the almost twenty-five years since the unit was installed.

I would like to walk in, go to the sink, and brush my teeth, but I cannot get past this point. I cannot force my feet to walk until I think about her.

And then, there it is in my mind: the claw-foot tub with the brass feet, the smooth porcelain flaking off the edges, revealing the black cast iron dots. It is filled with water. There is a towel on the floor beside it, but now I'm not sure why. Was Mom trying to keep from making a mess, or did she think she might change her mind and walk out of the bathtub? Under the water's surface lies a motionless body. Her eyes are open, but her face is so bloated it doesn't look like her; it looks plastic, like a doll. I am eleven, and it seems to me that what I am looking at must be a joke that I don't understand. I want to call for my mother; she will explain this to me. Is it some kind of twisted diorama she set up for an art project?

But even as the thought goes through my mind, I know it's not right. This is my mother, and my mother is gone. I know it because I am looking at her hands—hands, again, I keep thinking about her hands—and they are all wrong, so swollen they look like my father's. But she needs her hands for painting. She will need them once she gets better, but I know this is impossible. She will never need hands again.

I stand at the doorway of the bathroom gripping my toothbrush in its plastic travel case and my tube of toothpaste for what feels like a long, tiresome time. Finally, I realize I can't take another step until I say something to her. So, I do.

"Here's the thing, Mom," I whisper. I take a few steps into the room and close the door after me. "I'm thirty-six, you know? And I just came back from India. I carried everything I owned on my back. I drank tea every day, even on the hottest days. Somebody robbed my pocket money in Kolkata. Children clambered around me, they were so hungry, and they begged for a little change. You're not supposed to, but sometimes I gave them a few coins. There were temples, some small, some enormous. And so much color, color everywhere. Banners, lights, powder smeared over the gods, everywhere you look. So much color, it's . . . shocking."

I grip my arms and look for some sign that she has heard me, but nothing happens.

I clear my throat. "Inside the temples, people bring offerings to the gods—coconuts, sometimes, or milk—then the priest pulls back a curtain and you see the god, and it changes you. It's called *darshan*; it means 'seeing.' And I felt it. I felt myself start to change. I was starting to . . . let go of things a little." I look at the walls for any sign that my words are being heard. "India would have made sense to you, Mom. I would have loved to tell you about it."

I put my toothbrush and toothpaste on the counter. "Anyway, listen, I'm back now. And I need to brush my teeth and go to bed. I know I shouldn't let you hurl me from where I am in life all the way back to eleven years old, but it happens, every time. I don't know how to fix it, but can I just come in and brush my teeth?"

Suddenly, a thing happens that has happened before, but not for a long time, and it startles me: the water in the faucet turns on. Without my turning the handle, without my touching any part of the sink, it just turns on, water streaming steadily.

I know it's the plumbing, old pipes and crumbling stop valves. Still, I let myself whisper under my breath, "Thanks, Mom."

Finally, it's all done: my face is clean, my teeth are brushed, my pajamas are on. I slide under clean, crisp sheets and take a deep breath. The bed smells of the same cheap laundry flakes my dad always buys. I turn off the light; I am ready to give in to sleep . . . but I can't. My eyes remain open and I stare at the wall. Then, for no good reason, my mind flashes to another moment. A moment when something like an earthquake shook my life open.

I am in the hospital, in the ER, the place where I spent most of my waking hours for ten years. I am covered in the sour chemical smell of hospital disinfectants and antimicrobial pesticides. I have spent the day chasing down meds for one patient and a correct diagnosis for another, plus all the regular patient cases. The light is neon and white; I don't know what time of day it is, only that I am halfway through another twelve-hour shift. Suddenly, everyone is in motion, preparing for the arrival of an ambulance that's bringing a woman who was rescued from a bad car accident. The EMTs radio in that her condition is critical; she's unconscious. The next thing they tell us: she is pregnant, near term.

She will need an emergency C-section. There may not be much we can do for her, but we must try and save the baby.

The team preps the operating room, and within minutes, the EMTs bring her in on a stretcher. She's in bad shape, internal bleeding, possible hemorrhaging in the brain. The surgeon arrives and scrubs in, and within minutes the little girl is born, alive. She weighs only a few pounds, isn't yet physically ready to live in this world, and may also be injured, but she is alive.

But the mother is fading.

I watch the pediatric nurse bathe and weigh the tiny infant, then wrap her in a soft cloth and carefully set her into the rolling incubator, all soft and warm, that will keep the little girl alive through the next critical stage.

Suddenly, I hear the steady tone of the heart monitor alarm. The mother has passed. She lived long enough to let us bring her baby into the world, but that was all her body could manage. Then she left the world without ever even seeing her infant.

Usually, I can withstand tragedy without letting it sink me, but this one hits me hard. I look at the baby, so tiny and fragile, now wrapped in a clean blanket, the NICU nurse standing over her with a stethoscope, listening to a heart that's probably just a little larger than a jelly bean. All this girl will ever know of her mother will be photographs and stories her family tells her. I know what it's like, to grow up without a mother. *We have that in common, little girl*, I think. And in that moment, just before the nameless infant is wheeled away, something in my heart bubbles up to the surface, wordlessly announcing itself. I wanted a baby. I thought I needed a boyfriend first, a husband, a partner. But then I decided: no more waiting. I would have a baby.

In my childhood room, all these months later, I stand and go to the window, wrapping that pink bedspread around me for warmth. Sometime after I saw the baby in the NICU—weeks? Maybe a month or two?—my gynecologist told me that I had a condition I had never heard of before, polycystic ovary syndrome. I was taking birth control pills, which masked the symptoms, so I didn't know I had it. A hormonal condition, she told me, and I'd probably need fertility treatments if I wanted to conceive a child.

They don't know what causes it, she said. *Could be hereditary, could be environmental, no way to know.* But all I could think was that this was connected to my mother, and what she did twenty-five years ago. Since that moment, nothing in my life would ever be good and right again. I would never get married, I would never have a baby, I would be stuck in a tidal cycle that would bring me back to my eleven-year-old self, when I felt so useless, so hopeless, and so lost.

Foolish, all this self-pitying. But I am powerless in the gusting winds that push me around. Every time I stand up and decide I am done feeling that way, I get knocked down again.

Further from sleep now, I wander downstairs wrapped in the bedspread. In the living room, I squeeze between the piles of things to reach the kitchen and pour myself another glass of milk. I see the bottle and realize, oh, it's skim milk. Wretched stuff, skim, but that's all my father has. I squeeze back out through the stacks, and then I see, sitting on top of one of the boxes, a photo of Mom laughing, standing with a rocky beach behind her, wearing a big wool sweater. I think that must be Maine. She looks so young there, it must have been taken around the time she and my dad met. I take it and go sit on the steps and, in the darkness, gaze out the little window over the landing, onto the quiet street beyond. *Mommy, what am I supposed to do next? Do I stay and take care of Dad and Colleen and Riley? When do I get to do something for myself? When is it my turn?*

I hear Dad's footsteps on the hallway above me, and I wince when he switches on the hall light. "Jet lag?" he says, his voice crunchy with age and fatigue.

I laugh slightly and hold my hand over my eyes. "I'm too worn out to sleep."

I turn to face him as he walks down the steps. He wears faded pajama bottoms and a sweater over a T-shirt. He looks too skinny, and I wonder if he's eating enough. "Never owned a passport, myself," he says. "But all this jet-setting between time zones. It's got to mess something up."

I smile. "You're probably right," I say. Then I lift the cup of milk up toward him. "No more skim milk, Dad. Splurge for full fat. You need the calories."

"Fine," he growls. He sits down a couple of steps above me and takes the photo of Mom from my hands. "I always loved this picture," he says.

"Me too," I say.

"Your mother was so beautiful when she smiled," he says. Then he sets the picture back down on a pile. "The offer for bourbon still stands."

I push my back against the wall and pull my knees into my chest. "No, thanks," I say. "I'd take a double shot of milk, though, if it wasn't skim."

He chuckles. "She doesn't like my booze, doesn't like my milk. I'm sorry, Your Highness, your staff forgot to send me get your list of approved libations."

"Sorry, I'm just tired," I say, rubbing my temples. "No snow this year, huh?"

"Well, we got some before Christmas," he says. "But since then, it's been a dry winter. Cold enough, but dry."

"A little snow is nice," I say. "It gives winter some kind of grace. Like a reason to forgive everything else about the season." The words coming out of my mouth feel foreign and strange to me. Grace and forgiveness are not things I think much about.

Dad laughs. "That's easy to say if you don't have to shovel all that damn grace off the driveway."

I smile. "Well, I might have to shovel a driveway of my own this winter."

"Ahh, yes," he says. "The mystery house. So, what kind of a person leaves a house to someone they barely know?"

"She didn't have anybody else to leave it to," I say, sighing. "So strange the way things work out."

"Yes, very strange," Dad says, stifling a yawn.

"Go to bed, Dad. I'm fine."

"I'm in no rush," he says.

We are quiet, and I look outside through the little window at the trees bending in the wind.

"Well," he says. "I'm glad you're back, anyway. You don't think about what a comfort it is to know where people are . . . until you don't."

Chapter 5

Friday, January 31, 2014
Alex

I take a day to shower, do laundry, find my sweaters, and adjust to the time zone, and the morning of the next day, I go to the Newburyport Dunkin' Donuts to meet Pete Denton, the man who will give me a key to this house I've inherited.

I walk inside and a couple of people are in line, and a man is standing off to the side. "Are you Alex?" he says to me, tentatively.

"I am," I say. "You must be Pete."

"Nice to meet you," he says and reaches out to shake my hand. In his black wool coat and baseball hat, he seems friendly enough, a young, bespectacled attorney with dark hair, but he has a salesman vibe that reminds me of my brother-in-law, Eric. Also, I think he's the one who was bugging my father. I don't go out of my way to be cordial.

"You want to get anything here before we head over?" he asks.

I shake my head. "I'm good, thanks," I say. I have been drinking coffee since five a.m. when a garbage truck lumbered down our street, rousing me from a fitful sleep.

"All right," he says, gesturing toward the door. "Ready for the house on Killdeer Road?"

"Killdeer Road?" I say, pushing outside. "That's the address?"

"Yup," he says as we step on to the sidewalk. "It's named for a bird, a kind of plover."

I crinkle up my nose. People around here know all about plovers, tiny little birds who run around on the wet, sandy surface of local beaches after waves pull away, nibbling on whatever little bugs or crustaceans the tide brings in. I have heard of the killdeer before; the name matches the way the bird's song sounds. Still, it seems a strange name for a road.

"Why didn't they name it Blue Jay Road or something?"

"I don't know," he says. "Maybe you can petition the town to change the name of the street. Yours is the only house on it."

We go to our cars, Pete to his shiny Subaru station wagon with the car seat in the back and I to my just-barely-passed-inspection Honda. I follow him as he drives up State Street and turns left at the light to leave Newburyport, this lovely town that is too perfect and smiley, too browsy-shoppy-happy, too married-with-two-point-five-kids—too much my sister—for my taste. I follow him down High Street then onto Route 1A; now we are in Newbury. I have always liked this town, farmy and quaint with an odor of decay at the outer edges.

We continue driving deeper into Newbury to the bridge over Parker River. On one side the river leads down and opens into a sound. Beyond that, the Great Marsh stretches into the distance, massive and waterlogged, tall grasses topped with cattail flourish. The color palette is quiet right now, all shades of brown and tan. The treeless expanse beckons, but it's not a great place for walking or boating. It's a strange, flat song, a wide-open break in the landscape, welcoming to birds and water critters but not people. We stand on the edge and behold.

I keep driving, following Pete's Subaru. The marsh disappears behind some trees, but it will continue for many miles in both directions. A moment later, Pete slows down, waits with his left blinker on while another car passes, then turns and drives down a frozen little dirt road. An old sign on a rusted post reads, "Killdeer Road." It's not that the house is the only one on the street; it's that the street exists only for this house. We drive down a little way; after about a half a mile, big tangled bushes surround a little house, an old, small, weatherworn farmhouse. We turn past the bushes and into a crumbling driveway.

"Here it is," he says as we park and get out of the cars. "Welcome to Seven Killdeer Road."

And there it is, Number Seven, Marjorie's birding cottage. I huddle inside my winter coat and thick green wool scarf that still smell of the mothballs I packed them in last fall. The gravel grinds under my tentative steps. Paint peels off the planks, window sashes are cracked. The gutters are attached but rusted. Outside is a tangle of foliage, trees and vines that fence in the yard and wild grasses pounded down in winter's dry, frigid winds.

This house, any house that I might be custodian of, lurks like a marker on a map with a sign that reads "Here be Monsters." Cross into this threshold and you will not leave unchanged. The dangerous legacy of Ganesha, the dancing Hindu god with the elephant head. Maybe I can turn around now and not even enter, just sell the house without looking at it.

But I won't. I can't. This is what I came home to do; now it's time to do it.

"Shall we?" Pete says, gesturing to the door.

"May as well," I say.

We walk across frozen mud to the doorway. Pete carefully opens the screen door, and it creaks, dry and grinding. He inserts a key into the doorknob and tries to unlock it. It sticks, so he jiggles, jimmies, and pushes with gentle, measured control, but the knob will not turn.

"Let's try brute force," Pete says, and he winces hard as he slams his shoulder against the door. Finally, it opens.

Then, we're in. Pete holds the door for me as I walk into what I guess is a living room. Or what did they used to call this? The parlor. It's cold here. Freezing. Colder than outside.

"Is there heat?" I say, rubbing my arms.

"There should be." He goes over to a thermostat on the wall and turns the dial. "Let's see if it's as simple as that. It's an oil burner, so you'll want to schedule a delivery. You'll need to get the utilities in your name as soon as possible."

"Okay," I say.

"I wonder about the electricity," he says, and he flips a switch on the wall. A simple overhead light turns on, its pale-yellow glow barely visible in the white morning sunlight streaming through the window. "Look at that!"

"Great," I say.

I wander around the living room. Parlor. There's not much here. The windows are bare, no curtains or shades. A single wooden chair is pointed toward the window. One window has a simple window seat built into it. Nothing decorative on the walls, only cobwebs. The pine floor is stripped bare, no rugs, no shiny varnish, and my footsteps and voice echo through the whole house like a cavern.

Oh, Marjorie, is this what you brought me back from India for?

I gravitate toward the fireplace with its molded wooden mantle. "Do you think this works?"

He flips through some papers that he pulled out of his briefcase. "I wouldn't use it without getting it inspected. If the chimney isn't lined, it could be a fire hazard."

I stand by the fireplace. No ashes in the hearth, which tells me that Marjorie used it as a bookshelf; a few volumes sit stacked on the mantle ledge. I pick one up and blow away the dust. The title: *Birds.* They're all about birds. How to look for birds, habits of migratory birds, field guide to the birds of New England, birds of the Great Marsh.

And hanging on a hook beside the window, the newest, costliest thing in the room, maybe the whole house: a pair of binoculars. I slip off the cover and lift them to my eyes. Even now, I see them out in the marsh: little flyers, scouting, searching, soaring.

"See anything?" Pete asks.

I shrug and replace the binoculars. "Birds."

Within a couple of minutes, the house comes alive with banging and hissing. "Heat works," he says, looking satisfied. The dry dustiness is replaced with the musty odor of an old heating system. A good, thorough, inside-out cleaning would help this place. And some paint. Plus, I'm sure it needs new everything else: windows, floors, plumbing, appliances. I haven't even seen the kitchen yet.

Pete gets some papers out of his briefcase and comes to show me. "If you look on the survey," he says, holding out a crinkly old map that's actu-ally four pages taped together. "You can see the boundaries of the property. It's a good chunk of land, see, fifteen acres."

"Oh, that's quite a bit," I say. "Can I sell any of it?"

"Not for development. The marsh is protected, and the Newbury zoning board is pretty strict about issuing building permits so close to protected lands."

Wonderful.

"And out there," he says, looking at the map and pointing toward the woods behind the house, past the kitchen, "there's a small family cemetery."

I look out the window. "Really?" I say. "I don't see anything."

"In that direction, I think," he says, showing me the map, which means nothing to me. "Might be kind of overgrown. One of these days you can head back there with a machete and look for it."

I smile to myself. I left my machete in my other pants. "I'll let the next owners investigate that."

"Oh, so you're not keeping the place?"

I wander into the kitchen. It looks tired but functional. "I'll fix it up a little. But then, yes, my plan is to sell it."

"It's a nice place," he says. "Good bones, as they say. I bet you'd find a buyer pretty quickly."

From the kitchen I look directly at him through the doorway. "You want to buy it? I hear there's a cool cemetery in the woods."

He laughs. "The kids would love it, but Cindy? She considers houses built in the seventies antique. But me, I love the romance of it."

Oh, leave it to Cindy; she ruins everything. I stand in the kitchen looking at hand-built cabinets covered with grimy white paint that's chip-ping away to reveal blue-green paint underneath. I open one; the inside is raw, brown, unpainted. Someone put down flowery contact paper a long time ago, but that's all coming apart now. And dishes: three water glasses and four old mismatched china plates. Cardboard salt and pepper shakers.

"How many kids do you have?" I ask.

"Two, with another on the way." He looks at me with pride in his eyes, so pleased to be expanding his family.

"Congratulations," I say.

"What about you?" he says. "Any kids?"

"No," I say. "No kids." I don't need to elaborate, but still, it's an awkward moment. Because don't most people have children? Maybe. But Pete doesn't need to know about the moment in my doctor's office when she told me that my over-thirty-five-year-old body had dried up like a forgotten potato.

"You want to see upstairs?" Pete says, rescuing the moment from complete discomfort.

"Sure," I say, and, in our coats and boots, we clomp up the stairs. A small hallway leads to three doors. The first one I open, and we walk in; it's a bedroom with a sloped ceiling and two small windows. I open a closet door to an unpainted, dark cavity. A small rod crosses at the back on the left side instead of in the middle, and shelves on the other side hold plastic bins that contain pillows, sheets, blankets. The room has no furniture, only a small army cot folded neatly away in the corner.

"Funny that she never splurged for a bed," I say.

Pete shrugs. "I never met Marjorie," he says. "Was she a no-frills kind of gal?"

"I didn't know her well," I say. "I mean, she told me that the place was sparsely decorated, but just this seems . . . monastic."

We go back to the hall, and I open another door to another bedroom, this one long and slender.

"Kid's room," he says, then corrects himself. "Oh—or a guest room. Maybe an office."

Game room. Costco room. Wrapping-paper room. "Many possibilities," I say.

One more door down the hall. "Here's the bathroom," Pete says, pointing. "It's cute. It has a *This Old House* kind of charm."

I lean past him over the doorway and look. Toilet. Pedestal sink. An antique claw-foot bathtub. Of course, it has an antique claw-foot bathtub.

Of course, it does.

"Well, that's the house," he says as we walk downstairs. "Now, ready to sign some papers?"

"Ready as I'll ever be," I say.

He gestures to the kitchen table, the only thing resembling a flat surface in the whole house. We sit down at the little round Formica table in the corner, and he pulls out a huge stack of papers. I joke about how many trees must be slaughtered each time someone buys a house, and he just smiles and says that his firm uses recycled paper for just that reason.

"The taxes are paid up for this year," he tells me. "But you need to go to town and make sure they send you a bill for next year. Usually, that's handled through the bank that issues the mortgage, but you don't have one. Lucky duck."

I smile to myself. So lucky.

I sign and sign, rinse and repeat, and at some point, everything is done.

"Congratulations," he says, shaking my hand. "You are now officially the owner of Seven Killdeer Road, Newbury, Massachusetts."

"Thanks," I say.

Pete takes his papers, stacks them up, taps them on the table to straighten the pile, and then puts them in his carrier, smiling with satisfaction.

"Did you know Ms. Rosen well?" he asks.

Ms. Rosen? Oh, he means Marjorie. "I didn't. We only had coffee a few times," I say. I smile at the memory. "She liked Au Bon Pain; she loved their bear claws. She told me that she never would have eaten that if she was healthy, but she was so thin from the cancer, she was happy to indulge. I ate my fruit salad and told her to enjoy every bite."

"So she left you her house, but you weren't, like, the daughter she never had?" he asks.

"Not at all," I say. "Do you know if someone was with her at the end? She wasn't completely alone, was she?"

"Actually, I don't know," he says. "I think I heard that her brother—from Colorado, I think?—organized the service so maybe he was with her."

Marjorie, I hope it wasn't painful. I hope you had all the bear claws you wanted.

"Well, unless you have any more questions, we're all set," he says. "Are you going to stay here while you fix things up?"

"I haven't decided," I say. "Maybe. I have to figure out how much renovating I can afford. Say, the land alone must be worth something, right? If someone wanted to tear down the house and build something new?"

"Sure," he says with enthusiasm. "It's an amazing view."

I look through a window and see a break in the undergrowth, and from there, facing east, I see it, the marsh, extending past the road in a wide, flat expanse. And above that, uninterrupted sky, clouds breaking to reveal an expanse of blue illuminated by white-gold light from winter's midmorning sun.

And I have to admit . . . It's beautiful. I bet the sunrise here is amazing.

"Some people would love a view like that," he says. "Nature lovers, photographers. Heck, who wouldn't love waking up to that?"

"Nobody," I mutter.

"Well, enjoy your home," he says. He stands and walks toward the door, then turns. "Oh, the heat seems to work. You'll probably need to turn the water on from the basement, although you might want to wait until things warm up some. You never know with these old pipes."

"Oh, good idea," I say.

"You'll be okay here, then?" he says, sounding fatherly and protective. "Alone and everything?"

"Sure." But his face looks uncertain. "Is there something I should be worried about?"

"No, no," he says. "It's just . . . I think I would be spooked to stay an empty farmhouse like this . . . in the middle of the winter . . . all by myself."

"Spooked?" I say, laughing nervously. "Okay, if a family of four was murdered here, you have to tell me right now."

He laughs. "Oh, no, not that I know of," he says, clearing his throat nervously. "Hey, there's a decent pizza place ten minutes down the road toward Rowley. And keep going past that and there's a shopping center with a grocery store. Oh—my office will be sending some documents for your records, the title and all that. Should we send them here or to your dad's house?"

I stand in the hallway of the house that has found me, the house that has, somehow, unlikely as it is, brought me home. I am still mad at it for ending my trip, but it's mine now, maybe just for a short while. So, for now, I may as well stay.

"You can send them here," I say.

Chapter 6

Monday, February 3, 2014
Colleen

Today I visit Alex in her new, strange house. How does it happen, that a person inherits a house out of the blue? A person who never had a house, wasn't looking for a house, and did not want a house. I find the whole thing inordinately bizarre. I emerge from the shower, towel off, then dress in a sweater, jeans, and a light, printed scarf. Pretty, warm, but not overly fancy. I glance outside; it is a cold but dry February day. I'm glad it hasn't snowed this year. Spending the whole day stuck inside with the kids always made me restless. Eric used to march them a half a mile away to a hill for sledding, and they'd all come back cold and exhausted and ready for popcorn and a movie. I'm not up for the march or the sledding. Or the shoveling or negotiating with a plow person.

All the things Eric used to do. Went to every soccer game. Helped Ethan with the boy issues. Brought Maddie to every father-daughter dance. Took the kids to Water Country. And I helped with homework and baked for the bake sales and volunteered for the PTA. I thought we had a good balance of things. I still don't know why it had to end.

I look in the mirror to apply a little makeup in spare but noticeable tones: powder, blush, lip gloss, mascara. The usual daytime mix, just enough so I look like me. Or closer, anyway, to what I think I should look like.

Alex, my older sister who sometimes feels like a younger sister. Do we look alike? I examine my face in the mirror. A little, I guess. My skin is pale and slightly freckly; hers is the same, and actually, Riley's is like that too. My mouth is small, lips thin. Alex's mouth is wider, I think, sort of clunky. My hips are flatter, my build less bulky and I'm a little bit taller too. Riley, the youngest, is the tallest. And though she was slender when she was young, she's become downright skinny since she became a model. Alex's nose fits her wide face, slightly bigger. Riley and I have our mother's smaller, more delicate nose.

What about eyes? Alex has Dad's eyes, deep-set, brown. Riley's eyes are crystal blue, but shaped like mine. My eyes—the color is a murky dark green, papaya shaped. I don't like to look at my eyes; they are too much like my mother's.

I think of Alex's eyes, the light brown of autumn leaves, and I remember the time I saw a look of sheer, bottomless panic in them. Suddenly time flattens, and I am nine years old. Alex's face, filled with horror, even though she was smiling. Even that day she stayed composed; she was born to be a nurse. Her breath stuttered, and she ordered me, desperately but quietly, to bring Riley next door to Mrs. Herman's house. *Stay there for a while*, she said. *Ask her to make you chocolate milk. Ask her to show you the puzzles she keeps for her grandkids.*

I didn't ask what happened; I knew it was bad.

I think about Riley, how little she was, and how she wept—every day—for weeks. Strange that her grief was so overwhelming, but when she got older, she couldn't even remember that she had a mother, much less that she lost one.

I turn away from the mirror and look through a window, watching a few cars drive past. They don't know I'm up here; I am hidden from sight, just as I have hidden the truth about our family. I've told the fictional story to so many, the story feels like a sweater I put on to shape the person that people think I am. I don't see any harm in that. I am a certain kind of person in a certain kind of town, and if the facts of my life don't support who I am, I change them.

Looking back to the mirror, I like this scarf; it brings out my eyes. I tie it quickly around my neck, very French; then I undo it and tuck the ends under. That works. Now I am ready to go see Alex. There's a lot we need to talk about.

I stop for coffee and bagels, then drive through town into Newbury—there are sections of lovely new homes in this town, but it also contains wild, open spaces; farm stands; antique houses, some picturesque, some half-rotted, barely standing. In the luscious early fall, armies of sunflowers rise from these rolling hills, and the air is rich with the smells of manure and mulch. But now the fields are cold and quiet, empty as bones. I watch the side roads—Hay Street, Bayview Lane, Cottage Road—until I see the one I'm looking for, Killdeer Road. I have been down this way so many times, but until this moment, I never noticed that road.

I pull down the street, not much of a street, but this area is so choked with waterways and streams, all leading through the marsh, there's not much room for houses. I pull into the driveway, and there it is, another old, neglected farmhouse. The lot is surrounded by woods fully encroached by thicket. It desperately needs landscaping. And paint. Or maybe a wrecking ball.

I grab my bag of bagels and Styrofoam cups of hot coffee and walk across the sunken walkway slates. Alex opens the door before I knock.

"Let me get the door for you, it sticks," she says. "Welcome to my haunted house!"

"Alex, this is amazing," I say, trying to emit enthusiasm. "Hey, welcome home!"

We hug, do hellos, how are yous, etc. Alex in pajama bottoms and a big gray UNH sweatshirt. Her face is pale and tired, rings under her eyes. She tries to smile, but she seems exhausted. Did she lose weight in India? If she were really skinny, I would have been jealous, but either she didn't lose weight or her figure is covered up by that tent of a sweatshirt.

I bring my things into the kitchen and set the food on the faded linoleum countertop. "Thanks for the coffee," she says, helping herself. "I've been up since four."

"Four? Why on earth?"

"Jet lag." She pops open a little creamer and pours some into her cup. "I should have gone out for coffee, but I couldn't make myself face the cold."

"Alex, it's a beautiful house," I say. She gives me a dubious look. "With some fixing up, it could be gorgeous. So, how did this all happen?"

Alex sighs and plops down in one of the rusted, wobbly chairs around the table. "Can I have a bagel first?"

"Help yourself," I say.

She takes a bite. "I forgot how much I love bagels. No bagels in India. Only *idli*. They're fun, but they're not the same."

"Glad you like them," I say. "So what happened?"

She sighs, then tells me about how she met a dying woman who needed to leave the house to somebody. So she put Alex in her will and then croaked.

"I need to start being nicer to people," I say. "Maybe someone will leave me a house."

"Don't you already have a house?" she says. "Like a perfect house?"

"No house is perfect, Alex," I say. I look around. "You know, now that I'm looking at it, this place could be lovely. Paint the walls, polish the floors, make a few strategic updates, and you could probably get some real money for it. I could donate some furniture if that would help."

Alex gives me a bemused smile. "Thanks, Colleen, I'd be delighted to help you clean out your garage."

"Don't do that," I say, crossing my arms. "I am offering free furniture so your place feels less empty. I'm trying to be nice." She does not respond. "Well, can I have a tour?"

She gestures with her thickly cream-cheesed bagel. "Be my guest," she says, mouth full.

"Ahh, self-guided, I suppose." I stand up and gesture to a pizza box in the corner of the kitchen. "That's a nice touch."

"That was lunch yesterday, plus dinner and then today's early breakfast. I haven't been to the grocery store," she says. "And actually, I don't know how the trash here works. Do you know? Does someone pick it up?"

"I live in Newburyport," I tell her. "Who knows what they do in Newbury."

I wander into the front room and look out the window. The view of the marsh is startling, stunning. The marsh, flat like the Great Plains, but open and moving like the ocean, stretches out as far as I can see. Wisps of birds flit about—birds I do not know, do not recognize. These are the winter birds; come spring and summer, the air will be raucously thick with birds of all sorts, passers-through and year-rounders. It's kind of amazing. If I didn't have other things on my mind, I might actually be a little jealous.

I do not share these thoughts. Instead I mention bugs. "It's a great location if you like greenheads."

"Ugh," she calls from the kitchen. "I forgot about those monsters. When do they come out?"

"New moon in July to the new moon in August, more or less. They come right off the marsh with their little green jaws hungry for blood."

She comes into the living room still carrying her Styrofoam cup of coffee. "I plan to be gone by summer."

I float into the little dining room. The rooms are all stark and empty, no rugs, no curtains; my boot heels thunk loudly on the floorboards.

"Really? But I like this place," I say. "I bet you could ride a bike to the beach."

"Make me an offer, and it's yours." She follows me to the dining room. An old chandelier hangs in the middle of the room; I have to duck to avoid walking into it. The paint on the walls is peeling, and there is a distinct draft coming from the window.

"Sorry," I say. "My separation has put a serious dent in my ability to acquire real estate."

"Ahh, yes," she says. "Am I allowed to ask what happened?"

She leads me upstairs to see three rectangular bedrooms with funny little closets. What did happen? I don't want to tell Alex how I took Eric to dinner to tell him that I wanted another baby and found out he had a different plan.

I shrug. "We're reassessing. A relationship is a process, Alex. When you've been together for a long time, you sometimes need to take stock of where you are and the people you're becoming, and recalculate." I am regurgitating the jargon the therapist used with us, and I can see in her eyes that Alex is not buying it.

"Okay," she says. "So he moved out?"

I nod. "He moved into our condo in Newburyport, the place we owned before Ethan was born."

I bend over to look out a small window under the eaves of the house. I don't like talking about this. I wish I would notice some fracture in the house that I could bring up to sideline this talk. Nothing. Damn it.

"How are the kids doing with all of it?" she asks.

I open a closet, an unpainted enclosure with a rod supporting three or four old wire hangers that look like they've been here since the Great Depression. "Kids are resilient."

We wander into the bathroom; it's simple, looks like it was redone in the eighties with black and light-pink tiles that are now cracked, the grout between them crumbling. And the bathtub, cast-iron claw-foot. The kind some people covet. "Nice tub," I say.

"Yup," she says and quickly leads me back into the hall.

We walk back down the stairs and into the kitchen. I remark cheerfully about the house, call it homey and charming, point out that it could use a second bathroom. But there are real things we need to talk about. I have to tell her about Riley. I open my mouth to say it, but only more small words come. "I can't believe you went to *India*," I say.

"Me neither," she says. "Actually, I think I'm in shock. Part of me is still back there. Part of me is still in the airport, convinced they will never let me leave Delhi." She sighs deeply and leans against the wall in the dining room and looks out the window. "And some of me is here. So, I'm feeling a little scattered."

"You've been scattered for a while," I say. "You should stay here. Get unscattered. How bad could it be?"

She takes a drink of coffee and looks at me. "And do what?"

"Whatever you want," I say. "You don't have a mortgage, so all you have to pay is real estate taxes and utilities. You can take it easy. Get a part-time job in a doctor's office, weigh kids and give out flu shots. Go for long walks on the beach. Get a hobby; drink. I don't know."

"No," she says. "I want to go back to India. I didn't even make it to the clinic where my friend Maura was working."

"Was Maura at that brunch you gave last summer?" I ask. Alex nods. "She was so cute and young. What's she doing again?"

"She's a medical volunteer at a clinic," she says. "I was going to join her. I should show you her Facebook page sometime. She's doing amazing things, getting to know the people in the village, and starting health programs and all that. Learning the language."

"And you didn't even get there?" I ask.

"I thought I had . . . plenty of time," she says. "Maura told me I should see India before I got to the clinic. So I traveled and, I don't know, experienced things."

"Well, it sounds amazing, Alex," I say. "But we need you here."

"Colleen," she says, her eyes narrowing, turning inward. "You don't know how it is for me. I never found . . . a place in my life where I felt like I was where I was supposed to be. India is as close as I've ever come."

I blink at her in surprise. "What do you mean you never found where you were supposed to be? What about nursing?"

She shrugs. "I burned out. That's part of why I left. The hospital got sold and the new management company was going to cut our pay. Which is crazy; you don't know how hard everybody works. I got involved with the union, and then everybody was mad at me, management and other nurses. It was time to move on."

"So what's your plan? Just sell the house and go off again?"

She nods and plays with the plastic coffee cup lid. "Yup."

"Alex, I—" I begin. "Don't you think about . . . I mean, you're not a kid anymore. You might want to start a family."

She laughs and looks away with a very bitter expression. "You think I haven't thought about that? In the last ten years, twelve-hour shifts and double and triple shifts have been my life. I never had time to go see a movie, much less have a social life."

"That's what I mean. You've been working hard for a long time," I say. "Take a break."

She shrugs. "The thing is . . ." She stops herself.

"What is it?" I ask.

Her expression looks resigned, and finally she says, in a matter-of-fact tone, "Before India, I had this . . . almost panic attack. And suddenly, I knew that even though I didn't have a partner, I wanted a baby."

"Alex!" I say. My heart rushes into my throat. Alex has always kept herself closed, managing the crisis in front of her, but never talking about her heart. I am amazed to hear that she's even considering parenthood. "That's huge news!"

She shakes her head. "Well, it's not news. Before I went to all the trouble of picking out a sperm donor, I had my reproductive system tested. And I found out that I have a condition—" She stops herself and grimaces. "Anyway, my gyno told me that . . . conceiving would be hard. I could try fertility treatments, but it was going to be expensive and, I don't know, for a lot of reasons . . . I decided that route wasn't for me."

"I'm sorry, Alex," I say, and I am genuinely sorry. "What about surrogacy? Adoption?"

"Surrogacy is a hundred thousand just to get started," she says. "Even if I could somehow scrape together the money for that, I wouldn't have money left for daycare or . . . jeez, Friday night pizza."

"If you're sure you want a child, there are options," I say. "Adoption, fostering . . ."

"Thanks, but I've done my research," she says, and she goes to a door and fidgets with a knob that's on the brink of falling out. "Believe me. Sperm donation was the only option I could bring myself to invest in. Everything else was . . . just too much."

I want to hug her, but I feel like she is closed, mourning a child who was never born. "Alex, I'm sorry."

"Thanks," she says. "Then Maura went to India. I thought, 'I read *Eat, Pray, Love*, I'll go to India.' Once I decided, I bought my airplane ticket to leave in a month and had barely enough time to get in the shots."

"Wow," I say, which is all I can say. "But did you have a good trip, anyway?"

She thinks about that a moment. "Yes. It was beautiful. I saw things I never thought I'd see. The Taj Mahal, the Golden Temple . . ."

"What's the Golden Temple?"

She gives me a quick, awkward smile. "It's a Sikh temple in Punjab, northern India. It's incredible . . ." She glances at me, and I guess I have the wrong look on my face because she stops herself. "Don't worry about it. Anyway, sure, good trip. So, what's going on with Riley?"

I sigh, trying to absorb all that she has told me. "I wish I knew," I say.

She sinks down to the floor and leans against the wall, her knees pulled up to her chest. She grasps the ends of her curly dark hair and twists them. Just like she always did. "Any news?"

"No. She moved out of her apartment, but I don't know where she went."

Alex nods, leans her arms across her knees. "What happened when you called her?"

My gaze drifts down to a spot on the floor where large dark-brown knots in the wood form circles overlapping circles like moon craters. "She stopped answering. I filled up her voice mailbox with messages, but she never called back. Then her number was no longer in service. A couple of days ago, the agency gave me a new phone number for her. I called, left messages, but still, nothing."

"Did you try—"

I nod, because, whatever she's going to suggest, I have tried it. "Apparently, she's alive because she's showing up for work."

"Did you ask the agency for her address?"

I nod and pace the floor. "They refused. This tinny-voiced girl; she even sounds skinny. She just loves telling me no. I keep explaining, *I am Riley's sister, please, please tell her to call*—" My voice is cracking. I lean against the opposite wall.

Alex bites her bottom lip. "Any idea why she'd cut you off like that?"

I shake my head. "Last November, I called her to wish her happy birthday. We talked about her coming for Thanksgiving."

"And?" Alex says.

"Same as always. She said she'd think about it." I close my fist so my fingernails are biting into the flesh of my palm. "And I haven't heard from her since."

Alex sighs. "Maybe she just needs space. Maybe we should respect that she needs us to leave her alone for a little while."

"I know what you're saying, but I have a bad feeling." I pause. She won't like this next part, so I stall for a breath. "I hired a private investigator."

Alex looks surprised. She stands up and walks around the room. "An investigator?"

I nod. "He said he could probably find her in a couple of days online, but then he's been working on some other case and hasn't been able to focus on it." I'm embarrassed to have to tell her someone else's excuses. "But I already gave him a retainer, so I can't just pull out and hire someone else."

"Did you tell Dad?" she says. I shake my head. Alex pauses for a moment. Finally, she makes her pronouncement. "Can you cancel the investigation? If he hasn't done anything, maybe you can get your money back. Tell him you changed your mind."

I look at her. "I don't want to," I say. "I want to find Riley."

"We'll find her, Colleen," she says. "We have to."

I roll my eyes. "How, Alex? I've combed through all her social media stuff—which is, weird, by the way, this public side of Riley that she's trying to sell. I don't know where she's staying, no email, she won't answer her phone, and her agency won't tell me anything."

"Did you go to New York? Ask around her apartment?"

The tension in my jaw feels like it's about to snap. "Yes."

She pauses. "Could she be out of town?"

"It's been three months," I say. "Letters, emails, phone calls, texts, messages on Facebook, Instagram, Twitter. Give me one of those, and I'm with you, yes, things happen. I get it. Two weeks? Three? Sure. But it's been months." I pause to take a breath. Alex does not meet my eyes, which tells me that she's beginning to understand. "Plus, there's something I didn't tell you. A couple of years ago, she had a drug problem."

"What?"

"I saw her in New York. She was acting strangely, and she finally told me that she had just finished rehab. She asked me not to tell you and Dad."

Alex sighs. "What are we talking about? Narcotics? Meth?"

"Opioids," I say. "I thought . . . I thought it was over. I mean, she'd been to rehab. I thought . . . that was enough."

She shrugs. "Sometimes it is, sometimes it isn't. But let's not panic.

This is why we have a pact," she declares. "If we need help, we call each other. We call out a 911. We promised. We all did."

The pact; I think about our pact every day. Ten years after our mother died, Dad sent us to a therapist, a young woman in Danvers named Dr. Andrews—Annabel, she said we could call her. Alex was twenty-one, I was eighteen, and Riley was fourteen. We only went for a few sessions before we all got too busy, but Annabel told us that depression can be hereditary, and sometimes they saw clusters of suicidal behavior in families.

"You three seem so close," she advised us. "Lean on one another. When life gets hard, talk to each other. Nobody will understand better what you're going through than each other. That's a gift."

Afterward, we sat on our front stoop as a cold spring drizzle fell around us. As a family, we were never big on sharing our feelings, but Alex made us talk about it.

"So, any of us might be . . ." she said.

"Yup, suicidal," Riley said, her tone smug and sarcastic. She smiled and leaned back with her elbows on the concrete steps, her hair dyed black, her eyes ringed in eyeliner. Her punk rock phase. "I mean, it's not me. Is it you, Colleen?"

"Be serious," I said.

"I guess it's easy to think that way," Alex said. "That when things get hard, you could just kill yourself and the pain would be over. Sometimes I wish I could go away somewhere, you know, escape? But I don't think about . . . my own life."

"I don't think about it," I said. "I don't think I could go through with it, even if I did."

"I lied. I do think about it sometimes," Riley said. We looked at her, shocked that she would admit it.

"Oh, Riley," I said.

"You truly do?" Alex asked.

"Sure, sometimes, I guess," she said, shrugging. "I mean, it's not that big of a deal, is it?"

Alex looked down, her expression sad and thoughtful. "Maybe we can get ahead of this," she said. "Let's promise each other. We'll never do what

Mom did. If we're ever in so much pain that we're considering it, it's like Dr. Andrews said, we have each other. Let's talk about whatever is hurting us before . . . it eats us up inside. Until we can't see any other choice."

Calm, smart, measured. My sister Alex's superpowers.

"I like that," I said. "We can call it a 911. That way, we know it's serious."

"You good with that, Riley?" Alex asked. "Riley? Can you try to do that?"

Riley looked up, startled, like she was thinking about something else. "I guess, sure."

Chills go down my back when I remember that moment. Was Riley just being a brash teenager, saying that to get attention? There's no way to know. And now I'm even more scared.

"Alex," I say, pleading. "The pact is useless. If she doesn't want to reach out to us, we can't make her."

Alex crosses her arms. She is in triage mode. "All right, so what's next? She's alive, but we don't know where she is. Substance use might be an issue. You haven't moved and neither has Dad. She knows we're here."

"What if she's like Mom . . ."

"That's the worst-case scenario," she says, her voice strong. "Riley's not like Mom, though. Mom was so isolated. She had nothing of her own. She didn't have friends or a job. Aside from us, she didn't have family. She was far from home. She didn't have any support."

"She could have talked to Dad," I say. "And she did have friends. She could have called someone if she'd wanted to."

"Unless by the time she realized that she was depressed, she was in too deep to ask for help," she says.

I nod. "Exactly. By the time she realized that the thing at the door was a monster, it was already inside the house."

"The thing at the door," Alex says. "The anniversary is coming up, you know. Twenty-five years in April."

"I've been thinking about that," I say. "Should we do something? Plant a tree or install a bench somewhere with her name on it?" The ideas sound inane to my own ears, but those are the things that people do.

Alex shrugs. "To tell you the truth, I'm hoping I'll be gone by then."

"You're not even staying until spring?" I say. "For Pete's sake, it's just two months."

"I don't know. Everything depends on the house," she says. "You know, Colleen, I'm not crazy for this private investigator. It feels like we're betraying Riley."

"We have to find her, Alex," I say. "I don't know what else we can do. We can't wait until the monster is in bed with her."

Chapter 7

I wake up at once, panicked and filled with dread—Caleb! I bolt upright and realize I have to get him up, get him dressed, feed him breakfast, get him to brush his teeth. Breakfast, but I don't have any food. Why can't I manage it, why can't I buy a stinking box of Froot Loops and a carton of milk? I'm going to get this right. I have to.

Then I remember: Caleb is not here. He lives somewhere else now.

I hate myself in ways and reasons that I cannot fit to words. For a long time, I made it work. He went to a good preschool, not a baby ivy, but a nearby Montessori. I dropped him off in the morning, and for the price of a new car, they fed him lunch and snack and kept him warm and safe and entertained until six o'clock.

Then, if I was still working, one of the trio of college students who live a few blocks away would pick him up. Jaclyn, Marguerite, Stacie—the girls, I called them—all of them glued to their phones. Which I didn't entirely mind because when I texted any of them, they would respond almost immediately. The girls would give him dinner, and they watched TV or read until I got home.

Sometimes I was home when they got there, sometimes I'd get in at bedtime, just in time to kiss him good night. My baby would rush into my arms and give me one of those hugs you dream about. I'd bury my head in his neck, smell the smell that was him, and for one moment, everything was right. Then he'd show me all the things he made at school—crayon drawings, his name in glittery Cheerios, necklaces made out of beads of painted pasta. Constantly creative Caleb, my little artist.

Then, time for bed.

"What will you dream about tonight?" I'd ask, combing his hair back.

"You, Mama," he'd say, and I'd kiss him on the nose. He and his stuffed turtle would both be asleep before I left the room.

And as soon as I turned out the light, I went into the next room, sat on the floor of my room, and let it roll over me. The shakes. Silent sobs. A complete, all-over soundless meltdown. I would sit there and think about all the various ways I was failing as a single mother. All the other things I was supposed to be doing, that I just couldn't bring myself to manage. When his clothes were too small, Marguerite ordered new ones. When he had a fever, it was Stacie who noticed.

Where was Mama?

At ten o'clock on a Tuesday night while Caleb slept, Mama would be out on the city sidewalk. Smoking a cigarette, to see what it felt like to be completely disconnected from that life for a few minutes.

It was September, a pretty day, when they took him away.

I brought him to school in the morning, but for some reason, the school was closed. I texted all three of the girls. Marguerite didn't respond, Jaclyn was in New Mexico for the weekend, and Stacie was in class until lunchtime, but she said she'd come by after that.

But I couldn't wait for Stacie. I had a shoot, and I couldn't bring him with me; the shoot would include a dozen seminude models, plus the photographer's assistant was already mad at me for the time when I kept complaining that the concealed zipper of my giant hot-pink Galliano frock was digging into my side like an ice pick.

So I left him. My baby, Caleb. With the TV on his favorite channel and a bag of Goldfish crackers and a new box of crayons, a pack of sixty-four, complete with the sharpener, and a fresh pad of paper. Stacie would arrive soon, and then, I told myself, everything would be all right.

But it was not all right. When I got the call, I was getting changed out of a bulky gray dress that fit like a hot-air balloon on the bottom, with straps on top that concealed my nipples.

Even the way the phone rang sounded angry.

The woman asked if I was Riley Emery; I confirmed. She said her name was Christina Harris with the New York Administration of Children's Services.

"Your son Caleb is here, ma'am," she says.

My heart sunk.

"I don't understand," I said. "Stacie was supposed to be there. Where is Stacie?"

"Your son was on his own," she said. "He was found unaccompanied by a police officer on Eighth Avenue around eleven. Can you explain exactly why he was alone on a busy street in New York City?"

"Look," I said, frantic. "I'm a working mom, a single, working—"

"According to your son, you left him alone, ma'am," she said. "Apparently, he left the apartment because he wanted to see the subway, only he got lost and asked the officer for directions. Are you able to explain how this happened?"

I hunched forward with my head in my hand, perched on a stool in front of tall mirror, wearing white hose, high-heeled Zanottis, my face painted pale and ashen, breasts hanging out, nipples hidden by silicone covers. I felt nothing but exposed.

Caleb. He was my little boy. My soul hurt when they took him away.

The next couple of months were a blur. I took a drug test at the ACS and, of course, failed. Caleb was taken into ACS custody and put into foster care in a home in Brooklyn. Then there were criminal charges, and I hired a lawyer. Court dates. Feeling helpless in front of a judge. And the verdict: the criminal charges would be dropped but Caleb would be in foster care until I could get myself cleaned up.

Which, so far, I seem to be unable to do. Supervised visits? I made it to one, and it nearly crushed me. Not because Caleb was upset, but because he was okay. When we said goodbye, I could barely look at his beautiful face. After his foster mother drove away and I could not see him anymore, I walked to the nearest trash can and vomited.

Now, I get out of bed. I try to ignore the pit of guilt in my belly that sometimes almost corrodes a hole right through me. What do I need? A pill, just one, and a shower. I must not cry. My eyes swell up, and it takes me hours to get them to calm down. I check my face in the bathroom mirror. Even without the tears, my eyes are puffy. Lucia has some eye gel somewhere around here. She's so good with products.

While the shower heats up, I undress and sit on the edge of my bed wrapped in a towel, scrolling through my Instagram feed: #models, #modelstyle, #jcwmodels, #modelsofinstagram, #modelsofvogue. I post three pics from a photo shoot taken a week ago, #modelsofinstagram, and within seconds I'm getting views and likes and a few emojis. I scroll through and see pictures of people I've worked with, and people I've met, and people I've heard of, and people who are friends of people I've worked with, heard of, or met. The pictures are funny or tacky or serious or stupid or overly glam or very high fashion. My friend Sofia seems to be at a shoot in Paris, which I guess, now that I think about it, I heard her mention. Marsha is working on something with one of the big *Vogue* photographers, and I'm kind of jealous since I was available for that one. Still, I look and click the heart and comment "Wow! Luv!" and scroll and zoom.

By the time the shower is steamy, I'm basically caught up, although when I come out, there will be a hundred more tweets and grams and posts to check. And you have to stay on top of it because the moment you forget to check on everybody else, they forget to check on you. And suddenly, you're alone in the dark social media woods. Suddenly, you're forgotten. And *forgotten*, in this world, is as good as *never existed*.

I step into the shower. Still thinking about Caleb, the things I'm supposed to be doing to get him back. One is rehab. I keep planning to do it; I keep having my very last hit before I contact the center. Actually, I'm not sure how the whole thing works if the agency isn't arranging everything.

Not to mention paying for it. How much does it cost? How do you even find out? A couple of years ago, they put me through the one-month program at Linnea House, a beautiful New Jersey oasis. Organic food and daily "sharing groups." When I came out, I was clean.

Rehab. Why didn't it stick? I'm not sure. I can't remember.

Out of your mind, I tell myself, *put it all out of your mind.* Caleb is safe now. Safe and fed and cleaned, tended to and cared for. Some people are good at that kind of thing. And people who are good at things should do them. Other people should do other things. This is the way of the world.

A voice in my head says, *No, it doesn't work that way. He's your baby. He needs you.* I know this is true, but I don't know how to make it work. And suddenly, I can't stand, so I sit naked on the shower floor, my arms wrapped around my knees, and let the pellets of water pummel me. I want to wail like an animal, but I won't. I cannot walk past the people who live in this building and wonder if they heard me, if they are wondering what I am upset about. My life is none of their business. It's none of anybody's business. I wish everyone would leave me alone.

Instead, I keep going. I stand, wash and condition my hair, then get out of the shower and towel off my hair while I think about my day. There's a photo shoot for something—is today perfume or jeans? I need to check my phone. And I need to go to Sammy's place for a pickup. Or do I? Maybe I don't. There's the emergency stash, but I hate to take anything out of that. What if I have an emergency? I'll see how I feel if I don't go to Sammy's. Even as the words go through my mind, I know that whether I go or not, the pills will find me.

I toss on a T-shirt and grab my hair dryer—Lucia's hair dryer, that is. Maybe I won't go. Today I will pull it together and do what I need to do to get Caleb back. I'll find my money. I don't think I spent it; it's in an account somewhere. I will get a place of my own. I will decorate Caleb's room in dinosaur wallpaper and put pickup-truck sheets on his bed. I'll pull all his toys and books out of the box. I'll learn to buy groceries. I will. Starting today. Starting now.

But how can I start anything when I feel so low? One last pill. That's all I need.

Today is a studio photo shoot, and I figure it will be pretty straightforward. One person pulls and teases my hair then sprays it with parabens, then someone else paints a stranger's face on the surface of my face. Dress, shoes, props, then I'm ready to play whatever role they have in mind for me today. I'm so exhausted today, I just want to go back to bed. I should probably stop for a latte, but the idea of the taste of coffee makes my mouth feel dead.

I reach the office where the shoot is supposed to happen; I'm pretty sure I'm on time, but they don't look like they're expecting me. I root through my purse for my phone to double-check that I'm in the right place, but I can't find it. I might see better without my aviators, but taking them off would ruin my look. A girl at the desk gives me a stare that is total attitude. Her hair is dyed blueish black, and her nose is pierced. I think I've seen her before, but I can't remember her name.

"Six hours late," she barks at me. "What are you, high?"

"You're high; I'm on time," I say. I point to the back where other shoots seem to be in progress. "Wardrobe back here?"

"If they still want you," she says.

I dismiss her by flipping my hair and walking in. "Not over there. This way," the girl barks. She stands and gestures me to follow her to the other side. I go, but I walk in front of her, hands up, purse hanging on the bend in my elbow. Let's be sure about the pecking order.

"You were supposed to be here at ten. You'll have to wait until the photographer is free. Back here," she says, and she directs me to a room where two women are sorting through clothes on a rack. "But seriously, I'm going to talk to Marcella about this. We are running a business."

"Go ahead," I mutter. I know for a fact that I am on time. She hands a clipboard to one of the wardrobe girls and then struts out with a huff.

The girl looks at the board. "Are we still doing this one?" she calls out.

"I have no idea," the front desk girl calls back.

Wardrobe girl shrugs, then pushes through some clothes to find the right outfit. She hands me a simple white shift dress on a hanger. I take off my aviators and hold it up and look. It reminds me of a child's dress, simple and draping, sheer three-quarter sleeves, a modest sloping dip in the chest area.

"I love this . . ." I say. "It's like . . ."

"White tights," the girl says, not letting me finish my thought. Her dark, shiny hair has one of those Kewpie-doll cuts that almost looks painted on her head. The gloss is genuine plastic, but hey, it works. She hands me a package of hose and a pair of black shoes that look like shiny Mary Janes.

"Like a . . . like a funeral," I finally say.

"Not a funeral," she says, taking the dress from me and lifting up the hanger. "It's little-girly, see? Kiddie porn, that's what they're going for here."

The other wardrobe girl bursts out in laughter, her ponytail swinging. "That's disgusting!"

"Don't blame me," says the girl with the pixie cut. "Those are Jack's exact words."

I mostly tune out their chatter, but I stop when I hear the name. "Jack? Which Jack?"

"Jack Jensen," says Pixie Girl. "He picked the dress for you."

"Jack Jensen," I say. I smile a little, but I don't want to show too much enthusiasm. "I thought he was working in London these days."

"People do travel, honey," she says. She goes back to pushing clothes around. "I'm sure you've heard of airplanes."

I ignore the comment. "So, but he's actually here? Jack's here? Like, now?"

Pixie Girl looks at me like I am a tick she just stepped on. "Yes, he's actually here. You can change over there." She points to a standing curtain.

I take the dress, the tights, and the shoes and go behind the curtain. Slip off my jeans and top, and while I pull on the tights, I listen to the girls chatter about the clothes they are organizing for tomorrow's shoots—tomorrow's shoots? Seriously, what time is it?—and also about Jack. Most of their words are in one ear and out the other . . . until I hear, "I bet his fiancée was not too happy about that."

Fiancée? I stop and listen, but that's the only mention. They're back to yammering about tomorrow's schedule. Which has nothing to do with me.

The dress. It is a whisper of a dress, just a simple, breezy thing, and all I can think is, this is the dress version of me. I should get married in this dress. Jack was the one I thought I would marry. What fiancée? He told me he wasn't the marrying kind.

When I die, wrap me in this dress and throw me into the ocean. I will drift through the sunlight in the water, sinking slow and lovely, my hair submerging last, my face at peace in the light. As I fall to the bottom of the ocean, and the fishes feast upon me, this dress you can watch and you will know it is my spirit.

I put on the tights and the shoes. The girls place a thick covering over my head, and I go down the hall to makeup. Some guy is styling me today. He looks familiar but I can't remember if I've met him before. But wow, is he grumpy. Everybody is so short with me today, but I don't know why. The agency would have called me if I was that late, and nobody called. Plus, exactly what time is it? I am not going to ask. My head would get sliced off my shoulders.

He teases my hair, pulling it up off my scalp and scraping it with a comb so it stands up on its own. I am bored and fidgety, but I am trying to sit still. "You need some coffee?" he says. "Or a grape, perhaps?"

"Coffee, I guess. Black, with sweetener."

"Krista!" he shouts. The girl with the pierced nose appears. "Can you please bring Miss Emery a coffee with sugar-free sugar?" She hops off to fetch it. Finally. "I'm Tony, by the by," he says, but there is no smile in his voice.

"I'm Riley," I say.

"I know," he says.

"Oh," I say. "Hey, Tony, can you clue me in on something? Why is everybody so mad at me today?"

He takes a clipboard with the shoot orders on it. "Requested arrival time: ten fifteen. Actual arrival time: four thirty."

"What?" I say. "If I was so late, why didn't anybody call me?"

"I believe they tried to, dear," he sings.

"My phone hasn't rung all morning. I'll prove it." I grope around for my purse, but I can't find that now. I must have left it in another room. "Can you ask that girl to bring me my bag? I'll show you."

"You didn't say please," he says, not meeting my eyes.

I huff. "Please."

"Krista," he calls. "Please bring the lady's purse when you get a chance."

He starts in on the curling iron, then yanks my hair back hard. I'm getting it, I was very, very late. I am very, very bad. I just want to do the job and go home. I am dreaming of my bed, like it's calling my name. Maybe I'm coming down with the flu. Then, I'm suddenly hungry, and all I can think of is a hamburger, complete with greasy bun and lots of ketchup. Fries on the side. Someday I'll be able to eat that kind of thing. But not now. May as well dream of a celery stick.

She brings me a cup of coffee and my worn black Fendi tote from the wardrobe room, which she drops with a thud and then walks away. "Thanks," I say. Three years ago that was *the* bag you couldn't get anywhere at any price. Marcella gave it to me for my birthday that year. Now it looks tired; I am embarrassed not to have something new. God, this life.

"Hold on," I say to Tony, and I dig in past the shiny metal clasp and check the little sewn-in side pockets, three of them: nothing. I sort through the rest of the things in my bag, all of it tangled like a bird's nest: my cell charger and lip glosses, wallet, a religious newspaper some lady put into my hand in the subway, empty power bar wrappers, an extra pair of pantyhose, receipts for a million things I'm supposed to save for taxes, packets of artificial sweetener. A small Milky Way candy bar, which I forget why I have and keep meaning to throw away. Tony stands and stares. The whole thing is making me want to cry.

"Any luck?" he says, but he knows I can't find it.

I dig down to the bottom and find something else—a small photo of Caleb. It was taken at school, so the background is a fake path through a fake park. His dark hair is wavy, and his face is so sweet. The picture was taken last fall before he went away.

His first school picture.

"This is crazy," I say, continuing to rifle through my bag. Finally, I find it. "Of course, it's right here," I say. But something's wrong; it won't turn on. And then I remember last week when I slammed the life out of my phone. And then I remember that my phone has not, in fact, rung since then. I shake it slightly and it does wake up, although blinking and muddled; it tries to tell me that the time is 4:22 a.m. on October first. I'm completely confused, because it was working this morning. I posted things just this morning. A slight rattling sound comes from inside.

"Technical difficulties, I guess," I say, feeling like the wind has been sucked out of me.

Tony snorts and laughs to himself, then shakes his head in exasperation. "Oh, well," he says with a tone devoid of sympathy. "These things happen."

I look at my bag. I do not need this, I just don't. I want to leave; only one thing is keeping me here, and that's a paycheck. And the possibility of seeing Jack.

While Tony fusses over me, I look at my face in the mirror, and it's there like a map, like God has carved the story with His fingernail into the flesh of my face: I am getting older. Okay, older, yes, but we can tell the truth to the mirror, mirror on the wall: I am an addict. Under my eyes, those are not just bags, those are suitcases, earth brown and chicken fleshed. My skin is sallow, folded over on itself. My hair, soft yellow, looks all right thanks to Tony's styling, but let's face it, youth puts a kind of light in beauty, and that doesn't last. And there's no product in any store that can replace it. Once it's gone, it's gone.

And, baby, you are losing it fast.

I shove my things back in my bag, and Tony hands me a box of tissues. "Here," he says.

"Thanks," I say, taking the box.

"We still need to do makeup," he says. "Unless you need a few moments of silence to remember your beloved phone."

I look at him, my face twisting in disgust. "I'm sorry," I say. "Have we met?"

He grins, and not warmly. "Only a few dozen times, here and there."

I look him up and down. "I must have pissed you off somehow. Just tell me what I need to apologize for so we can move on with this, all right?"

"Thanks for the sentiment, Princess," he says. "People like you just think the world is sitting around, ready to jump when you say go."

"Jesus," I whisper under my breath.

He continues to preach, painting my face as he does. "No, seriously, people like you have a real problem . . ." And on he rants about how entitled I am, and how I need to get *over* myself and realize that other people have lives too. It's something he's always amazed about with models, he continues, because they should have realized by now that they don't have their own set of rules just because they're lucky enough to be born with cheekbones and size zero waistlines . . .

I actually do try to listen. And even though this tirade feels a bit much, I probably deserve it. Finally, he finishes and steps away from the mirror, wiping his hands with a towel, like he is wiping his hands of me.

What I see reflected takes my breath away. I look like the milky-white froth floating on top of a cappuccino. Just that breezy, just that sweet. My eyes are carefully lined into stylized almonds, brows penciled in with clean lines. My skin like a porcelain doll, lips pale. A vision of 1960s blanched modernity crossed with . . . yes, something like kiddie porn, but tasteful.

It's me as an innocent. The little girl I never was.

He gives me a hand mirror. "Tony," I say. "I'm sorry. I don't blame you for being mad at me, but wow, you do good work."

"Thanks," he says. "That makes me take exactly half of it back."

"Half," I say. "Well, I'll take what I can get."

"Beautiful," says someone with a British accent, and I look over my shoulder. "Breathtaking, really." It's Jack; he is here. Roguishly handsome as always, deep eyes, dark-brown hair, and just enough stubble around his face. He was always so lean, muscular; he still is, but maybe a little softer around the edges. That's okay; so am I. When he looks at me, I feel like I might burst from the thrill of his recognition. He will save me, save this awful day.

"You're back," I say.

"Just for a few days." He's wearing what he always wears when he's on a job: expensive jeans and a crisply ironed white button-down Oxford shirt. Jack takes my face gently in strong hands, touches the edge of my jawline, pushing my head first in one direction, then the other, studying my features in the mirror. The white dress and tights, the little-girl image I have been transformed into, this was his vision. He sees what I am inside. I want to kiss him, but I have a feeling Tony would explode if he had to touch me up. My heart beats fast under his touch, and I wish, so very much, that everybody else would disappear. I want him for myself.

"She look all right?" Tony asks him.

"Yup, good," Jack says. "Half an hour, love. I'll be done for the day, and then it's all you, right?"

"Okay," I say.

"You can, I dunno, read a magazine or something." He points at a lounge with his chin. "Your face is probably all over 'em anyway."

Not like I used to be, Jackie. And Jack goes away again, just to the next room, but I miss him. Again.

"She done?" The front desk girl, Krista, asks Tony. He affirms. "Riley, I've got your agency on the line. Bernie wants to talk to you."

Bernie, Berta, Bernadette . . . also known as Miss Seale, Marcella's assistant. Krista ratted me out. Thanks a lot. I get up to follow her, but then I look back at Tony as he wipes the makeup capsules and puts them away. "Tony," I say. "I'm sorry I wasted everybody's time. I don't mean to be a pain. Things just get away from me sometimes."

He stops what he's doing and looks at me, his eyes bearing a hint of forgiveness. "Okay," he says. "It's okay. I might have been a little harsh."

"Phone," Krista says. She turns and walks off, and I follow behind her.

I cannot believe Krista tattled. If I were a waitress, I would spit in her coffee. I lift the receiver to my ear.

"Hi, Bernie," I say. Three young models walk by on their way out. One of them looks me up and down. Don't judge me, kid. This life is merciless; it will grind you down.

"Hi, Riley," she says. "Can you come in on Monday? Marcella wants to see you."

It's bad. I bite my lip. "Bernie, hi! You will never guess what happened. My phone just died. You can check my Insta; I posted just this morning, so I totally don't know what happened. But I guess I got the times for this shoot all mixed up—"

"Honey, it's okay," she says. "Look, Marcella's at a recruiting thing right now, and I have to seriously go. What time works—is ten good? Eleven?

Marcella has some slots in the morning, but Monday night she leaves for Paris, so the schedule is kind of tight."

A recruiting thing. Where they harvest the new girls so they can replace the old ones.

"Riley?" Bernie says. "What time?"

I take a deep breath. Something great will soon die. "Eleven is good," I say. "I'll get a new phone this weekend." I swallow my tears and ask, "Will they just give me a new phone or will I have to pay for it?"

"I have no idea, honey, depends on your plan. Okay, see you Monday."

Bernie hangs up. I stand there another moment, the dial tone sounding in my ear. The clock on the phone says the time is almost six o'clock. How did it get to be that late? I feel sick, like the world is spinning too fast around me.

Suddenly, Jack runs past me on his way to the elevator doors, a bevy of girls on his arm. They're all giggling and relentlessly snapping selfies, pressing their faces next to his and each other's. I'm so embarrassed for them; he's not interested in a bunch of children and their games.

But then he calls out to me, "Oh, new plan, love. Ken's doing the shoot. These girls are kidnapping me. We're going to a torta truck that's supposed to be unbelievable!"

Don't go, I want to say. *Please stay with me.*

But there's nothing I can do but watch the girls spirit him away, squealing with laughter, flipping their hairdos as they push the little buttons on their little phones to post their little pictures.

Helpless in dress and makeup, I call out, "Are you around this weekend?"

"I am," he says. "Let's meet at that place, the bar we used to go to. I'll be in touch."

"I'll send you an email," I say.

I hope he heard me; the girls had him mostly out the door. I stand then, alone in that wispy white dress. The memory of Jack's hands on my face remains like an imprint. I ache with the memory of such tenderness; I wish I could keep that memory forever.

Chapter 8

The sky is a flat silver-gray and looks ready to drop a few snowy goose-feather flurries over the marsh. I am standing at the window in the dining room at Number Seven, Killdeer Road, gazing at the expanse. There's a dead tree on the other side of the street. Bark stripped, it stands with branches jagged, cracked and broken, the top snapped off and missing. It looks like a fractured hand reaching out; it looks like shattered bone.

Colleen has me worried. Where is Riley? She could just be busy, but this radio silence has been dragging on for a long time. And if there's a drug issue, things could be a lot more serious. Either way, we need to find her. We need to bring her home.

I wander aimlessly around the first floor. Colleen was probably right; the police probably can't help us, but I'm not sure a private investigator is the way to go either. What if we just leave her alone and trust her to come back to us? No, the risk that she might drift so far away that we can't find her at all is too big.

Addiction. I remember the ER, faces of families waiting for news of a loved one recovering from an overdose. My heart went out to them; to those who have not been through it themselves, addiction feels like a choice, like something someone chooses. That makes it a kind of sharp-edged anguish for the families of those who struggle with it. The self-doubt, anger, and frustration, the lack of answers and guarantees; what can you do for someone who desperately needs help but doesn't want it? Addiction changes a person from the inside out. The poisoned urgency of narcotics takes over every conscious part of human intent until the person they used to be almost evaporates.

And the worst part: it's all chemical, the way the opioids interact with the composition of the brain. We try to pretend that willpower has some role with recovery, but that's a farce. Once the brain tastes heroin, it changes. Once the brain tries heroin, it needs it.

I have to keep busy. I go to my backpack, toss all my clothes onto a sheet, which I tie into a bundle and toss into the car. Then, I drive to the laundromat in Newburyport, stopping first at the market for a box of laundry soap and a bag of Goldfish crackers.

It feels strange. I am driving through this cute little town on clean, paved roads, all of us drivers fastened in our seatbelts, signaling and driving the speed limit; it's all so calm. Not a full week ago, I was in a village in India, riding in a motor rickshaw whose skinny, mustachioed driver had the blood red teeth of a betel nut addict. He liked to drive extra fast on the unpaved shoulder of the road while keeping the rickshaw just vertical enough to not tip over. It was like a carnival ride.

I rip open the top of the Goldfish bag. How can this be the same planet?

Out the laundromat's wall-high windows, I see a few flakes begin to blow around against the dank sky. I shove my clothes into a machine and insert a bunch of quarters, then plop into an orange fiberglass bucket seat with my Goldfish and try to watch a game show on the flat-screen TV in the corner.

I am restless, though, and cannot pay attention. A young couple comes in and puts a load in, sitting in silence as they stare at their phones. Before me, suds splash and spin in the window of the washing machine, and I think about Marjorie, the dreaded angel of my eternal return.

Couldn't you have held out a little longer, Marjorie? Just enough for me to reach Kerala?

I met Marjorie in Boston two years earlier. There was a big snowstorm;

the weather people had predicted it, but somehow the volume and speed came as a surprise. It was a Wednesday night, and I was headed home after two twelve-hour shifts, taking the number four bus to the number twelve bus to my apartment. With rush hour traffic, the whole trip could take forty-five minutes, but after an hour and a half in the fast falling snow, we'd progressed half a mile.

The bus wasn't too full though, and I had two seats to myself. Inside, the bus was warm and so quiet, I kept dozing. Through the window the falling snow was lovely in a way that you can only appreciate when you're not in a rush to get anywhere, sparkling under the streetlights, covering the sidewalks with gleaming white. The only reading material I had was a free Metro tabloid, which contained four pages of generic articles about life in Boston. Once I'd read everything in it twice, I pulled out my phone and started to look for something slightly more substantial to read, but mostly I just wanted to go home, put on my pajamas, and go to sleep. But the bus driver informed us that traffic conditions were bad—the Mass Pike was full of cars, bumper to bumper, none of them moving. And the snow was piling up between them.

"Just like the Blizzard of '78," the driver said.

We passengers shook our heads and muttered "oh, no's" in response.

"That '78 storm was bad," said the woman on the seat in front of me. "People abandoned their cars right out on the Pike."

She turned at looked at me, a woman in her sixties, short salt-and-pepper hair visible under her knit hat. "My father actually got stuck in it," she said. "Even he ended up leaving his car right in the road. Can you imagine that?"

"I don't have to imagine, there's a photo of it right here in the Metro," I said. I opened up the tabloid to show her. The photo showed a road littered with unmoving cars, stuck in snow as high as their roofs.

"Well, good night, will you look at that," she muttered, taking the newspaper to look more closely. "We lived in Arlington, but my father worked in Boston," she said, handing it back to me. "When he realized that nobody was going anywhere, he just got out and started walking. When he needed a break, he knocked on some random door and found the nicest family. They let him in, fed him, gave him clean socks. Then he walked all night to get home. He walked almost seven miles that night."

"That's amazing," I said.

"Luckily, he was wearing sturdy footwear," she said. "Hey, are you hungry? I was just about to tear into this bag of craisins left over from a salad. Would you like some?"

"Sure," I said. She came and sat next to me and opened her snack.

Her name was Marjorie, she told me, and she admired my hat, a generic knit one with a gold and red pompom and a little patch that said, "Newburyport."

"Your hat looks warm," she said. "Are you from the North Shore?"

"It is," I said. "My niece goes to the high school in Newburyport."

"So you have family up there?" she asked.

"I do," I said. "I grew up in Amesbury. My dad is still there, and my sister landed on the other side of the river."

"It's beautiful up there," she said. "Ocean and marsh and cute little towns."

"It's lovely," I said. We started chatting then, and the bus grinded forward every so often. After three hours on that bus, we got to know one another a little. Marjorie was a professor of ornithology at Boston University. She had a cat named Tom Brady, a stray that she'd adopted who loved nothing more than hunting birds, though she tried to encourage him to leave the birds alone and go after mice. She was an avid reader and had loved Jane Austen since college. Her favorite food was chocolate anything, but she got hives when she ate it, so she had to be careful.

"I think of it as medicinal, not recreational," she said, smiling.

Finally, she revealed that she had ovarian cancer and had been at Mass General seeing her oncologist.

"I'm so sorry," I said. "May I ask, what stage?"

"Four, actually," she said. She looked out the window. "My oncologist just told me, today, actually . . . well, actually, she and I agreed. We're done with chemo. Done with treatments of all kinds, I guess."

The cancer was untreatable. It meant that she'd started what would likely be a slow and painful walk toward the end.

"Oh, Marjorie," I said. "I'm so sorry."

"Thank you," she said. "It's been a long journey." She began to cry, just a little and very quietly. "Oh, goodness," she said, wiping her eyes with a paper napkin from her pocket. "Your whole life, you think the one thing you'll always be is alive. And when you hear for sure that that's not the case, it's still a shock to the system."

"I can't imagine," I said, and that was true.

Eventually, the bus reached our stops, and before Marjorie and I went our separate ways, we exchanged email addresses. A couple of days later, she sent me a note saying she'd enjoyed meeting me and would love to have coffee. Sometime after that we met at the Au Bon Pain next to the hospital.

After we chatted for a while, she became serious. "Alex," she said. "I have to ask a favor. It's a strange one. I have a cottage up in Newbury, not too far from Amesbury or Newburyport. It's old, simple, you know, no frills. Actually, hold on."

She pulled out her phone and found a photo of a ragged little house, then showed it to me.

"There's no dishwasher, for starters. No satellite television. No washer or dryer. But it's very quiet. I don't have neighbors, and there's no traffic. I bought the place after my divorce when I needed a place to escape to. The bird-watching is spectacular."

"Aw, it's sweet," I said. "How can I help? Don't ask me to come and fix anything, I'm terrible with anything mechanical."

"No, that's not it," she said. "I'd like to leave it to you. In my will."

I thought she was joking, but her hazel eyes showed no sign of a smile. I remember her face, small and completely geometrically round. And, sharp little beady eyes, birdlike themselves behind spectacles.

"That's very kind," I said, leaning back. "But Marjorie, I couldn't—"

"I used to go there on the weekends and just, just *be* for a couple of days," she said. "A quiet place is like a car wash for your soul."

"It sounds lovely," I said. "But you must have a family member who would take it."

She shrugged. "My nieces and nephews are all in Colorado. And they're a different generation; for them, to live without a Starbucks nearby is sort of like jail."

I smiled. "Don't you have children?"

She smiled for a moment, or maybe it was a grimace, and then she grew quiet. "We couldn't have them, my husband and I. I mean, my ex and I."

It was a forward question, but I decided to ask anyway. "Why?"

She shrugged. "I kept getting pregnant, but none of them stayed. Three miscarriages." Then she winced as if holding back tears. "The fun part? My oncologist said that my cancer was likely brought on by the hormones I took to try and become pregnant."

I sat back then and took it all in. "Marjorie," I said, and it was all I could say. "I'm so sorry."

"My husband and I, we just wanted a baby," she starts and then stops herself, shaking back the tears.

I offered no words, but gave her a moment.

"One day after my marriage fell apart, I was driving through Newbury after a morning bird-watching expedition out on Plum Island. I saw the For Sale sign and drove down to look at it. What can I say? It was love at first sight. The place was a wreck, completely full of old lady stuff." She laughed. "All that crap! I bought the place for a song. 'As is,' as they say. So I got a dumpster and emptied the place clean out. I gave things away, sold things, chucked entire boxes of who knows what until the place was empty. Pristinely empty. I had planned to fill it up with new things. But once it was empty . . . I realized I loved it that way."

She looked around, as though she was suddenly surprised to realize that she was not there. "I thought I could just let it go after I die, let the town take it up as abandoned," she said. "But it's been bothering me. The house wants to belong to someone. Please say you'll take it. Sell it, tear it down, build something new, put in a golf course. I don't care what you do. But just, let me leave it to you."

"Marjorie, I—" I started, unsure how I was going to get out of this. "I'm not really from there anymore. I'm here now. And to be honest, I'm not really looking for reasons to go back."

"Alex, my friend," she said, taking a sip of her tea. "Your origins are part of your DNA. You can't change where you're from by moving."

The washing machine has finished its cycle. The couple has left, and the place is quiet again. I toss my clothes in the dryer, then feed it a few quarters. The dryer starts, and I put on my jacket and head out onto the cold sidewalk. I need to walk, breathe the freezing air, let snowflakes drift into my eyelashes, and feel my fingers turn to stone in the chill wind.

After that conversation, Marjorie and I had coffee a few more times, and eventually Marjorie got me to say yes. It all seemed so theoretical that this energetic woman could be in the final stage of her life. I didn't believe it.

That was before I stood in the emergency room and held the motherless baby, before I felt that flood of love, that urgency to become a mother. I remember now that Marjorie had felt that same longing, the seemingly simple desire to create a family. Marjorie would have been a great mother; I know that much for sure. Was the cottage like a surrogate baby for her? She was so concerned to find someone who would take care of it when she was gone. She must have loved it.

In some ways, I am honored that she chose me as guardian of this place that meant so much to her. But I'm still mad that I had to come back to claim it. Back when she and I were drinking coffee together, I never really believed that I would ever see the cottage. Never remotely dreamed that I would go to India, much less have to come back from India to complete the adoption.

India, where are you? In the darkness of the early dawn in the holy city of Varanasi, on the Ganges River, pilgrims are lighting tea candles and setting them afloat in small boats made of leaves alongside strings of orange marigolds, and I am not there to see them. Wait for me. I will come back.

Chapter 9

Saturday, February 8, 2014
Colleen

Saturday morning I wake early, before the kids, and go to the kitchen and make coffee. Alex came for dinner last night; I made a pot roast. The kids love it, and apparently Alex does too, the way she wolfed it down. Although maybe she was happy to eat something that was not pizza. The coffee finishes brewing, and I pour it into my favorite mug from TJ Maxx. It's simple, pretty, and bone-white. The shape seems perfect to me, just the right height, slightly taller than it is wide, and thick enough to keep the coffee at temperature without being clunky like a diner mug. I take a sip; it's the way I like it, strong but not overpowering. Eric's coffee—on the rare occasions when he made it—tasted like burned toast. Which is why he would then add a pile of white sugar to it, a habit I found revolting. But he was always so pleased with himself. *This is how they do it in the Middle East*, he would tell people. Which was funny because the closest he ever went to the Middle East was a falafel shop in Plaistow.

I stare out the big window at the backyard, which is now covered in frozen brambles. My husband doesn't live here anymore. Maybe I'm glad he's gone. All his bad habits; before we separated I always told myself not to dwell on them, but I let myself list them now. He took business calls during dinner. He criticized me in front of the children. He scheduled oil changes and pest control visits without telling me, on days when I had other plans. And I didn't like the way he talked to the kids, always belittling, comparing them to other kids. And those times when we would be at a party or a restaurant or one of Maddie's games, and Eric's eyes moved so slowly, so subtly in the direction of another woman. I wanted to hit him.

So why did I want to have another child with him? I wanted that feeling again. Bringing a new baby home means that everybody is filled with sweetness, awe, joy, and purpose. It always made me feel like we were all on the same team. I could use some of that about now, I guess.

I pound the counter again. My jaw is sealed shut so hard it hurts, and a headache is starting, one of the really fun ones that will persevere against coffee, ibuprofen, and acetaminophen. Today I will run, no question. I will let the kids zone out in front of their iPads, strap on my layers, my sneakers, and two pairs of socks because it is crazy cold out there. I will go outside and run before the sun sets on this frozen day.

I start to empty the dishwasher and stack the glasses on a shelf behind a cabinet door that hangs a little because the screw that holds it in place is loose. Eric promised to fix that for years. I decide that I will fix it. Also, I need a lawyer. Eric says it's not time for lawyers; he just needs a break. *Let's try marriage counseling,* he says, and then he barely shows up for it. It's so cute how he promises that we can take the pieces of this marriage, wipe them off, and put them back together as though a marriage is a carburetor. Does he think I don't know how things work? Marriages don't take breaks and get back together. Marriages are a gluing together of two lives, but the gag is, there is no glue. This life only sticks when the two separate parts choose to stay, when everybody chooses family. I chose family. Eric chose something else.

I need a lawyer. They say divorce is not a game you win or lose at, but I want to win. I want Eric to lose and know he lost.

No, I don't want to be that kind of a person. What is wrong with me? Who am I becoming?

Eric and I, so far from where we started. Once, we were college kids. Once, we were newlyweds. Once, we were so excited to welcome our first baby into the world, and then a second. We were a young family, filled with hope. But what happened? I still don't know.

The kitchen is still cold despite the fact that I put the heat on twenty minutes ago. My coffee has cooled too fast, so I put my TJ Maxx mug in the microwave to warm it up.

"Mom?" Maddie says. All at once my precious alone time pops like a soap bubble. Maddie yawns as she speaks and plops in a chair at the counter.

"What are you doing up so early, sweetheart?" I say. "It's Saturday. No school. Did you forget?"

"Nah," she says. "I just woke up. And then I was up."

I sigh. Maddie has been a light sleeper since she was a baby. I grab the cereal box off the shelf and put it in front of her, along with a bowl and a spoon and a half gallon of milk from the refrigerator. She can do these things for herself, but I do it anyway, out of habit.

"Sugar?" she says as she pours flakes into the bowl.

I look at her aghast. "What do we say?"

She rolls her eyes and pouts with her entire deflated torso. "Please. May I have the sugar, please?"

"Yes, you may," I say.

The bowl is on the counter in front of her, but somehow children and men never notice anything that is where it should be. Why is that? I push the bowl across a couple of inches. People usually notice motion.

She looks at the sugar bowl but does not touch it. Her hands stay in her lap. Her long, light-brown hair is still flat from sleeping. Her eyes aren't quite awake yet, but she looks at me and says, "It's weird having Dad gone."

I nod slowly. "Yes, it is. Weird." I cannot tell her that I feel like a piece of me has fallen between the cracks somewhere, and that I don't know how to find it.

She glances down, sighs, and pulls her bowl toward her. With shoulders hunched under a worn thin sweatshirt, she pours milk over her breakfast flakes, then sprinkles on the sugar. Maddie likes to soak her bowl, an ocean of white milk with just a small island of cereal in the middle. I watch her lift the spoon of cereal, dripping with milk, into her mouth.

"How are you doing? I mean, with all this?" I ask.

She chews for a moment. "Okay, I guess," she says. "Emma says that eventually, you'll get a boyfriend in, who knows, Chicago, and then we move there, and we won't see Dad until next year. And then you and Dad argue over who gets which holidays, plus we have to deal with this new guy's kids and all their problems."

"Madison Newcomb," I say. "You don't need Emma Pallazola telling how things are going to work. I don't have a boyfriend in Chicago; I don't have a boyfriend anywhere. And we are not moving. You and I and Ethan are staying right here, in this house. Your lives are our priorities. We're all going to do what we can to keep life as normal as possible. Got that?"

"Sure," she says. She perches her chin in her hand and stares at me with a doubtful expression. "It's your priority to keep everything the same until you can't, and then it changes. I get it."

This is thirteen. "Kid, I am doing my best here."

"I know, Mom," she says. "Sorry."

"This is hard for everybody," I say.

She nods, and then it's quiet between us for a while, and I gaze blankly out the window, looking, but not really seeing. Finally, I pick up my phone to review the schedule for the day. Maddie has soccer at nine; Ethan has wrestling at eleven. In the afternoon they're both invited to a friend's house for pizza and a movie. Somewhere in there, I need to pick up Maddie's costume for the school play from the mall, since dress rehearsal starts next week. Then maybe I can squeeze in a quick trip to Target to pick up some cheap pans and dishes for Alex.

I check my email; I half hope for something from Eric, though I know nothing will be there. And Eric has not disappointed me. But there is one from Mr. Hensler, my private investigator, sent last night. *Tracking some leads, nothing conclusive*, he writes. *Will alert you as soon as I have something concrete.*

Nothing conclusive. Except one thing: I would have looked so pretty in the earrings that money would have bought.

"Did you hear anything back from that guy?" Maddie asks, as though reading my mind.

I glance up at her and try to figure out if she can see what I'm looking at. I'm on the other side of the island from her. "You mean the investigator?" I ask, and she nods. "Nothing yet."

"That's weird too, how Aunt Riley disappeared."

"It sure is."

"I set up this thing on my phone," she says. "It's an app that tracks news about someone. So, if anything happens to her that gets in the news, I'll get some kind of an alert."

"Really?" I say. "That's great, honey. Have you heard anything?"

"Nope."

"Okay. Let me know if you do."

"I will," she says. "But, Mom, don't you think Aunt Riley can take care of herself?"

I look at Maddie and stall my answer by taking a deep drink from my coffee cup. "Of course, she can. But she hasn't talked to Pépé since before Christmas. He's worried. I'm worried. Aunt Alex is worried; we all just want to know where she is."

Maddie's jaw munches up and down. "If Ethan was missing, I'd be thrilled."

"Not if he was missing like this, you wouldn't. You'd be worried. I hope you would be worried."

She shakes her head. "It's not the same. You and Aunt Alex act like Aunt Riley is a baby who can't take care of herself."

"That's not true," I say.

"The way you talk, she never did anything wrong," she says. "She was always breaking the rules, and everybody would act like she's a genius. You always felt so honored if she happened to call you. But geez, what did she ever do for you? I mean, what's the big deal?"

A bright shaft of sunlight has crept through the window and falls over the face of my daughter. With Maddie, I often feel like I am talking to a brand-new person, someone I have never met before. That's how I feel now, but I forget that Maddie has been watching me closely for thirteen years, and I suppose I should have expected that the day would come when she would have opinions and sufficient vocabulary to explain them to me. Now my daughter is holding a mirror up to my face. The truth is, I don't like how it looks.

"She's my sister," I say, my tone steely because actually I don't like having a mirror held up to me like this. "And we went through . . . a lot when we were kids."

She shrugs and hunches over her bowl. "I know you did. We all know it was hard with your mom dying and all." She looks up suddenly like she's just had a brilliant idea. "Hey, do we have any blueberries?"

"Go ahead and check," I say. Maddie rolls her eyes, then slides off the stool and sulks to the fridge. She finds what she wants, then goes back to her seat in the diffuse morning light. For a moment again, we are both quiet. I am hoping we're done with this talk.

"Mom," Maddie finally says. "I was trying to figure out if I should tell you something, but it's kind of weird. It happened a long time ago. It's not bad, just strange. But I don't want you to be mad at me for not telling you before now. If I tell you, do you promise not to be mad at me?"

I blink. A hundred dreadful things go through my mind. "Maddie, what's going on?"

"It happened a long time ago," she says again. "It's something that . . . that I never understood. Something about Aunt Riley."

"Okay," I say. "What?"

She looks at me, her eyes more alert now that there's glucose in her veins. "I never told you because, I mean, I guess I always kind of thought it was a dream; like, I wasn't sure it really happened. But I've been thinking about it lately, and I'm pretty sure it was real. No, I know it was real. But I don't want you to be mad that I didn't tell you sooner."

I'm racking my brain, trying to figure out what this is about; did Maddie see something on the internet about Riley? Did she find some YouTube videos?

"She was here, Mom."

The words slap the thoughts out of my head. "In this house?" I say. Maddie nods. "No, sweetie, Riley has never been here."

"I talked to her. She was in my room."

I reach through my brain to figure out what she's talking about. "I think you're confused. Aunt Riley met you when you were a baby; we brought you to New York to see her. But she's never been here."

Maddie shifts in her seat and looks down at her bowl. "Remember that Thanksgiving, when Aunt Riley was supposed to come, but she never showed up? I think I was six or seven. Mom, she did come. She was here that night."

Now I am very confused. "No, she wasn't, sweetie. It was just me, your dad, Aunt Alex, and Pépé. Riley couldn't get here that day. Her rental car broke down in Connecticut, and she never got here."

"That's what she told you," Maddie says. "But she was here, in my room. When she left, she told me she would come back in for dinner, but she didn't. I guess she changed her mind."

I am without words, without questions, even. Maddie is describing something that never happened, that couldn't have happened. "It doesn't make any sense," I say. "We would have seen her. She wouldn't have just left."

Maddie gives me that thirteen-year-old look. "I am telling you what happened."

I look at the clock: six forty-five. There's some time before Ethan wakes up, as long as we stay quiet. "All right, Madison, I'm listening," I say. "Tell me everything."

What I remember of that Thanksgiving Day, 2007, the one where Maddie says Riley came to the house without us knowing, is that it was supposed to be magical. It was *my* turn to host *my* family in *my* new house, a big, new, stand-alone house with three bathrooms, two floors, and a finished basement. I was in love with the house and Eric, and my children. Ethan was five, a sweet, funny kid. Maddie was in third grade, and as close to being a young lady as we could then imagine. I had bought a pretty dress for her to wear for the special occasion: black velvet with white lace on the bottom and the sleeves. Of course, she hated it; she said it pinched, and she couldn't move in it. But she looked lovely; we took some beautiful family photos that day. I was so thankful.

I'd set the dining room table two days before, put out the good china, and the polished sterling flatware. I had a shopping list and a to-do list on the computer, and I was on top of everything. Eric picked Dad up from Amesbury; Alex had gotten the time off from work and was driving up from Boston. I begged Riley to join us; by some miracle, she wasn't in Paris or Milan, just New York, and she promised she would. I emailed her directions to our home. She would see the house and meet Ethan for the first time. Maddie was beyond excited to meet the glamorous fashion-model aunt whom she hadn't seen since she was a baby.

"Ethan and I ate mashed potatoes and stuffing for dinner," Maddie says. "In front of the TV. We watched *The Lion King*."

I look at her. "Yup, I remember," I say. "We were supposed to eat dinner at five, but Riley wasn't there and I didn't want to carve the turkey until she arrived. But you two were so hungry, so I let you have some of the side dishes."

Maddie smiles. "You seemed so upset. Then I went to the bathroom and Ethan took the remote and put on something I hated; I don't remember what. Race car driving or something. And I was mad."

"I remember that," I say. "I was already so anxious waiting for Riley, then the two of you were melting down." On top of that, Dad, Alex, and Eric were biding their time drinking ginger-cinnamon martinis that Eric was mixing. I kept putting cheese and crackers and nuts in front of them, trying to mitigate the effect of the alcohol, but it was no use. They were all drunk.

I was on my own.

"You told me to go to my room," she says. "I didn't mind going. I had my tablet, so I figured I'd just go up there and play until Aunt Riley got there."

I nod, trying to remember. "So, what happened next?"

"I went upstairs and sat on my window seat and looked out the window for a while," she says. "I hoped that I would see her car driving down the road, and I wanted to come and tell you. I wanted to be . . . the bearer of good news."

"Did you see anything?" I ask.

She shakes her head. "No, but now I think she must have been out there. She must have seen me. I sat on my bed and started playing with my tablet, and a couple of minutes later, there was a knock on my window. I looked out and saw . . . a woman there."

"There was a woman in your window and you didn't scream?" I say.

She bites her lip; she is looking for the right words. "Mom, it didn't feel real, exactly. But I wasn't scared. She was so pretty, and she smiled at me. I mean, for all I knew, she was the tooth fairy or something."

"And you let her in?"

Maddie nods. "I wanted to see what she was going to do."

This is the strangest thing I have ever heard. "How did she get to your window, Maddie?"

"There used to be a tree there. Remember?" she says. "She must have climbed up."

She's right, there was a tree in front of the house. We took it down a few years ago when our homeowner's insurance told us it was a liability. Chills go down my back as I realize that indeed, someone could have climbed that tree and accessed the window to my daughter's bedroom. I feel the color drain out of my face. I cannot believe that it never occurred to me that a simple tree could pose a safety threat.

I frown. I don't like this. What was Riley doing that night? She was invading my family's privacy; did she have any idea? No; I imagine that that was the furthest thing from her mind. She probably thought she was playing a child's prank. She wanted to see how much she could get away with.

"Okay," I say, trying not to think about little girls who were abducted from their bedrooms. "What happened next?"

"I opened the window for her, and she put her finger to her lips and went, 'Shh . . . You must be Madison.' I nodded. She said I looked like you. I told her everybody says that."

"Did you know who she was?"

Maddie nods. "Yes."

"But how?"

"Pictures, I guess," Maddie says, looking toward to the window. "And she was beautiful. I told her everybody was waiting for her downstairs, and she said she'd get there. 'They can wait,' she said. I told her you were pretty upset, and she just smiled and said, 'It's okay. I can handle my big sisters.'"

I sip my coffee. Maddie's story sounds more possible with every word.

"She was only wearing a little makeup, I noticed that," Maddie says. "And something about her face was like a little girl. She had freckles. I'd never noticed them in her magazine pictures, but now I realize it's because some makeup person paints them over. Or photoshops them out. I wish I could do that, just erase my freckles."

"Don't wish that," I say, touching her face. "I love your freckles."

Maddie ignores me. "But am I right? Does she have freckles?"

"Sure, right across the bridge of her nose and her cheeks. Just light little ones. All three of us have those." I cross my arms and look at my daughter. "How did she seem? I mean, was she in a good mood? Or upset or anything?"

"She was sort of all giggly and happy, but mostly because she was excited that we were . . . like, playing a trick on everybody," she says. "But under that, she seemed sort of sad. You know what I mean?"

I fold and grip my arms and look down. I am listening hard to her story and trying to tease out anything that helps explain this. Riley was a moody teenager, and she could swing from laughing to angry in a minute. "I think so," I say.

"She didn't stay long, only a couple of minutes," she says. "And she told me not to tell you that she'd come into my room."

Secrets between adults and children. A risky game.

"Is that why you haven't told me before now? Did you think I'd be mad?"

"Not really," she says. "I'd sort of pushed it out of my mind. It didn't matter anyway, until now."

"Madison," I start, placing my hand on hers. "No adult has any right to ask you to keep their secrets. If someone demands that of you, you tell me. No matter what. Even if they tell you that you'll get in trouble. Okay?"

"Yeah, yeah, yeah," Maddie says. "I know all that. But this was different, Mom."

She's right; this is different. But then again, it's also the same.

"What was she wearing?" I ask.

"She had on this really pretty dress with, like, fringes on the edge that shook every time she moved. Kind of like the dresses they wore in the twenties or something."

"A flapper dress," I say.

"Yes," she says, nodding. "Her hair was kind of crimpy curly and pulled back but loose, not like a tight ponytail or anything. Oh, and high heels. I remember that. You'd think someone climbing through a window in high heels would be, like, awkward, but she made it look easy, like she did it every day."

I cross my arms and smirk. Riley Emery is the girl who lives the dream: she went to Manhattan to become an actress but got spotted by a modeling agency; she's built a career on getting made up and wearing exquisite clothes; she's rubbed elbows with the rich, the famous, and the outrageously glamorous. Plus, she climbs trees at night in high heels and sparkly flapper dresses. And she was reckless with my daughter.

What do we do with you, Riley? How I wish I knew where you were so I could scold you.

"Riley makes a lot of things look easy," I say.

Maddie continues. "I kept thinking you were going to hear us talking and open the door. I mean, actually, I wanted you to. I remember, I kept hearing the hallway floor creak, and I was sure it was you, but you never came in."

I shake my head. "No, I didn't hear a thing. So she didn't stay long. Did she just go back out the way she came?"

Maddie nods. "She said she was going to join you guys, but she wanted to come in the front door. I told her she should just walk downstairs, but she didn't want to. She said she had a big surprise for everybody."

"A surprise?"

She nods. "She wouldn't tell me what."

"Any idea what she was talking about?"

"Nope," she says. "I kept listening for a knock on the front door, or the sound of all the grown-ups saying hi, or something. But it never came. After a while, I looked out my window to see if she was still out there somewhere, but I didn't see anything. I guess she left."

I open my mouth to speak, but the words slip away from my lips. The sunlight in the kitchen has grown so bright and sharp, it makes me feel that the air outside is ice-crackle cold. "No, she never came that night. She called and said her car had broken down," I say. "It must have been a little while after that, but I don't remember what time exactly."

"Yeah," Maddie says. "I remember we all sat down and Dad sliced turkey, but everybody was sort of tired and, I guess, drunk by then."

"And after all that, Ethan didn't touch the turkey," I say. "I just gave him pecan pie to get him to stop whining."

"I remember," Maddie says. "Why do you think Aunt Riley did what she did, Mom?"

I shake my head. "I wish I had even a guess," I say. "But I don't."

"Let's ask Aunt Alex what she thinks," she says.

I feel my face twist into a doubtful smirk. "We can ask Alex, sure. But I think the person who needs to explain this is Riley."

Chapter 10

Sunday night, I book three wake-up calls with three different companies on lovely Lucia's lucky landline to make sure that I am up early enough to buy a new phone and then get to the agency on time for my meeting with Marcella. My career might be salvageable if I can be on my very best behavior today. Step one, get out of bed. Done. Then get ready, get out. Once out, find a cell phone store. After that, I spend half an hour convincing a young hipster in a goatee and a suit that I have an account with them. Why can't he find my name in the system? And another half hour selecting a phone. For some reason, it takes goatee-suit-dude another half hour to switch the phone on for me. Why does everything take so long?

This time, I know I am late when I rush into JCW Modeling Agency. Bernie/Bernadette/San Bernardino sits at a desk outside Marcella's office, her straight blond hair wrapped in a tight bun. She's young but tough, and her fake glasses really do make her look smart. She gives me a certain look of pity, and my heart sinks. This is not good.

"I told you to be on time," she says, her shoulders falling. "Just couldn't do it, huh?"

"I have a new cell phone," I say, holding it up for her, this tiny little devil that I have no idea how to operate. "Can I give you my new number?"

"They couldn't switch it over to your old number?" she says.

I smile meekly. "I was ready for a change."

"Isn't that your third number in, like, two months?" She sighs but grabs a pen. "Go ahead."

I tell her the number. "Is Marcella ready?"

Bernie looks down at the office phone. "She's finishing up a call." Bernie turns around to catch Marcella's eye through the window that runs vertically beside the door. Marcella holds up one finger. I wait for a minute or two and try to seem busy by fidgeting around with my phone. Finally, the phone light goes off, and Marcella herself comes out to get me.

"Riley," she says, and her voice is strained. "How are you feeling?"

I give her a smile and hold up my phone again. "New phone," I say. "Yay."

"Come on in," she says. And then, quickly, to Bernie: "Hold my calls."

I wince when she says that. It keeps getting worse.

I go into Marcella's big bright office; one wall is adorned with a series of framed black-and-white pictures of her kids, two boys and a girl, Ryan, Mason, and Yvette. They are so beautiful with their open, curious faces and their hair, shimmering like gold; they should be in a movie. And then there's the window and that downtown view. Every time I come into this room I feel like I am flying over Manhattan. Suddenly, I am drenched in the sensation I had the first time I stepped in this office, that New York is the most magical city in the whole world, brimming with possibility, and terrified that I, a girl from tired old Amesbury, will never be enough for it.

And now we know: Riley from Amesbury will never be enough.

Marcella tells me to take a seat. I sit in one of the chairs facing her desk, but she stands in front of me. She is tall and gorgeous, as always, in a skirt and a loose, flowing blouse, her light-brown hair cut in a neat bob. Marcella looks down to collect her thoughts.

"Marcella—" I start.

"Riley, please," she says.

I went to her mother's funeral and to Yvette's fifth birthday party. She helped me when I first got to New York, and she helped me when Caleb was born. She visited me when I was in rehab. Marcella has been everything to me for seven years. This isn't just work. This is family; the family I chose.

She's not going to fire me. Nobody *fires* family.

"Riley," she finally says. "What's going on?"

"I'm sorry, Marcella," I say. "It's crazy; I lost my phone—"

"This isn't about phones," she says. "This is about business. When you don't show up for a shoot or a show or a fitting, dozens of people have to rearrange everything around you. And it makes you look like you don't care about anybody's time but your own. Which makes *me* look like *I* don't care."

The look on her face is so solemn. I hate that. "I do care," I squeak.

She holds up her finger. "And here's the kicker. You're older, Riley. You actually do know better. People aren't going to put up with foolishness just because you know how to work a catwalk. You need to hustle. That means you get places on time—early, in fact. You're not better than anybody; you're just showing up to do a job, same as everybody. Nobody's going to hire you for your looks or because of your name. They hire you because you know what you're doing. But these days, I'm not so sure about that."

I bite my lip. "I'm sorry, Marcella. I'll do better."

Marcella sighs, walks around to her desk, and sits down. "The behavior we've seen lately—blowing off shoots, arriving hours late, being rude—this isn't like you. What's going on?"

"Nothing," I say. My heart floats up and into my throat. I want to cry. I look down at my lap because I don't want her to see that my eyes are wet.

"I'm sorry," she says. "Riley, I know you're using again. I have to let you go."

"Marcella, don't," I say, gripping the sides of my chair. "I need the work."

"I know. You need the work; you need the money. It gets pretty expensive after a while, huh?"

"Don't do this," I say.

She comes around to the front of the desk and sits on the edge, across from me. "Take this opportunity. Quit. Clean yourself up, and pull yourself together. If not for your own good, then for Caleb."

Marcella sighs, grips her elbows, and turns away. I know I disappointed her; I could have been one of those models who embraced motherhood and added it to her brand, and dressed her kids in designer overalls, and brought them to photoshoots and posted them all over the Insta-Twitter-Face-gram world. I don't know why I'm not like one of them. I don't know where my whole life went off the rails. And I have no idea how to fix any of it.

"Don't talk about him," I say.

"Fine, Riley, don't do it for him, and don't do it for me," she says. "Do it for yourself. Because you won't make it to the other side. If you don't do something now, the drugs will kill you. They always win, trust me."

I stare at her and blink. "You think I'm an addict. I can't believe it. You guys sent me to rehab two years ago, and now you think I'm using again?"

"You're really going to deny it?" she says, her short bob bouncing. "Empty out your purse. Right here, on the desk." She taps her desk to show me where to pour everything out. "Better yet, here's a cup." She reaches into a drawer and slams a little clear plastic cup down in front of me. "Go to the ladies' room and give me a sample. Prove me wrong. I'd like nothing more."

I only look at the cup. I don't want to turn away from a challenge, but I had a pill parfait for breakfast. Happy little pills, and a snort of cocaine to cheer me up because I sort of knew what was coming. I don't touch it, but I meet her glaring eyes. Her face, her pretty face, which I have seen drunk and flirty at agency parties, pale and exhausted after twelve hours on a plane, fraught with worry for her mom, and exasperated by the drunken hijinks of young models, looks at me now with a derision I never would have thought she'd have for me.

She picks up the cup and puts it back in her desk drawer. "Damn it, Riley," she mutters under her breath.

I know how I look to her. Me, my own face painted in broad strokes to hide a geography lesson of lines and circles. My body, skinny and bony, not lean and muscular like it should be, like it once was. And my pretty Fendi bag, the one she gave me for my birthday, showing threads on the handles and scuffs on the bottom. I have nowhere to hide. For a few years, I fooled the world into thinking I was beautiful, but now they realize, as Marcella finally has, that I am a fake.

I want to go home and hide under blankets. A friendly, happy little pill, and this will all fade into some past so distant that it might have never happened at all.

"All right, then," I say. I stand up and whip my bag over my shoulder and walk to the door.

"You're breaking my heart," she says. "You're a smart girl; you have a lot of talent. You could have a great future, but you need to get clean."

I smile. "I bet you say that to all the pretty girls."

"I'm sorry, Riley. You have no idea how sorry I am."

My hand is on the doorknob, but I'm not quite ready to leave this room, where I used to be so welcome and safe. "I thought," I say, not exactly sure if I am speaking out loud, "that you were going to help me."

"I wanted to," she says. "But if I keep helping you, you will die right in front of me. And I'm terrified, Riley. It might already be happening."

Out on the sidewalk, I cry while I walk for two city blocks. And then it hits me—wait, I'm free. The future is wide open. I could do anything. Anything at all. I could go for a bicycle ride. I could take a cooking class. I could read the whole newspaper on Sunday morning and eat a bagel. An entire bagel. With regular cream cheese!

I will start, though, by going home and taking a pill and a nap, as long a nap as I want. Maybe, in fact, I will never wake up.

Chapter 11

I have taken to sleeping in my sleeping bag on Marjorie's army cot. Simple living; temporary living. This morning, I woke up when I heard footsteps— *dreamed* I heard footsteps—someone running up and down the hallway outside my door. They were so clear and loud, I almost believed there was someone out there that very moment. But when I sat up to listen, everything was quiet.

I remember what the lawyer, Pete, said right before he left to go to his lovey Newburyport McMansion. "I think I would be spooked to stay an empty farmhouse like this . . . in the middle of the winter . . . all by myself." Actually, Pete, sometimes, it is a little spooky here.

And still, I am moving ahead with plans. A couple of days ago, a real estate agent named Leslie, a friend of Colleen's, stopped by and tried to convince me that I should do a big renovation. *Two choices*, she said. *Do the upgrades yourself and make some real money, or do nothing and wait for who knows how long to sell at a minimal price to someone else who will buy to flip.* In the meantime, I'd be on the hook for state and local taxes as well as insurance. Nothing in life, as they say, is free. Sigh. Grumble. Great.

Then we went to the basement to view the house's major organs. The oil furnace is fine; it resembles a World War II tank, but it will last the winter and perhaps outlive humanity. Then we looked at the electrical box. It was rusted shut; Leslie, who is more resourceful than she looks, fished a metal nail file out of her purse and picked until it surrendered. The door swung open to reveal a panel of glass knobs, pretty and clear like ancient gems. And around them, a giant nest of wires, all colors, some bound by tape, everything tangled.

"Oh, God," she said. "You need a certified, insured electrician in here. And I wouldn't wait. This isn't safe."

"It's that bad?" I asked.

"Number one fire hazard in a home is bad wiring. And this is . . ." She points at it with lacquered nails. "I mean, I hate to say it, but it's not just bad, it's a disaster. Have you had a home inspection?"

"I didn't think I needed one," I said. "Marjorie used to stay here on weekends, and I assumed that if she did that it was safe enough . . ."

"With houses, you can never assume anything," she said. "I'd get the place inspected if I were you. Costs a few hundred dollars, but then you know what you're dealing with."

Oh, good, another way to spend money.

So, today, the electrician she recommended is coming by to examine the situation. I look out the window while I wait; it's warmer today, and the sky is gray. It feels like snow, but there's nothing in the forecast. A white van pulls into the driveway and a man gets out; his name is Chris, and he wears a jacket over a faded Patriots sweatshirt. His hair is graying and his eyes are lined, but I sense he is younger than I am. After introductions, and a few generic comments about the house—"Nice house; I love the old places. So cool, you know?"—he tells me about his life, about his kids, second and fifth graders at the charter school. Everybody around here likes to talk about their kids. Maybe everybody with kids likes to talk about their kids.

We descend into my dirt-floored basement, and he holds a bright flashlight up to the circuit box, the spaghetti tangle of wires, and the panel of jewels.

"That's some fancy wiring," he says. He touches a couple of fuses and tries to follow a wire back to its source. "Ben Franklin himself might have engineered this one."

I smile weakly. "Oh, boy. Should we call a museum?"

He gives me a face that's half smile and half cringe. We walk upstairs and wander the house; in each room, he points out code violations and safety hazards. I have too few outlets, he says, aluminum wires, no GFCIs around the kitchen or bathroom. And other things too. A veritable salad of electrical issues.

Finally, we sit down at the kitchen table. "So, what we're looking at here is basically a whole house rewiring," he says.

"Yeah, I got that," I say. "How much are we talking?"

"I'll write up an estimate and email it to you," he says. "I'd say at least two grand just to get you up to code. This isn't one of those, everything goes black when you use a hair dryer and a toaster at the same time. However, turning on a light could be a ticket to a bonfire. Hey, you got a fire extinguisher?"

My head is swimming with all he is telling me. "I . . . I don't think so," I manage to stutter. But yes, I need a couple. I grab a receipt from a pizza delivery and start to jot down a Home Depot list.

"If I were you, I'd put new batteries in all of the smoke alarms and test them. Make sure you have a couple in the basement. I didn't see any down there."

"Okay," I put batteries on my list, new smoke detectors too. "So when can you start?"

"I'm working on a house in Boxford now, but I might be able to shuffle things around to start next week," he says. "Don't want you having any unplanned barbecues."

"Thanks," I say.

Chris hands me his card, and I give him my email address. I thank him and show him to the door, then watch him drive away. How am I going to pay for this? I have a massive credit card bill on the way, paying for that last-minute trip back to the US from India. I have some money in the bank, but not much more than it would take to fix the electricity, and even if I foot that bill, then what will I live on? I need a job. But I'll need more.

I drive to Amesbury to see Dad. When I walk into the house this time, I'm hit by the old-man smell: some combination of menthol body rub, Lifebuoy soap, and instant coffee sediment in unwashed mugs. Plus all the detritus in the living room emits its own cloud of grime and mildew. And something else—the state of inertia, maybe.

Dad makes lunch, hamburgers fried in a cast-iron skillet, his specialty. We sit, and I tell him about the house.

"You should come see the house, Dad. You'd like it," I say. "It has that historic New England charm."

"I want to see it," he says. His bushy eyebrows go up. "I'm intrigued."

"Really? How about now?" I say. "After lunch? I'll drive. It's only fifteen minutes away. I mean, twenty if we get behind a tractor."

"I don't think today is a good day for it, Alex," he says, glancing down at his plate.

He won't leave. I didn't really think he would. I pause, wondering how much I want to push this. "Come on. It has a view of the marsh. And it's really set off. You wouldn't even know it was there if someone didn't tell you. It's a little . . . mysterious, actually."

"Sorry, Alex. I'm tired," he says. "I've probably been staying up too late, watching the Bruins."

"Oh, sure," I say. "It's that time of year. How's the team doing, anyway?"

"We have a pretty good lineup," he says. "But I don't think it's a Cup year."

I bob my head in understanding. "Dad, please come see the house another time." I sit back in my chair. I watch him eat, and I think about the person he used to be. He used to keep a little Sunfish sailboat at a dock in Salisbury. Many summer Saturday mornings before Mom died, he tiptoed out of the house before the sun rose and brought back the fish he caught. We girls begged him to bring us with him, but he just swatted us off and mumbled something about needing time away from females.

It could be so easy right now for him to walk out the door and do . . . something. Anything. But he doesn't.

"You weren't like this when we were kids," I say. "Even after Mom. We used to go places. Remember? Boston. Portsmouth. Maine in the summer. When did you . . . stop doing things?"

He shrugs and looks at his plate. "Maybe after I retired, or when everybody moved out. Now that I don't have you kids bugging me to take you places, I'd rather stay home, is all. And I don't need anything that's not here."

"Dad, you need to go out, get some air. Go to Portsmouth for an afternoon. Let's go to a Bruins game in person. I'll buy the tickets. Come on. It's important to get out."

He grimaces; the idea of going too far from home gives him vertigo.

"And if you don't want to do any of that, come see my house," I say. "Admission is free. Lunch is included. Reservations are not required."

He chuckles. "Sometime. Not today."

I sigh. Then I decide it's time to ask. "Pop, I talked to a real estate agent. Apparently, the wiring in my house is ancient like Egypt."

"Number one cause of house fires is bad wiring," he says. "You talk to an electrician?"

"I did," I say. "Place needs an overhaul. And a lot of other stuff too, a new roof, new plaster, refinishing for the floors. Landscaping. Appliances. I mean, there's a list a mile long. But I think if some of it got done, I could sell the house for some real money."

"Really," he says, interested.

"Well, it's in a good school zone; at least, that's what this Leslie tells me. And old houses, apparently they're not making more of them."

It's a small joke, but I'm trying. Dad puts his burger down and wipes ketchup off the corner of his mouth. "This is true."

"But I need cash, Dad. I can do a lot of the work myself, but I still need money. Any chance you could loan it to me? I'll pay it back to you after I sell. With interest."

He finishes his burger and wipes his face with a napkin, then pushes himself away from the table. "I don't have a lot, Alexis," he says, looking me straight in the eye. "I live off my pension, and it's not much."

"I know," I say. "And I know I'm asking a lot here. But I feel like we have an opportunity . . ."

He raises one finger to quiet me. He's not done yet. "But I have a little put away, maybe for a rainy day, or so you girls have something to inherit. Or in case I end up in a nursing home. So, what are we talking about? What will it take to fix up this ugly duckling?"

"I don't know exactly," I say. "I think twenty or twenty-five thousand would really help."

"Hmm," he says, sounding doubtful.

"We'll write everything down, Dad," I say. My hands twist and tangle. "The money, the interest. We'll draw up a serious contract. You're a bank, I'm a borrower. Simple as that. As soon as I sell it, I pay you back. I don't have a mortgage, so whatever I sell it for will be profit."

That's when Dad's face starts to change, like he's thinking about things, revisiting things, feeling things. He doesn't talk for a few moments; I almost wonder if he's forgotten that I'm waiting for him to answer my question.

"Dad?"

He rubs his forehead. "Funny, you and your sisters. You used to be the one who took care of everybody. Tell me this, Alexis. Let's say you sell the house. What comes next?"

I shrug. "I suppose I go back to India," I say, briefly daydreaming about packing for my return. "If this works and I make some real money, I could stay in India for a while. I mean, that was my plan, to work in the clinic, to help people." Then I realize what I'm saying, where he has pushed me. "Dad, I might really be able to help people there."

"All this travel," he says, shaking his head. "You used to be my little partner; you always took care of things. All the little things, so many little things I just couldn't ever figure them all out . . ." His mind is wandering, drifting in the wrong direction.

"I can still help," I say loudly, hoping I can interrupt his mental solar storm. "Look what happened this time, I came home. It wasn't just the house, Colleen needed me, and Riley . . ."

Dad nods and looks at the wall, thinking. Then he says, "Santa Claus, Easter Bunny. I didn't know about any of that. And the tooth fairy!" He laughs. I think he's trying to change the subject. "Poor Riley. All her teeth fell out at the same time, remember? She had a mouth full of gums for a while."

I sigh heavily and sit back. "Pops, what about the money? Can you help me?"

"I worry about your sisters," he says. "Where is Riley? I never heard of that before, someone just disappearing like that. Cutting everybody off. Why would she do that?"

I swallow. I guess I already know the answer to my question. "I wish I knew."

"And Colleen, with her marriage and all."

"Yeah, it's too bad."

"Yup," he says. "You know, with people. It's hard to make sense of. One day, someone's up and someone else is down, and the next day it switches, or it turns out that someone else looked up, but they weren't doing as good as they seemed. Everybody's got stuff, Alexis."

"I know, Dad." I feel like I am standing on a riverbank watching my money on a raft in the river, drifting out to sea. With each passing word he speaks, the answer is increasingly *no*.

He leans forward and turns his face toward the floor. "Alexis, I can't give you any money. I'm sorry."

"Sure," I say. "I understand."

I thank him for the burger and head out. My father thinks he can keep me home if he doesn't help me. But then I realize I can do it without him. I was a worker bee for at least ten years and saved money from every paycheck in a retirement account. I don't remember the rules; there will be paperwork and interest to deduct, but I know it's possible to withdraw some of it. And how much is there? I'll have to check my statements, but something, I think. Hopefully enough.

Sorry, Dad. Nice try.

I drive through Amesbury on the road that will bring me to the highway, but when I reach Main Street, I park in front of the library. This was my other childhood home, my refuge. I look at the brick facade, the ceramic owl beyond the second-story window. I need books now; I need to wander, feet and mind, to breathe in dusty stacks. I need information. I have to figure out what to do next.

Inside I sit down at a computer and search the library catalog. I dig through my purse for my wallet and pull out my old Amesbury library card—I still have it!—and find a stack of books about home renovation. Going through the books, I start a list of exactly what I need to do to the house; then I brainstorm for a while, scribbling my ideas on a scrap. I go to check out my books and see a sign at the desk says that the library is looking for help.

I think about that. A library instead of a hospital. Books instead of diseases. Nobody suffering or dying or sick, no telling terrible news to worried families. No life-or-death urgency. I mean, the money is probably not great, but the idea of it is more than a little appealing.

I fill out an application, and then Dolores, the head librarian, a woman in her sixties with blond hair that curls into a slight bouffant, emerges from a room in the back to meet me. She looks at my application through bifocals.

"You were a nurse," she says, looking down at me through the tops of her glasses. "We just need some part-time help shelving books and staffing the front desk. Are you sure this is of interest?"

"Yes," I say. "I'm looking for something a little different. I think this is exactly what I need."

"Wonderful," she says, looking again at my application. "When can you start?"

I shrug. "Whenever you need me."

"Monday morning at nine," she declares. "Don't be late. I don't care for tardiness."

"Neither do I," I say. "See you then."

Home, and then I am home. I have a job now; strange to think someone will be expecting my presence Monday morning at nine a.m. It's starting to feel like I am settling into this place, but I don't want to forget what I am here to do: get in, fix up, get out. I don't want to get comfortable.

Midwinter dusk comes early. I stand by the window for a while and watch the sunlight fade from the eastern sky over the marsh. Pieces of my talk with my father go through my mind. There's money, something for us to inherit. And I am the one who took care of everybody. *What comes next?* he asked. *India,* I said. And suddenly, the money is gone. Why? Because he knows that it's the beginning of a timeline that takes me to a place where he would not be able to reach me. None of them would. They'd have to get along on their own.

And this is just the way it always is; I don't pursue the things I love because my family needs me. My whole life I've been a good girl, a good daughter, a good sister. When I found my mother, my God, I was a child. I protected my sisters; I called the ambulance. I called the post office, told them it was a family emergency, and yes, please, could someone drive my father's route to find him and tell him to come home right away. I watched them drag her out of the bathtub. I watched a stranger put his face to my mother's, her body limp in his arms. I watched water spill from her mouth, knowing even then that she was beyond saving.

I saw everything, and I never told any of them what it was like. That has to be enough. There is a limit to how much one person can bear for a family. I have reached mine.

The worst part? I was almost free. I was there, I was away. But then this house. This house! Damn it. I should hate this house; I should leave right now and let it crumble. I am so mad and hurt, I kick the wall. When it doesn't shake, even a little, I kick it again, harder. I know, and know for sure, that if Colleen or Riley needed money, Dad wouldn't even blink. But when it comes to Alex, nope, she can do it on her own. After all, she got through college and nursing school on her own, right? She's tough, smart, resilient; she'll work it out.

I hit the wall with my fist so hard it hurts. I'm not so tough, Dad. I need your help this time. I wish I didn't have to do this alone. I stand in front of the window, staring into the foliage beyond and shaking my hand to quell the pain; I want to scream. My body is shaking. I don't know what to do with this anger. I watch my face, reflected perfectly in the darkened glass. Why is everything so hard?

I wipe a tear from my eye, and when I glance up, I see something in the reflection. A person, a man, is standing behind me.

Ice shoots up my back. I turn fast, but the room is empty. Yet I know I saw somebody. I saw the shape of his face this time more clearly than before, and now that my heart is racing, I can no longer deny that there was a before. The footsteps that awakened me this morning. And sounds; little ones that have no source. A sense of motion, something stirring behind me in an empty room. Doors that creak open for longer than they should. And the odd nag of being watched, of being not alone.

And in the rooms, lights flickering on, then flashing and going dark. But that's just wiring, right?

I don't know anymore. Maybe it's jet lag. Maybe I'm going crazy.

Panic bubbles in my gut as I stand in the living room, and then the old radio in the empty bedroom upstairs goes on. It plays jazz. My mom's favorite.

I cover my mouth to keep from screaming. But it's silly, I know it's only the electricity, a surge forging through, uncontained by old wires. It must be. I hold my breath. I don't believe in things I cannot see. The wiring is bad, yes, I know. That accounts for the lights and the radio, but what about the other sounds? What about the face in the window?

Upstairs muffled voices murmur through the tinny, twinkling notes of the music. I stand stock-still, shivering, straining my ears to make out words, but I can't understand anything they're saying. I want so badly to hear, to understand. Suddenly, the air is freezing, so cold my breath emits little puffs. I look around to see if a window or door has popped open, but I don't see anything. Did the heat just give out? Great, just what I need.

I turn to face the sink, eyes closed. And then I hear footsteps across the living room floor. Then the front door slams open and, just as fast, crashes closed.

The music shuts off abruptly, and then . . . and then . . . all is quiet.

I gasp for air and open my eyes. Everything around me seems still, the walls, the windows, the air itself is holding its breath. The temperature of the air is normal, but I am still shaking. I wait to see whether it will start again, but nothing happens. I look out the window over the sink; the late afternoon is pitch black. I turn slowly, tentatively, not sure what I expect to see.

The room is empty.

It's just the bad wiring, I think. And my mind's reach for a logical diagnosis is so quick and dispassionate, I almost laugh.

Sure, wiring. Let's go with that.

The air is tinted with the faint smell of candle smoke, and I wonder if the electrical system has finally exploded. I grab a flashlight, open the door to the basement, and shine the light down the stairs and toward the fuse box. There's no sign of smoke or fire.

And oh, I am not walking down those stairs right now. No amount of money could make me.

Now I just stand here, shaking, shivering. I put on my jacket and scarf; I need to go someplace with lights, people, noise. I go outside and get into my car.

As I pull out of the driveway, I think, cats. Maybe I should get a couple of cats. If only so that next time I hear things, I can just tell myself, *Oh, it must be the cats.*

Chapter 12

Friday, February 14, 2014
Colleen

Valentine's Day, and the last day of school for the kids before February vacation. We don't have any plans for the week; the three of us will just relax and make it up as we go, and next weekend Eric is taking the kids skiing. For Valentine's Day, the kids made me cards, and I bought myself a box of very expensive chocolate at the fancy food store in Newburyport and charged it to Eric's credit card. Truly, it's the least he can do. I am making the kids a nice dinner; I invited Alex too, but she says she has a headache and is going to bed early. I hope she's not coming down with something. Well, it will be a nice, quiet evening at home with my favorite people. I slice mushrooms and onions for beef Stroganoff and listen to cheesy love songs on the doo-wop radio station. Valentine's Day is not going to drag me down.

And yet, I am on edge. I finally talked to Nate Hensler. He texted me while I was in the drive-through line at Dunkin' Donuts; so, I parked and talked to him.

"I found your sister," he said. "She's safe, as far as I can tell. She's living in a nice apartment on the Upper East Side. It belongs to someone else, but she's there alone and she has a key, so I think she's borrowing it. But Mrs. Newcomb, I have reason to believe your sister is using drugs."

"Oh, shit," I said under my breath. "What do I do next? How do I reach her?"

"Frankly, I'm not sure what to tell you," he said. "I'm concerned that if you approach her, there's a good chance she'll just run away from you again. And I don't know her mental state. It could be that if she feels pursued, she'll feel forced to do something drastic."

I sat parked in my car, overlooking the traffic circle at Route One, sipped my hot caramel macchiato, and thought about my sister. I remembered trying to explain her algebra homework to her when she was twelve and I was sixteen. She let me help for a few minutes, but then she got frustrated, shouted at me, grabbed her homework, and ran outside, slamming the door behind her.

His instinct could be spot on.

"Maybe it would be better if you could watch her for a few more days," I said. "And let me know if anything changes."

"I can do that, but this week I have another case that needs attention," he said. "So I won't be able to follow her as diligently as I did last week. But I will check on her."

"Well, wait, I don't want her to do something . . . destructive or dangerous while you're not watching her."

"Mrs. Newcomb," he said. "If you are worried, feel free to call the police. But I can't babysit her every minute. I'll see what I can do, and I'll let you know if anything changes."

I rolled my eyes. I shook my head. I didn't like how this was going. "I don't want to call the police," I said. "I hate that these are my only choices."

"I'm sorry I can't do more," he said. "You're welcome to contact someone else. Maybe a psychiatrist, or a treatment center. Or call a private intervention service; you could probably find one online."

I guffawed. Sure, send a stranger in to talk to her. That would not go well.

"I just feel so helpless," I said.

"You're welcome to explore your choices," he said. "Won't hurt my feelings a bit."

I thought about it, and we talked about it, and I drank my coffee and watched the gulls fly overhead. In the end, I told him to stick with the case. *Do what you can*, I told him. *And send me an invoice because I don't like expenses to come all at once out of the blue.*

After that, I went to the grocery store and called Alex and filled her in. Then I called Dad. By the time I got to the checkout, my cart was full but I had no memory of putting anything in there.

But now I have a pit in my stomach; things are out of control. I hate it when things are out of control.

Maddie comes into the kitchen just as I am draining the noodles. "Dinner's almost ready." I tell her. "Can you call your brother?"

"Sure," she says, sampling the sauce with a spoon. "This is good, Mom."

"Glad you like it," I say.

She goes to the doorway and shouts, "Ethan!" at the top of her lungs.

Ethan runs up from the basement, abandoning his Xbox for food. He gives me a big hug, even while my hands are clad in giant pot holders that make them feel like lobster claws. "I love you, Mom," he says.

My sweet kid. He has no idea how much I needed that. "Thanks, Ethan," I say. "Me too." I hug him back and press my face against his hair and smell. It smells faintly of shampoo and the earth after a rainfall. Or maybe I'm imagining that part; it's how he used to smell when he was a baby. I never thought those days would feel so far away.

I kiss Ethan's head. "You two set the table in the dining room."

After dinner I give Ethan and Maddie the night off from chores, and I load the dishwasher. The radio is on while I rinse the dishes, but I don't hear it. I am thinking about Riley: how she is found but still lost, plus Maddie's story of how Riley stole into her room on that Thanksgiving night all those years ago. I don't know what to make of it, and I don't know what to do with it. Does the story hold a clue about what's happening with Riley now? If it does, I don't know how to decipher it.

Later that night I don my flannel nightgown and thick socks against the cold, then climb into bed alone on Valentine's Day. I turn on the TV and watch the news. My head is starting the familiar throb. The feeling clogs my ears, creeps into my temples, and stretches them hard until my head feels like it might burst. Tylenol PM will get me through the night and keep the poison head-wheels from turning. Two rooms away Ethan is playing video games online with his friends, and so I put on the puffy sleep mask that covers my eyes and my ears. In one moment, everything becomes dark and I fall fast asleep.

But this is no dreamless sleep; my mind is riddled with visions of Riley, filled with images from magazine ads. The camera flashes, and I see her, her face drowning under so much makeup, cheeks dark red, eyes purple-gray, her hair platinum and blowing around. She looks wild and absurd, and when I look closely, Riley is not there at all. Where she was standing a moment earlier, there is now only a column of smoke drifting in a dark room.

I want to keep searching for her; maybe she's just on the other side of the smoke. I feel like if I look deeper, I might see little Riley, stretching her hand to me to help her cross the street. I reach into the smoke, but all goes black. I stand in darkness, complete and sudden. Slowly, I come to, realizing that Maddie is beside me, shouting, shaking my body.

"Mom," she says. "Mom, you have to get up!"

An alarm is blasting. Ethan stands beside his sister, coughing hard. I sit up in bed. It's pitch dark except for the light from a flashlight that Maddie is holding.

"It's a fire," Maddie says. "We have to get out. I already called the fire department."

With that, I am awake. No more useless words. We go.

I grab Maddie's hand, and she grabs Ethan's. The halls are filled with rancid chemical smoke, thick and foul. It feels solid, like a wall, but we squat down and try to keep our bodies low to avoid breathing smoke. Breathing is not possible; our lungs will not accept the hot gasses that surround us. My eyes sting and water; the smoke burns my throat. I taste charring like toast.

We hunch down as far as we can and crawl carefully down engulfed stairs. My body hurts, desperate to breathe. I spit and sputter and keep climbing through the tar-paper blackness. When we reach the bottom, there is some relief. This staircase leads directly to the front door, a door we never use. But tonight I unbolt it, and we spill into the night air, gasping for breath, all of us freezing in our pajamas and bare feet. But out and alive. Thank goodness for that.

And then I see it through the side windows of the house: the kitchen is engulfed. The siren of approaching fire trucks overcomes the blaring smoke alarms, and I am granted one blessing. The car, parked in the driveway and not in the garage, and I remember: the keys are in it. Last night I left them in the car. I know that, suddenly, clearly and confidently, as though I can see the keys.

I look at my children, their faces painted with a fear I hoped they'd never know, coughing, sputtering, freezing. They grip their elbows and forearms and huddle together against the February wind, their breath breaking into the air like puffs of the smoke we just escaped.

"Come on," I say, and they follow easily; nobody argues with me now. We three fugitives run across the lawn to the car, like a lifeboat, a gift granted by my five-p.m. self to my three-a.m. self.

My hands do not fumble, and I am amazed that they do not, that I am able to function at all. One moment before the fire trucks pull in front of the house, the keys go into the ignition, turn, and we back out. We drive in reverse down the driveway—a million times I have done this, but this is the only one that matters—and pull onto the street and across it to park. The car is cold but sheltered from the wind, and the air will grow warm in a few moments.

"What happened?" Ethan says from the back seat, coughing.

"It was me," Maddie says from the front passenger seat, tears in her voice. "I'm so sorry. I'm so sorry, Mom."

"Shh, honey," I say. "Just tell us what happened."

"I was on my iPad watching the Olympics. Lindsey was watching too, and we were Facetiming." She's so upset, she's heaving.

"Sweetie, just breathe," I say.

Her long brown hair hangs limply around her red face. "I went to make popcorn on the stove, like you always do. But then I went upstairs for something, and then this amazing speed skating competition came on, and . . . I forgot all about the popcorn."

"Did you hear the smoke alarm?" I ask.

"I had my earbuds on," she says, squeaking through tears. "By the time I figured out what was happening, it was all . . . happening."

Why didn't the alarm sound in my room? Why didn't it wake up Ethan? I don't know. What matters now, I tell myself, is that we are alive. This is all that matters.

I take Maddie's hand in mine to comfort her, but I am in shock myself. What now? Where will we live? Eric—how will I contact Eric? My phone is inside. I rub my eyes; they are scratchy with smoke, and I stink with it. Do I have to go through all this by myself?

Firefighters climb out of the truck; two walk around the house, and one hooks up the hose to the hydrant.

"I have to go talk to them," I say. "You two stay here. The car will warm up soon."

"Mom," Maddie says. "I'm so sorry."

"I know you are, baby," I say. "Don't worry, we're safe and everything's going to be okay."

How will it be okay? I have no idea. But I need to tell the kids that it will. And if I tell them, I ought to try and believe it myself.

I leave the sanctuary of the car and run in my long flannel nightgown and bed socks through the icy night to the firefighters. I find the chief and tell him that we are safe; and no, we don't have any pets; and no, there were no guests and nobody else inside. The neighbors are starting to come out of their homes. They all ask if everyone is okay. *Yes*, I say over and over. *We are okay. We are all out of the house.* Someone wraps a warm coat around me and hands me boots. Another gives me a thermos of hot tea. Who gave me what? I cannot remember the faces, only the hands and the warmth. I am grateful beyond measure.

The lights from the trucks—eventually, three of them arrive—and all the neighbors swarming around make this feel like a big party. A radio inside the fire truck buzzes and beeps, garbled, disembodied voices. An ambulance arrives. We go over; they give Maddie and Ethan sweatshirts, socks, and cheap sneakers. The EMT checks us all for smoke inhalation. I am coughing but I'm all right. Ethan needs oxygen. Seeing him sitting there with the cup over his mouth is the moment when I fight back tears. Maddie sits beside her brother. Her face is pale; she's so upset. She takes his hand in hers, and suddenly, they both look like babies. Please, God, please, help us get through this.

Someone calls my name and runs toward me across the sea of faces and yards and houses that are not on fire. Our neighbor from down the street, Corinne, the mom to two kids the same ages as mine.

"My God, I came to see what was happening, but I didn't expect . . . Is everybody okay?"

"We're all out," I say.

"Thank goodness," she says, gripping her elbows. Her winter jacket over her pajamas is nothing in this kind of cold. "When everybody's in the clear, send the kids over to our house. They can get some rest, and eat something, take a shower, whatever they need."

I look at Corinne; the lines in her face are deep with concern. I should take her up on her offer and send them with her, but it's too close to the one I accepted all those years ago, refuge at a neighbor's house, where I went to drink chocolate milk while EMTs dredged our mother from the bathtub. I cough hard into my fist and realize my jaw hurts from trying to hold it steady against the shivering.

"Thanks," I say. "I want to keep them close right now."

"All right," she says. "But let me get you all something to eat. I'll be right back." Then Corinne disappears into the fog of everything. I sit on the edge of the ambulance with Ethan and Maddie, watching the mayhem. What happens next? I have no idea. Will we be able to rebuild? A couple of months ago, Eric mentioned something about our insurance policy, but now I don't remember what he said. Where is Eric? How can he not know what we're going through?

Several minutes later Corinne reappears with blankets, a stack of them, plus a thermos of hot Swiss Miss and several wrapped granola bars for the kids. I am overwhelmed—by everything, but in this moment, it's her kindness, everyone's kindness, that sends me over the edge. I start to cry. Corinne puts her things on the ground and wraps her arms around me, holds me while I fall apart for a moment.

"You're okay," she says. "Everything's going to be okay. You got everybody out of the house. Nothing else matters."

"I know," I say and wipe my eyes. I remember then that our neighbors do not know about my marriage, except that there's a certain car they might not have seen in a while. And Eric is not here now—Valentine's Day night—which must be a very obvious sign. But Corinne does not ask where he is, and this, I know, is an act of tremendous compassion.

"Have they told you anything about the house?" she asks. "Remember, everything can be rebuilt. That's what insurance is for."

"I know," I say. I look at the house, smoke pouring out of the windows that the firefighters smashed. My body is cold to the core, my throat and teeth hurt. This house. My house. The place where I was safe. It smelled the way I wanted it to smell; the furniture I'd chosen over so many years. It was all *right*. Curtains I sewed. Treasures I loved. Closets filled with stuff that I amassed. All of it now dissolved into smoke and ash, rising toward the starry sky in a frigid night where the hours are passing so slowly. A night that will never end.

I gasp as the sobs rise into my throat. I almost wish Corinne would go away and stop being so nice to me. In the face of such kindness, all I can do is weep.

"Please let the kids come to my place," she says. "It's no trouble at all, and you'll know exactly where they are in the morning. We're here to help. Truly."

I sniff and wipe my tear-covered face with my arm. "Thanks, Corinne," I finally say. "That would be great."

When Ethan finishes with oxygen, he feels a little better, but Maddie is still visibly upset. I tell them that they are going to Mrs. Rossman's house, and they look relieved; they are ready to go. Big hugs; I love them, I say. Everything will be okay. I will see them later.

As I start to pull away, I see Maddie watching me; there are huge tears in her eyes. "What is it, Cupcake?" I say. "Are you all right?"

"Mommy, I'm so sorry," she starts, and then big tears start rolling down her cheek. "I wish I could pay for this, but I don't have enough saved . . . and I'm just so sorry."

I hold her close, then I look her straight in the eye. "Maddie, I need you to listen to me carefully," I say, calm and serious, focusing intently on her. "Yes, you were careless, but I know you didn't do this on purpose. You made a small mistake, and, unfortunately, this time, it came with big consequences. We'll talk about how to be extra safe in the kitchen, but for now, I need you rest and relax. And don't let this fester in your brain. We have a problem that we need to take care of. But if you make yourself sick worrying about this, it won't help anything. You called the fire department immediately, that's the important part. And you helped all three of us get out of the house. Because you did those things, we're okay. If you hadn't reacted so quickly, it could have been a lot worse. All right?"

My sweet girl sniffs her tears away and nods her head.

I hug her again. "You two go with Mrs. Rossman and just rest. We're going to be okay."

I feel reassured hearing myself say it, for that reminds me that it's true; as long as we are safe, everything else will be okay.

Then, I stand alone, freezing but watching fire. The worst part is the fumes: they're awful, toxic, like the stench of all our possessions melting into the manufactured, formless plastics beneath the surface of the things themselves. A neighbor gave me a cell phone and now I am trying to call Eric. Eric. Eric. He does not answer. I send a text.

> Please pick up. It's Colleen
> calling from another phone.

I call again, but still no answer. I consider getting in the car and driving into town, but I'm not supposed to leave here, and anyway, I cannot leave while all this is happening. Even if I wanted to.

The fire is beginning to die down, or that's how it appears. I can barely look at the house; the whole back side is black. Broken windows, a gaping hole in the roof. I cannot believe this is my house. It's surreal.

The fire chief talks to me for a while about the cause of the fire. I explain about Maddie and late-night stove-top popcorn and Olympic speed skating.

"Did you talk to a board up company yet?" he asks. "Call your insurance; they might have a restoration company they work with."

He keeps talking about what I do next, and I only nod. I have a million questions, but if I open my mouth to speak, I will start crying. Mostly, I want to know, where is Eric? Talking to the fire chief should be his job. Calling insurance and finding a restoration company should be his job, no matter what state our marriage is in. The fire chief pauses and looks at the house. Only one truck remains now, and they look like they are getting ready to move out too. This part is almost done.

"The damage is pretty extensive," he says. "It's not a washout, but you'll need some serious reconstruction. Could take a couple of months. There's a lot of water damage inside, and a lot of smoke. Once things settle down, we'll need to inspect it. If it's structurally safe, then you should be able to go inside and get a few things. That usually takes a day or two."

"Okay," I say.

He looks at me; I must look like I am about to fall apart. "I know this is hard," he says. "You're going to be okay. Believe me, I've seen people come through much worse."

I only smile. He probably says that every time.

The fire chief finishes his pep talk, and I am left looking at my broken home. Around me, in the half light, neighbors are waking and emerging, wandering through a perimeter beyond me, asking each other the same questions: What happened? Is everyone all right? An insurance adjuster thrusts his cards into my mittened hands. My eyes ache. My cheeks burn from the wind. I wish I could get in my car and simply drive home, but I have no place to go. This *was* my home. Was it beautiful? It was so beautiful. And it's not a "was," it's a house that needs repairs. Insurance will cover it. It will be lived in again.

Corinne appears before me once again, a cup of hot coffee in her hand.

She takes the cold cup that I have been holding for hours from my hand and hands me the hot one. "Doughnut?" she says, holding up a bag. I shake my head. "How are you holding up?" I can only shrug and sip hot, glorious coffee.

"Thanks for the coffee, Corinne," I say. "Thank you for everything."

"The kids are fine," she tells me. "They took showers and put on warm clothes and now they're resting."

"Oh, that's a huge relief," I say. "What time is it?"

"A little after six," she says. "I can stay with you as long as you need. If you want to come over and shower, or rest, or anything, you're more than welcome. Okay?"

Stop being nice, I think. I can't really stomach it right now. "Thank you so much. You don't need to stay with me. I'm all right."

She puts her hand on my back. "If you need anything, just come over, okay?"

Corinne walks back to her undamaged house, and I stand looking at my fallen one. Then I am thinking about things, items, possessions, so much has been lost. Photo albums of our babies, which were kept in the living room; those might be okay. Our wedding album was in the same bookshelf as those. Some clothes might be intact; maybe I can recover those when the fire chief gives the okay.

I remember another thing, something packed away in a closet, which I dearly hope is not damaged: the only painting I own by my mother. I never put it on the wall; I couldn't stand the idea of looking at it every day, but I wanted it close by. Now I want to see the painting, the way I want a mother's hug.

The mayhem is over, the fire department is gone, and even the neighbors are dissipating, floating back into their houses to take hot showers and drink familiar coffee in warm kitchens. The Red Cross gave me some jeans and a sweater earlier; now I need a place to change. Maybe I'll go to Panera.

Sitting in the car, ignition on for warmth, and I get out this phone—who does it belong to? I'll look at the contacts later and try to figure it out. The next thing is to track down Eric. I breathe. I am keeping it together. I seem to be functioning and not weeping, and at this I am supremely amazed.

Eight a.m. Panera has supplied me with a breakfast sandwich and coffee, paid for by a stash of emergency cash I keep under the seat in the car, and a clean bathroom where I changed into the most unattractive, ill-fitting pair of jeans I have ever seen. I've had a chance now to sit and collect myself, and I'm ready to call Eric again. Finally, he answers.

"Hi, Colleen," he says. "Sorry I missed your calls earlier. Listen, I'm getting ready to go for a run, can I call you later?"

"Eric, wait," I say. And that's all I can say before my breath catches. Hearing his voice, so normal, so familiar, triggered something involuntary, and now the tears flow.

He hears my voice and understands. "Colleen? Are you okay? The kids?"

I shake my head and twist up my face to hold back the tears. "The kids are okay, we're all safe," I say. Deep breath. One, then another. "We had a fire last night. The house."

"Oh, my God—"

"Nobody was hurt," I say.

"Colleen, where are you? What happened?"

I blow my nose. It's all catching up to me. "I'm at Panera. It started in the kitchen. The rest of the house is . . . filled with smoke but basically standing."

"What about the antiques?" he says.

The question first shocks me and then irritates me. "What?"

"The antiques?" he says. "The family heirlooms. No, scratch that, how are you doing? Oh my God, this is not what I was expecting this morning."

"That makes two of us," I say. The tears are gone. I realize I am talking to another man who cannot help me.

"How did this happen?" he asks. "Were you cooking something?"

"It doesn't matter now," I say. "Eric, can you contact our insurance company?"

"Insurance," he says, speaking slowly as though he's thinking about something. I can almost hear him rubbing his forehead.

"Eric?"

"We might have a glitch to work through there," he says. "Technically speaking, we might not exactly have insurance right now."

I feel the blood drain my face, the breath leave my lungs. "What?"

"Don't panic," he says. "I was having a dispute with our agent about the fact that they were charging us for some cyber thing I never authorized, and I refused to pay until he fixed it. This is their fault. The guy even acknowledged it. It's just that . . . as of a couple of months ago, our insurance was . . . technically . . . canceled."

Insurance canceled? I feel hyperventilation starting in, but I can't let that happen. If I lose control, there's nobody to fall back on. "You fix this, Eric," I growl. "You fix this today."

"I will. I have emails from the guy promising to resolve the whole thing. It's just that, when last I heard, it hadn't yet been resolved."

"Jesus, Eric, I cannot believe you would let this happen." Now my voice is rising, I am almost shouting. When I notice people turning to look at me, I turn the volume down, but now I'm hissing expletives. "I'm not kidding. You fucking fix this today."

"Colleen, I will do what I can," he says. "Who knows if I can even reach someone on a Saturday."

Now I'm rubbing my forehead. Here comes the migraine. "You will reach someone on a Saturday. You will call them, and you will reach someone, and you will fix this. Look, Eric, I really need a shower. I'd like to go to the condo and rest for a bit."

"Oh," he says, again sounding doubtful.

"Actually, if we don't have insurance, we may all be moving in there, just like the old days."

He clears his throat. "Colleen, you can't come here now. Someone's here."

"Who? Did you get a roommate?" I say. But the words get out of my mouth, then I realize what he's saying. I can't go to the condo. Someone is there. "Oh," I whisper.

He whispers now too. "I just started seeing her, and last night she . . . I figured you had the kids this weekend, so we were planning . . . No, listen, just give me twenty minutes."

My house burned down, we have no insurance, and apparently there's a woman in my husband's bed. I stare out the window at the cars zooming past.

"Are you still there?" he says.

"Yes," I whisper.

"Colleen, I'm so sorry. This isn't how I wanted this to come out."

Now I know why, very late on Valentine's Day night, he was not answering his phone. He was celebrating the holiday in a more . . . traditional fashion.

The phone beeps; another call is coming in. It's some name and number I don't know, but the timing is good because I can't talk to Eric right now.

"I'll call you back," I tell him, and I hang up but click a button to ignore the call. Then I make another call. My friend Peggy answers immediately.

"Colleen, my God, I've been calling you all morning," she says. "Someone posted about the fire on Facebook. I saw the house, and I thought, 'That can't be Colleen's,' but then I saw the address. Oh, honey, I can't imagine what you're going through."

"Yeah," I say.

"Where are you now?" she says. "Are the kids okay? What can I do?"

Again, the tears surge into my throat and lodge there so I can barely speak. "I need clothes, Peggy. I'm sitting in Panera wearing these jeans that the Red Cross gave me and they're . . . big, they're droopy, and they're really, really bad."

She laughs. "Only Colleen Newcomb would worry about having charity jeans that aren't cute enough."

"I guess if I eat enough breakfast sandwiches, eventually they'll fit fine," I say. We both laugh. "But, oh God, Peggy, Eric's gone. It's over. We're getting a divorce."

"What? Since when?"

I can't answer. I cannot speak at all. "He moved out a few weeks ago . . . but now I think it's really over."

"Wait, so you've been on your own through this whole thing?"

I nod, aware that she can't see me. "I need a shower, Peggy. Oh my God, all I smell is smoke. It's all over me. I feel like a sausage."

"Okay, you, get over here," she says. "Whatever you need, it's yours. Shower, food, booze. All of it. Just come."

"Okay, I'll be there in ten minutes," I say. "Oh, hey, could you text me the number for Corinne Rossman? The kids are there, and I need to call them."

"You got it," she says. "See you in a few."

A moment later she sends Corinne's number to this phone I'm borrowing. So I call to check on the kids. *They're okay,* she says. Her husband made everybody pancakes, and now they're all slumped on the couch, watching TV. I tell her that I'm going to get cleaned up and be over to pick them up probably in about an hour.

Eric might be waiting for me to call him back, but I don't care. The phone rings again. It's Eric. I don't answer. And I won't, not until I go to Peggy's house and let her take care of me. Now I get it, Eric, you're not one of us anymore. And I don't care if you met this woman before you left or after, yesterday or two years ago. You're gone, and I can't care right now because I am done.

I get in the car, but driving on autopilot, I end up back at my house, my lovely, wounded house. I get out of the car and stand in front of it, breathing in the cold, smoke-filled air. Now that the fire is over, I want to torch everything that ever belonged to Eric: his clothes, his books, his stupid stack of *Economist* magazines that he refused to either read or get rid of.

Are the antiques okay? Those antiques, those lovely family heirlooms, the ones that were untouched in our house fire. They will not survive my rampage.

The fire chief said that I would be able to go inside at some point; I just had to wait for them to declare the structure stable. But I won't wait. I don't need permission to walk into my own house. I open the front door and go inside, just like always, except that this time, the stench of smoke saturates everything—noxious fumes that hurt my throat when I try to breathe. If I look to one side of the house, I will see the total destruction, so I don't look over there. On this side, windows are smashed, furniture and rugs are soaked, but much remains.

I want the clock. Eric's grandmother's antique mantle clock, the pretty one with the wooden case and the bronze fixtures, the inlaid detail and the Roman numerals. On its face is written its origin: "A. Golay, Leresche & Fils, Geneve." Made in Geneva a hundred years ago. I find the clock sitting where it has always been, on the mantle over the living room fireplace.

Poor little thing. I have always dusted it with extreme care, and gently wound it during the holidays so that its quiet ticking would be the heartbeat counting down until Santa came down the chimney. This time I grab it, take it outside; suddenly, in the warming daylight, the loaner coat feels heavy. I'm sweating in the twenty-degree air, that's how mad I am; I throw the coat off. I toss the clock on the lawn and think about someone sleeping in the condo that I actually own part of. She's blond; she is obviously blond. And young. And lovely with a long neck that curves when he strokes her back. With a grunt, I lift up my foot in my Red Cross sneakers and stomp the clock. It creaks and groans. Another stomp, and it breaks under my weight; that feels good, like a taste of blood. I pull off the glass cover and stomp its pretty face.

Now the wood is cracked and brass bits of motor spills out, but it still looks like a clock. I need a tool to finish it off. The garage is intact, so I walk in and find a sledgehammer. It's cold and heavy in my hand. Am I strong enough to wield it, even after a sleepless night? Oh, yes, I am. I swing up high, then pound hard. It only takes a couple of knocks to smash that pretty little antique *horologe* like a bug in the dead winter grass. Cars drive past my lawn; I can only imagine what the neighbors think.

And then my phone rings. I have to put the coat on to find the phone in my pocket. Peggy.

"Are you okay?" she says. "I thought you were coming over. Do you need me to pick you up?"

I stand and throw down the sledgehammer. I am panting with the exertion, sweating from the thrill. "No, thanks," I say. "I just had to take care of something at home." I wipe my damp head with the arm of my coat and begin to walk toward my car. "I'm on my way now."

What am I going to do next? First thing is to go to Peggy's and shower and change. Then I'll call Eric, because we need a plan. I need to pick up the kids. Where will we all sleep tonight? I'm not sure. Anyplace but a hotel; it would be too much like the night after Mom died. Little Riley jumping up and down on the beds.

I can't think about hotels right now. The kids are safe and resting at Corinne's house. Once I feel more like a human being, I will come get them, and we'll figure out what to do. But I leave the clock's carcass on the lawn for all to see. The neighbors will see it or maybe they won't notice; probably they'll decide it has something to do with the fire. Eric will see it, I hope, because at some point, he'll come to the house to see the damage.

And I hope he will know that the carnage on the lawn is something he caused. Happy Valentine's Day, my own dear husband.

Chapter 13

Riley

Monday mornings are the absolute worst day of the week, and the February sky is gray and muddy, with no hope of brightening until later this week. Coffee in a pretty café helps a little, and I'm sitting at a table in the corner, watching the people go past. There are things in my life that I know to be true. One, I have no career. I have been fired from the only real job I've ever had by a woman who I thought loved me like family. I could try to sign with another agency, but I know how this works. Everybody's talking about why JCW let me go. People don't get second chances. Not in this world.

Two, I fail Caleb every day. With every visit to Sammy, every pill I take, I imagine he feels the ache in his little bones. The visits I am not attending. The contact with ACS I am not keeping. It makes me sick to think that someone would treat their child this way, even though I am the one doing it. How can I live with myself? What kind of person am I?

But actually, I know the answer. Pretty and damaged, I am the daughter without a mother. I have no business trying to mother a child, this little tiny boy. He relied on me for everything. How could I let myself fail him? I thought having a child would change me, chemically, essentially, from the inside out. I believed that everything would find a way. And it shouldn't be so hard. A child is a bag filled with need, only. Caleb needs love and attention. He needs to learn, explore, run, create; he needs friends and a peaceful place to sleep; he needs a bowl of cereal in the morning and dinner at night. How hard could this be? But I don't seem able to make those things happen. It's like, something in my core is . . . empty. I let everybody down. Every time.

It makes me sick to my stomach, makes me want to fold over and weep. The only thing that holds back the rising tide is a pill.

Dreadful little pills. There. That's better.

Three, I'm done modeling. I should take any name branding I still have and transition to acting. I will start going to auditions. Maybe acting lessons. Maybe I could start a YouTube channel and put out some modeling how-to videos, just to keep my name circulating. It would be something I could post, just to tell people, *Hey, Riley's still here*. It could lead to work in the theater, or even TV spots, movies. Commercials, at the very least. I need to look at backstage.com and sign up for some real auditions. Maybe I'll get an agent who can make all those calls for me.

Four, someone is following me.

He is young with dark hair, dark eyes, and sharp features. He looks intelligent, like someone who reads for fun and likes to argue about the things he knows. He tries hard to make himself invisible, watching me from across streets, hiding in unlit corners and behind newspapers, discreetly looking at his phone when I pass by. I lean forward now to peer out the café window. Is he there? No. Come to think of it, I haven't noticed him in a couple of days. Either he's gotten better at following me, or he's on to someone new.

Is he a stalker? In his wool coat and blazer, he seems more like a banker. Maybe he's a lawyer. Does this have something to do with Caleb? What am I in trouble for now?

The cold day passes slowly, and I wander the city. Everything is gray, the sky, the sidewalks, the reflections in the windows. The only thing I'm looking forward to is seeing Jack tonight. Jack. It's been six months since he went back for London Fashion week and then decided to stay there. Even though we'd already broken up by then, I've missed him.

Actually, the last six months have been pretty awful.

And then, finally, night. I dress in a loose black top that shows some cleavage, a pair of tight jeans, and high-heeled boots. I paint lines around my eyes. I consider three lipstick shades—Vivacious, Sweet Young Thing, or Heat. I go with Heat for its brownish undertones. I fluff my loose hair and look in the mirror one last time. One last brush of color on the cheekbones, and I'm ready. I go to hail a cab and realize I only have a few dollars in my clutch, but I thought I had a fairly big wad of cash. Then I remember, I gave that to Sammy for my last hit, some of which is in my bloodstream right now. I go to the ATM but my balance is crazy low: twelve hundred plus change.

How can that be? I stand and look at the number while everything swirls. Am I really so close to tapped out? It doesn't make sense. Should I sign up for unemployment? Am I allowed to do that? There must be some work checks that haven't come in yet. And when they do, I owe almost all of it to Sammy. And Caleb's birthday, coming up in May. He's turning six. Is it possible? He's getting so big. Will he be home by then? I wish he could be, but I don't see how it would happen since I'm not doing any of the things ACS told me to do. But just in case, we should have a party, a real one, with friends and a cake and a pony. How much would all that cost? Will I have work by then? A place to live?

Everything is so in between, and I don't know how to push forward. My whole life, I've never felt so confused.

I can't work this out right now. I grab what I need for cab fare and move on.

I plan to meet Jack at that bar we used to go to. When I arrive, he is waiting for me at a tall table in the lounge, and immediately our eyes find each other. Oh, those blue eyes; I fall for them every time.

"You're here," I say, smiling coyly. "Thank goodness you made it. I wasn't sure what those girls were going to do with you last week."

He laughs and glances down. "What a world we live in. Riley, girl.

Good to see you." We kiss each other's cheeks, but slowly, reverently. It's quiet here, and I'm glad. "Did you get a sitter for Caleb? How is he doing?"

"He's fine," I say, and I leave it at that.

Jack frowns. "I heard about JCW. Was that because of what happened at the shoot?"

I smirk. "It was a lot of things. Marcella and I talked it over. We just decided we were ready to go different ways."

"Come on, Riley, it's me," he says, his voice low; his accent is street British, raspy and charming. "You and Marcella were tight. What happened?"

I look down at the faux leather-bound drink menu. "I don't even know. Just buy me a drink. What's that?"

"Same as always. Vodka on the rocks."

Some things never change. A waitress in a crisp white shirt with a bow tie appears before me, asks me what I want. Tequila. And since Jack is buying, I order from the top shelf. "Reposado on the rocks with a wedge of lime."

"Salt?"

"No, thanks." I don't need the extra bloat.

She goes off, and I look at Jack. He hasn't shaved today, and I want to touch the dark stubble around his chin. "I thought you said you were never coming back to New York. I thought you'd had enough of 'the scene.'"

He chuckles. "It certainly is a scene here. My God, it never ends." I don't hear it, but he detects a sound his phone is making, and he takes it out of his pocket and touches it. "Turn you off. I'm officially off duty for the night. I've been doing some work for Revlon's Euro market, and they decided to bring me in to consult on a similar campaign for America. So it's a short visit. Actually, I fly back day after tomorrow."

"Too soon," I say. The waitress puts a paper napkin on the table in front of me and sets my drink down. It is the color of smoke; this kind of gray I like. I sip, and immediately the smoke fills me, gloriously stirring the chemicals in my bloodstream. My lipstick called Heat burns a mark into the glass's rim.

He is the photographer and I am the model. I imagine how I must look in this dusky light, my light hair slightly curling, with the dark wood of the bar behind me, around me. I am dressed for darkness because I feel dark tonight. I touch my chest, my necklace, a little charm shaped like a line drawing of a sailboat sitting cold on the skin of my breastplate. I know his eyes will follow my hand, will wander down from there, down to the line of cleavage that rises up between the buttons of my blouse. Will begin to want.

"How's London?"

"Busy," he says. And he begins to tell me about all the great projects he's been working on. Not just fashion, art photography too. He's meeting with members of the royal family, and some old rock 'n' roll stars whose names are supposed to impress me, and a bunch of visual artists I've heard of, but I'm not sure why.

Someone's name I'm listening for but don't hear him mention, and I can't remember why it was important. I'm focusing on his face, mostly his blue eyes, how they scan the room, almost like he forgot I was there, then looking directly back at me. Smiling because he found me.

"I'm glad to see you," he says, and I remember how much I love that accent.

"Me too," I say.

Then he touches my wrist and slowly starts to speak. "Look, Ry, we've been through this before," he says, almost whispering. "Neither of us has time for games. You know what I want. Just tell me what you need, and it's yours."

I grin. I have been through all this before. And the older I get, the more I think I just need exactly one man in my life, not Jack but Caleb. I wish life could be that simple.

"Oooh," I say flatly. "An offer I can't resist."

He scoots his chair close to mine, slips his hand under my top so he's touching just under my bra. His mouth is in my ear. "I want you," he says.

My breath stops; his hand is easing up under my bra, and his fingers reach toward my nipple. "Quit it," I start, but the truth is, I've been lonely. And I'm so tired of feeling old and wrecked. Wishing there were a wrinkle cream that could make me twenty again. One orgasm, one really amazing hard-core, bang-me-over fuck, and maybe I could forget about how hopeless everything feels. Just for a little while.

Jack's fingers close around my nipple and squeeze; between my legs, I feel the surge, the softening. I look around in the shadows; nobody sees us. The bartender glances over to check our drinks. He smiles slightly, understanding that we do not need drinks. The only word in my head is "surrender."

"Here's what I suggest," he says, his accent so goddamn cute. "We go to my hotel. I do things to your body until you can't stand up anymore. We do a couple of lines and come at the same time. I've even got a little treat," he says, and pulls from his pocket a tiny cellophane bag stapled at the top, a picture of a black cartoon cat on the front. The words "Black Magic" underneath.

Heroin? Yuck. Injecting? No. I cannot have nasty gaping holes in my skin. And then he says, "Come on. Just once. Just tonight. You and me."

I couldn't. I won't. I refuse. "I can't inject. You know that."

"You're unemployed. Nobody will see it."

Someone will see it; I will. At some point, I get to meet with the Child Protection agents, and they will assess whether I will get to see Caleb and what I need to do to get him back. I cannot have track marks in my arm when I have that meeting. I can't do that to my son.

Still, right now, in this moment I am carried away, and I am desperate. I need to be touched, desired. I need to be overwhelmed, deprived of air. Just tell me what to do. Nothing matters. I don't care anymore.

I am starting to sweat. I don't understand the connection between beauty and desire; sexual satisfaction has nothing to do with bone structure or hairdo. And yet it starts from the face, the feeling of being pulled in, pulled down. And that's the feeling I have now; I want to kiss him wide and deep if he's going to touch me like that. And I do. I take his face in my hands and press it against mine. He kisses slow and long, and the want inside me grows. I wonder if Jack is hard; I tiptoe my fingers over to his lap, and yes, there it is. I'm barely sure we're going to make it out of here.

And we don't. First, I go to the bathroom, a little room with a male/female sign on the door. A moment later he follows. We lock the door. We try to be as absolutely quiet as possible. We do not flinch when someone jiggles the knob to see if it's locked. There's another bathroom. I suppose I somewhat expected this, because I am not wearing underwear. I pull down my jeans and show him.

"You," he mutters, and his mouth goes between my legs, licking, sucking. I slink down to the floor to make it easier, but the black-and-white subway tiles are cold under my bare skin. The room smells like pee and bleach, and the fan overhead hisses steadily. His finger inside me; I close my eyes. I am want. He takes his hand out, licks it while he looks hard at me. His jeans are off, and there he is, all of him. I am beyond words and thought; I cannot resist.

Then he turns away from me to prepare, pulls a syringe out of a bag I didn't realize he had, then uses a piece of tinfoil and a lighter to melt the chemical. He glances up at the sprinklers on the ceiling to make sure that the smoke from his little fire doesn't set them off; it doesn't. They're probably turned off for this very reason. He starts with himself, wraps up his arm, finds the vein after a couple of tries, then injects. I am next. I sit up, and this is the cold part, the clinical part. He wraps the tourniquet around my arm, then slaps the skin to pop a vein. He finds one, then plunges the needle through my skin. My blood absorbs the poison; I flinch, and it takes just a moment, then, so suddenly, nothing matters. Job, money, Caleb . . . all my worries dissolve. My brain loses all the words it ever knew, and that is a relief.

Jack puts on a condom, and his body sinks into mine. We meld, my body welcomes his, pushing in rhythm. We fall into each other on the cold tile floor with abject desperation. Nothing this amazing has ever happened before. Everything eerily noiseless, including our breath, like the world is under a silent spell. I let it all quietly happen around me, but without me. And pleasure—yes, yes—for me it builds and happens so fast: holding him tight as shocks pulse through me, starting in the middle and shouting outward. I grasp him hard, shivering. I feel myself float up and out of this place, and I wish I would just keep floating.

Jack is still going, and even after I am finished, he grips my shoulders and heaves into me, his beautiful body so powerful. When it finally happens, he burrows his head into my chest and grips hard to contain his growling moan. I kiss the top of his head. There has never been a love like this one.

He is done, and I am done, and we both collapse, staring at the ceiling and that humming fan covered in thick dust. We pant. My bra is rolled, pushed up to my neck; my jeans are discarded on the bathroom floor; my clean-shaven vagina open and empty. It's dirty here and gross. Love doesn't look like this in fairy tales. I should be disgusted, but I'm not. I look over at him, at his body, his strong chest and the hair upon it. I kiss his chest. His face looks so relieved, and he smiles at me and sighs.

"Needed that tonight," he says. "I needed you."

This is love. There is nothing I wouldn't give this man. I don't remember why he went to London, but now he needs to come home. Home to me.

I lie against him, steam, almost visible, radiating from my heated skin. I guide his hand down inside me and I kiss his face. "Take me away," I whisper. "A vacation. We always used to talk about that, but this time, let's really do it. Okay?"

I am starting to breathe in helpless pulses again, as his finger pushes up and down. We kiss, and I touch him. He is beginning to wake up again. His eyes are closed, and he chuckles slightly. "Don't know how my fiancée would feel about that."

"Fiancée?" Then I remember, ahh yes, this is what the girls were talking about the other day. "Who is she, anyway? A model?"

Is she prettier than I am? Younger? Smarter? Famous? Is she royal or rich? A model? A singer? Maybe an actress. Doesn't matter now; mine is the body his fingers are inside.

"Oh, no, love," he says, and his breath skips. "I'm ready to settle down. Have kids of my own, a little house in the suburbs near my family. Never saw any of that happening with a model." He opens his eyes and glances over. "No offense."

"It's okay," I say, still guiding his fingers. "So who is she?"

"You remember Sylvie? My assistant?"

"Yes," I say. I expect him to say that he's engaged to her sister or someone she introduced him to.

"That's her, Sylvie. My bride-to-be." He states this as though giving directions to McDonald's.

Sylvie. Simple Sylvie in glasses and suit skirts. Chunky Sylvie, always on a diet, but globbing blue cheese dressing on her salads. Conservative Sylvie who frowned when someone mentioned they'd had a threesome. Silly Sylvie, with clipboard and laptop, and a phone to her ear, in a constant state of panic and exasperation, imagining herself the only barrier between Jack and a speeding train.

What would Miss Sylvie think if she could see us now on the floor of a bathroom in a bar in Manhattan? With that thought in mind, I ease Jack down so that he is lying on the floor, then lean down and suck and blow Jack into the last orgasm I will ever give him. I take him by surprise, and he almost forgets to be quiet.

Afterward, I stand, wash my mouth out in the sink, unroll my bra and fix my blouse, then put my jeans on.

"I'm staying at the Ritz," he says. "Come back with me."

I look in the mirror. My eyeliner is smudged, my lipstick is completely rubbed off, and my uncolored lips make my whole face look pale. I pull out a paper towel, wet it in the sink, and try to fix myself. Once I am presentable, I look down at him, still handsome, even disheveled. "Oh, Jack," I say.

The bartender knocks on the door. "Hey, kids," he says. "Closing in fifteen, and you need to close your tab. Thanks."

"How about it?" I say, kicking his leg with my toe. "I get you off and you get the tab. Seems like a good trade."

He stands up and starts to put his clothes back on. "You seem mad. You're not mad, are you? Didn't you know about—oh, God, you didn't."

My head is spinning; I'm mad, but I'm high, and my body is still shaking in the aftershocks of what was, actually, a pretty good lay. I don't look him in the eye.

I put my boots on. "It's okay," I say. I'm done with this room and with Jack, and I unlock the door and leave.

"Riley, wait . . ." he says, but I don't.

Back in the bar, I go to where we were sitting and pick up my coat. The bartender looks over at me. "It's on him," I say. "He's a lousy tipper. Sorry about that."

A couple of other people in the bar, two guys talking, and one other man. A man in a black wool peacoat with dark eyes, drinking by himself.

He glances at me as I put on my coat, then he subtly slips some cash across the counter, preparing to leave.

Oh, that's the guy, I think. My friendly neighborhood stalker.

I go to the door and stand there for a moment, checking my purse and my pockets to make sure I have what I need: keys, wallet, phone—ahh yes, the infamous phone. Inside me is still wet-hot from Jack, and I will never see him again. He is behind me then, this man I do not know, like a little dog, and he acts like he's waiting patiently for me to move out of the way so he can leave. I feel like I'm about to cry, but the number one rule for walking home alone at two in the morning is to keep eyes up and do not cry. Never let them see you cry.

When I step outside, the cold, still night slaps my face. My stalker behind me, I take a few steps on the sidewalk, enough to get around the corner, then a few steps more so I am almost a full block away from the bar. I don't want to be there when Jack comes out. I want to be long gone. I glance behind me, but that man is still there.

"Excuse me," I say out loud, aware that he can hear me, aware that he's trying to keep enough distance between us so I won't think he's stalking me. "What's going on?"

He does not respond, then finally, I turn to face him. He's a few feet away, cell phone to his ear, pretending to talk to someone.

"Seriously," I say, pushing my hair out of my face with my gloved hand. "Are you a good guy or are you planning to murder me?"

He holds up a finger like he wants me to hold on a moment so he can finish his conversation, and he speaks some little words. "Okay," he says. "Sure. Yup, sounds good." I stand where I am; I can be very patient when I'm high. But after about a minute, that runs out.

"This year, please," I say.

Finally, he finishes, says, "Right. See you later," pushes a button to hang up the phone, and looks at me as though he's being terribly inconvenienced. "I'm sorry, have we met?"

I smile and feel very sly; it's a joke, and we're both in on it, but neither of us can speak it out loud, because nothing is more dangerous than the truth.

"Hi, no, I don't think we have. Hello," I say, reaching out my hand.

He takes it and we shake. "But you've been following me for several days now, so I'm just wondering whether you're the kind of stalker that's going to murder me in the park or if you're a gentleman who could walk a girl home after a really hard day. Sorry, make that a hard week. Actually, this whole year has been pretty terrible."

He looks right into my eyes then. His eyes aren't just brown, they're black. "Well, miss," he says, "I'm sorry you're having a bad year. But I assure you, I'm not following you. You have me confused with someone else."

"Okay, that's how we're going to play this," I say, and I shove my hands into my coat pockets. I wonder if he can smell it on me, sex on a bar bathroom floor. And a gaping hole in my arm. All so charming, this life of mine. "Look. You know where I'm staying. This might have been the worst night of my life and what's the punchline? I don't have money for a cab, and no, I cannot call an Uber because I have not set up my account on my stupid new phone, because I have no idea what my Apple ID is. So can you walk me home? If not, just say so."

He smiles and looks at me with something like pity or sympathy. "Come on," he says, and he jerks his head for me to come with him.

"Thanks," I say, and I wipe a tear out of one eye.

He starts to walk and offers me a chivalrous bended elbow. I link my arm through his. He's tall but not as tall as Jack; his shoulder is at the perfect height for me to sink my head against. He smells nice; I like his aftershave.

"Tough night?" he says.

"I don't want to talk about it," I say. My heart hurts. I just want to go home and take a hot shower. Alone.

My new friend and I stop at an intersection, and we're surrounded by short buildings with ethnic shops and diners. In a few blocks we will walk among tall shining buildings. After that, we will come up to the border of Central Park, New York's own fairy-tale forest, complete with lurking wolves and glowing moonstones to mark the path home. By then, I will believe that we live in the city of possibility, in a place so lovely there is poetry even in the cruelest of heartbreaks.

"Okay, we don't have to talk," he says. "Would you be willing to tell me your name?"

I laugh a little. "Please don't do that. Let's just walk, okay?"

"Well, you have to at least tell me your address, so I know where we're going."

"You know where we're going," I say. The light turns green, and we start to cross the street.

If you do decide to murder me on the way, I think, just do it fast. I'm so tired of pain.

Chapter 14

Tuesday, February 18, 2014
Colleen

The fire seems to inspire some fatherly instinct in Eric, because all of a sudden, he's going out of his way to be helpful. He invites Maddie, Ethan, and me to pile into the condo, so we do, and it becomes a refuge of sorts. Maddie sleeps in the extra bedroom that was her nursery when she was a baby; Ethan sleeps on a cot in Eric's room. I am on the couch. There is one bathroom for all four of us. Conditions are tight. Emotions are fragile.

Eric somehow feels the need to stay close to us and drives us to Marshall's to shop for new clothes. And the three of us need everything: shoes, socks, underwear, school clothes, exercise clothes, warm layers, winter coats, and many other basics. We needed to roam and gather; Eric needed to buy groceries.

"What should I get?" he asked. I was so drained, I could not begin put together a grocery list or to even answer such a ridiculous question.

"You know what we eat," I said. "Just get that."

Only, apparently Eric doesn't know what we eat, because he bought loads of exactly the things we do not eat. Cheetos. Coca-Cola. Frozen chocolate cake. Tater tots. Taquitos. Pizza rolls. Pop-Tarts. Frozen burritos. Presweetened oatmeal in packets and presugared yogurt in cups.

I get it, it's comfort food. I get it, he actually is trying to be a good dad, to take care of his kids. The kids eat junk every time they're out of my sight, so I try to keep the food at home at least somewhat nutritious. And his selections were not quite up to par.

As he unloaded the bags of groceries, I thought my eyes would pop out. I felt my lips curl into a sneer. But I took a deep, cleansing breath and tried very hard to look in the other direction.

Then it is Tuesday morning, our third morning crammed in here. I wake up on the couch feeling like I never quite went to sleep, my throat raw with exhaustion, my jaw tender from stress. My current pajamas are purple sweatpants and a long, sloppy T-shirt. I go to the little kitchen to make coffee, which Eric and I drink in flimsy mugs that we bought a few years ago for the renters. When the kids wake up, I feel another wave of confusion; I do not recognize their night clothes. Ethan in a T-shirt I've never seen before and blue pajama bottoms that look like surgical scrubs; Maddie wears a women's pajama set intended as a Valentine's gift for some lucky gal (and thus was on sale the day after)—a pink background covered with illustrated Hershey's kisses and long-stemmed roses.

They both look like burgeoning adults, and I am not prepared to see this.

The two yawn and bump into each other and us as they prepare bowls of cereal. Then Eric reaches into a high cupboard and pulls down a box of breakfast flakes.

"Here you go, buddy," he says to Ethan.

Chocolate Frosted Flakes.

"Yeah, thanks!" Ethan exclaims.

"Eric," I say, because now I can't keep myself from snapping. "What's the story with all this junk food?"

"It's not a big deal, Colleen," Eric says.

I watch in horror as my son pours milk over the flakes and they emit some kind of faux-cocoaesque substance that turns the milk mud-brown.

My son grins as he readies his spoon for plunging. There are a hundred things wrong with this picture.

"That's like having a bowl of ice cream for breakfast," I declare, incredulous.

"Mom," Maddie says. "It's okay, it's not going to kill us."

"Not even close," Ethan says.

And now I'm fuming because (a) I cannot just take that bowl away from him even though I want to, (b) I cannot pour the box of cereal in the trash, and (c) now my kids are talking back to me and questioning my standards. Not okay.

"Eric," I say. "Can I see you in the bedroom for a moment?"

He nods and follows me in, then closes the door behind us. "Colleen, I know you don't like the cereal, but—"

I stand before him, just under his chin. "You don't get to do this," I say, pointing my finger in rage. "You don't get swoop in here and pretend you're rescuing everybody and ply my children with what is basically food-safe poison."

"They're treats, Colleen," he says sternly. "The kids have been through a lot. They eat healthy all the time, they can take a break."

"I know they've been through a lot, Eric," I say, lowering my voice so the kids don't hear me. "I have too. And it's not fair you get to be the big savior and feed the kids garbage food. Now they're questioning the way I feed them."

"You are taking this too seriously," he says. "It's only Frosted Flakes."

"Stop trying to help," I say. "I work hard to curb their junk food habits. You are undermining everything."

Now Eric snaps. "Damn it, Colleen," he hisses. "Yours is not the only way that's right. Whether we're separated, divorced, or married, we are both their parents. I am allowed a say in how my children eat. Stop acting like I'm trying to corrupt them. I am their father."

"Yes, you are their father. So where were you when we needed you?" I ask. "Our house was on fire. We had to crawl down the stairs to keep from suffocating. I stood in my nightgown in the freezing cold while neighbors came out and watched the fire trucks."

"Look, I'm sorry, okay?" he says, sounding not all that sorry. "You know, one question I keep having is this: Why didn't you wake up when the alarms went off? How come our daughter had to wake you up?"

I'm so mad I get dizzy. My voice gets low and quiet, like a growling grizzly. "I had a migraine. I took a Tylenol PM, and I went to bed. Because I was by myself on Valentine's Day. Meanwhile, six weeks after you moved out, you were in your bachelor pad, entertaining, apparently."

His nose is flaring; he's angry now. "I told you I was sorry," he says, glancing toward the door to make sure the kids weren't coming through it. "But that's not a card you get to play every time you're mad at me."

"You think this is a game for me?"

"What I think and have thought for a long time is that nothing is more important to you than the welfare of your children," he says. "Not one. Single. Thing."

This time, his words hit me like a punch in the gut. Am I being punished for being a good mom? For putting my children first? I thought that was the point.

I cross my arms and pull back. "Is that how it feels?" I ask.

"Yes," he says. "I've always come second and third to them."

I pause, unsure how to respond. "I only wanted to give my kids a good life."

"I know," he says. "And I know that's because your mom wasn't there to take care of you when you were growing up. But sometimes I felt like I didn't matter at all. Not as a husband or as a dad. You took care of everything with the kids. Sometimes you didn't even tell me when there was a problem. Like when Ethan broke his arm—"

"He fractured his wrist! And you were in Houston," I exclaim, no longer able to keep my voice low. "All day meetings, you told me. Very big deal, you told me."

"I had a phone," he says. "I could have at least talked to him. I could have bought him a . . . teddy bear or something at the airport gift shop."

"He wasn't even in pain, except when he realized that he'd miss a few weeks of baseball. I thought I was doing you a favor by not calling you while you were halfway across the country, attending meetings that you

told me would make or break your career," I say. "So I took care of it. That's
what moms do."

"I never needed you to protect me," he says. "I needed you to include me."

"That's the thanks I get," I say. And now I hear my voice; it's nagging.
I hate that word, *nag*, what it means and the way it sounds; everything
about it is ugly. "Eric, this isn't working," I say, my voice audibly on the
verge of tears.

"Yeah," he says. He is quiet for a moment, and he rubs his forehead
as he thinks. "I'll find somewhere else to live until the insurance money
comes through. The three of you can stay here."

"No," I say. "I'm the one who should go. It's too much for me, being
here now. Some of my favorite memories happened in this condo. Plus,
now it's your place."

"You sure?" he asks.

I nod. "Peggy offered to let me stay at her beach shack. I'm going to
take her up on it. I'll be out of your hair tomorrow."

Eric's face crumples. "I don't want our lives to be like this," he says. "I
never meant . . . for it to be like this."

I sigh and rub my eyes. "The only thing that matters now is taking care
of Ethan and Maddie," I say. "I'll just be ten minutes away, and I can still
bring them home after school and stop by a couple of times a week and
cook dinner. I don't want them feeling like their mother abandoned them."

"Okay," he says. "Let's talk to them about it tonight."

"Sure," I say.

I walk out of the room gripping my elbows, feeling somehow like I
have done something very wrong.

Later in the morning, I meet Alex at a coffee shop in Newburyport. I told
Alex and Dad about the fire on the day it happened, but that was the only
thing I told them. My sister looks shocked when she sees me. I haven't been
to the drug store yet to buy cheap cosmetics or even a hair dryer.

"Colleen," she says with alarmed concern.

"I know," I say. "Let's take a walk."

We get coffee and head down the street and cross to the boardwalk along the river. In summer, this area can be teeming with children, walkers, tourists, but now it is empty.

"You look exhausted," she says.

I gaze out at the sloshing gray waters of the Merrimack River, a few boats across the way, all wrapped in plastic for winter.

"I am," I say, and I stop, stalling. "It's not just the fire, Alex. That morning, when I called Eric about the house . . . when I finally reached him that morning." I chuckle because it's all I can do. "Anyway, my husband has a girlfriend."

"What?"

I take a drink of coffee. "I guess I don't know if she's a girlfriend or a—what do they say now? A hookup? I haven't asked him to clarify. He says he wasn't having an affair. I think it's more pathetic than that. He didn't want to be with me anymore, but he couldn't stand being alone."

"Ugh, men," Alex says. "Colleen, I'm sorry."

"So, I guess my marriage is over. You probably already knew that, but I . . . had hope. Oh, and there's more," I say, smiling now, because this is absurd. I tell her about how our insurance lapsed.

"What does that mean?" she asks.

I shrug. "First of all, it means our house burned down, and the insurance company doesn't need to pay us a nickel. Second of all, it means . . . I don't know, the *first of all* pretty much covers it."

"How are Maddie and Ethan doing?"

"They're . . . amazing. It's winter vacation, and they're supposed to be relaxing and enjoying themselves," I say. "At least they don't have schoolwork. And Eric is cheering them up by letting them gorge on MSG and corn syrup. Now they're festering at the condo. They just don't have much to do until Thursday when Eric is taking them skiing."

"Wait, are you staying at the condo too?" she says. "Where are you sleeping?"

"On the couch," I say. But then the tears start again, angry and exhausted. I turn away from her and pull a tissue from my pocket. "Why is this all happening at the same time? I lose my house and my marriage on the same day? Why?"

"Colleen, I'm so sorry. He's obviously even more of a louse than I thought he was."

The wind comes up behind me and blows my hair into my face. "Oh, Alex. We can't call Eric names. He's the father of my children, and that's never going to change." I blow my nose. "Plus, I think he is trying to help. I just . . . I'm at my wits' end."

"Do you want to stay with me?" she says. "There's plenty of room."

"Thanks, but no," I say, turning my head to push my hair down. "My friend Peggy is letting me stay at her place on Plum Island. It's small, but it's right on the beach, not that that does me any good this time of year."

"Plum Island?" Alex says. "Are you sure that's a good idea?"

I look out toward the Merrimack River. Beyond where we stand, in the distance, a little strip of houses seems to almost float upon the surface of the water. That is Plum Island. The other side of the island faces ocean. "I'll be fine," I say.

I know what worries Alex. Plum Island was one of our mother's favorite places. She loved kicking off her sneakers and feeling the sand between her toes and the frothy ocean water under her feet, no matter how cold it was. She loved it in the winter, when almost nobody else was there and the fog came in thick and you could not tell the difference between sky and water. And though we knew that to the north we were looking at the city of Portsmouth and the Isles of Shoals, and to the south, the town of Ipswich and Cape Ann, in the mist those places appeared like distant, mysterious shores yet to be discovered.

"It's got to be awfully quiet this time of year," she says. "Don't you need more, I don't know, action? Things going on?"

"It's close to Newburyport," I say. "And I think I'll like the quiet. Heck, maybe I'll take up painting."

"Like Mom?" Alex says.

"No, not like Mom," I say. "Like me. Like I have always wanted to do, except I never had time because I'm always organizing everybody's lives. Anyway, I'm not worried. It's only temporary."

"If you say so," Alex says.

That afternoon Peggy drops off the key to the place before she brings her kids to North Conway for the week. At dinner, Eric and I tell the kids that I'm moving out for a bit. I reassure them that I will still pick them up from school and bring them to their activities. I will also be taking over as Grocery Shopper in Chief. They know what that means. Vegetables.

The next afternoon I am ready to go. I drive down Plum Island Turnpike, a straight, smooth road that leads away from the city and into an expanse of marsh that is wide, flat, and jagged with frozen mud. By the edge of the road there are a few houses, a few trees. I pass the little airfield where they host model airplane competitions on Father's Day. Just like always, there are two or three cheerful biplanes parked there. Then, on the right, I pass Bob Lobster, our favorite fish shack. Our family has spent many warm days sitting on wooden picnic tables, scarfing down lobster rolls, fries, and chowder. Now the sign says they're "Closed for the Season" and all is quiet.

After that, on the other side, the beloved and iconic Pink House stands alone, overlooking the marsh. You're not supposed to, because the house is now the property of the US Fish and Wildlife Service, but I pull over by the side of the road. The old foursquare is not as pink as it once was; nobody's lived here in years, and the paint is flaking off. But it still holds its glass cupola high, watching the wide and empty horizon around it. There's something haunting about this house, so solitary, so remote. My mother used to admire it. She thought it very brave of the house to endure out here all alone. The house isn't very big nor fancy, and there's no neighborhood, nor even a proper sidewalk for people to reach it easily. And yet, here it stands and here it remains, proud and beautiful after all these years, the silent matron of the marsh. A red-tailed hawk swoops in from the river and lands on the chimney; I don't know whether I should feel like I'm home or homeless. Frankly, I feel both.

I continue driving over the bridge, then I turn right to navigate through the narrow streets and to Peggy's cottage. It is the last house on the island before the wildlife refuge begins, which means there are no neighbors to the south. When I arrive, the cold wind off the ocean gusts so hard, it slices through my clothes. I burst through the door with bags of groceries and bags of clothes, the ones purchased yesterday at Marshall's, tags still on.

The cottage is right on the beach; glass doors open up to sand, but in this freezing winter, that fact only serves as a cruel joke. The place is simple, one open space, surrounded in basic wood paneling, basic kitchen appliances, an old bathroom with a shower. Peggy and her ex once planned to do a major renovation, a la Joanna and Chip Gaines, but they didn't make much progress before their marriage fell apart. Peggy got the house in the settlement, but she didn't have the income to implement the HGTV overhaul she'd daydreamed of, so here we stand.

I walk around and touch things, a shelf, a chair, a basket filled with seashells. I sit on the bed and take a used novel from the bookshelf. I don't notice which book it is, and I can only thumb through the pages mindlessly before I am exhausted by the idea of reading it.

The silence is already too loud here. It gives me too much space for thinking, and I use it to blame myself for everything that's ever gone wrong. Eric is right, I should have included him more. I shouldn't have been so controlling. I could have been a better wife. I should have talked to him more. I am not a complainer; I never complained, but what's the difference between that and telling someone how I feel? I just don't know.

How do I feel? Now, I feel lost, displaced, exiled, even though I'm the one who volunteered to come out here. What did I feel before now? What did I feel before Eric told me he was leaving? I'm not sure I know.

Pride, that was one thing I used to feel. Proud of our home and our family and our lifestyle. We lived in a beautiful home; I was married to a handsome lawyer. But the house was never ours; it was just a tease of fate, something God dangled in front of me to make me feel safe for a little while. We were the Newcombs, the neighborhood's golden family. I played the game and I played to win, but I failed. Turns out, Alex is the smart one—too smart to get trapped in this life of building beautiful things to protect yourself from the fact that life is temporary, and then ending up running ragged to keep the illusion going. In the end, everything goes up in smoke. In case you forgot for a moment, nothing ever lasts.

Chapter 15

Colleen knocks on the door, and there she is, right when she said she would be. She called earlier to say that Eric was taking the kids to New Hampshire to go skiing, so could she bring over Indian takeout? The answer, of course, was, *Yes please, always, anytime.* Now she's standing at my door, holding a big paper bag of from the place in Newburyport. Plus, two bottles of Kingfisher beer to go with it. Without makeup, her eyes look puffy, her face exhausted but open and childlike. I wish there were something I could do for her, but I have a feeling that just eating Indian food with her is the best I can offer.

"Hungry?" she asks, smiling weakly.

"Yes! That smells amazing." I am starved. I spent the day wandering around Home Depot studying tools and supplies and discussing my projects with various sales people, trying to figure out what I need and how to start. I feel like I deserve a big meal. We rip open aluminum foil coverings and tear lids off containers, then fill paper plates with steaming curries, rice, naan, samosas, *dosas*, and an extra greasy order of *pakoras*. The spice is fragrant and strong, and the food is satisfying. It's not India, but it's good for now.

Colleen takes small bites and eats as though the process is exhausting.

"Try to eat," I say. "It really will help."

She glances up at me with nobody-asked-you eyes. "How are the projects going?"

I clear my throat. "The wiring is done," I say, digging through the bag for napkins. "So, the house is no longer a matchstick waiting for a flint." I suddenly realize that this was the wrong thing to say. "Oh, Colleen. I'm sorry."

"It's okay," she says, pushing rice around with her fork. "Good that it's done. That's a big deal."

I nod. "It is. A big deal with a big price tag. Next, I need to fix the roof and install new windows, but I may have to wait until spring for those. But now that I have twenty-first-century electricity, I'm daydreaming about new appliances. Maybe even a washing machine."

"Oh, that's exciting," Colleen says. "Can I help pick things out?"

"You're welcome to ogle with me," I say. "But at the end of the day, I can't go too crazy. I'm on a budget."

"That's renovation math for you," she says. "Dreams divided by bank account. I wish we could pitch something in, but we're tapping into the college funds to rebuild our house."

"Wow, Colleen," I say, putting a samosa on her plate. "That's a bummer."

She shrugs. "Eric still insists that the insurance company owes us money. But until they pay up, Ethan's and Maddie's futures are lending it to us."

I shake my head in sympathy.

Colleen uses a plastic fork and knife to slice her samosa into manageable pieces. It doesn't work too well.

"You're allowed to eat that with your hands," I say.

"It's too greasy," she says. Then she pauses and looks at me quizzically. "I've had a lot of extra time for thinking lately."

"That sounds dangerous," I say.

She nods. "I think a lot about money. You have some of Mom's jewelry, right?"

"Sure, packed away somewhere," I say. Our father distributed it among the three of us after I turned eighteen, before I went to college. He put a pile on the kitchen table and told us to divide it among ourselves; he didn't care who got what as long as nobody was complaining. None of us wanted to take anything; it felt too much like we were taking pieces of Mom. I ended up with a couple of necklaces and bracelets. Classics of gold and pearl—pretty enough, but not really anything I'd ever wear.

"Why?" I say. "You think it's worth something?"

"I have some gold pieces," she says. "I'm going take them to a jeweler. Just to see."

"I always thought they were fake," I say.

"I don't know," she says, wiping her fingers on a paper napkin. "Sometimes I wonder if she came from money. She seemed different from other people. Not just because she was from California or because she was an artist. She . . . carried herself differently. Not in a snooty way, just a little more refined or something. Poised, I guess. Do you remember that?"

"I'm not sure," I say.

"She'd mention things," Colleen continues. "She took dance classes when she was young. Not ballet, but, like, manners class. What's that called? With white gloves. Cotillion. And something about how oyster forks are the only forks that ever go to the right of the plate."

"Why would that even come up?" I ask.

"Dad brought home oysters one time," she says. "We didn't actually have oyster forks, she was just teasing, like, 'Don't forget, Colleen, oyster forks go to the right of the spoon.'"

"That's funny," I say.

Colleen nods. "I didn't understand when we were little. But it's kind of coming back to me now." She dips a piece of samosa into the sweet brown tamarind sauce. "Like I said, I have extra time to think."

"Like I said," I say, "sounds dangerous."

Our mother is a puzzle, but the pieces are contained only in memory, an unreliable medium that shifts and changes beneath our very touch. There might be a picture, but we will never see it unless we figure out what the pieces are and how they fit together. And most days, I don't know how to start.

"Hey," I say. "Do you remember that Mom liked jazz?"

"Sure," she says. "She used to stay up in that attic room for hours, painting, and all we'd hear was muffled clarinet music coming through the ceiling."

"Oh, that's right," I say.

"Sometimes I'll be at a doctor's office or at a party and hear something she used to listen to, real classic jazz like Thelonious Monk or Duke Ellington," she says. "Then I feel like I'm back there for a moment, downstairs, while Mom is in the attic, painting."

"That's a nice memory," I say. "Can I borrow that?"

She laughs a little. "Help yourself."

After dinner Colleen and I toss the plates and napkins in the trash and put the leftovers in the refrigerator. Then Colleen goes to the other room and brings me something from her purse. "I picked this up for you. I have a friend who works in adoption services." She pulls a stack of papers and a booklet from her purse and puts them on the table.

"What is it?" I ask. She nods at the papers, so I touch them, look at them, not lifting them off the table. It's an adoption application and a booklet about how to apply. "Colleen . . ."

"I know what you're going to say. All you do is fill this out, and then somebody contacts you and walks you through every step. You'd have plenty of time before . . . you know, you actually get a child. This is just the beginning."

"Thanks, I know how it works," I say. "There's an application and an interview and somebody takes a dental pick and scrapes at all the messy little corners of your life to determine, *Oh, you don't have this, and you aren't that . . .*"

"It's not that bad, Alex," she says. "My friend said you'd be an excellent candidate. And with this company, you pay a fee and everything is included. The legal fees, the home visit . . ."

I laugh to myself. "First of all, those fees? Can run into tens of thousands of dollars before you've even bought a box of diapers. I don't have that. And the home visit, that's when they send someone over to examine the house, to make sure it's appropriate for children. Does this house look child-appropriate to you?"

Colleen sighs. "It could be. The schools around here are excellent. So, you tell the social worker you're renovating. Everybody understands a work in progress."

I grit my teeth. I don't owe her an explanation, but she's not going to leave me alone until I give her one. "It's not in the cards for me, Colleen. I don't have a partner. They'll want to know what kind of support system I have. And I don't even have a job right now."

"You could get a job any time. You work in health care. They're always saying there's a shortage of nurses."

My sister does not quit, and now we are shouting over each other. "I don't have a plan, Colleen. I can't say to them, *Well yeah, if you find a kid before I sell this house, then sure, I can stay and fix up a room and find a job and get, oh, I don't know, a stroller and a car seat and a nanny. But hey, adoption people, I'm not going to stick around if this process is going to drag on for a couple of years. So, if you need me, I'll be in India—*"

"Stop, Alex. Don't even say it," she cries. "Why are you giving up? If you want a child, fill out the application."

"You don't get it," I say. "I've moved on. Why can't you?"

"I didn't know this was a thing until two weeks ago," she says.

I take a deep breath and try to speak calmly. "If I was going to adopt, or try to, or even start the process, I'd have to decide that this is what I'm doing." I point frantically toward the ground. "This place, this town, this house, this way of life. But I don't want to. This house was not my plan. It would feel like I was giving in."

Colleen stands by the table, holding herself up, a hurt look on her face. "Is having a child the same as giving in?" she says. "Do you feel like I gave in? Like I settled for something?"

I shrug. "I don't know, Colleen. Was there something you wanted to do that you put off to raise your family? Is some part of your soul dying under the weight of your gleaming marble counters? Because I feel like mine might."

"You are not the only person with a soul, Alex. Mine was taken out from under me in ways that you cannot understand. And you act like I'm insulting your moral integrity by bringing this over." Colleen picks up the application and rips the sheets apart, then throws the pieces around the room. "If you don't want to fill this out, don't do it, but stop acting like you're the only person who has pain."

The look on her face is angry as she picks up the shreds of paper. "Don't," I say. "I'm sorry, Colleen."

"Forgive me for trying to help," she says, still scooping up the paper. "Forgive me for trying to bring something good into this family. After everything else . . ."

"Colleen, you don't need to—" I take the papers from her hand and shove them into the trash. Suddenly the lights in the dining room flicker and blink. Then they flicker and blink again.

"What's that about? New wiring shouldn't do that," Colleen says.

"It's fine," I say, because I think I know what's coming. "Don't worry about it."

"You need to call the guy and have him look at this," she says.

"I'll call him tomorrow," I say, gently easing her away from the light switch. "It's okay for now. Hey, Colleen, I'm sorry."

"No, it's okay, I get it," she says, and she throws her jacket on, grabs her purse, and dashes to the door. "I'll call you tomorrow."

I catch her before she goes out. "Thanks for dinner."

"You know, Alex, this house . . ." she says. "I know it wasn't in your plan, but it's an amazing coincidence, isn't it? Your own house, and it's right here. Near your family. It could be that everything's falling into place for you."

"Maybe," I say, but I don't meet her eyes.

She scoffs. "But if you don't want to be here, I'm not going to hold you back."

I smile sadly. "Thanks," I say.

We each smile a little and say our disappointed goodbyes. Then I close the door behind her, switch on the dim porch light, and watch her get into her car.

There is a knot in the pit of my stomach, a place in my body that knows that if I return to India, I will let people down. But I also know that I cannot live my life for anybody but me.

"It is not fair!" I shout out loud to the closed front door and the empty room. "This has been going on for twenty-five years, and it is not fair."

Before I turn back toward the room, the lights behind me flicker and blink, on, off, on, off. Oh, God, I think. I woke it up again. I shudder as the house begins to feel cold and small, and the shadows around me grow strange and alive.

And then it begins. It starts the way it usually does, with the sound of footsteps running up and down the hallway upstairs. A child's footsteps, I realize, or at least, something small. Something small, running. That could be squirrels in the attic. Couldn't it?

Then, in the living room, men's voices. Snippets of whispers, their sources unseen. No matter how hard I listen, I can't figure out what they are saying. Maybe it's not human at all; maybe it's animals behind the walls, making their nests and having their babies in whatever insulation is left. With this house, anything is possible.

I press my hands to my head to ward off a spasm of vertigo that I know will have the room spinning beneath me, which I am pretty sure is the beginning of a panic attack. I don't know how long I will be able to convince myself that these sounds are just coming from the house; I already only half believe it. I drift through the rooms, past the dining room and into the kitchen. The voices are upstairs now, muttering and flustered. Then, a child's low cry rings out. I hate that part.

"Stop, stop, stop," I whimper.

But it continues. And I stand with my back to the kitchen counter, gripping my head, refusing to believe what I am starting to believe. The sounds taper off into an uneasy quiet, and the dining room lights flicker again. The air around me is ice cold. The lights dim and blink.

I peel my hands off my head and look around. Suddenly—the lights are on and steady. The house is quiet, but it's a quiet I can't trust. "Hello?" I whisper meekly.

In that moment, the water in the kitchen faucet, inches from where I stand, switches on. I gasp, shudder, and cover my mouth.

Water streams from the spout, evenly and without malice. *See?* Just like Dad's, another old house with bad plumbing, old pipes, and crumbled stop valves. My hand shakes as I reach instinctively toward the handle to switch it off, then change my mind, then repeat the dance like my hand itself doesn't know what to do. Finally, I switch it off and quietly berate myself for being spooked.

On top of everything else, I need a plumber.

I feel my lungs tighten, and my breath becomes shallow and fast. I feel like I am drowning. "You can breathe, you're just hyperventilating," I whisper. "Get a hold of yourself." And I will. But eventually, I will have to walk upstairs alone, turn the lights off, lie there in the dark, and try to sleep.

Oh, calm down, I tell myself, there's nothing to worry about. It's only wind, rodents, wiring, squirrels in the attic, bugs in the walls.

The one thing it is not, I decide, is ghosts. I refuse to let this become a ghost story. But I'm not sure my shaking hands buy that.

Chapter 16

At about ten in the morning, I pull into the driveway of what remains of my home. The neighborhood is quiet. The clock I'd bludgeoned on the front yard is gone; if Eric saw it, he collected the pieces and never mentioned it. Which, actually, I appreciate. Over the past week or so, our interactions have been a bit friendlier. We talk every day to work through logistics: home renovation plans, insurance, the kids and who will bring them to the places they need to go to. I have been seeing the kids every day and cooking a few meals for them to eat at the condo (to supplement the frozen burritos and sugary cereal). Sometimes, I eat with them. Whatever else they eat is up to the three of them. Although I still remind Eric not to let the kids drink cola with dinner, because it does keep them awake.

Is this our new normal? It doesn't quite feel normal. But it feels like something we can do for a while if we need to.

But today, standing before the front door of my home, my gentle, wounded house, I have a mission. The windows are boarded up, and the house looks like its eyes are gouged out. We used to enter through the side door into the kitchen, but that is where most of the damage is, so I go through the front, unlocking it with the same key I've used for years. The door swings open into the living room; it's strange how unchanged it seems. The furniture is just where it was the last time I saw it. Bean bag chairs, the table, the big television. Everything covered with a gritty, black dust, probably from the smoke. There are signs that we used to live here—sloppy piles of board games and old issues of the Newburyport Daily News by the table; Ethan's sneakers under the table, still sitting at odd angles, where he tossed them haphazardly sometime in the days before the fire. People did once live here. But now it all looks strangely abandoned.

It is cold in here, surprisingly so. The earliest the place could be livable would be late spring, but I don't want to live here, not even then. I want a new home for me and the kids. Something small and cheap; we don't need much space. I will get a job. I've never done more than front register retail before, working at a Talbot's while Eric was in law school, but that counts as experience. And, I tell myself, I am trainable.

I wander through the house, and everything I see leads to a memory. The dining room table Eric and I bought used and refinished together. A wall with framed photos: our wedding day, my little girl holding her baby brother and flashing a broad smile—our boy and girl, so little—in bathing suits under a backyard sprinkler. The glass is tainted black from smoke, which makes it feel even more old fashioned, like it all happened in a different era. Which I suppose it did.

I leave the photos where they are but collect a few other things. Funny things. A pair of bronze bookends shaped like mallard ducks. Sturdy and unaffected by the fire, I like those; I need them. In a closet I spot a sack with a roll of yarn. A knitting project I started years ago but never finished. That I take; I'd like to do something useful with my hands. In the bedroom, under the bed, I find an old comforter sheathed in a plastic bag. I open it and take a sniff; I almost can't smell the smoke, so I grab that too.

And in the back of my bedroom closet, so far back, I have to scramble to reach it, I pull out something else. A square-shaped something, wrapped loosely in an old sheet. I pull the sheet away and reveal an oil painting. The brushstrokes are spare; that was Mom's style. It's the beach at Plum Island, with the sloping shore on one side and the ocean on the other, and in between, a good distance from the artist, three small figures walk away, leaving footprints in the sand. The figures are dressed in hats and pants and sweaters, with scarves around their necks. Two tall children flank a smaller one in the middle, holding her hands.

The children are us. One child carries a bucket; that one is me. I was always collecting things to remember the day by. The tallest girl gazes out over the ocean. That's Alex. And Riley in the middle; she is small, and we each hold one hand, lest she stumble over the cold sands of the midwinter beach.

I stare at the painting for a long time, studying the moments of color that my mother turned into a vision of a quiet walk on the beach. Gloves off, I run my fingers delicately over sharp tips and vales of hardened paint. What's that called? Impasto, the texture of the paint on the surface of the canvas. I am seeking clues. The child who is me turns her face to look at Riley, and her lips are red and almost smiling. Alex's face is turned toward the sea, her face visible in profile. She looks past the water, over the ocean's surface for something far away. Riley is the only one whose face we cannot see at all; she is a hat and a flying scarf, a pair of hands reaching.

Mom is in the painting too, though unseen. She watched us, and this is what she saw: three little girls, so fragile in a big world, but determined to make their way across the sand in sneakers, one step at a time. This is a painting that only a mother would do—a painting by a mother who loved us.

And if she loved us this much, why did she do what she did? Why did she leave? I will never make sense of it.

I am sitting in the house that burned, where everything I knew and loved turned to ashes, holding a painting my mother made, and suddenly, a wave of grief goes through me. I want my Mom. She is on the other side of this object, on the other side of those brushstrokes, on the other side of so many years. If I rip the fabric off the frame and claw away at the paint, maybe I could sink down into the painting itself and see her. Just for a moment. That's all I need.

Why did she do it? Every now and then, people in town used to ask me that, as though they assumed that there was one thing in her life that she just couldn't handle. Maybe Dad was having an affair, or the family had financial problems, maybe three children overwhelmed her. Perhaps she just couldn't take the cold gray of the northeast.

I don't know, I told them. *I wish I knew, but I don't.*

Suddenly, I am shivering. It's time to go.

I load up the painting, the knitting, the blanket, and the bookends and scramble to my car. I pull out of the driveway and do not look back at the house or the neighborhood but drive through Newburyport to reach the place on the island, my home-for-now. Inside, I shed coat, gloves, hat, throw them on the floor, put the blanket and the knitting kit aside, and set the painting on the small table so that it is facing me. She started that painting in this place, on the beach outside my glass double doors. Funny to realize that, again, I am in the right place but at the wrong time. Twenty-five years earlier, and we would all be here together.

Why can't we be together now, Mom? Just choose not to do it, and we'll start over. Let's have a—what do the kids call it?—a do-over. Maybe, if we all want it enough, maybe it will just be.

I look at the painting, half expecting it to respond. But the canvas keeps its secrets. I am festering here, in this place that has once again become too hot—these days, I am always either too hot or too cold. Am I in early menopause or am I having a nervous breakdown? Maybe both. I head out, slamming the cottage door behind me, and get into the car. Where will I go? Somewhere away from here.

When I have my coat on and my car keys in my hand, I get a text from Nate Hensler.

Can you talk?

I call him right back. "Hi," I say. "What's going on?"

"So, I talked to her," he says. "I didn't really plan to. I think she'd seen me watching her, which surprised me, frankly, because I'm pretty good at not being spotted."

"How did she seem?" I say.

"She was in rough shape. I think she'd just had a bad date," he says. "It was late, and she asked me to walk her home. Since then, I've learned that her agency fired her. I think it must be the drug use."

I pace the room. "So she's getting worse? Is that what you're telling me?"

"She might be, yes," he says.

"Oh, crap," I say. "What do I do now?"

"I had a thought," he says. "She and I kind of had a bit of a rapport that night. What if I approach her? She might actually be really glad to find out that someone's thinking about her well-being. I might be able to persuade her that she needs her family's support right now."

I sit down in a chair and lean my head in my hand. I like the idea, but what if he's wrong? What if she figures out what's going on and pushes even further away? I don't know that I can risk it.

"I'm not sure," I say.

"I know it's a gamble," he says. "And given your family's history, I don't blame you if you decide against it. Obviously, I'll do whatever you're comfortable with."

I squirm. I fidget. I run my hand through my hair and push on my eyes. "Damn it," I finally mumble. "Okay, look. Talk to her. Tell her we're worried, okay? Tell her we love her. Tell her that we are only here to help her. All right?"

"Okay," he says.

"Just be careful," I say. "Try not to . . . trigger her in any way."

"I understand," he says.

I hang up the phone. I'm mad now; I feel totally helpless. But I get in the car and drive. Somehow I end up in Peabody, of all places, at TJ Maxx, the Temple of Numbing Your Soul by Gazing at Planters and Pillows. I go inside; I appreciate being in a big, airy, well-lit store where they let you linger and peruse, let you float and stare into the distance. Nobody bothers you as long as you appear to be considering some kind of purchase, a handbag, a bedspread, Siracha plantain chips, or small tables shaped like the Buddha's head.

I don't know if I have made the right choice with Riley. Should I call Nate back and tell him to stay away, tell me where she is, we will go there and intervene? No, I keep telling myself. She's keeping away from us for a reason. If I, or any of us, just barge in on her, would she talk to us? Run from us? Call the police? Fall apart? I just don't know.

I leave without buying anything. Then, because it's good for sightseeing, I head to Michael's. I find myself in the aisle with the oil paints, just staring at the different colors. After standing there for a long time, I load up my arms with paints, a set of brushes, a can of turpentine, a flat plastic palette, a cheap easel, and a set of canvases. I pay for my purchases and head out.

Next, I head to Trader Joe's and pick up a chicken Caesar salad in a plastic box and the ingredients for gin and tonics, then drive back to Plum Island. I mix myself a cocktail (in a rather large tumbler; but really, most of it is ice cubes), some gin, some tonic. I slice a wedge of lime and squeeze, then taste the concoction. It tastes bitter and sweet and fizzy and limey.

I nibble at the salad. I sit at the table in front of the painting, waiting for it to tell me what to do.

My second drink comes and goes, and then a third seems to happen.

I stare at the painting. "What do you have to say for yourself?" I finally ask the painting. It does not respond; it's pretending to be an inanimate object. It thinks I'm going to fall for that. "You know what? You owe me an explanation. You owe us all an explanation."

The painting does not blink, does not wince, does not even shudder slightly to acknowledge that I am speaking to it. "That's how you're going to play this," I say. And then I am on the brink of tears. "Mom, for years I have been looking for you, some sign that you were with me. But you never sent one. I loved you the whole time, and I still do. I never learn, do I?"

Suddenly, the glass is empty, and I can't remember how many drinks I've had, but I am surprised that this brand-new bottle of gin is just about empty. My head is swimming. Then I am lying on the floor, and I guess I've been here a while, crying for most of it, because my throat hurts and my eyes are burning.

I stare upward; I consider trying to push myself up, but that's not an option right now because the floor is spinning like a carousel. I stay where I am and gaze at the ceiling, beams of bird's-eye pine, how they whirl, so fast.

I wish I didn't have to live through all this. It would be so easy to call everything done, just wrap it up. I have prescription painkillers left over from oral surgery—enough pills . . . don't you think . . . on top of the gin . . . Maybe fill a bathtub . . .

"Only, I can't!" I shout out loud. "I don't get to do that, do I?" This time I do push myself up to standing, stumbling-standing, because actually, I am very drunk. "I have two children, Mom. And they need me. Not to mention Riley. I have no idea how to help that girl. You got any ideas? Of course you don't. So, even though my life is crap—and believe me, it is!—I will be here for as long as my children need me. Even if it kills me!"

My hands on my hips, I feel fierce, defiant. If Mom were a ghost, I would not be surprised if she suddenly appeared before me, saying, "You can never understand what I went through." But all I see is the room around me, and all I hear are the waves, crashing in measured rhythm on the shore beyond the cottage windows.

And that's when the room starts spinning again; now the gin is fighting back. I race to the toilet just in time. The entire contents of my digestive system lurch out and into the Plum Island sewer system.

When my cell phone rings, I am still draped over the toilet's edge, wiping my face with a damp washcloth. I've been there for a while, but I don't know how long. I look around for my phone for a moment before I realize it's in my hand.

It's Alex. "Hello?" I whisper.

"Colleen, did you try to call me?" she asks.

When she asks, I remember that I did. That's why I'm holding my phone. "Yeah," I say.

"I've been trying to call you back," she says.

"Sorry," I say, leaning against the toilet and closing my eyes. "I'm a little under the weather."

"Are you all right? Do you need me to bring you anything?"

My head is still swimming, and my mouth tastes of gin-flavored vomit. I start to fall apart again, but I am tired of crying, so I don't. "Alex, the investigator found Riley."

"He did?"

I tell her all that he and I spoke about, and what I decided. "Did I make the right call?"

"I don't know," she says. "Who knows if there even is a right. There's just us doing the best we can."

I grunt in agreement, and suddenly another wave of nausea goes through me. I hold the phone away from my face in case I throw up, but I don't; I hold it down.

"You okay?"

"Sure," I say, wiping the sweat off my forehead. "I just drank a bottle of gin and threw up at least half of it. I'm terrific."

"Oh, Colleen. Gin is bad," she says. "Are you going to pass out? If you're at risk for alcohol poisoning, we should get you to the ER."

I pull some toilet paper off the roll and dab my forehead. "No, I don't need the ER. I just need to get it out of my system. Alex, I don't want this to be my life."

"Honey, you have a lot of major life stuff hitting you at the same time. This won't last forever," she says. "You're going to get through this."

I sniff. I blink. To hear her say it really does make me feel better. "You really think so?"

"I know it. Absolutely. But for now, let yourself fall apart. If you try to hold all this in, you'll explode. But gin isn't the way."

I laugh. "I might be done with gin for the rest of my life," I say. I sit back and wipe my head on a towel. "You know what? It's been a really crappy winter."

"I know," she says. "I know it has. Hey, maybe you shouldn't be out there by yourself. It's kind of depressing. Come stay here."

"Thanks," I say. "But your house gives me the creeps."

"Yeah, me too."

I stand and go back into the main room, and again, I see the painting, which grips my attention as though it's calling out to me. "Alex," I say, suddenly. "Mom . . . she must have been in so much pain. Whatever I'm going through now, it's nothing compared to what Mom endured. That she would leave us, that she would really go ahead with it."

"Don't try to imagine it, Colleen," she says. "Mom's pain was her own. It's a place we should not go."

Our mother's pain, a place we should not go. I know she's right. Mom felt her own pain so succinctly, in her grasp, it became diamond-hard.

"Don't you have friends you could stay with?" she asks.

"No," I say. I pour myself a glass of water from the sink. "I'm going to stay here. I'm getting used to it."

"When's the last time you saw your kids?"

"Yesterday . . ." I say.

"Okay, good," she says. "Maybe you should get away with them. Disney or something. Do something really, completely fun."

"They can't," I say. "They're so busy with sports and so many things they won't want to miss . . ."

"Ethan and Maddie can miss a soccer game to spend some time with their mom," she says. "You need to do this for yourself, Colleen."

"Maybe."

"And, Colleen? I'm really glad you called. Call anytime. Even in the middle of the night. Even if I'm in another country."

I guffaw at that one. If she's in India, she won't be available for her sister's nervous breakdowns. Or anyway, I wouldn't be.

"I mean it," she says. "Okay?"

"All right," I say. And I know she does, at least for right now. "Thanks."

Chapter 17

Saturday, March 1, 2014
Riley

Almost three weeks since I lost my job, but I keep moving. I've gone on a few acting auditions, but nothing has materialized into a job yet. The numbers in the bank account grow and shrink in ways that don't make sense to me. But who cares! I live in a beautiful city, in a heated apartment. I am carpe diem on the cheap. I talk my way into everything: museums, movies, even the ballet. I should write a book. *Penniless Poppy's Guide to Fun in Manhattan.* It will be a best seller, and I'll be set with money for life. See? Everything comes up roses.

Tonight, big plans: dinner and dancing in the Lower East Side with my friend Valencia and a few others. I put in two hours at the gym in Lucia's building, then go out for a walk and a kale and farro salad. I make my way back through the cold, clear city afternoon. On a Seventh Avenue corner, some crazy religious people shriek and chant and wave signs about the apocalypse. As I walk away from them, I glimpse the setting sun: light seeping out between buildings, gleaming wisps of yellow and rose. It is the last view of light as the edge of the planet rotates into darkness. I stop to watch, to let the flash blind me a little. All the noisy, crazy New York people swarm past me, but I stand still and watch. It's so beautiful, I almost can't take it in. The soul-shattering beauty of this earth is almost enough to make me consider staying.

Someone jostles my back. I sigh. No. It's time to go.

Back to Lucia's in time to get dressed. I slip on a tight, shimmery blouse (a classic from Lucia's closet), plus skinny jeans and black applique Valentino ankle boots (those are mine, rescued from my eviction). Tonight we're meeting for sushi and drinks at Kyo Ya, then going dancing at some new club in Alphabet City that's supposed to be a raging scene. I am frankly not in the mood for any scene, especially a raging one. But everybody's been on me about JCW: *What happened? What did Marcella say? What am I doing now? They never fire anybody!* I keep telling them all it was a mutual breakup. *I'm fine, Marcella's fine. Everything is awesome.*

I sit down in front of the mirror on the dressing table. What to do with my hair? I am uninspired. Curl or straighten? Put it up or wear it down? I examine, consider, and then I remember a picture of me. It was a series Jack took for a perfume ad. I was in a huge French gown, mimicking Marie Antoinette, sitting in a country garden, looking peaceful. No wig, just my hair, the colors on my face soft and natural. I looked pretty; I looked like myself. Jack showed me as I was on the inside. How amazing that somebody could see past the foolishness, straight into my broken soul.

Who is Jack sleeping with tonight? Could be anybody. Maybe even his fiancée.

I decide to wear my hair down in ringlets, lightly coiled. When that's done, I put on a dangly little bracelet—guess who it belongs to—and after I fasten it, I push up my sheer, loose sleeve and glance at the white inside of my left arm. There it is, the hole from when Jack and I shot up together. It's still red and puckering. I flex my arm to feel the infected sting. It's a pain that sickens me to the core, reminds me of that night. And even my revulsion excites me a little. It reminds me of Jack.

I throw my face in my hands and groan out loud. I should call Valencia and tell her I'm sick and can't make it.

Jack. Valencia. Marcella. Friends I don't like and lovers I don't have. Plus, a big gross hole in my arm. Here is the titillating life I abandoned my son for. I can't think about him, not now, but my throat clogs with the onset of tears, and I can barely swallow. Nothing in this world means anything, and even the daisies on the table, the ones I bought at the fruit stand today, are lightless and strained. I heave forward; what is the point of all this?

Everything is broken.

Time for a fairy tale. Once upon a perfect fall day, almost six years ago, there was a beautiful princess. Her career was going great, photo shoots were coming at a mile a minute, and people knew who she was. Of course, there were chemicals; some helped her feel confident and suppressed her appetite, others helped her stay awake, some helped her sleep. Then, one beautiful New York day when the air was clear and the light was luscious, the princess went for a walk wearing a really fun top with spaghetti straps and cute, expensive shoes that embraced her feet so her steps barely touched the sidewalk. She popped into a store and spotted a stunning beaded bracelet. It was on sale and cost almost nothing, so she bought it. Then she bought an ice cream, just a teeny one, to reward herself for running three extra miles that morning. It was hand-churned and cold, and the flavor dissolved on her tongue. A taste of heaven.

The princess's phone rang before she'd swallowed that last lick of sweet cream. She answered without thinking. *Hello, this is the doctor's office. Your pregnancy test was positive.*

The end. Fairy tale over.

I wanted an abortion. I had the money; I had plenty of money. The baby's father was some guy in LA who bought me drinks at a club. I had no way to contact him even if I wanted to; I didn't know his name, much less what club I was at.

Maybe I was lonely; maybe I thought a baby would keep me company. I was young then. Everything seemed possible.

Funny how things used to seem possible, used to happen without my wanting them too much. I barely showed up for anything, and yet, good things kept happening. Funny how fast that ends.

I was supposed to stop using. And drinking. I planned to, really, and each drink was the last one, and each hit the last. The doctor told me the risks, what to expect when you're expecting, especially when you're using. I tried to stop, and sometimes, I did. But then I'd start again. Which I guess is the opposite of stopping.

My baby. Born underweight with a high chance that he could experience some kind of developmental delay or intellectual disability, but to me, he was perfect. The first moment I held him, I felt overwhelming love. And pity; I felt so sorry for that tiny baby. The only protection between him and a world that eats fragile, sweet souls alive, was me. And I'm no help to anyone.

After he was born, I thought a lot about Mom. I wished I had her to tell me what to do, but I couldn't find her. Sometimes I can; she hovers in the corner of the ceiling. She looks like she did in the picture I keep tucked away in a little book: long hair, wide, deep eyes, pretty smile. I try so hard to find memories of her, but there's nothing. She must have spent time with me, right? But the only memories I have are photographs. And little stories I make up in my mind, to sit where the memories ought to be.

Caleb once asked me if he had grandparents. I told him he had a grandfather who knew how to sail boats and a grandmother who turned herself into a penny that I could never find again, even though I looked every place I could think of.

He liked hearing about the grandfather who knew how to sail boats. And for a while, he kept finding pennies on the sidewalk and asking if they were his grandmother. *No, baby*, I said. *That's not the right penny.*

I never told Dad or Alex or Colleen about Caleb. I meant to. I wanted to. Alex visited just after I found out I was pregnant. I planned to tell her, but I couldn't. I kept imagining my sister the nurse reciting all the terrible things that maternal drug and alcohol use does to a fetus. And I knew that perfect Colleen in her perfect house with her perfect children would tell me a hundred ways that I was doing everything wrong.

Nobody was going to tell me that I was making a million mistakes as a mother. I would wait and hear that from the police, thank you anyway.

God, Caleb, what have I done to you? I am so, so sorry, baby boy.

Before I go out the door: a pill for the road, and one more in my purse. With the chemical tucked in against my cheek, dissolving, I look at myself in the mirror.

I can't do this anymore. Tonight, and that's it. Everything ends tomorrow. Okay?

Okay.

Promise?

Promise.

My night out with friends is not what I needed. Sushi and selfies, dancing and drinking; I had hoped it would be ridiculous and delicious, like Saturday nights used to be. I had hoped I would lose myself at the club, stop thinking about everything in the pounding music and the pulsing light, revel in the fun of being one of the beautiful, untouchable birds on display. But I couldn't let go and simply be. Tonight, it was too much.

So I did the unimaginable: I walked out. I told my friends I had a headache, and they sent me away with aww-pity-feel-better faces. I felt like there was something else we should say to each other, but I couldn't think of what. I requested my coat from the coat check and left. Alone. At two a.m. Not something I usually do. It gave me a strange sense of power, but it's lonely too.

I look back at the door to the club and watch the bouncer admit three more pretty girls. The party continues without me. I guess that's how it goes.

Then I walk into the chilly night. The cabs that pass me are all full; I consider whether I should wait for an empty one or call an Uber. I look up at the streetlight on the opposite corner and watched the fine drizzle fall, catching the light with a shimmer that reminds me of sunlight on the surface of the ocean.

For no particular reason, I look down then, and in the shadow beyond the streetlight's beam, a man is standing, watching me with a quizzical expression. I watch him too, trying to figure out whether I know him, but it's hard to tell, and people keep walking past both of us. Finally, I recognize him—it's my stalker. I'm happy to see him, so I cross the street to find him. When he realizes I'm coming toward him, he starts to back away.

"No," I call out. "Wait. Hold on." I quicken my pace to catch up to him. "Hi," I say when I reach him.

"Hi," he says.

"How are you?" I say.

"Okay," he says. "Yourself?"

"I'm all right. Are you here stalking me?" I ask.

He chuckles. "In fact, no. I was heading home after having dinner with friends."

"Nice," I say. "How was dinner?"

He shrugs. "Great. They made swordfish."

"Delicious," I say.

He nods. After that, silence.

The next words come out without me exactly planning them. "Do you want to get a cup of coffee?"

He seems confused or surprised. "You mean now?"

"That's what I was thinking," I say. He hesitates and looks around; I get the feeling he's looking for a reason to say no. "Unless you have somewhere to be?"

He shakes his head.

"Well, then. Let's go."

He grins. "All right," he says. He offers me the bend in his elbow, and I link my arm through his. We pick a direction to start in, and I pull my scarf over my head to protect my face from the drizzle. I like how holding his arm feels; I like the smell of his aftershave.

It feels comfortable like this, which is strange since this is the second time we've met. Who is this man? I don't even know his name. He's been following me, but tonight's meeting seems like a genuine coincidence. I wonder if he's a stalker or more like a detective of some kind. He's not with the police, I don't think. I grip his arm as we walk through shining, cold streets illuminated under streetlights. I don't know what he knows about me, but in this moment, it does not matter. We are here, he and I, in this Manhattan night, and we are together, bounding down the sidewalk, searching for coffee. The scene and the moment are so perfect, I wonder if I am imagining them. But then I smell his aftershave and feel the cold spray on my face, and I know that I am not.

Chapter 18

The air seems milder today; I suspect the warmth comes ahead of the big storm we're expecting tomorrow, which makes it feel comfortable but ominous. I am in my father's cobweb-covered basement, digging through the half a dozen boxes I left behind before I went to India. I tried to keep things organized by labeling the boxes—Alex Clothes, Alex Bath, Alex Kitchen, Alex Books. But what am I looking for? It's not mixed in with books. Bathroom will be towels and linens. Kitchen, obviously, dishes, pots, and pans. Then I notice a smaller box atop two larger ones. I grab it, and in the light filtering in through the submerged window, I go up the stairs into the kitchen where Dad is sitting, reading the paper.

"Is that all you need?" he asks. "Don't you want to take some of your other things?"

"No, thanks," I say. "I'm trying not to unpack more than I need to."

He looks at me over the top of his reading glasses. "Oh. Okay," he says. "Well, what do you have there?"

Hopefully, this box contains all the small things from the bureau in my bedroom, including trinkets I bought myself over the years and rarely wore, and the fancier items of my mother's, which is why I am excavating it now. I consider telling him that this box might contain a new roof that I will sell for a ticket to India, but why rub it in. If he wants to tell me not to sell her jewelry, I don't want to hear it.

"Just stuff," I say.

"Big storm coming," he says. "You ready for it?"

"I think so," I say. "I have candles, matches, an emergency radio, extra batteries, bottled water, and junk food. What are you going to do? Do you need supplies?"

"I am always prepared for emergencies," he says, ruffling his paper. "But I'm going to Mrs. Moschella's house. She might need me to help her with her sump pump."

"Well, that's nice of you," I say. "All right. Good luck tomorrow."

"Don't be a stranger," he calls out as I begin to weave my way through the living room piles.

"Don't you be a stranger, Dad," I shout back. I want to yell at him to put his paper down and get in a car—any car, mine, his, even an Uber—and come see my house. But my father from Maine is more stubborn than molasses in February; he will not change a hair until he is good and ready to.

"I never am," he says.

I roll my eyes and head out to the car.

Fifteen minutes later I am back at the house, sitting atop my sleeping bag with the small cardboard box in front of me. I open it up; the top layer is dress scarves, for the rare occasion. Next, a few rolled-up pairs of socks, a few undergarments. Then I see the thing I am looking for—an old wooden folk-art box with a carving of trees in the cover.

I press the tiny hook-shaped latch and push the top open. And then the treasures. I lift them out carefully. Two small ceramic terrier dogs. A round pencil sharpener printed like a globe. A necklace with my birthstone that was a birthday gift from Colleen. A tiny paper valentine from my best friend in first grade. A few gold bangles, which also belonged to Mom. And under those, a felt drawstring jeweler's bag. It's heavier than I remember, contoured to the touch. I push the mouth open with my fingers and turn it on its side; the necklace slips out.

Mom's pearls. They're cool, heavy, smooth; they make tinkly music as they rub against one another. I have lived my whole life with no need for, or interest in, jewelry, but here I am, pulling out my mother's pearls and feeling like a paleontologist handling evidence of a creature who once roamed these lands.

I wonder if I could ever wear these. I hold them around my neck. They're just not me.

I study the necklace. The clasp is gold with little diamonds. Those couldn't be real, could they? Is the gold *gold*? What about the pearls? I always thought they were painted glass, but now they seem too heavy to be glass. I put one between my canine teeth and bite carefully; there is no give, no hint of cracking. I look at where my teeth hit the surface; no mark. The pearls are lovely, shimmery and luminous, burning cold fires in round bellies. I cannot imagine my mother wearing this necklace. She would have preferred something unusual, a charm on a chain, colorful glass beads, something that felt meaningful to her. She wasn't a "pearls to the country club" person. She wasn't an "oyster fork" person either, or at least, I never thought so before.

Anything else in the bag? I reach in, and my fingers find a small square paper. It's a photo of Mom that I've never seen. It must be her college senior picture, classic black and white, posed with a dark drape that half exposed her shoulders. Her blond hair is cut short and curled at the edges, and around her neck, this string of pearls.

My mother in pearls. Her lips are pressed together and her smile is barely there. She seems so stiff and formal, I almost don't recognize her. She looks like a child; something in her eyes looks pained, or do I imagine that? I reach in again to see if there is anything else—and there is something more. A small square cut from a newspaper:

Mr. and Mrs. William Montgomery of Sausalito, California, have announced the engagement of their daughter, Suzanne, to Jacob Gregory O'Dowd, son of Mr. and Mrs. Philip A. O'Dowd of Santa Cruz, California. Miss Montgomery and her fiancé are seniors at the University of California in San Francisco. A wedding is planned for next April.

Who are these people? Jacob O'Dowd and his parents, Mr. and Mrs. Philip A. Were they really married the next April?

I put the newsprint aside. There's another photo in the bottom of the box, one I saved. This is the mother I knew. It's South Williston, Maine, the summer when she met and married our father, and she's standing next to her bicycle wearing torn sneakers and a white T-shirt and denim cutoff shorts. Her hair is tied loosely back, and she's beaming. And in a milk crate strapped to the back of her bicycle, a canvas painting in progress, and a bucket filled with her painting supplies.

She must have been two disparate people—a debutante daughter of wealth, composed and contained in expensive pearls, and an artist, lovely, wild, and limitless. How did she manage being both, I wonder, or was that part of the problem? One of these was the person who made her parents happy; the other was who she was on the inside. She tried to shed the first one like a skin, tried to outrun it, but maybe it caught up to her.

I don't know, and the picture of her in Maine makes me so inconceivably sad, I cannot stand to look at it anymore. I grab a jacket and rush outside for air. The breeze is strong and I stumble through it, into the yard; the wind blows my hair into my face, and I peel it away only to have my eyes blinded by a dazzle of sunlight.

I gaze out onto the marsh as a million questions buzz in my mind. Who was this man, my mother's first fiancé? Where is he now? We never knew anything about my mother's life before Dad; we had no one to tell us. I shake slightly and try to catch my breath. When I stop shaking, I will call Colleen. But a voice interrupts my thoughts, and I am so surprised, I feel like the wind might blow me over.

"Hi there. Do you live in this house?" asks the man, whom I did not see approach.

I am stunned, startled. He must have walked down from the road above, which I have never seen anybody do. He looks to be decently well off, a pleasant man in his early seventies, I would guess, thinning gray hair, dressed in a warm L.L. Bean jacket and khaki pants. In better weather, I imagine he'd be on a sailboat, drinking a Manhattan.

I swallow; I compose myself, and in a moment, I remember how to speak. "Yes," I say. "For now, I do. I'm fixing it up."

"Oh," he says. "It's a nice house. I always liked it. I always admired its view of the marsh. That's a fine view."

I nod. "I agree," I say. "Do you live around here?"

"Me? No, not anymore, at least," he says. "I'm from Boston. My grandfather lived in Newbury at a farmhouse, just up the road from here. Growing up, we spent summers here helping him on the farm."

"Oh," I say. "So, did you used to know this house? Or, I mean, the people who lived here?"

"Not well," he says, smiling. "I mean, they bought milk and eggs from my grandpa, but aside from making deliveries down here, I didn't really know them."

I nod. I had half hoped that he might tell me something about the house and the people, something that would explain the . . . recent events.

"I'm always so glad to see the old places still standing," he says. "My grandad's house is still there, but it's been renovated so much, I barely recognize it. Old houses get torn down every day and new ones built, and only the old-timers like me remember the way things used to be."

"Old houses are a lot of work," I admit.

"Well, thank you for not giving up on it. Seeing it there on a day like this, it brings back so many memories. I can smell the salt marsh hay we used to pull into bales. I can even taste my grandmother's blueberry jam."

"That's lovely, sir," I say.

He begins to speak, then he stops himself and simply gazes at the house. "My memories aren't all so nice," he says. "My granddad, he was pretty ornery. I've learned to choose to remember the nice memories over the less nice ones. But it takes work."

"I have that problem myself, sometimes," I say.

"Something I wonder about," he says. "Do we choose our memories or do our memories choose us?"

I smile. It's an innocent enough question, and a ridiculous one, because obviously, our memories have no agency, no ability to make a choice. They are a part of us. Indeed, they are the basis of everything we are as human beings, our identity and all our abilities, everything we understand about ourselves and the world. I saw it so many times in the emergency room, a person whose memory was impaired by trauma, physical or emotional, who lost not their life but all awareness of everything that ever happened in it— every lesson learned, every person encountered, all the bonds ever created.

But for me, sometimes memory does feel like more than a biochemical, neurological reaction. It feels like a presence that grants us either sunken mothers with wide-open eyes or summer blueberries, warm from the sun. But I haven't figured out how to choose one over the other.

"I wish I knew the answer to that," I say.

Chapter 19

Sunday, March 2, 2014
Riley

This man and I do not speak as we walk, and I am grateful for the quiet. We are searching for a place to stop for coffee. I need coffee, and something stronger too; I need a pill. The one in my clutch pulses like a homing device. On East Tenth we find a small diner, very old school. Perfect. He opens the door and waits for me to walk inside. The place smells like greasy griddle cakes, bacon, and hash browns, and I know that those smells will stay in my hair until I wash it. The place is busy, but we spot an empty booth with red vinyl seats, and even though the table has not been cleared, we slide onto the benches. An unsmiling waitress hands us menus and takes away the dirty dishes then wipes the surface with a dirty rag. After that, a middle-aged waitress with light-brown hair and too much mascara, whose name tag reads "Veronica," comes to the table. We order coffee and pie.

Now, in the diner's florescent light, I really look at him. He is handsome; though it's not only because of how he looks, it's also because his attention is so focused, intense. His skin has a slight olive tint to it; his build slender, strong but not bodybuilder. He leaves his coat on but open when he sits down. He sits in his bench leaning away from me, staring at me as though he's trying to figure something out. After a moment, I think—oh, it's me, he's trying to figure *me* out.

What in the world is so interesting about me? I'm an open book.

I'll need a pill soon. It's starting to sprout into my blood, the itchy push of need, and until I find it, I will think of little else. I want to take one just so I can stop thinking about it. Being an addict is exhausting.

"Nice place," he says, smiling politely.

"I hope they have good coffee."

Veronica brings us mugs and a bowl of little creamers, plus two juice glasses of ice water. The coffee is hot and bitter. Would it be awful to take a pill right now at the table? I could tell him it's aspirin. But he would know. I have a feeling he would know.

I keep wondering whether there's a girlfriend or a wife; no wedding ring, anyway.

He pulls out his phone and looks at something, then puts it back in his coat pocket. "Somebody looking for you?" I ask. He shakes his head, grinning like he knows what I'm really asking.

Finally, the waitress brings slices of pie, and they're huge, like slabs of building materials. The berries in mine and the apples in his are gleaming jewels encased in pie crust, sweet and flaky, radiant with sugar. It's the most beautiful food I've ever seen. And after I admire it and salivate, I couldn't possibly eat it any more than I would eat a pair of shoes.

"Looks good," he says.

I nod. He eats; I watch him delicately cut a bite and then shovel it up with a fork and load it into his mouth. He gets to eat; boys always do.

He sees me watching him. "Something wrong?" he asks.

"No," I say. "Just . . . you haven't asked my name."

"I know your name," he says. "You're Riley. I overheard that man at the bar call you that."

I pick up my fork and try to imagine what it would be like to take a bite. I suppose it would be sugary, slimy, and crisp at the same time. I can't make myself do it, so I drink coffee instead. "You know my name because you've been following me," I say.

"I'm not following you."

I laugh. "Oh, I guess it's a coincidence that we just bumped into each other two times now . . . and I've been seeing you all over town, hiding in doorways and around corners . . ."

He shrugs. "That place Salty's is near my office, and sometimes I stop by for a drink after work."

"Your office?" I ask. He nods. "What do you do?"

"I'm an editor for a small quarterly scientific journal," he says. He pulls out his wallet and pretends to look for something. "I'd give you a card but I'm fresh out."

"Oh, that's too bad," I say, sipping coffee.

"Nate," he declares, and he thrusts his hand across the table.

"Hello, Nate," I say slowly, taking his hand and shaking it.

I study him, his face, his hands. He just doesn't look like an editor of a quarterly scientific journal. He also doesn't quite look like a common stand-alone stalker. Those guys always have something unhinged and creepy about them, a wild look in their eyes, a homeless vibe. But this one doesn't seem deranged. In fact, he's clean shaven, organized, focused. Even, I'll give it to him, a pretty decent actor. His cologne smells pricey. No, he's working for someone.

I change tactics to one that usually gets results. I swoosh my hair to the side and move so my blouse falls slightly, showing a little cleavage. "Come on! I just rescued your Saturday night."

He scowls. "Rescued how, exactly?"

"Before I came along, the most interesting thing that happened tonight to you was swordfish," I say. "The least you can do is tell me the inside scoop."

"Inside scoop on what?" he says.

"Come on," I say. "Look, you have to understand. When you're a woman alone in the city, especially one who makes a living being looked at, you learn to pay attention to who's watching. So don't tell me I haven't seen you," I say, "because I have."

He makes a face like he has no idea what I'm talking about, and maybe I'm just nuts.

"You're working for somebody," I say, pulling my top even closer in and sitting back.

"I work for the American Association of the Advancement of Science. They're my publisher."

I glare at him. "What kind of science, exactly?"

"All kinds." He takes a bite of pie. "The AAAS publishes six peer-reviewed journals . . ."

The itchy feeling is really starting to irk me, and I tap my fingertips against my warm coffee cup.

"I don't buy it," I say.

He grins. "It's good pie," he says. "You should have some."

The awareness is constant, of being seen or photographed and how the moment would appear were it frozen and flattened into an image, and more than anything, how I look in it. This photo would be an art shot, black and white, capturing the grit and grime of the early morning diner, a girl dressed to be seen, hiding now behind a cup of coffee, with uneaten pie on a plate. My eyes would be circled in kohl, and my hair crimped and covered in gel to make it look sweaty and druggie. Mostly, though, the picture is of me looking at him, trying to figure out who he is and what, exactly, he wants.

I push my plate toward him. "I'm not hungry. You can have mine."

Am I really supposed to believe the science journal story? I can't tell. I have seen him so many places, but he has me almost convinced that I haven't. This man—what was his name? Nate—with the dark hair and dark eyes is a bit of a mystery. Maybe I'm like that too—or maybe I used to be like that. These days I look older than jokes about New Jersey. His eyes are deep; there's more going on in there than I can see. Those are the kind of eyes that make you feel like you can tell him anything. The kind that make you feel like you will tell him everything.

He chews and swallows, then takes a swallow of coffee. "So, what do you do?"

"What do I do?"

"I told you what I do, now you tell me what you do," he says. "We take turns; we go back and forth. That's called a conversation."

"Yes," I say, "I just didn't know—" How far we were going to take this game. "Okay, fine, I'll bite. I'm a model. You know, runway shows, photo spreads, champagne in limos, parties with Anna Wintour, that kind of thing."

"The only thing I know about fashion I learned from that movie, *The Devil Wears Prada*," he says.

"Oh, do not even," I say, lightly touching my middle finger to my temple. "You cannot mention that movie to people who actually work in the fashion industry. Seriously, it's a bad caricature. Anna Wintour has a vision, and she's a perfectionist. Nobody whines into their latte when some man has to crack a whip to get something done right."

Suddenly I realize he's laughing and trying to conceal it like he's pretending to wipe his face.

"Why is that funny?" I say. "It's not funny."

"I'm sorry, it's a little funny," he says. He scratches his cheek like it's a habit, something he does to wake himself up.

"There's a lot to it, Mr. Science Journal," I say. "Anyway, are you from New York?"

"Brooklyn, born and bred," he says. "Before it was the new Manhattan. You from here?"

"No," I say. "Come on. You know where I'm from."

He gives me a blank look. "I don't. That's why I asked."

"Fine," I say. "I'm from Massachusetts, a small town north of Boston. Like, very north. Almost New Hampshire."

When I don't continue, he says, "And the name of the town is . . .?"

"It's called Amesbury. Used to be a mill town. It's cute but it's a little quiet for me. Although, my sister loves to email me that a new cool brew pub or coffee spot or crepe café just opened up in town and I really just *have* to come and try it."

He looks down and smiles to himself. "If I had a dime for every new coffee spot in Brooklyn . . ."

I smile. "With that many dimes, you could buy Brooklyn."

"Ha, that's right, I could afford to live there," he says, chuckling. "So, your sister's still there?"

I nod and absently stir my coffee. "She's in the area. My dad is in Amesbury," I say. "He's a mailman. Well, retired."

He's sitting back with his arm outstretched over the top of the seat. "Boy, that's a tough job," he says. "How's he spending his golden years?"

I grin and look down. "He stays quiet," I say. I pull up my clutch, a turquoise Gucci with a brass horse bit in the middle, and start to look through it. The shakes are starting to make their way to the surface, and I don't want him to see. I find my pillbox and grip it in my palm but keep my hand in my purse. "Kind of a recluse these days."

"When my dad retired, it made my mom crazy suddenly having him around the house all the time like that," he says.

"Your mom?" I say. Suddenly my mom is here with us, sitting at the booth, perched on top of the sugar shaker, even while my mouth is starting to water with the possibility of what's in my hand. It's only her head, actually, atop a pair of wings—insect wings, not angel ones—and she's hovering like she is also curious about the answer to the question. "My mom?"

"Well, I meant my mom," he says, taking a sip of coffee. "But we can talk about your mom."

"My mom . . . sorry . . ." I'm losing track of the conversation. "My mother died before I was born." I drop the pillbox into my purse, take a drink of coffee, and glance around. I don't want my mom to see me do this.

"She what?"

I realize what I said. "Not before I was born," I say. "But I was pretty young. I actually don't remember her."

"Oh no. I'm so sorry," he says.

I nod. "She killed herself," I say, even though he didn't ask. "Nobody knows why. She didn't leave a note or anything."

He looks at me hard, like he's studying me. "You ever wonder why she did that?"

I shrug. "Sometimes. I don't walk around with this huge emptiness in my soul," I say, and it sounds callous, even to my own ears. "My sisters might. But since I don't remember her, it's not like I lost something I had."

No, I think, it's worse than that. I lost my mother and grief left my father an empty shell. I was raised by two sisters. And though they loved me and cared for me as best they could, they could not keep me safe.

"Here's a question," he says slowly, tentatively, gazing down at his cup of coffee. "What if someone could tell you something about your mom. Something that might help you understand . . . what happened to her?"

I lean back and cross my arms. "Aha," I say. "You had me doubting myself for a moment. You really are a spy, aren't you?"

He rolls his eyes. "I'm not a spy. I'm a humble editor," he says. "It was a hypothetical question."

I stare at his face, trying hard to read between the lines. "That's not a hypothetical question. And anyway, no, there's nothing I want to know. My mother is a whole Pandora's Box that I prefer to leave closed and locked."

"All right," he says. "So, Amesbury. Now that I think of it, I feel like I've heard the name before. It's fairly rural, isn't it?"

I sigh. "There are a lot of farms. If you're into picking apples, go straight to Amesbury. It's west of Salisbury, where the beach is. If you reach Salisbury and keep going east, then you're on your way to Ireland."

He puts down his fork and wipes the corners of his mouth. "Well, you'd be on your way to Spain, or southern France, maybe."

"Excuse me?"

"Northern Massachusetts, that's the forty-second parallel." He draws an imaginary horizontal line in the air to illustrate. "France or Spain might be on the other side. Not Ireland."

I am amazed. We always used to say that anything we lost that went floating across the ocean was on its way to Ireland. "How do you know that?"

And now that we are at the beach, looking across to France and Spain, my mother flies away to the next table to see what's new with the gang of steampunk youth eating greasy burgers. Bye, thanks for visiting.

He gives me a sympathetic smile and taps his head. "It's a steel trap," he says. "Every little fact goes in and stays there. I'm killer at *Jeopardy!*"

"Really," I say, flabbergasted. "I can't imagine what that would be like." Outside the window beside me, two busses, lit up but empty, pass from different directions. "I barely remember anything. Sometimes I think it's better that way. My memories would be so sad if I actually remembered them."

Veronica refreshes our coffee, and Nate peels open a plastic capsule of creamer and pours it in. "I've read that drugs mess with memory."

"Is that so," I say. Once again, I have the feeling that he's talking about me, but I choose to ignore it. "So how do you end up with such a good memory? Is that a genetic thing?"

He gives me a funny smile, closed lips. "Just dumb luck, probably. I tell you, I'm about as dull as a . . . as a science journal editor. Let's talk about you."

I sit back, slumping. "That's hardly fair," I say. "You know everything about me. You've been watching me."

"I have not been watching you," he says, giving an exasperated laugh.

I cross my arms. "There are eight and a half million people in the Big Apple. I've bumped into this one stranger twice in the past two weeks and seen someone who looks just like you across the street from the place where I'm staying."

He looks at me with raised eyebrows. "It's called a coincidence."

"No, it isn't," I say.

"Fine," he says, leaning back as though he's giving up. "What if I am watching you? What have I seen you doing?"

I frown; blink. "That's hardly fair," I say. "You're not going to admit what you're doing, but you get to interrogate me anyway?"

He rubs his forehead. "I'm just trying to make conversation," he says. "Remember how that works? I say something, you say something . . ."

"Okay," I say, turning my coffee cup around by the handle. "What do you want to know?"

He shrugs. "Oh, I don't know," he says. "How are you?"

"Interesting place to start," I say. "I'm fine. How are you?"

"Can't complain," he says. "How's work?"

"Peachy," I say. "I was fired a couple of weeks ago. And I got kicked out of my apartment last fall, so that was fun."

"That's terrible," he says. "So, where are you staying now?"

"I'm crashing at my friend Lucia's place," I say. "Her dad is an Italian shipping magnate, and he bought her a one-bedroom in Lenox Hill to use whenever she's in the city. She's abroad at the moment, so she's letting me stay there rent-free."

"Did you say you have a sister?"

I glance into my clutch and pull out a lipstick. "Sisters. Two."

"Are you close?"

"All sisters are close," I declare with a flat smile. "My sisters and I are so very close. You know, geography notwithstanding." I press the lipstick to my lips and apply a ring of color, then meld my lips and blot them on a napkin. I know I have applied it perfectly, but I check it in my tiny lipstick mirror anyway. Yup, perfect.

"Where are they?"

As much as I love to talk about myself, this is actually getting tiresome. I sigh. "One in Massachusetts, near Amesbury, one is off gallivanting in . . . India, I think. Next question, please."

He leans in, puts his elbows on the table, and covers his mouth with his hands. "All right. Tell me. There's a child," he says. "A little boy. Who is he?"

His question shocks me; I clear my throat and think about how to respond. "What?" I whisper. "How could you know about him?"

"Well, okay, I do know you, a little bit," he says. "I'm sure you don't recognize me, but I follow you on social media. And somebody posted photos of a child and tagged you. The boy looks a lot like you."

"So you have been lying to me." I stare at the wall as I put my coat on. "Well, Nate, or whatever your name is, you know what? Not cool. You could have told me. Then at least I wouldn't hate you right now."

"Riley, I'm sorry," he says. "Don't go."

"Not so nice to meet you," I say. I flip my hair up out of the back of my coat and dash out the door. As I start down the sidewalk, a cold wind hits me in the face. Whether or not he's a spy almost doesn't matter. I'm used to being watched. But I wanted him to be a good guy. I wanted him to not be a liar.

"Wait," he says, running to catch up to me. "Wait, Riley, please."

"I have nothing to say to you," I say. And now I'm really crying, partly because I'm upset and partly because the wind is stinging my eyes.

And I really did like him.

"Look," he says. "I'll tell you the truth, as much of it as I can. Just come inside for a little bit longer."

"Tell me now," I say.

"I am a private investigator," he says. "And I have been following you."

"You jerk," I say, hitting him on the shoulder with my clutch. "You are a total jerk."

"Ow," he says, rubbing his shoulder. "Hey, that hurts."

"You are a terrible spy," I shout. After a few good bats, I stop hitting him and put my hands to my eyes to try and wipe away the tears. "Remind me to never hire you."

"Look, the truth is—I wanted to talk to you," he says. "I wasn't planning to do it tonight, but here we are."

I look into his eyes; something about the intensity in them, or just the way that he is, makes me trust him, or at least I want to trust him. I want desperately to trust him.

I sniff and look around. "Why?"

"I'm just trying to make sure . . . that you're safe."

"Is that the truth?" I say.

"It's the whole truth," he says. He lifts his right hand. "I do solemnly swear that it is nothing but the truth."

I look down, I don't want to meet his eyes. I also don't want him to leave me. "Did you pay for the coffee?"

"Yes," he says.

"Did you leave a good tip?" I ask.

"Almost as much as the coffee."

I nod. "That little boy on Instagram," I say. "I don't want to talk about him. At all. Understand?"

"Yes," he says.

Another burst of cold wind rushes into me. "And no more lies. No more stories. No . . . science journals. If it's not true, don't say it."

"Okay," he says quietly. "Let's walk. We can talk about anything you want. Or nothing at all. We can be totally silent if you'd rather."

"All right," I say.

Once again, he bends his arm and offers it to me. I hesitate a moment but then I take it, and we walk forward into the cold New York City night.

Chapter 20

Sunday, March 2, 2014
Colleen

I wake up early and do what I need to do, what I need to remember that I must always do: pull on my sneakers, wrap up in layers, and set my feet to pounding. I'm ready for it, and I crave it; I hate the fact that I let everything get out of control. Time to rein things back in.

Suddenly, a text comes in from Maddie.

> Mom, we're worried about you being on the island. Come here before the storm starts.

> Is that okay with Dad?

> It was his idea!

She adds a zany-faced emoji.
It's nice to hear they're thinking about me. It cheers me up.

> Okay, thanks. What snacks
> do we need?

> We have everything! Just come.

Then, an emoji face with tears of joy.
I send a thumbs up.

> Afternoon.

Okay, Eric. You get points for trying to be a good guy.

I take the road instead of the beach; behind houses, I am protected from the late-winter wind, slicing off the hard waves. When I think about my life during a run, there's a clarity I can't access at other times. From here, the wind burning cold and dry on my face, and I realize that my job is to take care of myself. I cannot wallow in hopelessness. I have to remember that I have children who need me. I owe it to them to be strong.

After my run I make coffee and sit down at the table. Looking out at the ocean, the low waves breaking, I decide. The storm will come this afternoon, but this morning, I will talk to my father.

But my cell phone rings before I am out the door. It's Alex. "Colleen?" she says. "I hope it's not too early."

"No, it's good timing," I say. Her voice sounds urgent. "What's up?"

"I found the pearls, Mom's pearls," she says. "I don't know anything about jewelry. They . . . might be real, I guess."

"Wow," I say. "So, take them to a jewelry appraiser and . . ."

"Colleen, was Mom married before Dad?" she asks.

It's a surprising thing to hear, and I laugh awkwardly and fumble with my words before I can respond. "What? Why?"

"I found a wedding announcement," she says. "The daughter of Mr. and Mrs. Montgomery engaged to marry Jacob Gregory O'Dowd of Santa Cruz. Do you know anything about that?"

"Uh," I say. "I never heard that she was. How funny. What was his name again?"

"O'Dowd," she says. "Jacob O'Dowd of Santa Cruz. In April of '77, I guess."

"I never heard about it," I say. "What do you think it means?"

"I don't know," she says.

"Well, I'm heading over to Dad's today; I'll ask him. Are you working? I can visit you at the library."

"No," she says. "I'm trying to squeeze in a trip to the paint store before the storm sets in, so just call me."

"Where did you find the announcement?"

"It was in the pouch with the pearls," she says. "Along with what I suppose is her senior portrait, where she's wearing the pearls. I guess I never looked inside when I got the necklace. Now I'm thinking, it's like she was two different people. Split right down the middle."

"Yes," I say, my gaze out at the rolling, crashing waves, the tide pulling back from the shore. "I'll let you know if I find anything out. What colors are you considering?"

"For paint? No idea," she says. "I thought I'd see what grabs me. Any suggestions?"

"Well," I suggest, "think neutral, at least on the first floor. People want to look at your house and imagine the colors they would pick and whatever décor they have in mind. So, it has to look finished, but it also needs to be a blank canvas. Nothing too distracting."

"Blank canvas," she says. "Okay, thanks." She sounds distracted, distant. "Colleen? Why did our mother have so many secrets?"

"I don't know," I say. "Maybe she thought she could leave something that didn't feel right behind her. Maybe all she ever wanted was a clean start . . . like, a blank canvas."

"Why didn't it work?" she asks.

I shrug. "Maybe the things you try to leave behind have a way of catching up to you."

We say goodbye, and I stand by the sliding door window and stare out at the water, the wind stirring it into frothy whitecaps in the distance. Starting over is never easy.

I put on my jacket and get in the car. I decide not to call ahead to let Dad know I'm coming. I'll surprise him. If he's not home when I get there, he won't be far. But then I stop and turn back. I want to bring the painting. I go back in for it and set it carefully on the floor of the back seat of the car. A simple frame of wood that my mother probably built, and a simple piece of canvas stretched across it. Hers were the hands that stretched it; her hands nailed it in place.

I look at it before I let go. For the first time I notice, the girls are in primary colors—tones straight out of the tubes, highlighted only in touches of white. Clean yellow, red, blue, crayon colors for three little girls in their hats and scarves. So simple. The sand, the sky, the ocean, those are more complex mixtures of pigment, blues swirled with white, with gray, flashes of ochre and crimson reflecting in the water, the sand in browns and pale yellows, like butter on toast. The girls and the sunshine upon them. A perfect winter's day. This is all she wanted to paint on her blank canvas. But in her heart, there were dusky shades underneath. A darker sky was always hovering.

I drive to Amesbury, pull up in front of the old house on Greenwood Street. Dad's old Buick sedan with the rusted hubcaps is in the driveway. With the painting in my hand, I walk up the porch and open the door, knocking at the same time. "Hello?" I call. "Anybody home?"

I expect him to come hobbling out of the kitchen or down the stairs, but he doesn't. "Hello?" I call again. "Dad? Daddy? It's Colleen." Nothing happens. "Anybody home?"

He must be out for a walk. I could drive around and look for him, but instead I stay and wait. I squeeze past the piles of newspapers and books and magazines in the living room. I imagine that there are creatures living among the piles and stacks, but I don't look for them and I don't see them and everything is better that way. The kitchen is somewhat tidy: two plates and a glass are drying in the old rack, and the yellow linoleum counter is wiped and the cracked, warped panels on the floor have been swept. He tries to keep house; it's just the throwing away he can't do.

I look around the house, mostly to make sure that my father is not living under a half-collapsed roof. I can just imagine that happening and him saying, "Well, I just put an extra sweater on, and I don't notice it." I set the painting on the floor, lean it carefully against the wall, then climb the stairs to the second-floor bedrooms. Then I see it in the hallway, a little trap door in the ceiling. I haven't thought about that door in a long time. A rope dangles, beckoning. I reach the handle and pull down a ladder that unfolds with some arthritic creaking and, after one more strong yank, sets on the floor.

My heart beats fast. Her studio; as far as I know, Dad has never cleaned it out. I look at the ladder rungs. It's sacred ground up there, and I'm not sure I should do this. I look and look some more, then I climb the rungs. A few steps and there it is; there she is. Not Mom, but the art that was her life. It's like a museum here, a long narrow room covered in cobwebs, and cold, for there is no heat here under the roof. Dad had set up half of the attic for just her, right next to one of two attic windows. He put up dry wall on one side and installed a neon light that snapped on with a metal ball chain, which I pull now. I hate the brash glow it casts, not to mention that maddening buzz; she must have too, because there are two other lamps fitted with incandescent bulbs.

The rest of the attic is behind where I stand, and she would not have seen it if she had been looking at the easel or out the window. The space still radiates fumes of turpentine and oil paint, mixed with attic dust. I love the smell of her art supplies. Her transistor radio! I could switch it on now and, unless the station has changed its programming in the last twenty-five years, I would hear saxophones, clarinets, and a snare drum beating in time through the crackling soundwaves. Mom's wooden easel stands right where it used to, stained with drips of paint; a pile of canvases is stacked on the floor, some blank, some marked with the beginnings of projects left unfinished. In the corner a small cobbled-together table, stained with paint drippings of all colors, holds her tools: brushes, paint tubes now filled with pigmented concrete, and glass jars, large and small, some with crumbs of dried paint in the bottom, others clean and shining in the morning light.

The light and how it changes the shape of everything, shifts color, forms mood. My mother studied light.

Against the wall, there is a stack of sketches; are any of those from the days leading up to her death? I consider lifting them to see, but still, it feels intrusive. And I don't really want to know what she was thinking or feeling in those last days.

"Strange car out front," Dad calls from the bottom of the stairs. I jolt, so surprised I need to grab the back of the chair so I don't fall. I look down the ladder, and there he stands, a rolled-up newspaper in his hands. "Morning."

"Hello," I say. Once my breath recovers, I carefully come down. "Where have you been?"

He helps me push the ladder back up into the ceiling. "Just to the diner for breakfast. Thought I'd get out of the house one more time before this . . . monster storm. Didn't know you were coming or I would've waited."

"It was sort of a last-minute thing," I say. "How're you feeling, Dad?"

"Pretty good and not too bad. Yourself?"

"I'm all right," I say, and I am trying to smile, but I feel like he sees through me.

"Colleen," he says. "I'm sorry for everything you're going through. It's a lot."

I nod slightly. "Thanks."

He starts to walk down the stairs, and I follow. We reach the kitchen, and Dad pulls out a chair for me. "What's the last time someone made you a cup of coffee? Sit down, put your feet up, make yourself at home."

My father can be sweet; sometimes I forget that. Actually, nobody has made me coffee in a long time. A few minutes later, the old plastic Mr. Coffee that I got him years ago for Christmas is percolating away, and we are sitting at the little kitchen table. The skin of his face is ruddy and prickly, and hair that used to be dark is thin now, wispy and white, some strands defying gravity. A year and some months before seventy, and he looks like an old man. But then, he looked like an old man when we were kids, or maybe he just felt old then, always grumbling that these girls were too much for him. And probably we were. Maybe we still are.

He pours us each a cup. "Thanks," I say. "Oh, it's good."

"Mrs. Moschella gets these beans at a place in Salisbury," he says. He tosses a teaspoon toward me. "She tells me they roast them right there. I don't know if that's a big deal, but she seems impressed."

"Mrs. Moschella always knows where to get the good stuff," I say. "How is she? I haven't seen her in a while."

"She's fine. Loves to tell me what great things her grandkids are up to." He gestures dismissively. "I don't talk as much about my amazing grandchildren. I hate to make her feel bad."

I laugh. "Oh, they are amazing," I say. "Those two are my heroes, they've been so great with all the madness. Hey, Dad, be careful with that attic ladder. I noticed a couple of loose boards."

"Yeah, I've been meaning to fix those. Probably need to replace the whole thing or build a real staircase."

I nod and stir my coffee. "And you still haven't—" I point at the mess in the next room.

"Nah," he says, shrugging. "One of these days. I'll have to if I want to sell this place. Hey, you need milk?"

"No, thanks," I say. "Are you thinking about selling, Dad?"

"Just something to consider," he says. "I've been in this house a long time."

"When did you move here? Was it after Alex was born?"

"She was a baby, I think," he says. "And she's, what, now, thirty-six? Yup, thirty-five years sounds about right."

I stare into the dark well of my coffee. Mom must have been young then, I think, maybe just twenty-two. A baby herself, with a husband eight years older. They had their summer fling on a small scenic Maine cove, complete with a rocky coastline and lush pine trees. The story he always told us was that when he asked her to marry him, he never expected her to say yes. Alex thinks she must have been pregnant, but Mom was gone by the time we were old enough to even have that idea. And Dad never told us.

"Dad, how did you and Mom meet?"

He shrugs and looks at the ceiling for a moment, like he's trying to remember. Finally, he twists up his face and speaks. "It was a small town. Everybody knew everybody." He sighs. "I was about to join the army."

"The army? I had no idea."

"Yup, I was going to sign up in the fall, so I spent the summer helping out on my uncle's fishing boat. I saw your mom all around South Williston, sitting by the cove with her easel; or biking around with her painting supplies strapped to a milk carton; or sitting on the beach, laughing with friends. She painted landscapes for tourists to buy in gift shops. Made decent money doing it too."

"Why didn't you stay? If people loved her paintings, she could have kept selling them."

"Life is rough in small Maine towns," he says. "Summers are beautiful, but they don't last. And winters can be . . . long and lonely. I thought she'd be happier in Massachusetts."

"Dad," I start. "I have a weird question for you. Was Mom married before you?"

He looks surprised. "What?"

"Alex found an engagement announcement," I say. "Someone O'Dowd."

He smiles and looks out the window and far away. "She never told me the whole story. Just that he was the son of someone her dad worked with. There was a big wedding and a fancy honeymoon. But a month later, she filed for annulment."

"And she didn't tell you why or what happened?"

He shakes his head. "Nope."

My gaze falls on the table. "Is that when she quit college? Did she . . . quit college and then move to Maine?"

"I don't exactly know. All she told me is that she left under unhappy circumstances."

"That's all she told you? Her own husband? She never spoke to her family again, and she never mentioned why?" He shakes his head. "But did you ask?"

He grimaces slightly and shrugs slowly. "If she didn't want to tell me, who was I to hound her? It was painful for her. I didn't want to make her dredge that up if she didn't want to."

I try to line things up in my mind, and I drum my fingers on the table. Her marriage to her father's business partner's son didn't work out, so she quit college—right before she graduated—and broke things off with her family and headed east alone.

Or maybe that was the punishment. If you can't make this marriage work, then you are hereby cut off from the family and from all the family money, including college tuition payments.

"Okay," I continue, feeling bold now. "Was Mom . . . was she pregnant before you got married?"

He frowns and wraps his hands around his mug. "All these things I never talked to you kids about. She was supposed to tell you, you know?"

"I know," I say. "But she didn't."

He smiles. "She was a golden girl from out of town, she could have had anybody, and plenty of guys tried, believe me. Local kids like me and the prep school boys on their fathers' yachts. Frankly, I was amazed she wanted anything to do with me. But she'd look at me and smile, and my day got good." His face looks far away, like he's watching her move through the house doing something wonderful like carrying a birthday cake covered in lit candles.

I blurt out my thought, because I never really understood before this moment. "You adored her."

He glances at me sheepishly, a little embarrassed. "Sure."

"All these years, I never thought about it . . . how much you must have missed her," I say.

He sighs. "I missed her a lot. Still do. I never thought we wouldn't grow old together. To answer your other question," he says, tapping one thick finger on the table. "Your mom was expecting Alex before we got married."

"She was?" I say. "But you're Alex's—"

He laughs. "Oh, yes, certainly. I always knew I was, but seeing her grow up, your sister has habits that I can trace back to every branch of the Emery family tree."

I laugh, but then my father's face becomes thoughtful.

"Sometimes, I wonder if we were ready for marriage. We tried to pretend, at least to ourselves, that her being pregnant wasn't the only reason we were getting hitched. But the truth is, it probably was."

"Daddy," I say, because I'm going the distance now. "Do you know why she did it?"

He considers this raw, awful question. He grimaces again; he's right to think carefully, because whatever he says next will be added to the montage in my head that plays over and over. These next words go down in indelible ink.

Finally, he takes in breath and speaks. "Your mom had an illness. She did what she did because she was sick."

Okay, this we've heard before. Suddenly I feel desperate. "No, Dad," I say. "There must be more to it. She was alive one day, and the next day she wasn't. Something happened. Someone said or did something. If it's something I did, or one of us, you can tell me. Don't think I can't hear it. I can. I would rather know."

He stands then and lumbers across the room to lean against the kitchen counter with his arms crossed in front of him. "Sweetie, you must never think that what your mother did was because of you. She loved her girls. All of you." He looks down and sighs. "Susie and me, we got married in the town hall with a couple of friends as witnesses. It was late September, but a heat wave made it feel like the height of summer."

"Sounds romantic," I say.

"Well, it was simple. Not like her first wedding, but that's how she wanted it," he says. "And we didn't have any money. After that, we went on what we called a honeymoon, just one night because I was due to take the civil service exam two days later. We packed a few things, got some bread and cheese, a bottle of wine, and headed off in my pickup truck to a small lake. We had the place to ourselves, and we pulled out sleeping bags and lay under the stars and talked about the future. You know, the kids we'd have, the life we were planning. All that."

As he talks, the memory registers on his face like he is there, drinking in the Milky Way, gasping at every shooting star.

His face shifts then, a gravity darkens his eyes. "She was so small in my arms, like a child, and I kept thinking what a miracle it was that I'd been entrusted with not just one beautiful life, but two. And for a while that night, she was happy, but then something in her changed. She became quiet. Then she started to cry. 'I'm going to ruin your life,' she said. Over and over, 'I'm so sorry; I'm going to ruin your life.'"

Then, my father, who I don't remember ever seeing cry, begins to weep, but so quietly someone else might almost not realize it was happening. He rubs his forehead, like the very remembering of this is making his temple throb. "I told her, 'No, it isn't true. I love you, Suzanne. You *are* my life. You and this little being. It's going to be a whole new world for us.' But she kept crying. Nothing I said could calm her down."

He is silent then, his gaze away from me, and I do not speak. "I wanted to protect her from what was hurting her. But when I couldn't . . . when she . . . I'm the one that failed her."

I realize that I have forgotten about my coffee. I put my hands around the mug, but it has become cold. "You didn't fail her," I whisper.

He grins, like he appreciates my effort. "That day, I mean, the day *it* happened, someone chased me down on my route to tell me to go home, but they didn't know what the emergency was. I got home and saw the ambulance parked in the driveway, and Alex standing in the front yard, her face blank with shock. They were bringing the stretcher out of the house, and I convinced myself that the person under the sheet was someone else, someone I didn't know. But it only lasted a moment."

I pull a pack of tissues from my purse and offer him one, but he wipes his face against his sleeve. "I wish I could have saved her. She seemed so helpless against it . . ."

"Against what, Dad?" I say.

"Sadness, I guess, or depression, that might be the technical name these days," he says. "When the sun was shining for her, everything was A-OK. But when it wasn't, the pain she carried was deep. It destroyed her from the inside."

I don't know what to say. To that or any of this. "Did she ever see a doctor?" I ask.

He shrugs. "She wanted the sickness to go away, and she thought the best way to do that was to live as though it wasn't happening."

"Oh, Dad," I say.

"She talked to her regular doc, but he . . ." He stops and stares at the floor for a moment, then sighs. "He gave her Valium for anxiety. I told her pills never fixed anything. They sure didn't this time."

"The pills she took that knocked her out . . ." I say slowly, because I'm forming the thought as the words come out. "Were those the . . . Valium, the ones that she . . . ?"

Daddy nods and looks down. "She'd saved them up, then she took them all at once with vodka. The coroner told me later. It made it easier for her to not resist drowning."

"Oh, Dad," I say. And suddenly I have heard all that I can hear for today. I stand up. "Daddy, I'm so sorry."

He nods. "This family has been through a lot," he says. "And I wish it hadn't turned out this way. But I loved your mother. I'm still proud that she picked me. And I took care of you three the best I could, although I think I didn't do a very good job."

"No, Dad," I say. I hug him. "You did a great job."

Then I pull away. "I should go," I say, and I go to the painting and lift it up like it is the hand of a child I need to take home with me. I grab my coat and my purse and my jingling keys. "Thanks for telling me the truth, Dad. I mean it. It's better to know the truth than not know."

"Take it easy with the storm," he says.

"You too," I say.

Then with my painting in hand, I walk out into the temperate winter's day under a sky that turned slate gray while I was inside. I want to go home, I think, and I walk away from the house of my childhood toward a borrowed cottage on the beach.

I drive away from Dad's house and into Amesbury Center, where I park in a bank parking lot and dial Alex's cell phone. "Are you in the car or at the paint store?" I say.

"I am counting shades of white," she says. "There's pinkish-white and purple-white and brownish-white and creamy-white and light-bright white and muted white and a few dozen more, and that's not even including ivory or beige. It's making me seasick. How was your talk with Dad?"

"Good," I say. "I have news. Do you want to meet for lunch?"

"No, let's talk now; this storm is making me nervous," she says.

"All right, well, find someplace where you can sit down," I say. "This is interesting."

Chapter 21

Sunday, March 2, 2014
Riley

Nate and I meander through night streets in the East Village in the early morning, unnoticed as ghosts. I decide I can forgive the fact, finally uncovered, that he has been following me, and that he knows about the one thing in my life that I try to keep totally private, my son. I forgive because with him, I feel steadied, and I am grateful for his company. The blowing wind is cold, parching my cheeks, burning them or freezing them. It's here now, still, again, that sticky, retchy feeling of withdrawal. My heart is racing, and my mouth is dry as baking soda. I would sell all my secrets to the FBI for a bottle of water, but I don't want to let him see me take a pill. Maybe he already knows about all that, but I want to preserve some part of the illusion of the person I am playing. Who is that person? Pretty Riley; not an addict, a woman with a few life things to clean up and flowing locks and easy laughter. A person I never was, so it's nice, at least, to pretend.

He and I are quiet as we go. Finally, he speaks. "Do we—are we going anywhere in particular?"

"I don't think so," I say, looking up. "Do you have any ideas?"

He thinks for a moment. "One time, years ago, I was out all night, probably drinking," he says. "It was a group of us. But at dawn we ended up on Williamsburg Bridge, watching the sun rise. Have you ever seen that?"

"No," I say.

"It's neat," he says. He stretches his arms out in front of us, like he is unveiling something wonderful. "It's like time stops. Golden light illuminates the city of Manhattan. All the buildings in the East Village . . . they gleam. I don't want to get too sentimental, but it's . . . worth seeing, anyway."

He smiles at me with a genuine kindness and warmth that I don't experience very often. The sun rising over the Williamsburg Bridge. It sounds amazing. And this, I decide, is what I want this night. To see the sunrise with him.

"The Williamsburg Bridge isn't too far from here, right?" I say. "Can we go there?"

"Yeah, we're pretty close already," he says. "The sun should come up a little after six." He checks his phone. "Six twenty-seven, to be exact. But we should be there before that. So we have two hours."

"Let's do it. Please, can we? Please say yes," I say, grabbing the bottom of his jacket like a child.

He smiles, laughs. "Okay, okay. What do you want to do until then?"

I say, "Just this, I guess. Walk around."

"Riley, wait." He looks into my face, his eyes meeting mine with a quizzical expression. "It's late. If you're tired, we don't need to do this."

"I'm fine," I say. I smile and gesture, "Let's go!" with my head. But the truth is, I'm exhausted. And my Valentino boots are soaked. My feet ache so much, each step is a struggle. I don't know if I can make it. Please, to all the forces of the cosmos, let me hold my breath long enough to see the sun rise over the East River. Give me this one night, one morning, one last sunrise. And then, I promise, I will go home and do what I have decided to do. What I have promised. I will go to sleep, the last sleep of a long day.

"Wait," he says. "You're shaking."

He takes off his coat then takes off his blazer, then puts his coat back on. "No," I say. "You don't need . . . you'll be cold."

He slips my coat off and helps me put the blazer on. His blazer. Then he puts my coat back on over it.

"Better?" he asks.

I smile. "Yes," I say. "Thanks. You're sure you're not too cold?"

"Don't worry about me," he says.

"All right, which way do we go?"

He looks up and down the street, then he looks at his phone and picks a direction. "This way."

We cross a street and then stand on the next corner beneath a streetlight. We wander the sidewalks of Manhattan's Lower East Side, crossing streets quick and lithe, the way starlight crosses dimensions. My mind snaps back to how we look in the magazine spread of my imagination, and now I've called in wardrobe for a switch: he's wearing a well-cut suit, I am in a white slip dress under a mink coat, my hair glossy white with a thick curl to it, like Jayne Mansfield. Our eyes are locked on one another, and I smile knowingly, my ruby red lips pressed closed. Click.

We cross another street, and suddenly, I am drenched in fatigue and nausea. I would feel better if I had a drink of water. I would feel better, so much better, if I simply took a pill.

"You're quiet," he says.

"I like just walking with you," I say.

"Me too," he says, and he looks at me and smiles for a moment.

It makes me happy when he smiles at me. But now that he's looking at me, I am suddenly aware that if I feel like a mess, I probably look that way too. I can feel my hair frizzing and the skin under my eyes beginning to swell. We walk past a grocery window, and even in the dull streetlight, I can see it, my makeup fading, my smile melting. Some concealer, I need; and dry shampoo would help; but I can't carry any of that in my tiny clutch. I stand for a moment before the dark, reflective glass. "Hold on a sec," I say. I take a sample packet of hand cream from my purse, tear it open and smear it on my fingertips and touch it into my hair. If that's the least I can do, I'll do at least that.

"What is that?" he says, laughing.

"Just need a touch-up." I dab it lightly onto the strands of my hair until

I look a bit smoother, not photo ready, but better. Then he stands beside me, peering in the shop window.

"Cigarettes, lottery tickets," he says, reading the signs inside. "Tangerines on sale."

I stop fixing my hair and look at the reflection of the two of us in the window. Here we are, two strangers on a New York street. I wish we were friends. I wish we were lovers. I wish my life had gone a different way; maybe we could have gotten married. A small wedding, a chapel service in the morning, all sweet and white, with a chamber quartet playing Pachelbel's Canon. My hair curled in golden ringlets that flank my face. My dress would be just simple and white. Caleb would be so handsome in his suit.

Would Nate and Caleb get along? This is all a daydream, so why not? Nate would adopt Caleb. We could start over, the three of us. It's too much to imagine, but I let myself do it anyway. I would give my sweet, serious boy a father, one who's smart like he is, and funny in his own way. I look over at Nate, who is gazing around us, hands in his pockets. He would make a good father. He'd help Caleb with his school work. He'd take Caleb to the park on Saturday mornings. Caleb could make Father's Day cards for him at school. I imagine Nate reading *Pete the Cat* to him, and next year, helping Caleb read by himself.

Maybe I could get through all this if I wasn't alone. I would give up the drugs. I would find other work, maybe I'd even finish college. I'd learn how to make dinner, how to shop for groceries.

My mind spins with dreams; I shake my head to ward off the daze. I don't know anything about this man. Why am I letting myself get carried away? But then again, something about being with him feels right, so why not? Maybe this is the night I let myself get swept off my feet.

"It's hard to imagine that the city that never sleeps could be this quiet," he says. "Only time I ever see it like this is when it snows."

"I love the city in the snow," I say. "It's like magic, everything glistens. It hasn't snowed at all this winter, has it?"

"We had some flurries," he says. "But nothing big."

I look around. Again, I am completely confused about where we are. I could check the map on my own phone but my hands are cold and I want to keep them in my pockets. "Which way is the river? Is it over here? Let's please go."

"We're on our way," he says. "No need to rush." He checks his phone. "We still have more than an hour."

The air is changing; it's becoming misty and slightly warmer. The traffic is growing busier, and the air is thickening with sounds of cars swishing through the streets.

"But where are we?" I ask.

"Well, that's East Houston, so we're close." He punches something else into his phone and shows me the map. "Twenty-minute walk. All right? Here, let's sit down for a bit. There's a bench right over there."

"Okay," I say. I sit reluctantly; I don't want him to see how uncomfortable I am. My throat hurts, my head hurts, my legs are freezing, and I feel like all possibility is leaving my body. I need a pill, just one. I think of the ones at home, the whole huge pile of them. Just waiting for me and all the pain they will erase.

And yet—why not simply feel all this? There is no other moment for me but this one, this beautiful moment, filled to the brim with pain and beauty and love and heartbreak.

We sit on the bench, and almost without thinking, I squeeze up beside him. "You're still shivering," he says.

"I'm okay."

"Please let me take you home," he says. "You need to rest."

"Not yet," I insist, sitting straight up.

"Why are you so intent to see the sunrise?" he says. "The sun comes up every morning, every day."

Tears are in my eyes. I look into his face. *Not for me.* But these are words I cannot speak out loud.

"Nate," I ask. "What will you tell them about me? I mean, whoever's looking for me."

He looks down. "I don't know," he says, sitting on the bench beside me. "I'm not supposed to be doing this, you know. This strange Manhattan walkabout."

"What you're not supposed to be doing is talking to me," I say. The traffic a few feet from us is stalled at a red traffic light; the light changes, plastic green now, and they all make their way forward, into the gloom of the quickly fading night. "Who is it? Who asked you to spy on me?"

He looks away, mouth flat, eyes searching. "I can't . . ."

"Yes, you can," I say. "I need to know who's so curious that they had to hire a detective?"

He turns to me and looks at my face. "Someone who's worried about you and wants to make sure you're safe."

Aha, if my safety was at risk, there could only be one person. "Colleen, then. Yes?"

"Riley, stop. It doesn't matter."

I sit back and cross my arms. I sigh. "Please, when you talk to her, tell her that I'm all right, okay? Tell her—make sure she knows—that I have problems, but they're my problems. I know she would have liked to help me, but the truth is, I'm beyond help."

"Riley, why so many secrets?" he asks. "Why don't you just tell your family what's happening in your life? They can help you. Let them try."

I consider what it would feel like if I told them about all the mistakes I've made, and then the further mistakes, mistakes upon mistakes, covering up the first round like sloppy brush strokes of clotted white-out, and mucking it all up worse. It's almost funny to wonder, how did I get here? It started, I suppose, in Amesbury, at the small house with the white picket fence on Greenwood Street, with the gutter hanging off the roof and the rusted swing set in the backyard. And the loss of the one person who could have saved me. And the boy down the street, and a violation that never left my body or my heart.

The very idea of telling my family anything about my life is overwhelming. I laugh a little then sink my head into my hands in despair.

"If I ever told anybody," I say, vaguely aware that tears are streaming from my eyes. "If I had to listen to myself speaking those words out loud, my heart would simply break."

"He's your son, isn't he?" Nate asks, his hands in his pockets, gaze down, like he cannot meet my eyes. "The boy in the pictures."

I sigh. I don't have the energy to resist this anymore. "His name is Caleb," I say.

"Yes, Caleb," he says. "Riley, I . . . I accessed the New York Child Protective Service's databases. I know about the order of disposition."

"Tell me you didn't," I whisper.

"You made a mistake, Riley," he says. "But the order of disposition is a legal plan, it's a list of things you can do to get your son back. You were supposed to get clean, take a parenting class, attend supervised visits with your son."

I glare at him. I am at once furious that he has hacked into this part of my life, and yet, grateful. I'm glad he knows. Now I won't have to tell him.

"All those things, you could do them. You can get him back," he says. "In fact, the state desperately wants to give him back to you. You can start tomorrow. If you at least try, you could have him back by summer."

But Nate, I think. *You don't understand. He's better off without me.* The tears fall straight down from my face into my lap.

"Riley," he whispers, "please, don't cry." He puts his hand on my cheek to wipe away my tears.

I look into his dark eyes. How I wish we hadn't met this way. If only we'd found each other in a different place, at a different time. Tonight is too late, like meeting someone on vacation while you're on the bus to the airport to catch a flight home.

"I know," I say, and another tear falls. He brushes it away with his thumb.

The sky is one more shade lighter, as though the layers of darkness are being peeled away.

I can't keep thinking about this, so I force myself to get to my feet. "Please can we keep going," I say. "If we get there late, we'll miss the whole thing."

"Riley—"

"Come on," I say. "It's not far. Please?"

"Can we talk about this later?" he asks.

I look away for a moment. "Yes. Later. But for now, let's find the bridge."

He stands up, groaning with exhaustion, then off we go, continuing our wander in the direction of where the sky is lightening fastest.

We walk, and I realize, I truly am comfortable with this man. Until I was fired, I was almost constantly surrounded by people, but sometimes I felt so lonely. This man beside me, I keep looking at his face and feeling so happy to see him. With him, I don't feel so alone.

Is this how falling in love works? I'm not sure. I've never done it before.

A few moments later, I see something across the street. I stop and turn to look.

"You okay?" he says.

The street is empty in both directions for a moment, and I step off the curb and begin to cross.

"Wait, where are you going?" he says.

It is a storefront window for a travel agency, a display of different posters tacked to a board and lit from underneath. The posters are sending you on different vacations—one to Greece with its sky-blue ocean, one to the Cayman Islands for sailing, one to the Grand Canyon where the cliffs form clay-red sculptures. And another to Key West, where you will scuba dive. This is the one that transfixes me. The poster depicts a sea turtle with its powerful flippers, its serious face, and dark, wise eyes. It is the turtle that I see, that has called me across the street.

My hand floats up and touches the glass.

"What's going on?" he says.

I start to open my mouth to talk, but no words come out. Finally, I whisper one word: "Caleb."

And I remember that day, a really good day. Caleb was four, and the air was warm and summery. I had taken him to the Museum of Natural History, and we had spent over an hour in an exhibit about sea turtles. When he spotted a stuffed turtle in the gift shop, he begged me to get it for him.

"Please, Mama, please?" he said, jumping. "I take good care of him."

What did we name the turtle? I hardly ever remember because we usually only call him Turtle. Oh, yes! Lester Hard-Hat. Lester quickly rose in ranks to become my boy's favorite lovey. His green fur lost its luster, and his shape went from firm to squishy. He wasn't shiny anymore, but he was loved beyond measure.

The morning I got the call from ACS about Caleb wandering the street, my heart stopped and my blood ran ice-water cold. I knew I had made a mistake and I knew it was a bad one. All I needed them to tell me was: how can I get Caleb his turtle? Please don't be so horrible as to deny a boy his turtle.

I was allowed to bring a bag in for him. Lester was the first thing in.

Caleb and his turtle. Caleb, turtle-like himself, with a wisdom that seemed turtle-ancient, a heart with a thick shell around it, and a home that he'd learned to pack into a small space that he could carry with him. My baby boy, who clung to whoever was caring for him; somehow, he realized that I was the one who was fragile. When I said goodbye the day he went into foster care, he did not cry. He seemed ready, like he knew it was coming and had expected for a long time.

Lester, I think, certain that with my hand on the surface of the glass window he will receive my message, *please take care of my boy. Keep him safe always. Make sure he feels loved and cared for. Find the people who will care for him.*

"Riley," Nate says. "Are you all right?"

I turn to look at him. What does this man know about sea turtles, who cross thousands of miles of open ocean to find the place of their birth? Without a map or a compass or a GPS, their hearts are simply pulled to the place where they are supposed to be. They know in their physical cells what direction they need to move in, and somehow, they always find that place, their true home.

May we all be so lucky.

"Riley?"

My eyes fill with tears. "You don't know. You can't know. I hate myself. When he was taken away, there was a pit in my stomach. I wanted him back, but . . . what if . . . why did I think I could take care of another person? I can't even take care of myself."

It's too much to bear, so I lean my forehead against the cold concrete wall of this building.

"Riley," Nate says, trying to envelop me. "Okay, listen to me. We're going to get you help. It's not like you made a choice; addiction is a sickness. We're going to get you into therapy. You will get your son back. You can turn this around."

I push myself back from the building. My face feels hot and swollen.

This is not a moment for Instagram. I smile slightly; his optimism cheers me up. "I like hearing that," I say. *But Nate*, I think. *It's already over.*

I look at his face, so earnest in the chill morning. I dab my eyes with the sleeve of his jacket.

"I'm worried about you," he says quietly.

"Don't be," I say. "I'm just a little exhausted. Hey, do you have a tissue?"

"Check my pocket," he says. "I might have a spare napkin from a bagel I had for lunch."

I find the napkin and blow my nose. "Sorry," I say. "So unladylike. Which way do we go now? I still want to see the sunrise."

I glance around and suddenly notice a bridge's rectangular tower in the distance. "Oh, is that our bridge?"

"It is," he says. "But I'm not sure the best way to get to it from here. Let me check." Nate checks his phone, looking around to get his bearings.

As he studies the map, I look back at the poster of the turtle. "Don't forget, Lester," I whisper. "Take care of my boy. You promised."

"We need to get to Delancey," he says. Then he points. "We'll go down East Huston then cut across on Ludlow Street."

Now that we have a plan, we walk with purpose down East Houston, passing shops and cafés and restaurants and smoke shops, almost everything closed and locked up with a few more hours still before the gates go up and they are open for business. I am quiet, and my eyes are so tired. Our arms are linked again, and it feels right. I keep forgetting that he's been hired to follow me. Why did he switch from following me to accompanying me? And what, exactly, does he know about me?

Does it even matter? I'm not sure.

A few minutes later, Nate steers me to the right, another street full of restaurants: Chinese, Thai, Italian, Mexican. Does anybody in this city cook? I don't see why they would bother.

We cross a street and then finally, amazingly, we are standing at the gate to the bridge.

"Are you ready?" Nate asks.

I smile, I nod, and so we begin making our way up the slow slope to the bridge.

The footpath is paved, the dark asphalt decorated with loads of color-ful graffiti. Cars cross the bridge on a thoroughfare below the footpath, and there is a subway track below us as well, and every now and then we hear a train rumbling into or out of Brooklyn. Around us in all directions are the massive steel-iron elements of bridge structure, all painted a faded red: teeth, ribs, fingers, arms, girders, beams, pipes, supports. It feels alive.

We walk for what seems like a long time; we don't walk slowly, but we don't rush either. And even though it is early on a Sunday morning, a handful of cyclists pass us, and a few pedestrians too. But none of them stop to see what we are following: to the east, a crack in the darkness that is quickly leaking sunlight. We smile at each other. The crack melts into a swath, and the sky above the horizon looks as though it is melting. We keep walking, and finally, Nate and I are high up over the river, standing in the cold wind, and the water far below us swirls and churns in the wake of a barge passing through. My hair blows in all directions; I grasp it to keep it out of my eyes. The molten orange becomes a band of pale winter yellow that quickly turns gold. The buildings of the Manhattan skyline in front of us appear in dark profile against the dawn. Nate leans on the fence that separates us from the tall partition that serves to discourage jumpers. I put my hands on the cold railing for support. We watch—witness—the stretch of orange spill its brilliance through the whole sky.

"Look," he says.

I do look. I am looking.

Suddenly, the orb of the sun approaches; a moment later it bursts above, and the star itself rises. It's still New York and the morning is not silent; cars and trucks thunder along beneath us and the train lumbers trough periodically. But this does not lessen the magic. It still feels like the world is holding its breath, witnessing the cracking open, the spilling forth of all possibility. In the fractured light, the tall beautiful buildings of Manhattan, capture the radiance and glow as though on cold fire.

This is the kind of thing God gets up early to see.

"See how the sun is just above the horizon?" Nate says. "Photographers call this the Golden Hour."

I nod.

And now the sky is whitish blue; it is simply daybreak. A group of joggers runs past us. This is my city; this is my home. I am not from this place, but I have become who I am here. So much have I grown here; and much have I lost. Here on this bridge, I am hovering above a landscape of concrete, buildings and lots, and the swirling surface of the East River.

The city is an ugly beast; I love it like none other.

I turn away from the cold wind to stand close to Nate, and I put my hand upon his face. We do not kiss, but I press my face against his. I breathe in the aftershave on his coat.

I wish we could stay like this.

He pushes me away slightly and takes my hand.

"Sunrise. Now," he says, "let me send you home."

I nod. And we turn and walk back down the path on the bridge to Delancey. The sun is fully up now, and the city has resumed its usual pace of wide awake and breathlessly busy; the night and the sunrise are both long gone, almost forgotten.

"I'm going to hail you a cab, but take this," Nate says, and he digs a business card out of his wallet.

"Oh, you found one," I say, remembering how he tried to give me a fake business card so many hours ago.

He smiles, chagrined to be caught in his own story. "Okay, that's my cell." He points to the number on the bottom of the card. "Go home. Get some rest. Call me later. Promise."

"Only if you buy me breakfast," I say.

"Absolutely," he says. Nate hails a taxi and helps me get in.

"Where can I take you?" says the driver.

"Home," I say.

He sighs heavily, loudly. "I don't know where that is, lady."

Me neither, I think. But I give him the address to luscious Lucia's lovely lair.

As the cab pulls away from the curb, we watch each other until we no longer see one another. What does it matter that he was hired to follow me? It could have been the most adorable meet-cute on the Fifth Avenue cocktail soirée circuit.

Could have been? Almost was. Never will be.

The cab brings me to Lucia's apartment building, and I let myself in; it feels cold and empty. For the next hour, I lie on the mattress in my coat, wearing his jacket, listening to the sounds of neighbors awakening: footsteps clunking, voices speaking, showers humming. Then I rise, drink several cups of water, and take a hot shower. I put on clean clothes: a pair of jeans, a white shirt, and the blazer. His blazer.

It still smells like him. I didn't imagine it. He was real.

Then I sit down with my clutch and take out my beloved pill. I take it out of the pillbox and put it in my cheek. I suck slightly, letting it dissolve and melt into my bloodstream. I feel the narcotic taking effect; the pain in the bottoms of my feet and the horrible cold are receding from the surface of my skin. When I feel better, I take the big bottle from the back of a cabinet in the kitchen; this is the stashed-away stash.

And I begin.

These I swallow. I swallow a pill, and I swallow a pill, and I swallow a pill. I drink some water, then stop for a few moments; I'm hoping that going slowly will help me keep everything down. Then I swallow two pills, and two pills, and two pills. Another break. Nausea surges through me, but I sit and tell the heaving to stay calm. Pain leaves my body like I never knew what it was. I am filled with a sense of relief—relief that I am doing this, relief that it's almost over.

But what about Caleb? How can I do this to my son? This that was done to me. His face when they tell him; I can see it crumple with disbelief and heartbreak. The moment you break a child's heart is the moment you wish you'd never breathed on this earth.

But the effects of the chemicals take me over, and these thoughts dissolve from my mind. All at once, I am beautiful and loved. I am a child treasured by my family; I have friends and loves without number. I have a love, somewhere in the city, who will come find me later—he knows where I live! And he will hold me and comfort me.

And we shall all live happily ever after.

I turn on the news and snuggle way in deep under the covers. The weather report comes on just as I begin to doze. *A big storm is coming,* says someone on the screen, a man or a woman, I'm not sure; I can't really see past the map of the region behind them. *Big, big storm*, they say. *Rain and wind up and down the East Coast. High tides and storm surge could mean problems for coastal New England. Batten the hatches, everybody . . . gonna be a doozy . . .*

Chapter 22

Sunday, March 2, 2014
Alex

Even the girl who checked me out at the paint store this morning asked if I was ready for the storm. I told her I was, and left it at that. She doesn't need to know that I'll be hunkering down in a house that has the structural integrity of a wood pile. If the storm goes the way they're predicting, it could be impressive. High winds mean likely power loss and a good probability of storm-surge flooding. The good news is that it's the new moon; a full moon high tide with a storm like this could really cause problems.

Can the house withstand what's coming? I guess I'll find out.

I asked Colleen to stay with me, but she has a better offer. The truth is, I don't want to deal with this thing on my own. And if the power goes out, I don't want to be by myself in the dark. Actually, that terrifies me.

The weather report says that the storm will start in the afternoon. By lunchtime I'm home from the day's errands and spend the afternoon looking out the window every five minutes as though waiting for party guests. Around two o'clock the rain begins in earnest. The tiny hairs on my arms stand up; something is coming.

I make myself a cup of tea and sit at the kitchen table and listen to rain on the windows, watch gray sky weep over the brown marsh. At three thirty the power goes out. I try to call Colleen and realize that my cell service has stopped working. Now I'm nervous; I hope she reached her family safely. Between the rain on the roof and the wind battering the house, the sound of rattling and pelting is steady, and I constantly wonder if *it's* starting again. The rain and wind bring down a year's worth of dead leaves and twigs, covering the yard. I'm not excited about cleaning that up. The work never ends, the list of projects just keeps expanding. Still, I am starting to feel a kind of fondness for this place.

I need to be on my guard with this house. I will begin to feel like I belong here, like there is a connection between us, and it will be too hard to walk away. Make no mistake. I plan to walk away.

I fold myself up in the window seat and try to read a paperback novel in the daylight that filters through the clouds. It is quite possibly the worst book I have ever read, but I don't want to put it down; it's my only source of companionship. As the afternoon proceeds, I feel more distracted; I have now read the same paragraph so many times I've almost memorized it.

At five the rain comes down in thick sheets. I look outside; the sky is darkening with a sunset that happens behind black clouds. Night falls, and the sky becomes pitch dark; the only light in the house is the three emergency candles I have lit in the living room and the flashlight I am trying to conserve. I've consumed some of the snacks I stockpiled: the Saltines, paired to perfection with crunchy peanut butter and the occasional garnish of M&M's. The rain is steady, but the wind is growing stronger. The strange rattling throughout the house continues. I know that I am here alone, but still, I keep wanting to call out, ask if someone's out there. Trees in the woods behind the house creak achingly, like bone scraping bone. The wind breaks against my windows, howling like a creature lost in the storm. These are the sounds invoked in fairy tales, and for good reason: they remind us that home, safety, shelter, it's all an illusion.

Sounds that remind us that what's outside must not be let in.

And then, in the darkness, it begins: footsteps overhead, first slow and tentative, then fast, someone running back and forth. Shards of voices whispering. Suddenly, the room is freezing.

I don't know what is happening, but I won't let it scare me. "I don't believe it," I say aloud, though I don't sound very convinced. "No ghosts, no goblins; there is nothing here."

And yet, something is here. I listen as hard as I can, trying to make out words, like eavesdropping on a bus. The voices are calm and hushed, an occasional sad whimper. Girls' voices mostly, but then it's men talking again, and a child crying out. That is the worst. I sit straight up and shudder.

It's time to open the wine. With a shaking hand, I pour it into a glass, then go back to my perch at the window. On the way, I walk through something damp, wet. In the flashlight's beam, I look around. Rain is pouring in through a gap in the window frame.

"Oh, great," I say. I put the wine down and go to a stack of towels in the kitchen and grab two. One I use to wipe the perimeter of the window then put down where the water is pooling on the floor. The other I use to dry the places where the water is splattering, then drape over my shoulder.

Later, I need to go upstairs and look for leaks, but not right now.

The things I hear cannot hurt me; they're only noise. At least, this is what I tell myself. The wild wind shrieks, and the house shudders in response. We are a ship on the ocean, casting about in boiling waters, almost toppling over but not quite. I wish I had a cat. I desperately wish I had a cat.

Footsteps in the room behind me halt, as though the walker noticed me and stopped to see what I would do. I don't turn around. I pick up my wine and sit in the window seat. "You are not there," I declare aloud.

A gash of lightning hammers the yard, and I yelp in shocked response. I look outside; for one moment, everything is lit up like daytime, like fire. Outside, at the edge of my peripheral vision, I glimpse a figure. I shake my head and reject the idea. Nobody is in here; nobody is out there.

Upstairs, then, voices ring out, muddled. I still can't hear the words, but I can make out the tone. The voices are not angry, I decide. They are urgent. Suddenly, I'm less scared; I'm curious. I stand and listen. They are men's voices, enmeshed in something critical. This time, my ears tease out the words, "What's your name?" And a moment later, "Miss, you need to go outside."

Miss, you need to go outside.

This is not just voices, it's a memory—my memory. I leave the glass of wine on the mantle and walk to the foot of the stairs and stand there in deep wonderment. It's that day. I remember now . . . I called 911, and it seemed like I had barely put down the receiver when the police arrived. Ambulance and fire truck would follow, but the police came in right away. They pounded the door and it swung open; there were two men in uniform.

"Are you the little girl who called us?" asked one.

I held my breath. I knew that if I tried to speak, I would burst out in tears.

"What's your name?" he asked.

"Alex," I whispered.

"Can you show us where the bathroom is?" he asked.

I pointed up the stairs and one of them went up while the other stayed and asked me questions. Where was my Dad? Where were my sisters? Was there a neighbor I could go stay with? Was there a relative they should call for me?

I don't know how I answered any of it, or if I spoke at all.

"Dave," called the officer who was upstairs, "you got to come up here."

The officer I was talking to looked at me calmly and said, "The ambulance will be here in a few moments. I need you to go outside and wait for them, so they know they're at the right house. All right?"

I nodded, but as he walked up the stairs, I did not go. I couldn't leave them—or her. I quietly walked up the stairs and stood outside the bathroom where the two men were leaning over the bathtub, trying to pull her out.

One of them noticed me. "*Miss, you need to go outside,*" he shouted.

Their sleeves rolled up to their biceps, arms in the water, trying to hold her up, hair dripping, water sloshing all over the floor.

"Alex," called out the first one. "Honey, please go outside so the ambulance can find the house."

I stood there and shook and said nothing.

Eventually, I was outside. I know that because I remember standing there and watching the fire truck pull up at the curb and then the ambulance. Soon after that, Dad came home.

I was eleven years old, in sixth grade at Amesbury Elementary School. My biggest frustration the day before had been that I had gouged a hole in my favorite stone-washed jeans when I tripped on the blacktop at school. And I was sick of hearing Madonna on the radio. I was learning clarinet, I loved whales, I wanted to be a marine biologist when I grew up. My sisters and I were like any family: we played board games, fought over everything, rode our bikes, griped about chores and homework.

But after that day, everything changed. Dad shut down, and Colleen and I had to grow up on the spot, raising Riley, making sure there was food in the refrigerator, buying clothes, folding laundry, booking dentist appointments, and calling the plumber. Our childhoods, all three of them, dissolved that day. When we were scared at night, we had to comfort ourselves; when we wanted dinner, we had to make it. Colleen and I hopscotched into adulthood, fueled by a maturity born, not of experience, but of necessity.

The girl who played baseball in the street with the neighborhood boys went away that day and never came back again.

Miss, you need to go outside, barked the policeman.

Is it possible that I have been painting this memory on these walls since the moment I walked in here? Maybe all that has been happening in this house hasn't been from squirrels or bad wiring, nor spirits of former residents. Maybe these are my memories, hung around me like laundry on a clothesline.

Do memories choose us or do we choose our memories?

I don't know, but maybe a memory can put itself before you and insist that you reckon with it. "I remember," I whisper. "Yes, I remember."

But why this, why have I been replaying the moment the police found my mother's body?

Because, whispers a voice in my head. *This was when you forgot.*

"Forgot what?" I say out loud in the darkness.

That I loved you.

And it's true. In that moment my eleven-year-old self decided that my mother must not have loved me. If she did, she wouldn't have made me see that. A mother protects her children from the world's horrors, but mine put the worst one right in front of me. I don't know why, and I never will. But maybe I can try to remember what came before. The love that came before.

"I'm sorry," I say out loud in the dark house, trying not to let my voice waver. "I didn't mean to forget."

And suddenly, the sounds fade; the footsteps walk down the hallway above me and don't return. The voices dwindle. This time, there is no dramatic exit out the front door, no faucet turning on. The whole thing dissolves like a movie fading to black. And once the last of it ends, the house becomes . . . quiet.

And then I know that now, it's over. Whatever this was, whether it came from inside me or outside me, it's done.

I breathe in the air, which smells like smoke from emergency candles, brackish from cold, salt-marshy wind beyond. The air in the house feels less charged, clearer. So, what to do next? I have another sip of wine, looking out the window to see if any lights in the distance have come back on. Nothing; the distant horizon remains dark. I breathe deeply, rest my eyes, place my palm over my chest to try and quiet my fast-beating heart. Sleep seems like a good enough option, or maybe I should go crouch under the blankets and read by flashlight. Now, in this house where the spirits have been properly exorcised, I can rest.

And then it happens, the thing that stops my heart midbeat: a full-on knock at the front door.

I gasp and stop breathing for what feels like a full minute. Another knock, and I realize it must be Colleen; did she not make it into town? Finally, my breath begins again; then the blood goes back into my legs, and I go to the door. Flashlight in hand, I open it a little; the rain has stopped. Only wind now, blustery and powerful. Strange, warm wind that has all the trees around the meadow at its mercy.

"Hello?" I say. "Is someone there? Colleen?"

"Alex, it's me."

Colleen is not standing before me. Riley is. I can't believe it; I don't believe it. I look for a long time, but there she is, tall and slim, her buttery-yellow hair loose on her shoulders. The sister I have not seen for six or seven years. I open the door the rest of the way.

Finally, she speaks. "Hi, Alex," she says quietly.

There is a lump in my throat, and I can barely force words to come out of my mouth. "Riley," I finally say. I reach out to hold her, and I wrap my arms around her, my little sister who is a full head taller than I am. And so skinny I feel her bones against my skin. Her skin is cold but not wet. "I can't believe you're here!" is all I can say, and I say it over and over.

"Where have you been?" I say, touching her arm. "Is it really you? We've been searching for you. Are you okay? Wait, how did you find me?"

"That's a lot of questions," she says.

In the flashlight's beam, I beckon her inside. I can't believe she's here, and I'm a little too excited to stop with the questions altogether.

"I'm so glad to see you," I say. "Did you come all the way from New York through the storm? How did you get here? I didn't see a car."

"The car . . ." she says. "There was mud . . . I just left it out there . . ."

"Is your car stuck in the mud?" I ask. I look out the window, searching through the mist. "Where is it? I'll call Triple A."

"No need," she says. "I'll get it later."

I offer to take her jacket, which looks too big for her, like a man's suit jacket, but she wants to leave it on. I lead her into the kitchen and offer her wine and Saltines. I skip the peanut butter and M&M's and instead offer spray cheese, certain, for some silly reason, that she will prefer it.

Of course, she does not eat. I can't get past how strange it is, that she would appear on my doorstep like this.

And for a while, then, we talk. We talk about little things: how long it has been, why I am in this house, the day, the storm.

In the flickering candlelight, her unpainted face looks like a child. Her eyes are not red, and her skin is porcelain clear, but something about her seems heartbroken and raw. I hope she will stay the night; she will be warm and safe here. Then we will call Colleen, and the three of us will go out for breakfast, hot coffee, pancakes, hash browns, sausage.

We will be sisters again. Riley is home now, and we will find our way back to being a family.

"Alex, can I ask you something weird?" she says. I nod. "I always imagined you with kids."

I frown. That is a weird question. Did Colleen tell her to ask that? I shrug it off, hastily explaining that a child is simply not in the cards for me. I don't want to go into it with her, and my answers are light and abrupt.

"Come on," I say. "Let's go to the other room."

I lead her into the living room. She sits down on a wooden chair—I wish I had something nicer to offer. Something about the room and the candlelight flickering on the walls. Something about the uneven, unpolished wood floor beneath our feet, and the wind still beating the windows, and glasses of wine in our hands. She feels like a visitor from another time.

"Riley," I say, sitting on the floor and holding my knees to my chest. "I can't believe you're here. I have so many questions."

"Please," she says, smiling. "Please, can we skip the questions? At least for now?"

"Just tell me, where have you been?" I ask. "We've been trying so hard to find you."

She sighs, looks around. "I've been working a lot, Alex. There was a special project. And it really did take all my time."

"Didn't you get Colleen's phone calls? She's been frantic searching for you."

"I'm sorry if I worried anybody," she says.

Her eyes are dull; her whole face looks tired. She's been working too hard. She needs a break. So, we won't stay up all night talking. We'll talk until we're tired and then go to bed and sleep late. I will give her my sleeping bag and I will sleep on the floor with Marjorie's old blankets.

But for now, we sit together and talk. We have the conversation we always have, have had over and over again since we were children. About Mom. *What happened that day*, she asks. Why did she do it? What do we remember about her? Riley remembers almost nothing; I lend my memories to her.

But not all of them. I wouldn't do that.

When we are out of words, Riley looks around. "I like this house," she says. "So old and quaint."

"It is," I say, also glancing around. "I might have liked something a bit more updated, not that the choice was up to me. I guess it doesn't really matter. I'm not sure how long I'll be here."

Riley nods blankly. "Marjorie loved it here."

"Marjorie? How did you know—"

Riley only smiles. "Is that the right name? I don't even know. It just popped into my mind."

"That's right," I say. "Marjorie. I just can't remember mentioning her . . ."

"I guess you must have," she says. Riley leans forward in her chair, rests her arms on her legs, and hangs her head down. "Alex," she says. "I can't remember anything about Mom. Sometimes I think I remember, but then I realize I'm thinking of photographs. Or imagining things people told me. Everything secondhand."

"I know," I say. "We all feel like we didn't know her."

"Tell me something about her. What did she love?"

"She loved you," I say. "She used to wrap you up in a little blanket and coo to you, and rock you to sleep in the rocking chair. And if any of us made too much noise or woke you up, she threatened to sell us to the gypsies."

I get up off the floor and find another chair to sit in. I keep talking, and Riley laughs a little. Riley, my sister. She is almost hard to look at now, all luminous and blue in this dark house. Her face is so fragile, it might be made of glass. She glances around as though she has lost interest in this conversation.

Lightning flashes beyond the window, silent but powerful, lighting up the whole window frame like daytime. This time I don't flinch, and neither does Riley; we simply watch in awe.

"Riley," I say. "I have to ask you something. Do you . . . Are you having a problem with drugs? I might be able to help, you know. I mean, I know a little about addiction, from the ER."

She does not respond but looks down and clears her throat.

"Did you hear my question?"

She looks at me with an expression I can't interpret, a flatness of hurt, confusion, and disinterest.

"Alex, I have to ask you something."

Her voice sounds serious. "Okay," I say. "I'm listening."

"Do you remember Mrs. Rhinehold?" she says. "The widow who used to live down the street from us. She took care of me while you two were at school. After Mom died."

I sigh. She's not going to answer my question, so I may as well answer hers. "Mrs. Rhinehold," I say. "I do remember. Colleen and I used to pick you up there on the way home. Why?"

"Do you remember her son, Arthur?"

Their family moved to New Hampshire the next year, so I haven't thought about these names in a long time. I remember that Mrs. Rhinehold had a son and that he was older than I was, maybe about four years older. Now that we're talking about it, I remember that he was strange. Slowly I remember more . . . he was home a lot. Why? He had problems at school. And he refused to play with the other kids in the neighborhood. He was tall, heavy, kind of a big kid.

Colleen didn't like him, and neither did I. We worried that Riley was over there when he was home, worried that he might hurt her, either on purpose or by mistake or something in between.

"Mrs. Rhinehold watched you while we were at school," I say. "We didn't have much money, and I think Dad was desperate."

Riley looks down. "She was a nice enough lady," she says. "She used to play blocks with me, those little wooden ones with the letters. I probably learned the alphabet because of her."

I'm confused, because this story doesn't feel happy. "Well, that's good," I say.

"It was her son," she starts. But she does not finish the sentence.

"What?"

She shakes her head, and, looking away from me, her face crumples in an expression of disgust.

I feel my eyes tearing up. We would know when Arthur had been home from school because he'd be watching cartoons on TV when we picked Riley up—mean, violent cartoons, with the volume up loud. Mrs. Rhinehold would apologize about him with an awkward chuckle when we went to pick Riley up. On those days, we asked Riley if she was all right, had she been hurt; at bath time we checked her arms and legs for bruises.

We never saw a mark on her body. Not even one.

She looks down. "He used to . . . do things. To me."

My blood runs cold. I suddenly understand that we were looking for the wrong kind of mark.

"Riley, no," I whisper.

" . . . molested me," she continues, her eyes cast down. "That's what it's called, I think. What he did to me. Not rape, but . . . other things . . . bad things."

Disbelief dries my throat. I can't talk. I can't quite breathe. A battering of wind against the house outside. I shake my head slightly. "Riley, no," is all I can say.

How could he do that to our sister? She was only a baby; she had just lost her mother. My God. Then, I remember: she used to refuse to eat, cried easily, couldn't sleep at night. How could we not have seen it? I guess because we were children.

The experience of sexual abuse in childhood does not end with the conclusion of the abuse. It's trauma. It gets replayed over and over a million times in the mind of the survivor. It makes feeling safe ever again difficult or impossible; survivors sometimes turn to drugs to blot out the memory.

These are things I know and have learned from work. What I never knew until this moment was that my sister had been living with this, keeping this secret from the ones who loved her all these years. If I had known then what I have learned since then as a nurse, I would have understood. I would have seen it. She wouldn't have been alone. We could have gotten her help.

"Did his mother know this was happening?" I ask.

She shakes her head. "He did it when she was out running an errand or outside talking to the mailman. He said that if I ever told anyone . . . I don't even remember anymore what he was going to do. There were a few different things, I think."

"Riley, no," I whisper. "I am so sorry."

She smiles slightly, in an expression like gratitude.

"Ri, are you seeing a therapist?" I ask. "If you're not, let me help you find someone. People can heal, they can put their lives back together after abuse. It just takes time . . ."

She holds one hand slightly up to stop me. "Alex, I'm not telling you this because I want you to solve anything. And I don't blame you or Colleen, not in the least. I need you to understand . . . my life hasn't gone the way I wish it might have. Some of the unraveling started there, I think."

Suddenly, I realize I am full-on crying. "Damn it, Riley, you were so little," I say. "How could he do that to you? How could that woman let her son do that? This makes me so mad!" I want to find this Arthur and rip him apart. "What about now? Are you safe?"

"I'm here with you, Alex," she says. "I have never been safer my whole life."

"Riley," I say. "I am sorry."

"I know," she says. "I know."

We are quiet for a while, this terrible truth filling the space between us. But I feel her pulling away, and there's something else I am still hoping she will answer tonight.

"I have to ask you a question," I say. "Remember Thanksgiving a few years back? Colleen's daughter, Maddie, said you snuck through her window. You talked to her for a while but left and never came to dinner. Is that true?"

Riley looks up, but her gaze passes me. "I think the wind is calming," she says. She rises from her seat and walks across the room to the tall window. "It's starting to clear."

Yes, out the window a few stray stars are visible in the night sky.

"Family plot," she mutters.

"What?"

"Out there," she says, pointing. "There's a family plot, out in the woods."

I stand and go to the window. I don't know how she could possibly know that. "Yes," I say. "The lawyer told me about that when I first came here. I've never seen it. How did you know it's there?"

"How? Oh, I didn't," she says. "They're pretty typical in New England. I once did a report on it in school. A couple of generations ago that's what they did, bury family on their own land. It's cheaper that way. The do-it-yourself method."

"Oh, sure," I say.

"Do you know who used to live here?" she says.

"I looked up the family names," I say. A chill wind blows up against the window, and I wrap my arms around myself. Riley does not shudder at the wind. "For a while, I was having some . . . disturbances."

"Oooh," she says. She looks at me, her eyes bright, her smile funny. "You mean, a haunting?"

"Something like that," I say. "Riley, what happened that time, that Thanksgiving? Why didn't you come into the house? We were all waiting for you. Nobody's angry, but why didn't you come?"

She sighs and puts her hands in her pockets. "Alex," she says. "Life is complicated. I wish I'd done things better, or, at least, done things differently. There's so much I'm not proud of."

"Like what?" I say. "You can tell me anything."

"And I will," she says. "But listen, it's late. I should go."

She stands and starts toward the door.

"Go?" I say. "Go where? You can't go out there; the roads could be flooded. I thought you said your car was stuck in the mud—"

"No, it's fine," she says. "All my stuff is—at the place . . ."

"What? Where? Are you checked into a hotel?"

"Sure, a hotel. My things are there. My clothes, toothpaste, everything."

"Riley," I say, hands on my hips. "This is an inlet on a floodplain. It's a miracle that you got here. Listen, I have plenty of toothpaste. I even have a spare toothbrush."

"Alex, I can't stay."

"But what hotel is it?" I ask. "In Newburyport? Where?"

"I forget what it's called, but it's in the middle of town. Don't worry about me, I'm fine, okay? I'm completely fine. I'm in a really good place in my life. I'm exactly where I need to be. Just know that."

Finally, I give in. "Okay, I can't make you stay. But before you go, just tell me about that Thanksgiving."

She stands facing the door, all I can see is her back, her oversized men's suit jacket still on. Her head falls to her chest. "Alex," she says. A small sound comes from her, like a whimper. "Have you ever made a mistake?"

"What . . ." I say. I go to her, but I feel compelled to keep my distance. "Everybody has." She turns toward me and touches her eyes lightly with her fingers, trying not to smear her eye makeup.

She turns to look at me. "You and Colleen . . . you were my heart. I couldn't breathe here, that's why I went away. But when I left, I had no heart. Or maybe it was my soul that I lost; I don't know. Maybe if I had had a mom, or at least remembered her, I might have had something to hold on to. I might have gotten something right. But I didn't. I failed."

"Why do you think you failed at anything?" I say. "As far as I can see, you have everything you ever wanted."

"Everything I ever wanted?" she says. Then, she looks me in the eye and smiles. "I wish I could laugh at that, but honestly, I think I'm too exhausted."

"Riley, what's going on?" I say. "You keep talking in jigsaw puzzles. I feel like you're trying to tell me something, but I can't figure out what. Just tell me, okay? I can't help you if I don't understand."

"That Thanksgiving," she says, raising her voice. "I wanted to see you, all of you. But I couldn't do it. I couldn't go there, to that beautiful house where everybody was all dressed up and happy inside and lay my ugly life in front of you and say, *Here you go, folks. This is me. Have at it.*"

Her face twists in a way that's not so pretty, and once again there is a silent flash at the window.

"Not that everything in my life was ugly," she says, on the verge of tears. "Parts of it were beautiful. Even some of the mistakes were beautiful."

"I don't understand—"

She cuts me off. "That time . . . I thought, if I could see Maddie and see what was possible, maybe something inside me could be, I don't know, convinced or healed. But, Alex, she was so . . . perfect and little. I couldn't . . ."

She stops talking. I wait for her to finish, but she doesn't. "They're not so perfect," I say. "The Newcombs. Eric and Colleen are getting a divorce." I watch her face looking for a shocked reaction, but it doesn't happen. "Nobody's as perfect as they look."

Riley, my sister with the smooth honey hair and the beautiful face, smiles slightly. "I know," she says. She opens the door, and we stand out on the landing in the cool, sea-salted night mist. Then she turns to me and looks me in the eye. "Alex, I have to say something, and I need you to listen."

"What is it?" I say, gripping my arms against the cold.

She looks away, grimaces, then turns back to me. "If there ever happened to be . . . a child, one who was, you know, lost, maybe just completely lost. I don't mean in a store; I mean, in life. You'd help them, wouldn't you?"

I stare hard at her face; I have no idea what she's talking about. "Of course."

She pushes her hand against her cheek like she is wiping away a tear. "If the time came, and you were helping this child, could you do me a favor? Could you try and remember . . . a mama loves her baby. Even a mama who isn't very good, a mama who failed over and over. Even then, she always loved her little one. Would you . . . tell the child that, from time to time? Can you do that?"

Her words are confusing; it's like she's talking in riddles. "Riley, sweetie, what are you saying? Is this about Mom?"

She shakes her head. "Never mind. Tell Colleen, none of it is her fault. There's nothing she could have done to change what happened."

"Riley, everything you say sounds so final," I say. "Tell her yourself, you'll see her tomorrow."

"That's a good idea. I will. Bye, Alex," she says. "Thank you. For everything."

I hug her, it's all I can do. Then she begins to walk down the steps, and I follow her to the edge of the first one. I go all the way outside, but I still don't see her car. "Riley!" I call out. "If the road is impassable, just come back. Okay? Don't try to drive through water."

She only turns and waves and keeps going, moving quickly toward the road, like she's being beckoned by the mist.

I grip my arms; the air is suddenly colder than I expected, or maybe I'm just noticing it now. Riley disappears. I do not hear the sounds of her car doors opening or the car starting; they must have been swallowed up by the wind. I watch from the steps of my house, the door at my back, but I do not see headlights. The mist must be so thick, I think. Thick like the dirt above your grave.

I turn and go inside. I blow out the candles and take my flashlight and go upstairs. I should feel relieved to have seen Riley, to know she's all right. But I don't. I feel confused. And sickened about what she told me about the boy down the street. I cannot believe she endured that. I cannot believe that we let that happen.

Even when I am upstairs, wrapped inside my sleeping bag, I cannot stop shivering.

I hope the electricity comes on soon, because some radio chatter would be a relief right now. The house is silent, and for once, I wish it would wake up and make a little noise.

Chapter 23

Monday, March 3, 2014
Colleen

I spent Sunday afternoon safe and sound in the condo with Eric and the kids. We ate Pringles and onion dip, plus chocolate chip cookies that Maddie made. It was like old times, only, maybe better because I think, deep down, we were all glad to be under the same roof, and the only storm was outside.

And as promised, the storm was bad. In the middle of the afternoon, we lost power and cell service. After that, we played board games and watched the rain.

This morning the power came on but until a little while ago, the phones were still out. We checked the local news; the schools were open, so the kids went off, and I got ready to head back to Plum Island.

Just as I was getting ready to leave, cell service came on. Immediately, my phone lit up with messages and failed calls. Three calls and three messages from Nate Hensler. Several other calls from numbers I didn't know. Now I am looking down at the alerts on my phone, shaking.

"What is it?" Eric asks.

I shake my head. "I'm not sure," I tell him.

I call Nate. He answers immediately. "Good morning, Mrs. Newcomb," he says. His voice is craggy, worn out.

I say simply, "We had a huge storm here, lost cell service. What's going on?"

"Mrs. Newcomb," he says. "I'm so sorry, your sister passed away."

My knees give out, and I sink onto the couch. "What? How?"

"She overdosed on Fentanyl," he says.

"But you—you were supposed to talk to her. What happened?"

"I did talk to her," he says. "I want to explain everything, but it would be better in person. Can you come to New York?"

Eric sits down next to me and puts his hand on my back. "Yes, of course," I say. "I need to talk to my family. We'll try to get there tomorrow. I'll call you when we have a plan."

I don't believe it. My bones don't believe it. Eric turns on his laptop and looks it up. He finds articles confirming that Riley Emery is dead. He starts to read one of them to me, but I can't listen now. I can't absorb those words. I look at it over his shoulder, letting terms ping-pong through my brain. *Overdose, found in a friend's home, rushed to hospital, dead on arrival.* Like oil poured thick on the surface of skin, it does not sink in but sits atop in a glossy puddle. I long to push it off, but it is not sleek like oil; it is permanent, like glue.

I need to see Alex. I need to see her face, to hug her, I need to make sure she's all right.

"Thanks," I say to Eric, stuttering, stumbling, shaking.

"You okay to drive?" he asks.

"I hope so," I say.

In the car, I try to call Alex, but her phone is off, routing me to voice mail almost before I finish dialing. So I drive; I drive down Route 1A to the edge of Killdeer Road. A large oak tree was felled in the storm right across the road, dragging a power line down with it. A crew of men work a chain saw to dismantle the tree, one limb at a time. I cannot drive past them, so I park my car on the opposite corner of the main road, away from the machines, and walk down the wet, sloshing road to Alex. My walk becomes a run, the bottoms of my jeans get soaked in the drenched road. In a moment I see it behind the high bushes, Alex's house, strange like an apparition, the house that brought our sister home. But I guess Alex is not our sister anymore. She is only *my* sister. We girls were three, and now we are one plus one.

I go to her door and knock. Nothing happens, so I knock again. "Alex?" I call. Then I open the door and put my head inside the living room. It feels stark and grainy white in the diffuse morning sunlight. "Sweetie, it's me. I let myself in." Finally, Alex comes down the staircase wearing gray sweatpants and a sweatshirt. She is smiling, but there are rings under her eyes. How do I explain what has happened? This is not right.

"Hi," she says happily, rubbing her eyes. "Why are you here so early? Did Riley call you?"

"What? Did who—" I say.

"Never mind," she says. She looks at me with narrow, scrutinizing eyes. "No coffee?"

I shake my head. My eyes are hot. How can she still not know? I haven't told her. And I realize I don't want to say it out loud. I wish she would just know. "Alex, there's something . . ."

"It's okay, we'll get coffee later. Colleen!" she says, almost singing. "The craziest thing happened. Riley was here last night. Oh, but you already know that."

I stand in her living room because there is nowhere to sit. Her words don't make any sense.

"She was?" I say. Alex nods. "No, Alex, she wasn't."

"No, she was. She talked to you, right? She's coming back this morning so we can go to breakfast. Oh, wait, let me get dressed. We were going to surprise you, but now you're here, so that's even better." She starts toward the stairs. "I guess that was a silly plan. Riley's in Newburyport, so we should have just met her there. Oh, well. Be right back." She heads quickly up the stairs before I can say anything.

"Alex, stop," I say. "Alex!"

"Thirty seconds," she calls down from her room.

I hear her walking around upstairs; I feel like I should go up there and grab her shoulders and shake her and tell her. But I can't make myself speak those words. And anyway, she may as well get dressed. It hardly matters. I'll give her a few more moments of not knowing.

She emerges in a pair of dark jeans and a light-green sweater.

"You look nice," I say, almost whispering.

"It's not every day I go out for breakfast with my sisters." She looks around. "My cell phone died last night. Oh, there it is," she says, spying it on a box in the corner. "I was going to see if Riley called, but she can't because my phone is dead." She goes to the light switch on the wall and pushes it up and down; nothing happens. "And I guess the power's not back yet. Colleen?"

She says my name so abruptly it surprises me. "Yes?"

She stares at me like she's just noticing me for the first time that morning. "What's going on?"

I open my mouth, hoping that the words will just spill out. But they don't; they won't come unless I speak them. "Alex," I say. "Riley's dead."

Chapter 24

"Riley's body was found last night in a Manhattan apartment," Colleen says. "She overdosed."

"No," I say. "That can't be right. She was here."

"That's not possible, Alex."

I feel like she is trying to purposely kick the air out of my lungs. "Colleen, it is possible. It happened. Riley was here. Last night. You talked to her, didn't you? That's how she knew where to find me."

"No, Alex, I didn't—" she starts, but I cut her off.

"Yes, you must have," I say. "Because she was here. She came inside, we ate spray cheese on Saltines, we drank wine. Colleen? Are you listening? I'm telling you the truth."

My voice sounds like it's coming from somewhere else. But Colleen's face is so pale, grief written in salted pencil upon her face. But I don't know why she's so sad; this is all a mistake. "Riley is in Newburyport," I insist, "at some hotel, but she couldn't remember which one. She's coming to get us for breakfast. She could knock on my door any minute now."

Any minute. Now.

Nothing happens. We two are the only ones here. Come on, Riley, I think. Walk through that door. Prove Colleen wrong.

"I'm sorry, Alex," Colleen says quietly.

"Did they check dental records?" I say. I hear myself say it, my voice shaking. "If they didn't check dental records, we don't know for sure that that's Riley."

Colleen sighs. "It was her face, Alex. People know what her face looks like."

"I know what her face looks like. I saw it last night! Look, Colleen, she's coming here this morning. You can ask her yourself when she gets here. Ask *her* who was staying with her, who overdosed in her apartment."

"Oh my God, Alex," Colleen says, pressing her hands to the sides of her forehead. "Would you listen to yourself? Stop. She is not coming. She wouldn't even be able to get onto your road unless they finished clearing it."

"Why not?" I say.

She sighs. "There's a tree down at the top of the road. Nobody can drive in or out."

"Well, that's why she's not here," I say, grabbing my raincoat and high boots. "She's stuck. Let's walk up there, she's probably trying to call me right now only that's not working either."

"Alex, stop! Stop it!" she shouts. "How could that possibly have been Riley last night? How could she have known where you lived?"

It occurs to me, finally, that she's trying to tell me that she never spoke to Riley. I stop, then, I do stop. I stop and breathe. "Maybe Dad told her?"

Colleen's face twists in a skeptical grimace. "You seriously think Riley called Dad? And said, *Hey, where can I find Alex?* And then Dad said, *She's just down the road; let me get that address for you.* And then Riley said, *Great, I'll put it into my GPS and pop by for a visit.*"

I freeze in my footsteps, and my hand falls off the front doorknob. When she puts it like that, there's nothing I can say. My legs melt underneath me, and I sink to the floor. She is looking at me with a serious expression, and it feels like she's won.

"*In the middle of a terrible storm,*" she continues. "*What a good time to visit Alex, the sister I haven't seen in years,* she thinks. So she gets in her car in

New York, but she has never owned a car, so maybe she rents one or borrows one, both of which require some degree of planning, which has never been her strong suit, and heads north through the same huge rainstorm that was so intense, it shut off the power and cell service of everyone in the area."

Colleen is right. I shrug and stare hard at the floor, aware now of what a fool I've been. "Some people might do that."

"Yes, some people might. But not Riley. And Dad wouldn't just talk casually to Riley—Riley, who's been missing for months—and give her your address, if he even happens to have that written down, which he probably doesn't, much less directions, because, as we both know, he's never been here."

Finally, I swallow. "I don't understand this, Colleen." I sink down to the floor. "What happened to your investigator?"

She sits down beside me. "He's the one that called me to tell me. He said he talked to her. So, I don't know what happened. He wants to talk to me in person, so I need to go to New York. I think we should all go."

"Colleen, I can't believe this," I say. "Does Dad know?"

"I haven't talked to him yet."

I hate the idea of having to tell him. "She can't be dead; she was here last night."

"What time was it?" she says.

"I'm not sure," I say. "The power was out. It was dark. After dinnertime for sure. Maybe sometime after seven? Do we know anything about . . . what time she died?"

"Not that I've heard," she says. "Tell me exactly what happened."

I shrug. "She walked in the door and we talked."

"What about?"

I look at my sister, her tired face, her eyes, alert now, inquisitive. My mind is blank. I can't remember any of it. "Just things."

"Well, did she use anything or leave anything?"

I shake my head. "We were in here, in these three rooms the whole time. If she left anything, it would be here."

Colleen stands up and looks around, walks through rooms where the sun illuminates the windows like it's a regular day, even brighter than usual, for the sunshine is reflecting on the wet pavement outside. It feels like the sun does not know that Riley Emery has died.

I scan my memory for clues. Did she use the bathroom? No. She drank wine from a glass and left on the ridge a pale smudge of lipstick. I washed it last night, and the cup is still beside the sink.

I stand up, go to the kitchen. "Colleen, look," I say, pointing to the juice glasses beside the sink. "Two glasses. One for me, one for Riley." I turn to my sister, look in her face. "I didn't dream this. She was here."

"Alex," Colleen says, sighing. She looks so sad. I want to shout *No*, over and over, until the world stops and finally works the way I have it in my brain. In that world, Riley is alive. She's in a hotel somewhere nearby; she's on her way over for breakfast.

Colleen's phone rings and the high-pitched tone startles both of us. She pulls it from her jacket pocket and looks at the caller ID. I stare at her wide eyes, half expecting her to say that it's Riley. "It's Dad," she says. She doesn't answer it, and a moment later her phone beeps, indicating a message. "We have to talk to him," she says. "We have to tell him. Or maybe—maybe he knows. Maybe he's calling to tell us."

My throat tightens, and I hear myself gasp. "What's the date today?" I say.

She looks at her phone. "March third," she says.

"So yesterday was the second," I say. "March second."

"One month before April second," she says. "The day that Mom . . ."

"Twenty-five years ago," I say. "And now Riley."

"Oh, hell," Colleen says.

Colleen's phone rings again. She whimpers slightly and mumbles, "It's Dad, again. I can't, we can't . . . I have to." She shrugs, then pushes the talk button and says, solemnly, "Hi, Dad."

He knows. And Colleen tells him, *Yes, we know*. She tells him, *I'm here with Alex*. She hears his words and repeats them to me, calmly patiently. "Riley's agency called him," she tells me. Pause, listening. "They don't know much right now except that she overdosed." Listening, and then: "Toxicology report . . . will take weeks . . . settle her estate . . . no will . . ."

I am starting to believe it: Riley is gone from us. What happened last night? My time with her does not feel like a dream. It feels more real than this does. My head pulses with confusion. I want to blame Mom, because all of this started with her. And that boy down the street, the one splayed on his couch, watching mean cartoons. How could he do what he did to a little girl who'd lost her mother? How could any of us have let that happen? How could we let her down and not see what was in front of us?

Then I realize—Colleen doesn't know that part yet. I will have to tell her.

How will I tell her?

I feel the familiar old anger starting in my chest again, and it makes me want to bury my head away or flee. No, I think, I won't give into that this time. Remember the love, I tell myself. With Mom and with Riley too. Don't let grief choose your memories.

Colleen gets off the phone with Dad, and we are both quiet, both looking down. Slowly, this is becoming real.

I walk into the dining room and look at the floor, staring hard, wishing I could make her footprints materialize on the floorboards. "She overdosed, Colleen," I say. "She did this to herself."

Colleen leans against the wall, holding her hands behind her back. "I know."

"She always said she couldn't remember Mom. What about our 911? Did she forget that too? Did she forget about us?"

She looks at me and shrugs. "Maybe. Maybe she chose to forget."

I feel tears preparing to surge, like a wall of water, like a tsunami. I have one last breath in me before the onslaught. "She never belonged to us, did she?"

"No," Colleen says. "That's what they always say about children. But still—"

"Still," I say, whispering. And finally, I am able to cry, which I think means that now I believe it. I sink on to the floor and Colleen sits beside me, and then we're on the bare, dirty floor of an empty room, the one where our sister walked a few hours earlier, leaving no visible footprints. We will grieve our sister; we will wear black and go to New York and gather what remains of her and bring her home. We will support Dad and get him through this; maybe that's our most important job now. But after all this, I realize, we need to let Mom and Riley fade into the history of our lives and think of them gently, cautiously, lest we create rivers of grief so wide and deep, we ourselves might drown in them.

When we are ready, Colleen and I walk up the road to her car. The marsh smells sweet and clean in the morning air, but the road is littered with waterlogged sticks and tree limbs that snapped off in last night's wind. The men have finished working, and I wonder whether electricity will be restored by the end of the day. Then I can charge my phone, and then Riley can . . . but no, I guess she won't.

We reach Colleen's car. She slides in and I touch the door handle, but then I stop. I need to tell Colleen what Riley said last night. About Mrs. Rhinehold and her son.

"You okay?" Colleen asks from the driver's seat. "Is the door stuck?"

"No." I open the door and get in. Colleen starts the car. "Hold on a minute," I say. "Something strange came up last night that I need to tell you about."

"What do you mean?" she says.

I shake my head because I'm still confused about what exactly happened. "Do you remember our neighbors, the Rhineholds? A woman, a widow, I think, and her teenage son?"

Colleen turns the car off and swallows. Her face turns pale. "Oh, God."

"What?" I ask.

"The woman was Riley's babysitter, right?" she says. "And her son. What was his name? Arthur."

"Yes," I say. "What do you remember?"

"A couple of years ago, there was a story on the nightly news about a man who worked at a preschool in New Hampshire, some town near Plaistow," she says. "He was arrested for abusing the children. The name sounded familiar, and I wondered if he was the same guy whose mother had taken care of Riley . . ."

"Could have been," I say. "Remember? We didn't like him. He gave us the creeps."

"I remember," she says. "Do you think he—"

My head hangs. I nod. "Yes. I think he did. Riley told me that that was where, what did she say, some of the unraveling started. Like, her life's unraveling."

"Oh, no," Colleen says, covering her mouth with her hand. "Oh, no."

I realize that I am telling her something that was conveyed to me by someone who was not exactly my sister, or who was my sister but wasn't exactly with me. I don't understand it; but what I do know is that the confession felt very real, and Colleen needs to know.

"Did she tell you what happened?" Colleen asks.

"Not specifically," I say. "Just that he molested her when his mother wasn't around. And threatened her."

"That was just after Mom died," she says. "Riley, she was so little."

"She was so little," I say.

And for a moment, we are quiet together, watching the mist over the marsh, heartbreak in our throats, bitterness in our bodies. So much had been taken from Riley. And now she's gone.

"When I saw that bit on the news, that thought went through my mind," Colleen says. "Maybe I kind of knew. But then something happened, who knows what, the phone rang or one of the kids needed something or dinner was ready. I forgot about it and never thought about it again."

I nod. "Colleen, we were children when it happened."

"I wish she had reached out," Colleen says, her voice shaking. "If she had just told us, we would have gotten her help."

"I know," I say. "I know."

After a minute, we realize we need to get to Dad's. Colleen turns on the car and drives up the road; in town, we pick up coffee, then drive to Dad's house. He's happy to see us, but we can tell he has been crying. He's been on the phone all morning with someone from the coroner's office in New York, taking notes on a yellow legal pad. We three sit at the kitchen table, and Dad puts on his reading glasses and reads them to us, pausing sometimes to make out his own handwriting. Riley had been staying in a friend's apartment; someone asked the police to do a welfare check on Riley, and they did. When she did not respond, the police called an ambulance. Riley was pronounced dead on the scene.

Dad looks up at us and his eyes seem very big. He speaks slowly. "I asked them to cremate her. We need to decide what to do with the remains." Colleen and I look at each other blankly. "You two think about it. I'll go along with whatever you decide."

"All right," I say. Colleen nods.

He puts the pad down and takes off his glasses. "Funny," he says. "You always think you'll see your kids again." He grabs each of our hands and squeezes them tight. "They might fly away to New York or India, or even Newburyport . . ." We smile. "But it seems like they're still with you. Then you get a phone call and . . ."

As the events of the previous night fade, a veil grows between me and my Riley, our strange time together. I accept that she is gone, and I stop talking about what happened, since I cannot explain it. I do not tell Dad that I saw her, or what she told me about being abused by the boy down the street. There's nothing we can do to change that now; we don't have any idea where that man is, and if it occurred to anyone to report him to the police, of course, the victim is now deceased, plus the statute of limitations probably ran out a long time ago. Maybe someday I will talk to Dad about it, but not today.

The next morning Colleen and Dad and I take the nine a.m. train to New York. We reach Penn Station around noon and take a cab to our hotel. After we check in, the three of us retreat briefly to our separate rooms to tidy up. When Colleen comes out, her hair is pulled back in a tight, smooth ponytail, and she is wearing black slacks, black blazer, black boots. She is dressed for mourning and for business. We go to a café to meet Colleen's investigator. When we walk in, she spots him sitting at a table, drinking coffee and looking at his phone.

"Mr. Hensler," Colleen says, giving him a flat, polite smile. "This is my sister, Alex, and my father, George."

Mr. Hensler greets us with hellos, how-do-you-do's, call me Nate. A waiter takes our orders for coffee and pastries, then we talk. Dad's expression is gruff, his arms are folded across his chest. This can't be easy for Nate, to meet us all under these circumstances; that fact makes me want to be slightly more amicable. Plus, I don't forget: he is our only connection to Riley's last day. If we are brusque or unfriendly, there's nothing stopping him from walking out of here, and I want to know what he has to say.

"I am so very sorry for your loss," he says.

"Thank you," I say.

"Can you tell us exactly what happened?" Colleen says.

He plays with his water glass and hesitates. "Sorry," he says. "I'm not sure where to begin. Your sister was doing drugs," he says, setting his water glass down. "I believe she had become a habitual Fentanyl user."

"Fentanyl?" I say. "What was she—" I stop myself. I don't even know what question to ask. Fentanyl, a potent synthetic painkiller, similar to heroin, but so much stronger. Actually, it almost makes heroin look like aspirin. "Why do you think Fentanyl?"

"The medical examiner told me that he suspected that's what she overdosed on. The toxicology screen won't be back for a couple of weeks to confirm, but the initial autopsy indicated visceral congestion and pulmonary edema," he says, "which are common indicators for drug overdose."

I sigh, and my gaze goes down to the table. Visceral congestion, lots of blood in the organs, and pulmonary edema, foamy blood in the lungs. I don't know what to say next, so I say nothing.

"You told me you talked to my sister," Colleen says. "How did that conversation go?"

Nate nods. He folds his hands together and sets them on top of the table, shoulders tense, torso hovering forward over the edge of the table. "It wasn't what I expected, to be honest. She'd been at a dance club with friends and left the club around two or two thirty a.m. I happened to be in the East Village having dinner with friends, and I was heading home. She spotted me at a corner waiting for the light to change, and then she invited me out for coffee. She wasn't drunk or high or compromised in any way. So, we went out for coffee and talked."

"What did you talk about?" Dad asks.

"Our lives," he says. "The only way I can explain it is, we talked as though we were friends."

"Did you mention that you were working for me?" Colleen asks.

"She guessed it," he says. "I told her that I was only making sure she was safe. I told her that her family cared about her and wanted to help. I told her that addiction is a sickness and not her fault."

"Did she seem depressed?" I ask.

"Yes," he says. "But I never expected—I never thought—that she might end her life. If anything, she was thinking about the future. The last thing we did, before she went home, was go to the Williamsburg Bridge and watch the sun rise." Nate hangs his head and smiles bitterly to himself. "She was exhausted," he says. "And I told her to go home to rest. I told her the sun comes up every day . . ."

My father puts his elbows on the table and sinks his head into his hands. This is a lot for him.

Colleen sighs. "I guess I should expect a bill for the extra work?"

Nate hesitates a moment, then answers, "No. This case affected me personally and continues to. Mrs. Newcomb, when you shared with me that your mother took her own life, my first thought was that someone who has survived the suicide of someone close to them, especially in the case of a parent, the risk of their own suicide is elevated. So it seemed like a warning sign to me that Riley had stopped communicating with you."

"That was exactly what we were worried about," Colleen says.

"There are other warning signs," I say. "Some people say goodbye, or give things away, or have a calmness about them, like they're relieved that the decision is made. Did you observe any of that?"

He holds his hands to his mouth and nods in thought. "I am aware of those, and to be honest, for most of our time together, she did seem calm. She also expressed intense feelings of failure, which made me think she was experiencing a form of clinical depression. But we talked about how she might try to get her life back in order. I never realized that she . . ."

Colleen sighs and shakes her head. I cannot think of what to say or what to ask. All I know right now is that my beautiful sister is gone. And still, I don't understand what happened at my little house in Newbury, which now seems very far away. A strange visitation, Riley appearing in the darkness, telling me something that I know in my bones is true, that she was abused by someone our family trusted at the time when we were most vulnerable.

"Nate," I say. "I'm trying to figure something out. I know this sounds crazy, but Riley . . . she tried to contact me . . ."

"Alex, stop," Colleen says, hissing.

"The night of the storm," I continue. "Was that the night you two met?"

"No, the night before." He takes his phone out of his pocket and thumbs through. "Let me look at the calendar. The storm was on the second, right? She and I were out in the early hours of the second. What do you mean she tried to contact you? Did she text you? Call?"

My father looks at me with curiosity. "It's hard to explain," I say. "Do they know what time she died?"

"The coroner's preliminary report states that she died sometime between noon and four p.m.," he says.

"Between noon and four," I say. She died sometime in the afternoon of the day that she came to my house. I touch the table and push myself back into my seat and let out an uneasy breath. By the time she arrived at my house, Riley was dead, her body slumped in some New York apartment. My blood goes cold, feverish cold, and icicles shoot up my arms. I excuse myself, stumbling over chairs and my own feet, and rush to the restroom. I lock the door behind myself and grip the sides of the sink. I stand there, shaking.

All I know is, it happened. Riley was in my house. I don't know how she found me or where she went afterward, but she was there. She wasn't a see-through specter made of gossamer and light reflecting, and she was no memory replaying itself like a hologram projected on blank walls. She was herself. And she told me about something she endured when she was four years old. Four years old. She was a baby.

I press my hand against my mouth to silence the sob that wants to pour out of me.

A moment later someone is knocking at the door. It's Colleen. "Alex, are you okay?" she says.

I exhale, try to catch my breath, try to calm down. "I need a minute."

"Please come back," she says. "Nate needs to talk to us about something else."

It takes me a moment, but finally I answer. "Okay." I splash cold water on my face and dry myself off with a stiff brown paper towel. I breathe deeply, then I open the door. There she is, Colleen, my only sister.

"I don't know what it means, or what I saw, or how it's possible," I tell her. "But it did happen." She looks at me with doubt, a little like pity. "It did, Colleen. I wouldn't make this up, you know that."

She nods. "I know. It's just strange. But if you say it happened, I believe you. Let's go hear what else he has to say."

We walk together back to the table, but still I am shaking on the inside. Dad smiles at us. Nate asks if everything is okay. We both tell him, *Yes, it is.* And mostly it is, but also, it's not.

Nate sighs gently. "Listen, there's another thing I need to tell you all. I got curious about your family's history. I looked up your mom's maiden name, Montgomery. Is this your mother?" He slides a photograph in front of us; the photo shows two attractive young people, dressed formally, standing stiffly beside a Christmas tree and smiling flatly.

"Yes," Colleen says. "I don't know who the young man is."

He nods while Dad and I look at the photo. "The woman pictured there is Suzanne Montgomery, photo taken in the late seventies. The man is her younger brother, Robert, Rob."

"I didn't know she had a brother," Dad says.

"He passed away a few years ago," he says. Nate brings a folder out of his bag and places his hands on top. "Your mom grew up in a small, affluent community north of San Francisco. Your grandfather, Bill Montgomery, ran a company that manufactured farm equipment. M&O Tractor Company, Inc. It sounds humble enough, but it was quite an empire at one point."

"So she came from money?" I ask.

"Yes," he says.

Colleen and I exchange looks. "I thought so," Colleen says. "She held herself a certain way. Like she grew up with someone telling her to remember who she was."

Nate nods. "That sounds like the kind of family it was. Her brother had two children, Dennis and Rebecca, both still in California. I got in touch with Dennis and asked him what he knew about his aunt, Suzanne Montgomery."

Dad, Colleen, and I all lean slightly forward to listen. Nate pulls a piece of paper out from the folder. "He said they knew about Susie but didn't know what happened to her or where she ended up. Eventually, Dennis and Becky worked out some of the story." He looks at the paper, apparently a printout of an email. "Susie left home when she was twenty-one after a very brief marriage to the son of Philip O'Dowd; he provided the *O* in M&O Tractor, your grandfather's company."

"That must have been Jacob O'Dowd," I say.

"That's correct," he says, scanning the email. "The marriage was annulled after a month, and after that, her family basically disinherited her."

"How about that," Colleen says. "It was an arranged marriage."

"Any idea why the marriage didn't work out?" I ask.

Nate gives us an expression of curiosity. "I looked up Jacob O'Dowd. In 1986, he died at the age of thirty-two after being cared for in San Francisco's General Hospital Ward Eighty-Six. His obituary said he died of spinal meningitis."

"San Francisco, 1986," Dad says. "Any chance what really got him was . . ."

Nate nods. "General Hospital Ward Eighty-Six was famous for caring for AIDS patients. I don't know it for sure, but my strong suspicion is that Jacob O'Dowd died of AIDS. Again, I don't know the circumstances, but it's easy to imagine that Jacob was gay, and maybe Jacob's family wanted their son to marry a nice girl, to maintain appearances. The families set up the match, threw a big wedding. And maybe your mom found out, decided she didn't want to continue a sham marriage."

"So she had the marriage annulled . . ." I start.

"Apparently, your grandfather's partnership with Phil O'Dowd broke up shortly after that," Nate says. "M&O Tractor never regained the standing they had in the fifties and sixties. In 1980, your grandfather died of a heart attack."

Dad gets a sad look on his face. "All I knew was that the marriage didn't work out," he says. "I had no idea that her family disowned her because of it."

Colleen and I both take this in, glancing at each other and mumbling variants of "Wow" and "Well."

"So, here's where it gets interesting," he says, pulling a small neat envelope from a folder. "Dennis sent me this and said to give it to you." Nate looks at the envelope, it's addressed to Mrs. William Montgomery. "There's no return address, but it's postmarked from Amesbury, Massachusetts."

"What does it say?" I ask.

"The envelope is sealed," he says, turning it so we can see the smooth triangle, still glued neatly in place. "They found it in a drawer in your grandmother's bedside table about fifteen years ago, after she died. Rebecca always suspected it was from her aunt Susie, and she planned to open it someday. But she felt badly reading mail that wasn't meant for her."

"How do you know it's from Mom?" I ask.

He shrugs. "I don't," he says. "But my hunch is that your grandmother, Paula, who enjoyed luncheons at the yacht club and trips to Europe, didn't have many connections to the East Coast, much less in Amesbury, Massachusetts. I want to prepare you though: it's postmarked a week before your mother died."

I take the envelope from him and look at it, the paper browning, address written in Mom's neat cursive in faded ink.

"Funny," Colleen says, her arms crossed. "We've been looking for signs of Mom for so long, but now I'm not ready to open that envelope."

He shakes his head. "No, of course not," he says. "But take it. And open it when you're ready."

I take the letter and tuck it carefully into my purse. "Thank you," I say. I look at my father. He looks tired, overwhelmed. "How are you feeling, Dad?"

He sighs. "This is all a lot to take in," he says.

"Colleen, we should take Dad back to the hotel," I say. She nods. "Thank you for everything, Nate."

He reaches out his hand and we shake.

"Please know, I am so sorry about Riley," he says.

"Thanks," I say. "Do you have any other ideas about why . . ."

He glances down, considering. "My guess is that everything started to come apart when she started using drugs again, heavily, anyway, last fall. Around the time that Caleb was taken away."

Caleb. It's a name I haven't heard before. "Was Caleb her boyfriend?" I say.

"Boyfriend? No," he says slowly.

Colleen looks at Nate. "Who is Caleb?" she says.

"Caleb," he says. He looks at us and sees that we didn't not hear his words, we don't know what he's talking about. "Her son."

"Whose son?" I say. Now I'm the one who is confused.

Nate's face becomes very serious. "Riley. Riley's son. You—you didn't know she had a child?"

I feel the blood drain from my face, and I cannot speak. Riley's words go through my mind: *If there ever happened to be . . . a child, one who was, you know, lost, maybe just, completely lost. I mean, in life. You'd help them, wouldn't you?*

"She had a son?" I whisper.

"Oh, dear God," he says slowly. "She was very private about him, but I never guessed that you didn't know he existed."

Chapter 25

Tuesday, March 4, 2014
Colleen

My feet are itching to run; I am desperate for sneakers. I am so close to freedom . . . I cannot take any more talking. I get it; Nate wanted to help Riley, but he didn't understand that she was a ticking time bomb. There was no way he could have known. And we didn't know how much pain she had. We didn't know what that creep down the street had done to her. We didn't understand until . . . what, until after she died and appeared to Alex? Is that really what's happening here? No wonder my head is throbbing.

But then Nate says one word that none of us understand: "Caleb." What's he talking about? Riley had a son? Caleb, his name was Caleb. Was? Still is, because he's alive and well in Brooklyn. In ACS custody—what's that? Administration for Children's Services. Foster care. Riley's son had been removed and put into foster care.

My throat goes dry like roasted earth. "I don't get it," I say, is all I can say, like what he's said is a joke whose punch line I don't get.

My father's face is stricken. He looks like he is staring straight into the eyes of a ghost.

"She had a son," he tells us.

We all stare at him in disbelief, vaguely shaking our heads. Is there some chance he means something else?

A million questions in my head; I don't know which one to pick first. "How old is he?"

Nate looks at me with raised eyebrows. "He's five and a half," he says. "Started kindergarten last fall."

"Wait, I'm still lost," Alex says. "Riley had a son, five and a half years old. That's what you're saying?" Nate nods. "Who is his father?"

"I don't know," he says. "I assume that if his father were involved, he'd be with his father now. I never uncovered anything to suggest she was co-parenting, so I get the feeling he's not involved."

"Why wasn't he living with Riley?" Dad demands.

"The basic story, as I remember it from her file with the Administration for Child Services, is that one day last fall, his school was closed. Riley had to be somewhere. When she couldn't get a sitter, she left him at home in the understanding that the sitter would be there shortly—"

"She left him alone and went to work?" Alex says.

My mother's horror kicks in. "You can't leave a five-year-old alone," I say.

"That's what they told her," he says. "He got taken into ACS custody. In the report, Riley insisted that she had never done this before and never would again. But a drug test came back positive for opiates, so she was deemed an unfit parent. And Caleb was put into foster care."

"Is that where he is now?" I ask.

Nate nods. "They went to court, and the judge issued what's called an order of dispensation, which is basically a list of things Riley needed to do to regain custody," he says. "But she wasn't working on them. After everything that happened, I think she lost hope. She was resigned to losing him."

I nod and feel my face furrow. "Why didn't she tell us that she had— Jesus, a five-year-old. Was she ever going to tell her father that he had a grandson? This is crazy."

My palms hurt, I realize, because I've been holding my hands in tight fists. Then I notice that Alex is staring at me. I meet her eyes.

"We need to find him," she says. "And more than that. Colleen, this kid needs a—" The words stick in her throat. "He needs a home."

I nod.

"We're talking about a little boy who has lost his mother," Dad says. "He's gone through a lot. You two know that better than anyone."

We both nod. "We need to bring Caleb home," Alex says.

We pack up our things and hail a cab to take us back to the hotel. We go into my room, and Nate gets out his computer and starts typing.

Nate calls the New York ACS office. Someone tells him that the case-worker is a woman named Liz Davidson, and he writes her number down on the hotel notepad. When he hangs up, he looks at the notepad, then picks it up and gestures with it.

"At this point," he says, "I think it's best that you three take this phone number and contact Liz yourselves. These are matters for your family to consider and decide."

I cross my arms and nod my head. "You're right," I say. "Well, thank you."

I shake his hand and then Alex does, giving him a warm two-handed handshake.

"Mr. Hensler," Dad says, extending his hand as well. "You're the last person to see my daughter alive. I feel like I'm supposed to blame you, but I'm not sure what for."

"I'm sorry, sir," Nate says, shaking his hand "I desperately wish that this had ended differently."

"We all do," Dad says. "Thank you for befriending her."

"I won't soon forget Riley," he says. "I promise you that."

He gathers up his coat and his laptop, I open the door for him, and he's gone.

Now there is nothing more to do but call this woman . . . what was her name? I look at the note that Nate scrawled. Liz Davidson. I look at Dad and Alex.

"Are we ready for this?" I ask.

They both nod.

I look at the phone number, then breathe and blow out. If Riley was taking drugs while she was pregnant, this child could have any of a variety of psychological, behavioral, or emotional challenges. She was a single mom; we don't know anything about her parenting strategies—if she even had any—and we don't know anything about who has been taking care of this child. He is in kindergarten, I guess we know that much, but we don't know where he's attending school. He's my nephew, and we don't know a single thing about him.

I'm anxious. Alex will make the case that he should come and live with me, and I will be expected to open my arms and welcome him in. Into my broken family, into a burned-out house. The truth is, right now, I have nothing to offer this child.

"Are we sure?" I say to Alex.

She shrugs. "I think so."

I pick up my phone and dial the number, feeling like we are all holding our breath. The call goes to the woman's voice mail, and a crisp, perky woman's voice tells me to leave a message for Liz. I explain as quickly and succinctly as I can who I am, why I'm calling, and of course, my number.

I put my phone down and minutes pass, and I feel like we are all staring at it. My teeth grind. I hate being in the city without Riley; my sister should be here. How could she have had a child and not told us? So many secrets. Then I remember: the Thanksgiving when we almost saw Riley, the one when she crawled through Maddie's window only to crawl back out and leave, was seven years ago. She must have just found out she was pregnant. She must have come to Thanksgiving to make a grand gesture, lifting up the curtain with a great Ta-da, *I'm having a baby!* but when she arrived, her bravado failed. All she could do was climb through the window of my young daughter and talk only to her. They were two children, giggling, sharing secrets.

Suddenly, my phone rings. I look at the caller ID—Liz Davidson. My throat goes dry and my mind blank. I can't answer. I hand the phone to Alex. She looks at me in shock, then answers.

"Hello?" she says. We hear only her side of the conversation. First, she explains again who we are, why we're calling, who we're looking for. "Yes, that's the one," she says. "Caleb Emery, five and a half years old, I believe . . . My name is Alex Emery, I'm his mother's sister, his aunt. I'm from Massachusetts, and I'm here in a hotel room with my father, George, and my other sister, Colleen Newcomb . . . No, we never knew, even that he existed, before an hour ago . . ." Then, Liz talks for a while. "Yes, Riley Emery . . . Correct, Massachusetts," Alex says. Then, quiet. "Oh . . . I never saw that . . . If my father did, he never mentioned it." Alex looks at me and Dad with questioning eyes. "Hold on." She holds the phone down for a moment. "Dad, she says they sent letters to you and me telling us that Caleb was in foster care. I didn't get anything, did you?"

First, he looks blank, then somewhat embarrassed. "After delivering letters all those years, I'm not always so good about opening them."

Alex nods and adds, "If a letter came while I was getting ready to go to India, I could have easily missed it."

I roll my eyes and turn away.

My sister puts the phone back to her ear. "No, for whatever reason, the letters were never received." Then it's a few minutes of *yes, okay*, umm-hum, *I see, of course, absolutely*, and *yes, certainly*. My hand drifts up to my face, and I hold it against my mouth. I breathe, or at least, I try to remember to.

Finally, Alex says a few more words into the phone. "Email would be great," she says. "You can email them to me at . . ." She spells out her email address. "If your supervisor approves, when we will get those? A couple of hours. All right, I'll check this evening. Ms. Davidson, thank you so much for all your help, we really appreciate it. We'll talk tomorrow. Thanks."

She turns the phone off, then she sits down in a chair, looking into the distance. "Coll," she says, "could you grab me a bottle of water?" I grab one from the mini-fridge; she takes it and drinks, then looks away again.

"Well?" I say.

"Umm," she starts. "He is Riley's son. I was all prepared to explain everything about us; I thought she'd want to know all about Riley and why we think she never told us she had a son, and where we've been all these years. I thought I'd have to, I don't know, defend, explain."

"But she didn't ask?" I say.

Alex shakes her head. "She wanted to know exactly one thing: if we could be a resource for Caleb. I kind of got the feeling that if I said no, she was going to tell me to have a happy life and get on to the other things on her list."

"Resource, what kind of a resource?" I say. "That could mean a lot of different things."

Alex looks like she is only barely hearing me. "Right. And she understood that. And actually, she said she didn't need me to nail down what that meant, just yes or no, could I or we be a resource for the little boy. I told her we had no idea he existed until a few moments ago. She said we were all probably in shock and needed some time to process."

"She's right about that," I say. I breathe in, blow out. "Is there any chance we can meet him before we go home?"

"No," she says. "They need to do background checks on all of us. It'll take them a couple of weeks . . ."

"Weeks? Why weeks?" I say.

"I don't know, these things all take time," she says. "But even then, they won't let us see him unless . . . we . . ."

"Commit to becoming resources, whatever that might mean?" I say.

Alex looks at me. "Right," she says. "But she said that if her supervisor approves it, she might be able to email me some photos of him."

"Good," Dad says. "It would help to see pictures. Because right now, this doesn't feel real."

Alex and I look at Dad. He's sitting on the edge of my bed, his head in his hands.

"That's true," I say.

"Dad, how are you handling all this?" Alex says. "This is kind of a shock to the system. If you need to eat or lie down, just let us know."

"I don't need anything," he says. "I wish we could meet this boy in person."

"Me too, but maybe it's good that they won't let us," Alex says. "We might think we could pop in and say, *Nice to meet you, now we're going home*. If we're not going to get involved with him in a serious way right now, maybe we shouldn't meet him. He's going through a lot."

"But what counts as involved?" I ask. "I don't want to be crass—"

"Colleen . . ." Alex says.

"What, I don't!" I say. "But I don't think I can get much more involved than hugs and birthday presents right now. I mean, I'm sorry; I'm just being honest. I have a lot going on."

Alex sighs. "Okay," she says. "It's been a very long day. Let's all go back to our rooms and take a break. What time is it?"

"It's four," Dad says, looking at his wrist.

"She said it might take a couple of hours to get me pictures," she says. "Let's get together at six and see if they've come. Then we can go find some food and figure out, I don't know, what to do next."

"Okay," I say. "Good plan."

Though I know I will spend the next hours looking at the clock and pacing my room and thinking about Riley. Which is pretty much what I did last time I was in New York.

Chapter 26

We all go back to our simple small rooms, which are in a tidy row off the corridor on the hotel's sixth floor. I lie down on my bed. I'd forgotten how nice a real bed can feel, and this one is soft and so warm. I turn on the news and doze restlessly, waking with a start every so often.

Two hours later my cell phone rings. It's Colleen.

"Did I wake you up?" she asks.

"Not really. What time is it?" I say, sitting up, rubbing my eyes.

"Quarter after six," she says. "I'm here with Dad. Did you check your email?"

"Not yet," I say. "I'll be right there."

I get up, grab my phone, throw on shoes, and head over to Dad's hotel room. Colleen and Dad stare at me as I walk through the door.

"Well, did you get it?" Colleen asks.

"Hold on," I say.

I type in the password to open my phone. I press the button for my email. My thumb misses the target though, and a map opens, and I can't make it go until it loads all the way. Finally, my email opens. I scroll through but I don't see the one I'm looking for. I go back to the top, and this time

I see it. An email from Davidson, Liz, with attachments. Suddenly, my face feels hot.

"Here it is," I say. I click the email to open it. The message is simple.

Please see attached photos. Contact me tomorrow if you have any questions.

Best regards, Liz

I click one of the photos with my thumb, and the little animated wheel spins.

The first picture loads, and a little boy's face comes into focus. "Look," is all I say.

The boy stands in front of a playground tree on a day that looks sunny, but the temperature must be cool because he's wearing a hoodie, his shoulders hunched against the cold. His hair is brown and shaggy and a little windblown. His eyes are light brown and squinting a little; probably shrinking from the sun and wind. His mouth is shaped in an almost smile, but a reserved one with lips pressed together, an expression that seems slightly worried. Maybe he doesn't want to sit still for a photo. Maybe he just wants to play.

"He looks like her," Dad says.

Dad's right, he does look like Riley. The shapes of his face and eyes are so familiar. I feel like I'm looking at someone I've known for a long time.

We are all quiet as we look at the phone, silently holding our breath. You can't know someone's personality from a photo, I think, but there is a warmth to this child; he looks thoughtful. Then, I think of Riley. I see her figure in my living room, tall and slender, silhouetted against the candlelight. I hear her footsteps against the hard wood of my floor, and I remember her words: *You were my heart. Alex, you and Colleen. When I left, I had no heart. Or maybe it was my soul that I lost; I don't know. Maybe if I had had a mom, or at least remembered her, I might have gotten something right.*

You got him right, Riley. Wherever you are now, please know: you got him right.

I look at his picture, his eyes, his face. What are we doing? Looking at this picture of a child . . . Why? He's our family, and we know this; we don't need to look at a photograph to tell us what we need to do. Caleb needs to come and be with us. I look at Colleen; she stares intently at the screen in the dim light of this clean white hotel room. Is she considering bringing him home to live with her? I can't tell. A thought occurs to me. I can't figure out if it's crazy, so I imagine speaking the words out loud: *Caleb will come and live with me. I will raise him in my house in Newbury, near the line with Rowley, overlooking the Great Marsh.*

Is that crazy? It sounds crazy. A single mom living in a haunted house.

But that was the original plan, wasn't it? Have a baby and raise it by myself. It's the same plan. Plus, the house isn't really haunted. I'm the one who is, or maybe was. Maybe I'm ready not to be.

Dad looks at the phone through the bottom of his reading glasses, frowning in concentration. With his hands in the pockets of his dungarees, he shakes his head and shrugs. "Why didn't she tell us about him?" he asks. "We would have helped her. We would have done anything."

"That's the big question, Dad," Colleen says. "Why didn't our own sister tell us that she had a son?"

"That we had a nephew," I say. "That you had a grandson. There was so much that she never revealed to us. I don't think we'll ever know why she kept this secret."

I look at my phone and scroll to another photo. The child in these pictures has been through things we can't understand. He lost his mother and probably believed he was all alone in the world. I look at his face, and a surge of tears rises in my throat; I wish I could scoop him up in my arms and hold him and care for him the way I wish Riley had been cared for, the way I wish we all had.

In this photo, the little boy holds his animal up to the camera. The critter looks worn and beloved. One eye looks like it might be about to fall off. The animal is front and center, and the boy's face is only slightly visible behind it, but his eyes are squinting with a smile.

"Oh, look," Colleen says. "It's a turtle."

A bit later, when the sun has gone down behind clouds and the New York lights are glowing bold and bright, we leave the hotel for dinner, just to a place around the corner that serves burgers and beer, nothing fancy. Colleen and Dad look deflated; I probably do too, but I feel relieved. Today we found Caleb. We order our food, and then we are quiet. Nobody knows how to begin this conversation.

"I still wish I knew why she didn't tell us about him," Dad says. He takes a piece of bread from a basket on the table but puts it on his plate and does not eat it. "Why did she keep so many secrets?"

"It breaks my heart that she didn't take better care of him," Colleen says. "How could you leave a child on his own like that? Anything could have happened . . ."

"It doesn't matter now," I say. "She's gone."

"She could have done better." Colleen looks at us, at our faces. "Actually, you know what? I'm mad at her. She should have asked for help. There's nothing we wouldn't have done to help her." She glares at me. "Tell me I'm not right."

I don't know how to answer that, and neither does Dad. Colleen looks at us defiantly, like she's daring us to respond. And we don't; it seems better to let the live wire fizzle on the floor.

"This is just like when she was five years old," Colleen continues, "and she decided to paint her shoes with nail polish and the nail polish spilled on the carpet. Do you remember that Alex?"

Yes, I nod.

"We always clean up after her. Just like with Mom, we get stuck with the mess of life. It's like . . ." She catches her breath, a choke of tears, her voice low. "It's like, if we don't have the courage to just end it all outright, then we get left behind to manage everything for all the people who do." She starts crying and pulls a tissue from her purse. "And I hate it. We already did this, remember? And now here we are again. And it's not fair."

My gaze goes down to the table. I don't know what to tell her. I am depleted.

"She should be here." Colleen grits her teeth, her voice louder now. She pounds the table with her fist. "Riley should be *here*."

Dad drinks his beer, and a moment later the waiter puts our plates in front of us. Colleen pushes the lettuce and croutons of her Caesar salad around on her plate for a few moments but doesn't eat anything. "I'm sorry," she finally says. "I need to go for a run. I'll see you both for breakfast."

And she leaves. I don't have much appetite either, but I take a few bites of my burger, mostly to keep Dad company.

"It was nice to see pictures of Caleb today," Dad says. "I feel a little like I met him."

I smile. "Yes."

"I wonder how we will do this," Dad says. "We're the only family he has, and we're so far away."

I nod slightly.

"And the way we live is so different from what he's used to. City people, they like their crowded streets, their smelly subway stations, all the noise and hustle bustle. Is it like that in India? It must be."

I laugh slightly. "A little."

"You still thinking about going back?"

"I'm not sure." I chew my bite of burger, then take a sip of water. "Dad, I have a new idea. I think I want to adopt Caleb." This is the first time I've spoken it out loud.

His head bobs as he thinks about it; I'm grateful to him for not laughing. "Colleen will think I'm crazy. Or . . . assume that she needs to take him in since she knows how to raise kids."

"Well, even when things get back to normal for your sister, her life is never going to be like it was before."

"I can't . . . figure out, though, if this is a big mistake," I say.

Dad reaches for my arm. "Alexis," he says wearily, "there's nothing you can't do if you make up your mind. So there you go; just make up your mind."

I can barely speak. I reach over and hug my father. "Thanks, Daddy," I say, wiping tears away with my sleeve. "I already have."

And then a picture pops into in my mind like a postcard: a little house in Newbury, down a quiet street, overlooking the marsh. When I return there, I will need to buy furniture, toys, books, clothes. I will need to get a full-time job and find out about schools. I will need to transform Marjorie's cottage from a house that I inherited and hoped to sell, into a home for a little boy. This little boy. My nephew.

Chapter 27

Tuesday, March 4, 2014
Colleen

Finally, finally, thank God, I am free and running. My hair is tied back in a sloppy ponytail that bobs. I am running through the rainy city at night, in the night that's dark and wet, and my feet pommel the pavement, and I am going, going, gone. I am wearing my cold-weather gear, which is a little water resistant but not really. All I know is the bounce under my feet as I hit the hard sidewalks, squeezing past and through people—*Pardon me, excuse me, sorry*—and the traffic lights at every corner and how they turn from red hand, stop, to white figure, go.

And I run. I run.

For a while I am in a zone, hitting each street corner just in time to see the light change. As I dash across, I try to avoid crashing into cars or people. But my hair and clothes are drenched, and my eyes are bleary from the electric glare, the rain and the night. It's hard to see. It's hard to think. But frankly, that's what I want.

Anger, hot and thick, an ignition beneath me. I could run all the way to New Jersey. My breath now, pushing, grunting each time my feet hit the ground. I am eagle-focused, all I see is the next traffic light; when it is red, I concentrate to change it. I reach the corner, and it's go. So, I go.

These women, my mother, my sister, so fragile, so breakable, so foolish. If having children was going to ruin your life, why have them? They both had a choice; they could have ended the pregnancies or given the babies up for adoption. Mom made her choice twenty-five years ago, and it's like the three of us have been carrying her body in a bag slung over our shoulders. Riley, our sweet Riley, was the worst off because she never knew that she was one of us. She thought she was immune because she didn't remember. She was carrying a dead woman's corpse the whole time and had no idea. If only we could have reached her, we would have warned her—*Riley, open the sack. Do you see? It's Mom! You can't take another step in the world until you look at what you have and set it down.*

A puddle on the sidewalk ahead of me; I swerve to avoid crashing into people, then try to reach the edge in time to jump over it. I miss and splash right into the center. Now my sneakers are soaked. My throat hurts from the cold, from the rain, from everything that's happened today. How is it possible that Riley had a child? She had become someone we didn't know; that's what we've learned today.

So much strangeness. How in the night, in the dark, in the storm, Alex says that Riley appeared and told her that she was abused by her babysitter's son after Mom died. Is this true? I don't know what to make of it. I remember so clearly that Alex and I never liked that kid—what was his name? Arthur. We were children ourselves, and even we knew. We knew it in our bones.

It hurts my head when I try to understand it all, and nausea pushes through me, so I run harder and faster, still. I turn the corner onto a more residential street, running past brownstones, under streetlights, some lit, some dark. No more traffic lights to try and change with my mind, but plenty of people to squeeze past. My feet splash as I run; I have no idea where I am or where I am going, and I can't slow down to think about it. I look at street signs, read the words on them, but I'm not even sure what they say.

A bag of trash left on the street, spilling onto the sidewalk. I will leap over it like Wonder Woman. But I slip during takeoff and land smack in the middle. Now I'm covered in trash. Some young people stop to help me, ask if I'm okay. I don't care about being okay; I let them help me stand up, shake the trash off, and then I have no words of thanks. I push away and keep going.

I have always been polite and appropriate. I follow the rules, I cooperate, I dress for the occasion, I bring something delicious for the potluck. Sorry, *that* Colleen isn't available right. You'll have to leave a message.

I turn another corner onto a busier street; there, I stop and catch my breath. I look down at my knee; my favorite leggings are torn, and now I'm furious almost to the point of tears. I start running again, and I imagine my rage pounding the ground with each pump of my legs. Everything I always thought would save me has failed. Everything I love is ending. Was being married to me really so bad, Eric? Every moment of my life was for you and them. I never asked for anything in return.

Sharp raindrops fall in my eyes, stinging them. My hands are freezing. When I was eight years old, I didn't understand why people had to leave and I still don't.

My breath heaves with an onslaught of tears, but I am bone weary of crying, so I let it out with a roar. People turn to stare, and I pound past them, stinking like trash. I look through lit windows of shops and cafés where lovely people have their lovely evenings; wouldn't it be nice to be a normal person tonight?

I run down a street past some big industrial buildings. New York is lousy tonight. I am past the café area now; how quickly the neighborhoods change in this city. How fast I go, even in this weather. Now I am surrounded by dumpsters, scaffolding, run-down stores with neon signs, gas stations, shops with window signs in other languages. I pass two or three homeless people slumped by the side of a building, and a man walking his dog. I do not look at any of them. I do not smile. I run.

Two plastic crates stacked by the side of a building. I push myself, bound up and over. In my mind, I look like a Nike ad. I slide a little on the landing, but I keep going. My knees ache. *Pain doesn't matter*, I tell myself. Pain isn't real, is just a sensation. A busy intersection up ahead; I feel like I need to go that way. And suddenly, I am in a weird new place, filled with strangers and abrasive light, and loud, frantic laughter.

I stop to look around and realize that now, I am really lost. But which is the way back? I hate cities. I look in different directions, but nothing looks familiar. A couple of streetlights are out, and I can't figure out where I am. I start to move, just a light jog at first. Then someone brushes against me, and I panic. I have to get out of here. I start jogging harder, faster, then I build up to a full run.

I am going as fast as I can manage, grunting with each pulse. But then—my foot hits a slippery spot, and my torso shoots sideways, then hurtles into a brick building, in the dark and the rain.

Crash.

It takes me a minute to gather myself, to even figure out what happened. A couple of people run over to help me; I don't look at their faces. They prop me up, ask if I'm okay. I insist that I'm fine, that I don't need help. I don't exactly yell at them to take their hands off me, but almost. As I insist, they back away.

I need to breathe. I cradle my soaking head in my hands while I try to catch my breath. My head hurts; I banged it up. Then I examine my leg, which is starting to throb. It's the other leg, and now *that* knee of my leggings is torn. I shout an obscenity out loud. The blood is starting to flow. The pain is beginning to bloom.

I press my hands against my head and whimper pathetically. Sitting in the rain, bleeding, bleating, gasping for breath, while my life falls apart around me. I am embarrassed, but this is what I am right now, world. This is the only me I have to offer.

The pain grows more intense. I pull off the tank top under my jacket and wrap it around my leg to stall the blood. I stand, I try to walk, but I can't. All I can do is limp. I find the doorway of a darkened shop and stand under it. Just then, the real rain begins to fall. A downpour, as if everything before now has been prologue.

I wrestle my cell phone out of my zipped pocket and press a button; it dials. After one ring, a voice.

"Mom, hi," Maddie says, and she sounds happy to hear from me. I am overwhelmed to hear her voice, and I cannot speak. "Mom, are you there?"

"Hi, baby," I finally say.

"Are you okay?" she says. "I called you earlier. Did you get my messages?"

"I haven't checked, sorry."

"Is that rain?" she asks. "I can hear it."

"Yeah, I was out for a run. Here comes the deluge." I reach my hand out and let the cold rain fall through my fingers, just like Maddie and Ethan used to do when they were little. "I miss you guys."

"Me too, Mom," she says. "I've been thinking about you. I'm so sorry about Aunt Riley."

"Thank you, sweetheart," I say. "Listen, I have to tell you something important."

"Okay," she says. "It sounds serious . . ."

"I need to tell you the truth, Maddie. Your grandmother, my mother . . . She . . ." But I can't say it. I can't push the words from my lungs.

"I can't hear you, Mom," she says. "What about my grandmother?"

"She didn't die of cancer," I say. I have to whisper to keep the tears at bay. "She committed suicide."

For a moment then, nobody speaks; there's only the sound of rain pouring down.

"She did?" she says.

"Yes," I say. "I didn't tell you before now because . . . I guess there are a lot of reasons."

"How did she—?"

"She drowned herself in our bathtub."

Maddie takes a moment to digest that. "Mom, that's so sad."

Tears start streaming down my face, but you would not know from looking at me whether they were tears or rain. "Listen, Madison, I want you to know. I plan to be in your life for a long, long time. I will see you graduate from college, I will walk you down the aisle, and I will hold your babies."

"Mom, I—"

"I mean, if that's what you want," I say. "If there's something else you'd rather do in your life, Maddie, you or Ethan, I want to be there to cheer you on, no matter what it is. Okay?"

She laughs a little. "That's what you always say, Mom," she says.

"Well, I will. I promise, Madison."

"I love you so much, Mom. Come home, okay? We miss you."

I nod. "I will. I love you too."

I take a cab back to the hotel. My leg is pulsating, and my head aches so much, I'm almost dizzy. In my heart I feel like something in me has been pushed to the end, driven hard and broken. I feel exhausted but released. I want to remember this feeling. Exhausted but released. This is what I need.

Inside my room I peel my leggings off carefully; there is blood, a good amount, and a mean bruise. I take a hot shower, and then I am cleaned of the rain and the tears and the stink of city trash. I wrap a small hand towel around my leg to contain the bleeding, put on clean clothes, then call Alex.

"Hi," I say, aware that I behaved badly earlier. Aware that an apology is owed.

"Hi," she says.

I'm not sure what to say next, so I go straight to logistics. "I went for a run and hurt my leg. Do you mind taking a look at it?"

"Sure," she says. "Come on over."

I go to her room. She's drinking red wine from a hotel water glass.

"Colleen, what did you do?" she says, touching my head.

"I slipped," I say, wincing. "The roads are wet."

She sits down in front of me and examines my leg. "Good grief," she says.

"I didn't realize how bad it was . . . and then I couldn't walk."

"I'll bandage it up. Have you taken any aspirin?" I shake my head. "Actually, Tylenol would be better. I have some; let me grab it."

She brings out the bandages and the antibacterial stuff from her first aid kit and fixes up my leg and my head. When she's done, I look like a war hero. "Thanks, Alex," I say. "Do you bring all this stuff with you wherever you go?"

She scoffs. "I just carry the basics. If you were having a heart attack, I wouldn't be much help."

I laugh a little. "Alex," I say. "It's just you and me now."

"I know," she says. She shakes an instant ice pack and puts it on my injured leg. "Hold this right there."

I shudder at the pain, but the cold begins to numb it. "I'm sorry I walked out on dinner," I say.

"That's okay." She gestures to me to sit with my back up against her headboard, then puts two pillows under my leg to elevate it. "How's that?"

"Better. Thanks." She pours me a glass of wine, and I take it gratefully. "One thing I can't stop thinking about. The detective talked to Riley because I gave him permission. So, I don't know if I—did Riley overdose because of something he said or did? Should I have told him not to talk to her and just called, I don't know, a psychiatrist? A mental hospital? The police? Should I have gone to her myself? Or you, maybe, or Dad?"

Alex shakes her head. "I don't know."

"Alex, I knew, we knew, that this was . . . possible. And I could have helped her, but . . . I didn't do it right. I let her down."

"Oh, sweetie," she says. "Okay, I have to tell you something weird. Just hear me out, okay?"

I grab a tissue from the hotel tissue box and listen.

She looks at me urgently. "This is from . . . that night. Right before she left, Riley told me to tell you none of this was your fault. She said, 'There's not anything you could have done to change what happened.' It didn't mean anything to me at the time. But now, I wonder . . ."

My head stings, and I wince and put my hand to it.

"Do you want another ice pack?" Alex asks.

I shake my head no. "Damn it. I don't know what to do with that either," I say. "Finding out what . . . what that boy down the street did to her, and now this . . . afterlife exoneration. Do we just accept it all at face value? I mean, I believe you saw something, and I believe that you don't think you were dreaming, and I don't think you made it up . . ."

"I've been thinking about this too," Alex says. "I don't usually go around saying that I see dead people, right?"

"Not before now," I say.

"Okay. So tell me: When I told you about that kid down the street, didn't it make sense?" she says. "Like, suddenly a lot of things made sense.

And I wouldn't have come up with that on my own. I barely remembered that those people existed."

I nod slowly. "And we let that happen to her . . . What kind of sisters were we?"

Alex looks down, her brow wrinkled in thought. "We were children, Colleen. We didn't know what to look for or what to ask. We thought she was in good hands. And Riley was so little, she couldn't tell us. Especially if he was threatening her. All those nights, we thought she was crying because of Mom. And she was . . . but that wasn't all. There's no way we could have known."

"Maybe," I say.

"As for this other thing Riley said about you," she continues. "I mean, I don't know. Even if it was a dream or wishful thinking, or something that I convinced myself happened or outright made up. I mean, the search for Riley didn't turn out the way we hoped. But there's no downside to accepting that it's not your fault. Or anybody's fault."

"Sure, but—"

"Then don't take it from Riley, take it from me," Alex says. "Colleen, you did all you could. Please, please do not blame yourself for this. Or for Mom either, for that matter. We're only human. And these cycles we get ourselves tangled in don't do anybody any good."

"You're probably right," I say, dabbing my eyes. "Oh, I hate it when other people are right."

She laughs at that and pours some more wine, then sits next to me on the bed. For a while we are both quiet.

"So, did you ever suspect there was a Caleb?" she asks.

"Nope," I say, taking a sip of wine. "Did she say anything about him that night?"

She nods. "I realize now that she was talking about him in code. Of course. Hey, Colleen. Want to hear something really crazy? I'm going to adopt Caleb. I want to bring him home to Newbury."

For a moment, I don't know what to say. "Wow, Alex."

"I don't know what's involved with the process," she says. "I'll need a job, of course. I'll need a lot of things. But I—I feel in my gut like this is what I need to do."

"What does that mean for India?"

She shrugs. "I guess it will have to wait."

"Yeah, that little boy needs some stability."

"I know," she says. "You think I'm up for it?"

"I'm not going to lie to you," I say. "It's tough to raise a child with a partner, harder still to do it alone. And work full-time. Have you thought about what you'll do for childcare?"

"I haven't thought about much at all yet." She thinks about it for a moment. "The weird thing is, I believe that everything will fall into place. Maybe I'll find a job that has day care, or maybe Dad can watch Caleb after school sometimes. Maybe his teenage cousins could hang out with him from time to time, or maybe his aunt?"

"You can depend on us for whatever you need," I say. "Are you kidding? Maddie and Ethan will be thrilled to hear they have a cousin."

Alex nods. "This is the right thing to do. And I believe that if I do the right thing, the stars will align and the logistics will fall in place. Right? Maybe not all at once, but over time."

I adjust the ice pack on my leg and think until the words of my question organize themselves. "Alex," I start. "Are you doing this because it's the right thing to do or because it's what you want to do?"

She looks down in thought. Then she looks up at me and nods. "I want this."

A million questions go through my head, and I consider them as I stare at Alex. Will it be hard for Caleb to leave the city? What if Alex resents not going back to India? What if Caleb has mental and emotional problems and needs more support than she's ready to give him? What if Riley took drugs and drank while she was pregnant and now Caleb has neurological problems? All those questions, but the next moment, I am filled with warmth and none of those questions matter.

Finally, I just smile. "I'm glad you're adopting him. I'm glad he's . . . coming home."

"Me too," she says. "Colleen, I want to see these kids grow up. I want to know who they'll all become. And I want us to get old, you and me."

"Me too, I want all that too," I say.

"Let's make it a plan, okay? To stick around."

"Do you think we can make it?" I ask.

"Not if you keep up these kamikaze stunts . . ." she says, smiling.

"I'm serious, Alex."

"Okay," she says, seriously. "Yes, I think we can make it. It's a choice. But we have to choose, every day, every *single* day, to stay until the next day. It's that simple."

"And that hard," I say.

Chapter 28

The next day Colleen and Dad and I take the train back to Boston. We carry with us the simple white box that the crematorium gave us to transport Riley's ashes. We climb on the train and find four seats facing each other with a small table in between. Dad, Colleen, and I each shove our luggage onto the storage rack overhead. I sit on the aisle, and Dad sits next to me by the window. Colleen places the box on the seat beside her. Riley gets the window. I look at the box; I should feel like Riley is with us somehow. I don't. I feel like she's been gone for longer than we knew.

After we get settled, the train heaves itself with great volume and slowly begins pulling out of the station. Our car is thankfully quiet. I have a magazine with me, *This Old House*, but I am not ready to read. I can't take my eyes off that white box.

"I always forget that Riley was short for Aurelia," I say. "What a beautiful name."

Colleen glances up from her magazine. "The name Riley, it just . . . suited her."

"Your mother picked that name," Dad says. "Alexis is named after a poet your mom liked. Colleen was my mother's name. Aurelia was from your mother's side. Her mother, maybe, but I'm not sure."

I peer at Colleen. "What did Nate say Mom's mother's name was?"

She thinks a moment with lips pursed. "P something. Polly? Paula?"

"That sounds right. I wonder who Aurelia was," I say. We both shrug and are quiet for a while. I cannot look away from the box. "Any thoughts on what we should do?" I say. "With . . . her?"

"I was just wondering the same thing," she says. "Dad, what do you think?"

He looks at the seat beside Colleen, his expression tense. He does not speak, but he has not forgotten the question. Finally, he opens his mouth, but he changes his mind and closes it again. He tries again. "She should be with her mother."

"Union Cemetery?" Colleen says. "We can inter her ashes."

Dad and I nod. I say, "It will be nice for Caleb to have someplace to visit her."

"Do you think he'll want to?" Colleen asks.

I consider it. "I don't know. I hope so. Maybe not at first, but later."

That's as far as we get, and then we don't talk about Riley anymore. The train starts rolling. After a few moments, Colleen and I turn to our magazines, and soon after, Dad falls asleep. Every now and then I glance up at the Riley box and then stare out the window. When I get hungry, I rifle through my purse for a little bag of almonds from the hotel. I see them, then, something I'd forgotten existed—a small sealed envelope, addressed to a woman in California, a woman I've never met. "Mrs. William Montgomery," says the name on the envelope.

I hold it up. "Colleen," I say quietly.

She glances up. It takes her a moment to recognize it. "Not now," she says.

"No," I say. "I just don't want us to forget I have it. I'm curious about what's inside."

She nods; she sighs. "Me too."

I glance at her magazine and read aloud the name of the article she has up in front of her. "'Ten Versatile Pieces You Need in Your Closet This Season.'"

She looks down. "Is that what I'm reading?"

I look back down at my magazine. "I've been looking at the pictures of this 1850s town house for an hour, and I still can't figure out what city it's in."

Colleen glances at it. "Atlanta," she says, pointing. "Says so there in big letters."

I smirk. "Thanks."

Dad sleeps soundly, lulled by the movement of the train. When his snores get so loud that Colleen gives me a look, I shake him a little to change his position, and he quiets down. Then I give in to my state of utter distraction and stare out the window past him. Cities and towns, graffiti-splayed walls and wrecked-car junkyards, and the occasional glimpse, brief but lovely, of pristine blue moments of bays and oceans.

My beautiful sister, Riley, Aurelia. You didn't know what she looked like if all you saw was her image enticing you to buy perfume or jewelry. That was not who she was; that was an illusion she created. Of which, it turns out, there were many. We might have found her, I think; we could have found her, and we almost did. Who fell down on the job? Me, Colleen, that private detective?

God?

What did I see that night? Was the thing that ghost-Riley told me about being molested true? It must have been. Maybe the actual fact of it doesn't matter; my sister is dead either way, and she's dead because she could no longer endure her pain, whether it came from assault or grief or losing her son, or other things we don't know about, or all of it altogether doesn't matter. It was too much for her to carry alone, and instead of turning to us, she let her sadness erode her from the inside out until she was empty. And maybe that was part of our mother's legacy as well: Riley didn't know that she could ask for help because she had never seen someone do it.

The train rumbles along beneath us. A heavy man with a beard and a Red Sox cap crowds past me on his way to the bathroom, then jostles me on his way back. Haunts and spooks and all those ghosty things in my house in Newbury, none of them supernatural. But then, there was a ghost, wasn't there? And when the ghost herself actually entered my house, she knocked on the door and entered on two legs. Riley, Aurelia, what happened? Why didn't you tell us about Caleb? Why didn't you reach out to us sooner? You could have come home. The questions spin around my head as the train rumbles on, and I can't stop asking them, though I know they have no answers.

The train rolls into Boston's South Station around six in the evening and pulls to a hissing stop. We head out to the platform in the dry and chilly day, and as we go through the station, the distinct smell of Dunkin' Donuts coffee welcomes us. Our little family walks together, quietly, toward the parking garage. We find Colleen's car and begin the drive back to Amesbury.

After almost an hour on the highway, we reach our exit and turn onto the local roads that will take us home. At once, the landscape is familiar, the air tasting of salt from the ocean kingdom of Salisbury on the other side of the highway.

At the house Colleen and I try to help Dad with his luggage. "I got it," he says.

Inside, the living room looks different. Before we went to New York, Dad managed to clear away some of the piles and boxes. Some still remain, but they're stacked against the wall. Colleen and I look around, amazed that now some sections of the rug are exposed.

"Dad, you didn't clear this out yourself, did you?" I ask. "You shouldn't be lifting heavy boxes."

"Nah," he says. "I paid a neighbor's kid and his buddy to come over with a pickup truck. I decided I didn't need to look at everything. I just needed things out."

"Wow, Dad," Colleen says. "What got into you?"

He shrugs. "I don't know," he says, sitting down in his soft chair. "Girls, I've been thinking. It might be time to sell the house."

Colleen and I pull chairs from the kitchen and sit down beside him.

"When I got the news about Riley," he starts, his face heavy with grief, "it was a shock. You're not supposed to . . . see your child go before you do."

Colleen touches his arm. "I'm so sorry, Dad," she says.

"I know, hon," he says, patting her arm. "But it made me think about my life. And you girls. And everything we've been through. I know I wasn't always the best father in the world . . . especially to three little girls who needed a mom."

"You did your best, Dad," I say. "We know that."

He dips his head slightly. "What I realized when Riley died is, I would change any of this, all of this, if I could. But I need to move on. I'm selling the house this summer."

Colleen and I exchange looks. "This is a big decision," she says.

"But, Dad," I say. "Where will you go?"

He shrugs. "I always wanted to live near the water, get back to fishing, maybe get a little Sunfish sailboat. Maybe I'll find a cheap place to stay, Salisbury or Hampton. Someplace small, anyway."

"I can help you fix this place up," I say. "I have some experience."

"We'll all help. Even Ethan and Maddie can pitch in," Colleen says. "I'm going to miss this house. A lot of memories."

"Too many memories," he says. "Too many."

After dinner we say good night to Dad, and Colleen drives me back to my place. As we ride, we both feel it, a combination of grief, relief, and exhaustion. We get to my house, and Colleen lets me go with a goodbye hug. I walk through the house and switch on the lights; I brace myself for sounds, footsteps, voices, but there's nothing. I go sit on the floor in the living room. How could Riley have been here, in this exact spot? How did any of it happen?

And a new development: Caleb coming home to me, home to this place. What would Riley think of that? What did she say—she always saw me with kids. I shiver a little when I remember. That makes two of us, Riley.

I wander through the empty rooms and consider how I will go about preparing for Caleb. I walk upstairs and stand in the threshold of the room that will be his bedroom. He'll need a bed, for starters. And a desk. A nice, warm, cheerful rug. A television! But not in his room, just in the house. He'll need bookshelves and books to put in them. A toy box and toys. He'll need new sneakers and high boots for exploring the marsh. He'll need a bathing suit for the beach, and sunscreen and a bright-colored pail and shovel. He will need a butterfly net for spring, and a Mason jar for fireflies. He will demand a dog. And maybe we'll get one of those too.

But if we get a dog and bookshelves and stacks of books . . . I will have to make peace with the fact that it might be a very long time before I get to India. It's bittersweet, but maybe it's okay. India will be there when I am ready.

And in the meantime, I will make a life for myself in one place, a surprising life in an unlikely house, close to where I grew up, the last place I thought I would land. It's the lesson my mother taught: you can create a new life for yourself, but you can't cut yourself off from the person you used to be. Like Marjorie said, *Your origins are part of your DNA*. You can't change where you're from simply by relocating.

There is a brave new world for me ahead.

Chapter 29

Wednesday, April 2, 2014
Colleen

Early in a misty morning, Alex, Dad, and I visit the cemetery, acknowledging twenty-five years since our mother passed. We lay a bunch of fresh daisies on her headstone, and another bunch on Riley's. The cemetery is a pretty place just after sunrise, peaceful with birdsong and no other people around. Early spring after a snowless winter, and the world is softening, buds beginning on the trees, grass struggling to find its green. We speak little. There have been words, so many words, and now we are ready to simply stand beside those we love, quietly aware that this grief is a difficult one, one that puts us at odds with the one we lost, puts us at odds with ourselves and those around us.

But being angry at them won't bring them back. Nothing will; so, I admit, to myself at least, that my heart is broken in a way that will never mend. Once that's said, maybe I can pick up the pieces of my heart and move forward. Yes, that's what I hope for.

Later in the day, the sunshine has burned off the morning fog, and Alex and I sit on the beach in hats and sunglasses. Riley has been gone for one month. Alex is doing what she needs to do to bring Caleb to Massachusetts: filing paperwork, scheduling home visits, and all the rest. Liz, Caleb's caseworker, assures Alex that the process is slow, but that's the process. She thinks we will meet our nephew before the end of summer. Alex doesn't let the timelines scare her. She is dedicated. She's taking an online course on caring for children with trauma. She has joined a couple of support groups, one in person and a couple on Facebook as well. I introduced her to the Newburyport Families Club so she can connect with area families. She is devoted to making this work, and I am here to help.

And in three weeks, my children and I will move back into our house, all painted and fixed up since that night in February. Eric finally resolved things with insurance, and they will pay the reconstruction bill. I will spend the rest of the school year fixing things, painting, buffing floors, boxing clutter, hiding away the detritus of our old lives to make the place look pretty as a picture, and then we will put the house on the market. Then, another move, hopefully the last one for a while. I don't know where we'll end up, but I hope it's small, simple, clean. I may have to shed my beloved private master bathroom. That's okay. I will shed the things I do not need and savor the things I love.

The ocean before us is calm today; the end of winter brought gentler winds, and the water rises up into waves that roll and slide into an easy surf. Today the breeze feels tender, a relief under the strong springtime sun.

"How's the new job?" I ask Alex.

"Fine," she says. "I'm getting back into the swing of working nights. It's nice working in Newburyport; the commute is easy. And I get the feeling they don't see anything too crazy in this emergency room. I'm glad to be back at it, actually. The routine of having a job is kind of comforting. How's therapy?"

"Good," I say. "She told me not to just talk about painting but actually do it."

"Wow," she says. "And?"

"Well, I started a painting class at that art place in the Tannery. I just don't think I have any undiscovered talent."

"I don't know, Colleen," she says. "Maybe enjoying it isn't so different from having talent. If you like doing it, then you do it, and you get better."

"Maybe," I say. "I'll let you know if that happens."

Then we are both quiet as the wind burns our cheeks and the waves tumble and crash. A mother and two small children sit down the beach a few feet away from us. The children wear sun hats and long-sleeved T-shirts, and they put their toes in the sand and scream as they run in and out of the frothy, foamy tides that spill onto the sand.

Alex reaches into a small bag. "I brought peanut butter and jelly," she says, pulling two square packages wrapped neatly in wax paper. "It's what I've learned to cook so far."

"You have to start somewhere," I say as she hands one to me. "Did you bring juice boxes?"

"Lemonade in a pretty bottle," she says, presenting the bottle. "From the fancy place in town. And Dixie cups."

I smile. "Perfect." She pours two cups of lemonade and hands me one. I hold up my cup. "To Mom."

"And Riley," Alex says. We knock our cups together and sip.

Then Alex brings something else out of the backpack, a small envelope. It flutters a little in the breeze as she holds it up. A twenty-five-year-old letter written by a woman who would soon end her life. "Do you want to do the honors or shall I?"

"I'll let you," I say.

She sips her lemonade, then twists her cup into the sand and takes the envelope again out of the pack. She holds it up and looks at it.

"Mrs. William Montgomery," she reads. "Sunshine Avenue, Sausalito, California. How could anything bad ever happen on Sunshine Avenue?"

"Sometimes rain falls, even on Sunshine Avenue," I say. Indeed, I think, that, in a nutshell, is the story of my life.

Alex laughs, then continues. "The letter went to Mrs. William Montgomery. But we think her name was Paula, right?"

"Let's call her that," I suggest. "Or let's call her Grandma. Oh, before we do, we should ask. She might be one of those ladies who feels that being called 'Grandma' makes her feel old."

"Like she's somebody's grandmother?" Alex says.

"Right." I lean in slightly and whisper. "Don't tell her that she's a great-grandmother. That could send her over the edge."

Alex holds the envelope in her hands, barring against a gust of wind. "Are we feeling a little punchy today?"

I laugh and push my hair out of my face. "Maybe a little."

"Anyway. Postmark is dated . . ." Alex stops and swallows. "March twenty-sixth."

I nod. "That was just about a week or so before Mom . . ."

"Yup," Alex says. Then sun goes behind a cloud, and she pushes her sunglasses up off her face. She takes a plastic butter knife and slips it under the crease, then slices the envelope open. "And here comes the letter." Alex pulls a yellow folded sheet from the envelope and unfolds it. I expect it to look old and crinkled, but it looks surprisingly preserved.

"She typed it," Alex says. "Remember that great old typewriter she had?"

"I used to write my school papers on that thing. It was like a tank."

"That's exactly what it was, a tank," she says.

I press my hands over my eyes so I can listen completely. "Okay, read the damn thing, already."

"With no further ado," she says. "Ahem. 'Dear Mom . . . I was trying to decide whether to write this or not, and I guess I decided to write it. I wanted to let you know what I've been doing since Dad informed me, oh, so calmly, that I was no longer part of your family.'" She stops for a moment, then repeats slowly. "'Dad informed me. Oh, so calmly. That I was no longer . . . part of your family.'"

"Disinherited," I say. "And he did it without raising his blood pressure."

"Boy," Alex says. "You know, we're pretty lucky. To have a dad like Dad."

"We are," I say. "I'm glad Mom had him in her life."

Alex nods then continues reading. "'How long has it been? Many years. I think about you every day, Mom. I miss you. I think about Nan too. And I wonder . . .'" She pauses, takes a breath, and glances at me.

"'I wonder why you always seemed so angry at her and why you lied to us about her. Don't be mad at Nan, Mom. A person has to feel a lot of pain and hopelessness to do what she did. A person has to be just about desperate.'"

Alex stops reading again. "Nan," she says. "Does that mean 'grandmother'?"

"I think so," I say.

Alex rereads that part, her hair blowing in the wind. "It sounds like maybe she . . ."

"Was a member of that same club," I say. I look down at the sand and think about the words in the letter. *A person has to feel a lot of pain and hopelessness . . . You always seemed so angry at her . . . You lied to us about her.* Our mother's grandmother; sounds like she struggled with at least depression, maybe more. And Paula, our grandmother, tried the same trick I tried: don't tell the kids, but grandma has a darker side. Maybe if Paula had known better, she could have opened up the truth about depression, exposed it to sunlight, talked to her daughter about it. And maybe if she had . . . maybe our mother would have had more insight into what she was going through . . .

It was a different era, I tell myself. I sigh. *We all have to stop not talking about this.*

Alex continues. "'I named a daughter after her . . . Aurelia. I pray that my Aurelia, whom we call little Riley, has an easier time of it.'"

I look up. "You must be kidding," I say quietly.

"Nope," Alex says. She reads from the letter again. "'I have two other girls as well!'" She looks at me. "That line is followed with an exclamation point!"

"Wow!" I say.

"'My first is Alexis, but we call her Alex. She's smart, independent, and fiercely curious. My second is Colleen, named for her father's mother. You'd like her very much.'"

I look at Alex and smile. "Granny likes me more."

"A dubious honor," she says.

The corner of the towel beneath me flaps up in the breeze, and I smooth it down. Alex keeps reading. "'I got married, for real this time, and we live in Massachusetts. We live close to the shore, and I love that. The winters are hard here, but they have their own beauty.

"Listen to this," Alex says. "'I was in touch with Jake during his final days, and I sent a condolence card to his family. This AIDS thing is a horrible, cruel disease. Mom, Jake was the one who wanted . . . to annul the marriage. He insisted. I told him I didn't mind, but he said he cared about me too much to let keep me from having a regular life and a family. He was a good friend and a decent person, and I miss him.'"

She puts the letter down for a moment, and we look at each other.

"Oh no," she says. "We were close but we had it wrong. They were friends."

"I wish we could have met him," I say. "I wonder what he would have told us about Mom."

Alex sighs then continues. "'I still paint. I try to do something every day. But not enough to make any real progress in my technique, plus the cost of materials is a burden on our family. George is a mailman, and we have what we need but not much more. Maybe when the girls are older, I will figure out a way. Maybe when my little one is a bit older, I'll find a way to make money teaching art.

"'It's hard, Mother. Harder than I can explain. I look at something I might paint, and in my mind, I take apart the pieces, separate line from shadow, figure out the light, dissect the colors, work out the shapes, and imagine how I would compose the image. But I can't stay there for very long because there is a child, always, whose nose is running, who needs juice, who can't find their shoes, who has spilled the glue.'"

Alex and I glance at each other again.

"'And I don't wish you were here, Mom,'" she continues. "'But I wish you were here every day. And if you were here, I would not leave you to babysit my girls, but if you did, I would go and live in that other world in my head for a few hours, and I imagine it would be bliss.

"'Because . . . because . . . this is torture. The pain is physical. Every day I am torn apart like a paper doll. And some days, I don't know what to do, and I feel . . . so alone in this world.'"

"Damn it," I say.

Alex shakes her head. "'I miss you every day, Mom. I'm so sorry for all the trouble I caused. I never meant to be a burden. But I always loved you. Sincerely, Suzanne.'"

Alex puts the letter down. For a moment, we are both quiet as try to absorb this eerie dispatch. "And she never read it," I say.

"Not a word," Alex says. "Not a single word."

"She was too busy worrying about oyster forks," I say.

I look out at the gray-blue ocean before us and imagine my mother twenty-five years and eight days ago. Feeling so hopeless, she pulled out her typewriter and poured her soul into a letter. Sent the letter off, and a few days later, she simply gave up. On everything.

The waves roll before us; the tide starts to crawl up the slope of the sandy beach. The children squeal in delight when they uncover a perfect white sand dollar. Their mother calls out, "Look at that!"

Funny to think, all this time, Alex and I were looking for a big bang, the reason and the moment behind the decision to end our mother's life. But it was a slow erosion, I realize. Many years of trying to stay afloat, then she just stopped resisting.

I sigh and stare at the water, the ocean, the waves. Amazing, it seems to me, how everything continues in constant cycle. The currents flow and rise, push up and gather into a wave, then build until they crash in a frenzy of foam and churning sand. And then the calm, soft spilling onto the beach, and this is where the children play, giggle, and scream as the cold water rolls over their toes. And how it continues through the seasons and the year. Unless the moon fell out of the sky, nothing could stop the tides.

"Riley was named for our great-grandmother," I say. "Mom never told us."

"A family tradition, huh?" she says. "Why do you think she never read the letter? What do you think she was afraid of?"

I shrug. "After a couple of weeks of not reading it, it didn't matter anyway. Mom was gone."

The daylight is lemony yellow shining through a pale-blue sky. I let it shine down on my closed eyes, warming my face, and then I remember something Mom once told me. *Everything you see changes with the light,* she said. *The shapes of things change, and so do the colors. Time of day, weather, direction of the light source, if you're inside or outside, everything that effects the light will affect how you recreate it on a flat surface.*

"She must have felt so free when she left everything behind in California," I say. "It's kind of amazing how she ventured across the country alone." I laugh to myself. "Oyster forks. For God's sake."

Alex smiles too. "And pearl necklaces with gold-and-diamond clasps." She watches plovers peck at the sand. "That kind of freedom, though, Colleen? It's terrifying. It's like, you look over the edge of the world, and it's not just a place on a map, it's your soul, and you have no idea what's down there, but you know you have to look with eyes wide open."

"That's kind of where I'm at now," I say.

"I know," she says. "And I am setting up a home. I think we swapped places."

"I think you're right," I say.

Then we are quiet, my sister and I, listening to the waves. Maybe our mother never found what she needed here either. I think about the painting; my mother was the woman I saw behind it. In the middle of a brutal New England winter, she could find one sunny, mild morning, and she'd wrap us up and scoot us to the beach so she could spend a few minutes out in that salt air, trying to capture the light, trying to explain in solid color, in physical matter, something so elusive as love.

Everything you see changes with the light. And suddenly, I understand that the only thing we see in this world is light. Sometimes, though, it's not the light from the outside that matters but the light inside that shades everything, that determines which colors you see.

If you want to paint, she told me back then, *you need to learn to read the light.*

"Colleen, no more secrets," Alex says, turning toward me. "We can't hide anything from our kids or each other." I nod, and Alex and I embrace. "The next person that dies in this family," she says, "needs to get hit by a bus or catch a flesh-eating virus. Seriously."

"Alex!" I shout. But I am laughing. And both of us are laughing and crying at the same time. We hold each other in the warming sunlight. It feels good. I am happy.

Chapter 30

Monday, August 11, 2014
Alex

And then a child comes into my life. I am ready and I am not ready. There has been a lot of paperwork, a lot of legal terms, a lot of hurrying and waiting to hear. Bureaucracy, forms, signatures, home-visits, caseworkers, courses. But I cleared every hurdle, and now it's time. I am giddy and elated. I know how he ended up here, I am the one who brought him, but still I am in shock. I do what I can to prepare, and I feel ready for the challenge. I am also, at the same time, completely terrified and have no idea what I am doing.

I sold Mom's jewelry; the pearls were real after all, and the money let me fix the house up so it felt ready for Caleb. Thanks, Mom. In a few weeks, I filled the house with things, dreaded things, the kinds of things that slow you down when you're trying to make a quick getaway. Rugs, which silenced the hollow echo of footsteps through the house, but also required that I purchase an upright vacuum cleaner. Curtains and shades. A cozy living room chair with a little side table for a lamp and a cup of hot tea. A few prints for the walls. Beds! Twin size for Caleb, full for me. Bureaus for sweaters, trunks for toy boxes. Plus, proper sheets and blankets. A nice white-painted table and chairs, came from a yard sale, and then I needed dishes, utensils, and pots and pans, which Colleen helped me buy on sale at a department store.

There are other things I have had to find as well. A pediatrician, a child psychologist. I enrolled Caleb in Newbury Elementary School for the fall and met with the principal to explain our unusual situation. I learned the bus schedule and figured out where I would take him to catch it. I got him his own library card and brought home the library's calendar of events, which I posted on the refrigerator with bright plastic letter magnets, which I also have now. The psychologist suggested I ease him into physical activities, so I'm researching swimming lessons. Before summer is over, I will bring him to the beach at Plum Island, Sandy Point, and he will run and play and splash. I imagine us bringing a picnic, staying until the sun goes down. Maybe his cousins will hang out with us. There's just enough summer left.

And for Caleb, I know that this quiet house in the middle of nowhere, with no other children around, will be a shock to his system. The case-worker suggested I send him pictures of the world he's coming to, and so I do. I snap dozens of pictures—the house, his room, his bed, the art kit with crayons and markers that I bought him, the marsh, the school, his new teacher, the kids in the classroom, a cheese pizza—one of his favorites—ice cream cones, the beach, the town, even some deer that I spotted on the side of the road. I made a little book and sent it to the foster family to give to him. I hoped he would look at the pictures and start to understand some of what this place is about.

I hope he knows how much he is welcome and wanted here. Because he is.

Sometimes, amid all the busyness, I take a moment to stand in front of the living room windows and look out at the marsh. I can see how Marjorie loved it so much; now that the marsh grasses are turning green, it's truly beautiful here. But it's different from New York City; its charms are not always so obvious nor easy to find. They're quiet, simple. I'm hoping, praying almost, that over time Caleb will come to love it here.

On a hot Monday morning, I drive to Connecticut to meet the case-worker, Liz, who has brought Caleb to a Starbucks. The moment he walks in the door, holding Liz's hand and clutching his stuffed turtle, I recognize him; he is quiet and wide-eyed. Liz buys Caleb a muffin and the three of us sit together. While she and I talk, Caleb pulls his muffin into a million pieces, none of which he actually eats. After a short visit, Liz leads me to her car and hands me two trash bags full of Caleb's things. She walks us over to my car where we all hug goodbye, and I thank her for all she's done. Caleb climbs in, we wave to Liz, and then he and I are on our way home. The drive is a couple of hours, and Caleb sits quietly in the back, doodling with markers and stretching the putty I brought for him. A couple of times, we stop at McDonald's.

Finally, we exit the highway and drive through Newburyport, past the town and onto the quiet, rural section of Route 1A. Caleb sits up and puts his hand to the window, watching as small city gives way to country. I pull the car down Killdeer Road, and a moment later we stop at the house. I open the door for him, and he is home. Caleb is home.

He looks around for a few moments before he gets out of the car, Caleb and his turtle. Finally, he does, and carefully, quietly, follows me to the front door and into the house. Now that I have had the doorknob replaced, the key unlocks the door without any trouble.

"This is it," I say. I squat down to look him in the eye. "Welcome." I smile at Caleb and pat the turtle's dark green shell. Now that the turtle is in front of me, I see that the fur is faded, some of it missing, and one plastic eye is hanging on a thread. He has been very loved by this little boy.

"Does this fellow have a name?" I ask.

"His name is Lester Hard-Hat," he says, biting his lip and not quite meeting my eyes.

"Hello, Lester," I say. "Nice to meet you. You know, I have a sewing kit. If you want me to fix up his eye, I can do that. It won't hurt at all. Turtles are very brave."

He looks anxiously at his good friend. "Umm . . ."

"We don't have to do it today," I say. "Lester seems like he's getting by okay without any trouble."

"Yeah," he says.

"Let me know, okay?" I say, and he nods his head. "Let's look around the house. I want to show you your room."

I lead him up the stairs, and he follows tentatively. "Does anybody else live here?" he asks.

"Nope, just you and me," I say.

"Nobody upstairs? Or downstairs?" he says. His voice cracks with amazement. "No other kids?"

"Nope," I say. "The whole house is just for us. I know it's kind of quiet. But there are playgrounds in town, and we'll get to know other families and kids. How does that sound?"

He shrugs. I bring him to his room. He stands in the doorway and looks through.

"Here it is," I say. "Does it look familiar? From the pictures I sent?"

He shrugs again and looks through the doorway.

"I added a few things," I say. I point to a trunk in the corner that has a line of five stuffed bears carefully laid out on top of it. "The bears are from your grandfather, Pépé. Do you remember the picture of him?"

He nods and squeezes his turtle close.

"You'll get to know those guys," I say. "Turtles and bears get along great."

He does not look at me; his gaze is soft, like he's not really taking any of this in.

I sigh quietly. I am so nervous about how I speak to him. Whatever words I choose, whatever tone I take, I hope so much that it's the right thing, that he won't take something I say in a way that I do not mean it. I know that coming to live here is a big deal for Caleb, this child whose life has been turned upside down and shaken hard in the past year. I know that adjusting to all this will take time, years, in fact. But I want to get this as right as possible.

"You have your very own bed," I say. "Your own closet, your own desk. I heard you like to draw pictures, so I got you an art set."

I'd left the briefcase-shaped kit open so he could see the laid-out array of crayons, markers and discs of water color paints arranged in rainbow order. A look of sadness crosses his face.

"And paper," I say. "Lots of nice pads."

"Okay," he says shyly, trying to smile.

"If there's anything you need, Caleb," I say. "You just have to let me know, okay? This is your home now. I want you to like it here."

"I like it," he says tentatively.

He walks carefully to the window and looks out at the marsh, now visible since I took down all the mangy shrubs.

"What's out there?" he asks.

"That's the marsh," I say. "I'll take you out there sometime. A little stream goes through parts of it. Maybe we can go kayaking sometime. I bet you'd like that."

"What is that?" he asks.

"Oh," I say. "A kayak is a little boat you push through the water with an oar, a kind of a big stick. Like a canoe, but easier to use."

"Did my mom ever do that?" he asks.

And at those words, my heart sinks. This is what he and I share—we both lost Riley, we are both still grieving. I will never replace her in his heart, and truly, I don't want to. I just want to give this child a safe and happy home. Then suddenly, I feel relieved that he's asking about his mom. If he is curious about her, it means he hasn't closed his heart. That's a good thing. That's a great thing.

"I don't think so," I say. "I didn't try it either until I was a grown-up. But tomorrow, I'll bring you to see your grandfather, Pépé. He still lives in the house where we all grew up, me your mom and our sister, your Aunt Colleen. You can see your mom's old bedroom. Would you like that?"

He smiles slightly and nods, and I stand beside him, and the two of us look out on to the marsh, the sky, the rain.

That night I make dinner. His foster family told me that he loved mac and cheese, so I make a big pan of baked macaroni and cheese, complete with a crunchy, buttered breadcrumb topping and a salad. When we sit down to dinner at the little table in the little kitchen, he picks at the food, tentatively takes a few bites.

"Is it okay?" I ask.

A strained look comes over his face. "It's good," he says.

I take a bite of mine and chew. It tastes fine to me, delicious, actually. But then I notice a few boxes of Kraft macaroni and cheese sitting on the counter.

"See that blue box over there?" I say, pointing. "Do you like that kind?"

He nods.

"Would you like some now?"

He nods again.

No problem. I go to the stove, open a box, and a few minutes later, I serve him a bowl heaped high with warm tubes coated in milk, butter, and powder from a packet, colored nuclear orange. He devours it.

And so goes my first lesson at the school of Caleb: he loves mac and cheese, but the boxed stuff is better than homemade, and the kind with the sauce made of mixing orange powder with melted butter and milk is better than pourable Velveeta. The organic brands are acceptable, but the blue box is the best. I cringe when I think about what it's made with, but I can worry about that later.

After that, we watch movies: *Cars*, then *Cars 2*. Afterward, Caleb puts on the faded, worn pajamas that his foster family gave him, brushes his teeth, and begins his first night in Newbury, Massachusetts.

But of course, it's a tough night. He's exhausted, but he can't sleep. The pillow is too hard or too soft, the room is too warm or not warm enough. The turtle falls out of the bed and cannot be found until I come in and find him. In the end I bring my sleeping bag and pillow into his room and sleep on the floor beside him. Finally, we both get a little rest in the short time before the sun comes up. In the morning Caleb wakes up and looks out the window; when I notice that he's up, I see his face. His expression looks simply bewildered.

Each day since then has had ups and downs, and all of those get us a little closer to the day in the distant and unknown future when this new way of things doesn't feel so foreign. For Caleb's first two weeks in Massachusetts, I negotiate with my boss that I will take unpaid leave so I can help him acclimate. But I have hired a sitter to care for Caleb when I'm back at work, and now she hangs out with him while I do errands, just so they can get to know each other. Her name is Sandy, she's a young grandmother from Byfield, whose hair is dyed blazing red and cut short to show off crazy earrings that she makes as a hobby. She also works at a boarding stable and brings books about horses to read to Caleb, which he loves. I feel sad that I won't be the one who tucks him in every night, but this is the dance of single mom and worker bee that I always knew I would have to learn if I wanted a child in my life.

The weather has been breezy and warm, and Caleb and I do as many fun things as we can stand: visit the local playground, the bike path, the aquarium, the children's museum, the zoo. We cart plastic buckets and sand toys and sunscreen by the liter to the sandy local beaches. I introduce him to the lobster roll, which comes with fries; I eat the lobster, he eats the fries. But Caleb is still adjusting, and sometimes his struggles manifest in tears, angry and hot or sad and choking. I either hold him close or give him space, and I pray for the wisdom to know the difference.

Nights are trickier; for Caleb, sleep never comes easy. Even when he's completely worn out, it can be hard getting him to settle down, getting his mind to clear out for the day. We settle on a routine that starts with turning off the television, followed by pajamas and brushing teeth. Once he does those, he gets to sit with his markers and crayons and doodle for a little while before I come in and read. After that, we say our good nights and Caleb snuggles his turtle close.

Tonight, he wears his new Red Sox pajamas to bed—I'm starting to convert him. As usual, I pull his sheets up around his shoulders, switch on the night light, kiss his cheek, and leave. I go to my bedroom where I sit at my small wobbly desk and start in on the stack of bills. I need to pay the balance to the contractor who fixed the roof. And other bills: electricity, gas, water. I'll have to pay the minimum on my credit card this month, which I don't like to do, but we have a lot of extra expenses right now, and I need to be careful.

What about the long-term financial questions? I have life insurance through work. And I'm putting money back into a retirement account, just the minimum for now, but I will increase it. And I need to open a college savings account for Caleb. He inherited some money from Riley, and I need to make sure that that goes toward his future. Colleen told me what college plan she started for her kids, but I can't remember what it was, so I email her to ask her to remind me.

I'm typing this when a small figure in red and white appears in my doorway.

"Hello?" I say softly.

"I can't sleep," he says.

"Aww, sweetie," I say. I turn off my laptop, take his hand, and gently lead him back to his bed. *Why can't he sleep?* I ask. *Does his belly hurt? Is he thinking about something? Is he feeling sad or lonesome for his old home?* Each time he shakes his head, no. He's tired, I can tell. It's just that sleep refuses to cooperate. We repeat this in-and-out-of-bed dance three or four more times. *Does anything hurt?* I touch his forehead; no fever. *Is Lester talking too much?*

No, Aunt A, I just can't sleep.

Finally, when I am too exhausted myself to keep this up, I offer: "Caleb, how about I come sleep on your floor tonight?"

"Yes, please, Aunt A," he says.

And so, I bring my sleeping bag and my pillow and spread out on the floor of his bedroom.

"May I borrow one of your bears?" I ask. Caleb smiles and hands one to me, it's the one he named Honey. I snuggle him in close, the way Caleb does with Lester. But the floor is not comfortable, and in this night, unusually hot for this late in summer, his fan does not quite combat the humidity. One a.m. and I'm wide awake. I think about finances, budgets, and expenses. I think about the house, what more there is to fix, replace, and decorate; how will I afford everything? Can I really manage this life? It would be easier if I was two parents. There will be things Caleb will want to do that I won't be able to afford, and then what?

I spend the night as Caleb does, tossing, turning, occasionally dozing, then tossing some more, staring into the darkness, ruminating.

I can't tell if Caleb is actually asleep, but if he's not, he's staying pretty quiet. When I wake up again from dozing, I check the time on my phone, both hoping that morning is near and wishing I could rest for a little longer. Almost five a.m. Then, out the window that is beside Caleb's bed, I see that the color of the sky has turned from pitch black to a lucid sea-glass blue. Caleb sits up and looks out the window.

"Caleb, you're still awake?" I say.

He turns and looks at me. His eyes look red and tired. And suddenly, they remind me of the little girl I once held close when the night was so long and dark. In those sleepless nights, we did not understand what was keeping Riley awake. Now we know. I wish I could hold that little girl now.

"I have an idea," I say, siting up in my sleeping bag. "Put on your flip flops. We're going for a walk."

The very idea of it shocks Caleb, and his eyes grow wide. "In pajamas?" he says.

"Yup," I say. "Let's go."

And the two of us throw off our covers, go downstairs, slip on sandals that we tossed by the front door yesterday, and don our windbreakers. Then, with Lester Hard-Hat tucked under one of Caleb's arms, we venture out into the dawn where the horizon is beginning to glow in shades of pink and yellow. The air is fresh and damp, and the marsh around us is flat and rich with wild green grasses that hide critters of all kinds—including turtles! A fact that enchants Caleb to no end. This place is so different from the frozen tundra it was when I first came six months ago, it almost feels like a different place. In the distance, an outcropping of oak trees, thick with leaves, on an island of soil in the marsh, and forests of them on the far edges. The world is silent except for birdsong, and their music is so loud I don't see how anyone can sleep through it. I imagine that mornings like these made Marjorie's heart swell. I do not know the names of most of those birds, but maybe, in time, I will learn them. Caleb seems to love it too; his face bears a look of abject wonder, as though we have tumbled through the wardrobe and landed straight in Narnia. This is where we live every day, but at this hour, little miracles abound.

I hold Caleb's small hand as we walk down the lane, and suddenly, there's change in the air. The sky becomes crimson, becomes gold. Suddenly, the blazing edge of the sun begins to peek up behind the distant trees of the marsh.

I squat down next to Caleb, still holding his small hand, and point. "Here it comes," I whisper.

Caleb stops and gasps. "Is it a balloon?" he whispers back.

"It's the sunshine. That's today's sunshine just coming up."

He watches the sphere rise, the sky turning all the colors, pink, yellow, orange, but mostly flaming golden. Caleb's jaw drops slightly open as he takes it all in.

"Where did it come from?" he asks.

"Nowhere, it was always there," I say. "The sun never moves; it's the Earth that turns, just like a beach ball. At night, our part of the Earth turns away from the sun, and in the morning it comes back. But the sun is always there, just like the stars are always in the sky."

"They are?" he says. "But I can't see them now."

"They're just on the other side of the sky," I say. "We can't see them because the sunshine is filling the sky. But they're still out there, all the same."

The Earth keeps turning, every day, every night, each time giving us the chance to start over. In the night's darkest moments, we so easily forget that morning will come. We can't stop it; it simply happens, just like spring follows winter, just as the tides of the ocean rise and fall.

This moment. It is not the sunrise over the River Ganges in the holy city of Varanasi, where pilgrims wrapped in orange and white chant the ancient Sanskrit texts to call the sun into the sky. It is not the Taj Mahal or Kanyakumari, the island temples at the southernmost tip of the subcontinent, or Kolkata's Kalighat Temple, where the Great Goddess dances. But it is a good moment. Maybe a lifetime favorite.

I wish my mother were here. I wish my sister were here. I wish all these stories had had different endings. But I feel this warm, small hand in mine and look up as a flock of joyful sparrows hovers and swirls overhead like a magic carpet, and I think that I can welcome whatever is ahead. And be infinitely grateful for it.

Suddenly the look on Caleb's face changes from happy to worried, and he bursts out crying.

"Oh, sweetie," I say. "What happened?"

I wrap my arms around this small child clutching his turtle and stand up, holding both of them. Caleb buries his face in my shoulder and tries to talk through tears but mostly I can't understand what he's saying. I touch the back of his head and try to comfort him.

"Caleb," I say. "What is it?"

"I'm tired," he squeals.

I smile. Of course, he's tired. He's exhausted. I pick him up, hold him close, and carry him home, his head resting on my shoulder. Maybe now that he knows that all those things we cannot see—the sun at night, and the stars in morning—never disappear but only wait in another part of the sky, maybe now this little boy will tuck into his bed, hold his turtle close, close his eyes, and sleep.

And maybe I will do the same.

Acknowledgments

Writing a novel is very much like traveling; you start in one place, and you have no idea where you will end up. But if you're lucky, you meet some wonderful people along the way, and they become the signposts, pointing you in the best direction. Thank you so much to my early reader/editors who did exactly that: author Jenna Blum and Book Architecture founder and principal Stuart Horwitz. Many thanks to Sheila Smallwood for creating stunning visuals when I thought I would be going solo. I have been so grateful for the support and encouragement of the Newburyport Writers' Group including the wonderful children's book author Maggie van Galen; also, the New Hampshire Writers' Project, especially the Portsmouth Writers' Night Out group, organized by author Jeff Deck. Thanks also to Steve and Marilynn Carter for letting me talk on their WPM podcast—twice!

I am incredibly honored by and grateful to Blackstone Publishing for taking me on, especially to Addi Black. So much gratitude to my amazing editor, Jennifer Pooley, for her combination of wisdom and vision, and for giving me the feedback I needed to push this work to the next level. Thank you so much to the rest of the outstanding team at Blackstone Publishing: Hannah Ohlmann, Megan Wahrenbrock, Josie Woodbridge, Kathryn

Zentgraf, and Alenka Linaschke who created a STUNNING cover. I am so grateful for all the thoughtful and creative work everyone has added to this project.

This book would not have been possible without support and information provided to me by kind and generous friends and folks from all corners of my community. Huge thanks to my incredible web and design squad, headed by the incredibly talented Lauren Georgiades, with help from Soks Gemma and Dana Robinson, both also incredibly talented. Many thanks to Chief Fred A. Mitchell, Jr., Fire Chief of the Georgetown, Massachusetts Fire Department. At the eleventh hour, I needed to reach out to experts to double-check my facts, and my bacon was literally saved by a bevy of people I have never met: VaLynda Robinson, Joanne Robinson Peterson, and Stacey Sullaway. Thank you for your invaluable help, and for sharing your personal stories with a stranger. I also got help from a few parents in my daughter's Brownie troop. Thank you so much, Sean Sanderson, Erin Pallazola and Lori Kloc. But my very best last-minute informant was Cristine Alello, a friend from college with whom I re-connected on Facebook. Thank all of you times a hundred!!

Thanks to my favorite cheerleader (and Sunday morning exercise coach) Jerri Ortiz-Greenler. And a BIG THANKS to Julie Corwin, for all her encouragement and support.

This last part is for the long-time supporters. I am grateful to my sisters-in-law, Elayne Livote and Ilse de Veer, my sister, Anne Dailey, and my parents, Jim and Jane Mitchell for all the encouragement through the years. I have so much gratitude for the community at St. John's Church in Gloucester, where I work, for cheering me on, giving me time and space when needed, and for being patient when I lost my cool. This means you, Sue Lupo, Marge Bishop, Mark Nelson, and The Rev. Bret B. Hays.

I am grateful beyond measure to my amazing literary agent, Steven Chudney of the Chudney Agency, for his faith in me, and for all his support.

Finally, last but not least, so many thanks, plus kisses and hugs, to my wonderful husband Bram, and our daughter Amelia. I simply couldn't have created this without your support, love and patience, and for all that, I am eternally grateful.